THE TABOO SCARF

AND OTHER TALES

THE TABOO SCARF

AND OTHER TALES

GEORGE WEINBERG

ST. MARTIN'S PRESS—NEW YORK

Production Editor: David Stanford Burr

Design by Judith Dannecker

Library of Congress Cataloging-in-Publication Data

Weinberg, George H.
    The taboo scarf and other tales / George Weinberg.
        p.   cm.
    ISBN 0-312-04434-8
    I. Title.
    PS3573.E3916T3 1990
    813'.54—dc20   89-77846
                                            CIP

First Edition

10 9 8 7 6 5 4 3 2 1

CONTENTS

ACKNOWLEDGMENTS

As practitioners must when they write about their work, I have altered these stories to make them unrecognizable. All names, physical descriptions, places, times of occurrence, and identifiable events have been changed. Obviously, my patients have a right to absolute confidentiality. Still, I have tried to remain loyal to the psychic biographies of individuals in these stories, to their conflicts and their essential voyage, to the course that my therapy took with them, and to the outcome of our work together. And these stories underwent still another form of change. In each case, the real events were forgotten and then retrieved, so that my own contribution to them was unwitting as well as deliberate. Like the "screen memories" of patients themselves, they bear the stamp of the person doing the remembering.

I would like to thank Dianne Rowe for her close work on the manuscript, and Margaret Scal, who worked on this book at every stage. Also Olivia Katz, and those at St. Martin's Press who helped me and encouraged this book along: Tom McCormack, Bob Weil, my editor, and Jon Gertner.

Also contributing important insights and ideas were a handful of professional psychotherapists, Drs. David Balderston, Jean Balderston, Henry Katz, Helen McDermott, Cindy Mermin, Louis Ormont, Joan Ormont, and Hank Schenker.

In nature there's no blemish but the mind:
None are call'd deformed but the unkind.
Virtue is beauty.

From *Twelfth Night* by
William Shakespeare

THE TABOO SCARF

AND OTHER TALES

PROLOGUE

I am a psychotherapist in New York City. The stories in this book come from my practice, though, technically, this book is in no way a collection of case studies. Much more is included in these tales than my patient's personal histories. My own reactions to the people I worked with, their meanings to me, and other aspects of my own life evoked by my experiences are mentioned at times.

Nor do I think, after much self-scrutiny, that the choice to include this material is simply self-indulgent. In recent decades, taking account of the observer, what has been called "relativistic thinking," has become commonplace in even the most objective disciplines, like physics. The importance of such material has always been appreciated by psychotherapists when they talk privately. But, above all, these are personal stories, as you will see.

3

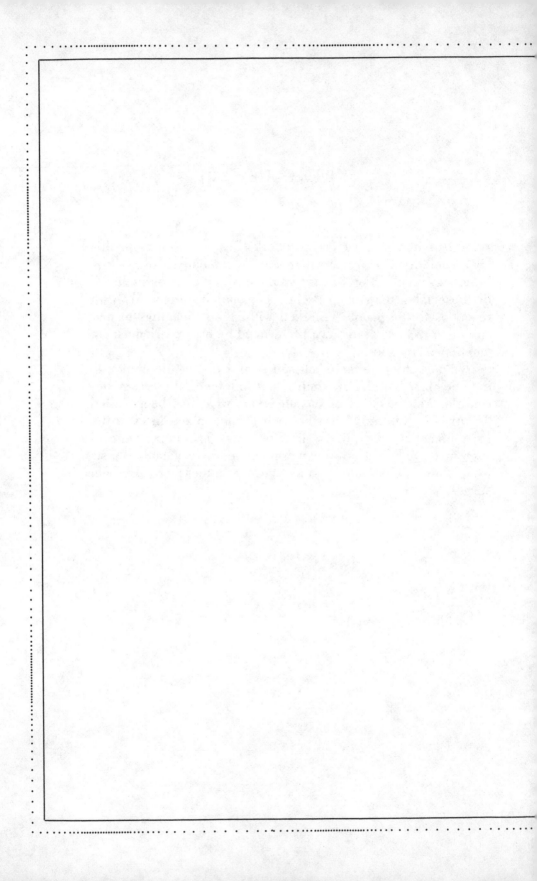

THE BEACON

I didn't know what I wanted of Susan, and the best defense against saying anything stupid was staying with the obvious.

Her face was still beautiful, an arched nose and high cheek-bones. She was tall and leggy, and in her flowered silk summer dress she was, if anything, thinner than when I knew her. Maybe I was still in love with her. But she was in my office for a consultation, and that was that.

"How have you been?" I asked insipidly.

"Fine. Doing a lot of things. I'm worried about Lisa. Really worried."

We were both fumbling and vague—I because it mattered and she because she knew it had mattered to me.

"I understand. I'm sorry to hear that," I said.

"She lives alone, in an apartment so shabby that you wouldn't believe it. She has no friends, only cats. I don't know how many by now, four last count, I think."

"No friends," I said.

"No. George, I'm afraid I haven't done a very good job. Marianne expected more of me, Lisa did too. I guess I don't even know what it is to be a mother, but I certainly want to do what I can."

"She was very little when your sister went to California and left her with you, wasn't she?"

"She was six. Oh, I forget it's been such a long time since we've talked."

"That's okay."

"Marianne took her two sons when she went off with that doctor. He didn't want any daughters, I guess. My sister's still out there, remarried again. But Lisa won't have anything to do with her, won't even talk to her."

"And Lisa's father?"

"Dead. Oh, dead for many years. I guess I haven't done a very good job."

"Look," I insisted, "you took her when her own mother didn't want her. You did your best. You stuck with her. You were the only one who did."

"I know. I had a good apartment, enough money. But I obviously didn't give her what she needed."

And Susan still had money, it would seem. She wore a black opal ring, surrounded by diamonds, a bit garish, like her gold bracelets. I could recognize the expensive shoes, though when I used to see her every day, I didn't know one pair of shoes from another.

I had tuned out for a moment, but returned to hear her still berating herself. "My values were, maybe still are, shallow. You knew that, you always knew it, you tried to help me. I can look great on the outside, but there's very little inside. Lisa's the proof. I think she hates me."

"There's got to be more to it than that," I said.

"You've always been so supportive, George. That's why I came here. It's gotten worse since she was in college. She was nearly an A student at Brandeis. But she didn't *talk* to anybody. Can you imagine it, an A student at Brandeis, and now she's working as an usherette, walking up and down inside the Beacon Theater with a flashlight, showing people to their seats. An usherette. Living alone. A college graduate

living in the dark, and rushing home. That's what I produced."

"I'm really sorry to hear about that. But maybe she isn't so
miserable. It's not what you want for her, I know."

"Not what I want for her! Not what I *want* for her!"

Perhaps my comment was a bit fatuous, but I was stunned at
the celerity of her anger. It didn't go with that porcelain facial
expression. I elected to say nothing.

"What I want for her is a full life. Friends, a husband,
interests. A vacation now and then, to go somewhere else. I'm
not saying she has to be a jet-setter. But I would like her to
have a life, that's all, just a life."

I looked at her directly for the first time. She was still ash
blonde, with a deep, sexy voice. She still had fantastic hands
with long fingers. "You understand what I mean, a life!" she
was saying.

But something was hollow about her, the years had done
something to her. Her self-evaluation had not been totally
wrong, perhaps even the implication that she had failed to
convey some elixir of life, of hope, to Lisa.

". . . the way she dresses, the way she lives, the way
she *moves*. I must have done something wrong. Terribly
wrong."

"You're still on good terms?"

"We talk. She knows I'm coming here to talk to you. If you
could cut down on the number of stray cats she has in that
apartment, I'd appreciate it."

I said, "I don't know that she even wants therapy."

"Doesn't want it. What are you talking about?"

Now that I dared look at her more closely, I saw that it
wasn't age itself that had changed her. Age can adorn if it
brings complexity, if it replaces innocent love with another
kind. Her face was pretty, but there was something vapid
about it, as if a light had dimmed. Her eyes, which to me had
connoted the ever-widening future, now gave a continual message of impatience, of joyless haste. I could imagine Lisa feeling discouraged by them.

After a pause, Susan said, "I'm sorry, maybe I haven't been clear, but there's a lot you don't know about her." She tried to say that warmly.

But I felt her apology was more manipulative than sincere.

"George, I've talked about you a lot, how bright and caring you are. I show her your articles sometimes, in *Glamour*. I've shown her your books. I have two of them, I don't remember the names."

"But we don't even know if she'll go to a therapist. You think there's a lot wrong with her. But does she?"

"She agreed to go."

"She's been in therapy before?"

"Never. You're the only person she'll see. If you agree. I promised her not to tell you anything about her. Maybe I said too much already."

It crossed my mind that other people must have loved Susan over the years, and fallen by the wayside. I wondered if any of them still felt the way I did.

"Look, Susan, maybe you're right and she does need therapy. But I don't think I'm the person to see her."

"Why not? I'll pay you whatever you want. Don't worry about that. I have money."

"No. It isn't that," I protested.

"Well, why not then? You're the one she trusts."

"Well, I know, but—" I started to say it was because of our relationship, but caught myself. What? A relationship twenty-five years ago stopping me from working with someone else! And I'd only seen Susan once between then and now. She would never understand. I wasn't even sure I did. How could I say, "Susan, I'd think about you too much, it wouldn't be fair."

I said nothing.

"Please, you're very well known now," she said.

"Well known? Hardly."

"Well, you're certainly doing well. And I don't trust anybody else. If I ever asked you anything, I'm asking you this. I've already spoken to her. I wouldn't know what to say if you said no."

She saw me hesitating. She said, "I told her all about you. Really."

"Susan, you know if I did work with Lisa, you and I couldn't talk anymore. It wouldn't be fair to her."

"Of course," she said, as if it didn't matter. It obviously meant a lot more to me than to her.

"Okay," I said. "Have her call me."

"I don't know if she will."

"She'd have to. I can't chase her. It wouldn't do."

"Of course. I understand."

She would understand the value of being solicited, being a high-level call girl. At the idea, I stopped myself forcibly from thinking of her that way.

"I'll have her call you. I'm so glad you're willing to see her. We consider it a compliment."

"Well, it's hardly that, Susan." I felt brokenhearted, and instantly regretted having consented.

As if on cue, she softened. "Are you still reading poetry, George?"

"Yes, I do. Not as often as I'd like, but I watch a lot of Shakespeare videotapes. I have a whole library."

"Oh, that's wonderful. How should I pay you?"

Something told me to resist the impulse not to charge Susan for that session. I said, "I'll add it on to Lisa's bill if she calls. I have your address."

"Well, I guess I'd better not take any more of your time."

We rose simultaneously.

At the door, I told her, "It was great to see you. I'll do my best."

It was a stupid final statement, I thought to myself.

The way Renoir must have touched his nearly finished paintings with hints of vermilion that gave them supernal life, the next day tinged my consciousness with memories of Susan when we were both seventeen. I could see her again, cool and fresh, her thick hair falling softly over the sides of her face, her white blouse contrasting with her deeply tanned neck.

Both of us were poor, going to City College and working in
the library after hours, but we found time for long walks down
Riverside Drive. Feeling completely unworthy of her, I'd never
dared make a sexual approach, which I felt might ruin everything. We shared the dream of becoming great writers, and I
pictured our names etched in gold on adjacent black leather
volumes of the Harvard Classics. Our two books would speak
to lonely people as yet unborn, signaling them to awareness of
the earth's magnificence.

One summer day, Susan and I had paused to lean on the low
railing and gaze at the Hudson River, not far from the Soldiers
and Sailors Monument. I recited Tennyson's line to her, "We
dipped into the future, far as human eye could see." Her eyes
sparkled as she looked unforgettably at me, and I will always
think that she loved me in that moment.

She said to me, "George, I really want to give something
beautiful to the world."

How could I have guessed that her willowy body and perfect
oval face were to be her gift?

Already she was being pursued by much older men. I pictured them as coarse, wrinkled people in fedora hats, the kind
who gauge everything by money and what it can buy. They
brought her to shows and restaurants, but none of them ever
recited poetry to her or believed in her the way I did.

One in particular offered to buy her a whole wardrobe if she
would sleep with him. "I hardly know the man," she said to
me, and seemed as repulsed by the offer as I was. I guess I
imagined, What did she need money for? She could take out
any book in the library, and that was what counted.

Naturally, she didn't inform me when she started accepting
payment for sex. Her earrings, her new dress, she explained
by saying that she had found a wonderful discount store downtown. But the lines I discovered and memorized and recited to
her began to mean less. And one day she surprised me by
saying, "You really could be a very attractive man if you
learned something about clothes." I felt confused and angry,
not at what she said but at the distance from which she saw me.

Then she broke an appointment to meet me after an English class, and I didn't see her for months. When I met her by accident on Broadway, she told me she'd quit college, and I saw her no more.

I thought about her when I got into Columbia graduate school, when I got my doctor's degree, and in spot moments later on. It even crossed my mind that maybe I was betraying her by staying away and that if I had any integrity I would have shouted at her to come back, not to me but to life. However, I sensed I would be rebuffed, and so I didn't.

Lisa arrived ten minutes late, looking somewhat as Susan had led me to picture her. In a worn cotton dress, she seemed roundish. She wasn't unattractive, but she had inherited none of the beauty of Susan or her sister, and she obviously wanted none of the life-style that Susan had paid so dearly for.

She pointed at me as she said, "You're George Weinberg."

"And you're Lisa."

After sitting down, she asked, "So how do we start?"

I told her I'd spoken to Susan briefly about her. "But you tell me why you came here."

"My mother wants me to see you."

I asked her what she thought her mother was concerned about.

"She wants me to dress beautifully, exercise, and be gorgeous. She doesn't like the way I live. She doesn't like anything about me. She doesn't like the way Henry, Olivia, Honey, or Marshall live either."

I surmised that she meant her cats. "Why not?"

"They sleep too much, I guess. They don't go out and meet anybody, and they're satisfied with me."

"You have four of them?"

"She's never seen Miss Prim."

"Oh, I see. Why not?"

"When I found her, she was in an alley with her two dead

kittens. Miss Prim is dying too. I don't want my mother to see her, do you understand?"

"You don't think your mother might help her? What exactly is wrong with her?"

"Her eyes look cloudy, and she has a big tumor near her tail. She can hardly move. She doesn't eat, except when I make her. That's enough about Miss Prim."

Lisa wasn't looking at me, but at the wall.

"Meanwhile," she said, "my mother wants me to lose twenty pounds so she can give me some of her dresses. And she wants me to find a fancy place to go in them. She'd like me to marry a doctor, maybe an ugly doctor because I'm ugly, and give him plenty of sex."

"She said that?"

"Not the sex part, but I know that's what's on her mind. But she knows I hate doctors, they're all ugly, really."

"What do mean?"

"Well, they all experiment on animals in medical school, don't they? They kill dogs and cats and mice, at least a few, don't they? They'd kill Miss Prim if they found her.

"I guess you'd like me to get a better job and to get married and to give up my cats, wouldn't you? And not to work as an usher, wouldn't you? To do everything different."

"Lisa, why do you say that?"

"I don't know."

But here I felt it was important to push. If she truly assumed I was against her, our work, whatever it was to be, would be over before it began.

"Lisa," I repeated, "why do you think I want you to change your whole life?"

At first she didn't answer. "Well, it would be the smart thing to do, wouldn't it?"

"Lisa, that's not my aim. Believe me, if you're happy, I'm happy. If you're not, if you're unhappy about something, if things aren't working for you, that's where I want to help, if I can. I don't tell people how to live."

"Well, I have no desire to get married or to find the right

man or to leave my apartment. It would be more than enough for me if Miss Prim didn't die. Much more than enough, whether you believe that or not, it's true. Whether you believe that or not, it's true."

With that, she tucked her feet under her, resting the soles of her badly cracked shoes squarely on my couch. She was making a statement, whose import I already knew was more sweeping than I could read at the time.

I chose the route of expressing my own annoyance as a way of reassuring her. "Listen, Lisa, you can believe this or not, but it's true. I don't give a damn if you stay in your job and in your apartment forever. Or if you never get married. Or if you never lose weight or go out on a date. I'm not here to tell people how to live. There's a lot of ways to live. Millions, maybe billions. Some work for the person and some don't. Do you believe me?"

Without bothering to look at me, she said simply, "No."

"Why not?" I asked.

"Mother said Doctor Dubman would help me. I talked to him for three months, he didn't say much of anything, except that he was helping me. Then I found out he told mother everything I said. They used to talk on the phone once a week."

"How did you find that out?"

"How did I find that out? How did I? She knew that I had found another cat. She asked me about the Sufi group that I visited, if they used drugs. She didn't even pretend. He told her everything. She said it was for my own good."

"You told him how angry you were?"

"No. I just never went back. Why should I educate him about how he fucked up, and help his practice, help him ruin some other lives. Doctor Dubman. Dummery after dummery."

I felt hurt that Susan had lied about my being the first therapist. Maybe she'd felt that by the time I found out, it wouldn't matter—a curious form of mother love.

"So I'm condemned as an enemy, and there's nothing I can do, even before I start."

Lisa didn't answer.

Then I suggested, "Maybe a vet could help Miss Prim."

"Yeah. Four hundred dollars and then maybe. I talked to Phil's vet. He's supposed to be very good."

"Who's Phil?"

"A waiter in the diner next to the Beacon. Where am I going to get four hundred dollars? Susan won't give it to me. She won't lend it to me, not for a cat. I can't ask her for that. And Miss Prim doesn't eat. I bring her with me to the job, and leave her in the projection room, and I feed her sometimes and I talk to her, but she's on the way out. That's enough about Miss Prim."

She was twisting her hair.

"I'm sorry," I said.

She seemed reluctant to talk about her background when I asked and gave me only sparse facts. She mentioned the private school she had gone to and just one friend, an autistic girl whose family had liked Lisa. But the family had moved across the country and she never heard from the girl again. In school, Lisa had done especially well in history; she volunteered that she loved animals. "Anything that lives and doesn't bother you."

I thought of Miss Prim, but this time Lisa's mind went elsewhere. "Did you know that termites, when they're under attack, create more soldiers than usual? In one week, they give birth to ten percent warrior termites instead of two."

"Really!"

"Yes, they have many different kinds of specialists in the colony, the warriors, the queen, the drones, the ones whose job it is to move the queen out of danger, that's me." She enumerated the rest.

"What do you call those who move the queen, your job?" I asked.

"The 'royal chariot.' They push her into some safe place when the ants attack."

Now she was twisting her hair violently, and I could virtually see her experiencing the onslaught.

"How many ants at a time?" I asked.

"Maybe three million. But the termites hide. They build walls, they have specialists at making paste so tough the ants can't get inside. But the warriors, they're outside fighting, and the walls get sealed up behind them. And they know they can't get back. They'll never get back. They know it, but they keep fighting. In the Middle Ages we used to do that when the thane was dead. We'd fight, and we'd fight until we collapsed. We knew we had to die."

She went on about the termites and about history, and I let her, knowing that people never just talk randomly, and glad that she was willing to talk about anything. It was her role to talk, and mine to translate, to accept that she was describing herself in whatever language she chose to speak.

Apparently, she'd first gotten interested in termites after seeing the movie *The Hellstrom Chronicle*. She'd seen it many times and then gotten books out on the insects.

"What do you call those termites who keep the queen out of danger, the ones like you? I don't understand that, by the way. What do you call them?"

"The royal chariot," she said, in a very definite voice.

"And you're like them?"

"Of course. My mother's the queen. I protect her. That's my job."

"What do you mean?" In retrospect, I'm sure I would have asked, even if I'd had no residue of curiosity about Susan and the way she lived.

"I lie. When men call up, I say she isn't there. If they're the wrong ones, I make up stories. I protect her. Once I actually called the police to protect her. That's enough of that."

I showed my deference to her wishes by returning to the termites. "How many are there in a what-do-you-call-it?"

"A colony. Could be twenty million. Even a billion, I think. But this isn't helping Miss Prim, and it isn't helping me."

I thought she felt uncomfortable about having been so talkative.

Suddenly she pointed to one of the two big plants in the

corner of my office. "Look at that bromeliad. Why don't you let
it dry out so it can think?"

She got up and rushed over to it and touched the thick,
veined leaves. "You're killing it with kindness, just like my
mother. The poor plant, it can't even think."

"I didn't mean to hurt it," I said feebly.

"'Didn't mean!' That's what my mother says. They get more
light on the forest floor than they do here." With that she
scanned the room. "This is a grim place. Grimmmmm." She
shuddered, insultingly.

Toward the end of the hour, I realized that she would expect
me to go right back to Susan with everything she'd said. How
could she possibly think otherwise or trust me after what had
happened with Doctor—I couldn't remember the name, only
the word "Dummery"! I realized that nothing short of beseeching her for confidentiality could show her the force of my own
commitment to it, and even doing this would be only a start in
allaying her fears.

I announced, "Look, Lisa. Please don't talk about anything
we say here. It's very important that you don't discuss with
Susan or with anyone else what either of us says, and I won't
either. Okay?"

She just listened.

"And I won't be talking to Susan about you or anything you
said. That would destroy everything. We need strict confidentiality. If she calls, I'll tell her to call back when you're
here, so you can know for sure that I'm not talking about you.
Is it a deal?"

She nodded.

On the way out, she said, "I'll be back Tuesday. What time
have you got open?"

I suspected that she didn't fully believe me about the confidentiality, but the hour hadn't been all bad for her.

My session right after Lisa was lively; it was with a couple,
Maria and Arthur, married for nine years. Arthur had just

been caught in yet another extramarital affair by his wife. As
Maria vented her rage in sobs and in curses, I could see that
she still wanted things to work out. Her love cried out through
the depths of her injury. I remembered Shakespeare's confession to the lover who cuckolded him, that he too could not
fall out of love so easily, that "Love bends not with the re-
mover to remove" but stays even when the other person takes
his love away.

Was I thinking of my own feeling for Susan, and possibly
delighting in Maria's letting off steam because it was my steam
too? Not guilty, I thought; she needed to deliver her rage, and
she obviously wanted to do so with me in the room. Whatever
else her diatribe meant to me, it was therapeutic to let her go
on. They would have their only chance to reconstruct, if indeed there was one, if they first cleared the air.

When they were gone, I waited a good five minutes so that I
wouldn't run into them. Then I switched off the lights and left.

It was a July evening. The city was cleaner and cooler than
during the day. I walked along Columbus Avenue, lined with
stores and restaurants with new awnings and splashy signs; the
streets were thronged with people, confident, sophisticated,
the men in jeans and brightly colored shirts, the women fresh
and young. Through the dark interiors of the restaurants, I
could see lovers leaning toward one another or opening their
menus and reading them in candlelight. None of this was for
Lisa, I thought, nor did she want it. As I reflected about her, I
liked her enormously. So what if she lacked the luster so often
incident to her period of life; she had a candor and a clarity
that sparkled in their own way. She had lived her own life,
with inhibition, perhaps with irrational fear, but so far as I
could tell, with far less self-deception than most indulge in.

And there was something else about her that moved me, that
I sympathized with profoundly, and could not yet grasp. I
strained for it, the wraith of a truth that might help her and
me—me mostly, I realized when I touched it. Lisa had op-

posed Susan and her way of life, opposed it on every front, fought it in the streets and on the rooftops, in a way that I had never dared to, or I would have been far more outspoken with her than I was. In a curious sense, Lisa and I were allies and she was the bolder one.

My last thought before meeting my friends for dinner was to remind myself to keep Susan out of the therapy—not merely excluding her from information, that would be easy, but in spirit. Though I applauded Lisa's refusal to buckle under to Susan's values, I had better remember that she hadn't fought them to vindicate me and that her triumph had doubtless been costly, as all rebellions are.

Over the next few weeks, I began to see how sweeping that rebellion had been. Susan's involvement with appearances, with wearing the right outfit, the right dress, shoes, jewelry, had resulted in Lisa's rejecting anything that suggested concern with appearance. She said frankly, "I was always ugly," and it crossed my mind that this belief had led her to feel that any effort to look pretty would be a travesty. And so she had renounced the outsides of things, their shape and form, to an extraordinary degree. She was utterly indifferent to the surfaces of things. However, she had substituted an almost bizarre emphasis on what went on deep inside of them.

Those comments she'd made in the first session, about what the termites knew and about my plant being "unable to think" because I'd overwatered it were not metaphors. She really believed that she could read the thoughts not just of people but of plants, termites, and inanimate objects. In contrast with Susan, who cared little, Lisa seemed desperately involved with what went on in the very depths of beings, and of nonbeings too.

This disparity between her mother's emphasis on the outer and hers on the inner life had resulted in many clashes, but none more notable than the one three years earlier which had provoked Lisa into moving out.

Susan, after repeatedly berating her for wearing a torn coat
that didn't fit, had, while Lisa was at the museum, bought her
a brand-new one and thrown the old one out. Not believing her
at first, Lisa had scoured the apartment for it, and when finally
convinced that it was gone, had almost fainted.

After lying down for ten minutes motionless, she sprang up
and savagely demanded to know what Susan had done with the
old coat, where she had put it. Shouting "It's lonely, it's lost,
it needs me, it was always so good to me, I promised I'd keep
it forever," she had ransacked closets and strewn their contents all over the floor, still hoping that Susan had stowed it
somewhere.

She had begged its forgiveness, and then had gone rushing
through the streets, searching garbage cans, but the garbage
truck had passed through the neighborhood, and it was gone.
Her frantic call to the disposal dump that night had reached
deaf ears. Apparently, it had been shredded and burned.

She had moved out the next day.

I questioned her at length about her feelings, about what the
coat had meant to her.

"What did it mean to me? I betrayed it. They left it in my
care and I betrayed it."

"Loyalty is one of your most important values, isn't it?" I
said.

"Loyalty?" She seemed shocked. "Loyalty is everything."

It crossed my mind how much she must have suffered at the
thought that her own mother had abandoned her. But in our
first month, she had never brought up the subject of her natural mother, and I sensed that I shouldn't either. Susan was her
mother now, she used the word "mother" readily about her,
and despite her fury, it was obvious Susan meant a great deal
to her.

And Lisa's loyalty extended everywhere.

She told me, "I saw a big brown captain's chair in the
street. I started to bring it home, it was in good condition, and
then I realized I couldn't."

"Oh, no? Why not?"

"My little yellow one would be jealous."

"How can you be sure?"

"I'm sure."

Not that I had any impulse to debate the matter, but I wondered, If I had been the delegate for the more sensible, more scientific point of view, how could I have argued such an issue anyhow? "Chairs have no feelings, they have no memory, make no comparisons."

And if she'd asserted, point-blank, "They do; how do you know they don't?", I would have been left merely mouthing my assumption, as unprovable in the end as hers. Even if I had said, "But feelings require a brain, nerve endings," she could have rebutted me in the same way. After all, had not the great René Descartes maintained that animals feel no pain, being without a soul! And surely, I'd rather have been on Lisa's side than with the modern-day empiricists who hold that we can't believe that a thing exists until we can measure it. And so I found it not unpleasant to enter her world, suspending disbelief as it were.

After a while, though I never truly adopted her view, I found it effortless, and even curiously defensible. Suppose, indeed, that she was nearly always wrong in her attributions of inner life. But suppose that on rare occasions she was right and saved those objects of her love from disaster. Could not an argument be made that her intervention on behalf of the one or two was worth the pointlessness of the rest, that her two truths per hundred more than compensated for the ninety-eight fallacies?

I didn't know how she felt about me, but I suspected that she might be testing me by dressing in her most tattered T-shirts and never combing her hair. Her appearance on that first meeting had been by far her most elegant.

She had dinner with Susan one night a week; Susan insisted on it, but I think that Lisa took sustenance from it, though she would never say so. "I meet my mother tonight," she formally announced several times. Then once she added, "She wants to call you."

"Fine, so long as it's when you're in my office, so you can hear everything—unless you don't want me speaking to her at all."

"No. That's okay. She just wants to know things are okay."

"What should I tell her?"

"Whatever you want."

Later that session, something happened proving that Lisa, far from being blind to the surfaces of things, was indeed an incredibly keen observer. I realized that she was sensitive to minute visual detail, and that she differed from others essentially in how she construed what she saw. Lisa regarded all exteriors as mere manifestations of what lay below, as epiphenomena, unimportant except in so far as they represented a great play of "human" forces, which others missed entirely but which often led her to laugh or weep.

Toward the end of the session, I must have wanted emphasis, and I gestured, pointing not at Lisa but in her direction.

She laughed.

"What's so funny?" I asked.

"Now I see why you point with your left hand."

"What?"

She was giggling, as if unaware that she might be hurting my feelings. "Can I see your right hand, please?" she asked.

"What are you talking about?"

"Show me your right hand," she insisted.

I extended it, and she looked at the fingers.

"I never knew that," she said.

"What!" I was feeling exasperated.

She said, "I wondered, why do you point with your left hand? You're right-handed. You write with your right hand, you picked up that plant with your right. The only thing you do is point."

She was excited over something, and I was becoming terribly uneasy, though I didn't know why.

"Let me see that finger," she said.

When I showed her the ring finger on my right hand, she said, "No. Not the middle one. The pointer."

Even before I extended it toward her, I knew.

"Oh my God, look how crooked it is," she said. "That's funny. Oh, you poor thing. Hiding that crooked finger all those years, pointing with your left hand. How did that happen?" She giggled.

"I broke it playing baseball, when I was, maybe, twenty."

"Really!"

"Yeah, a guy was running home, and I reached for the ball before it got there, and crunch."

"You poor thing. So you pointed with the other hand all those years because you're ashamed of it."

I felt flashes of fury at her as she repeated, "And you're embarrassed about that finger."

But, of course, she was right. I could even recall the decision back then to hide that finger, a decision I'd long ago forgotten.

"You're right, Lisa." I felt it was my duty to confess, but I was still furious. I could imagine how many times a day she must have punctured Susan's facade and tormented her like a picador. One could easily yearn for such a keen observer and intrepid action-reporter to disappear.

So her dauntless truthfulness, too, was part of her counter-reaction to Susan, who often made up things expediently as she went along.

After that, I felt strangely transparent, wondering what other frauds of mine she would bring to light. However, I actually felt better about myself and traced it to her reliving that lifetime of dishonesty about my right index finger and sympathizing with me.

But after she was gone, when I remembered that Susan was to call with Lisa sitting in front of me, I felt afraid that Lisa would note something in my reaction to Susan, see it or imagine it, and regard me as superficial, or even worse, as a traitor.

Two days later, when with Lisa present, Susan did call and ask if there was anything I should know, I was icy.

"No. Nothing. Lisa's here now, and we're working together. She's a wonderful human being."

That last came easy. I really thought so.

I was glad when we hung up.

"You know," Lisa said, "I mentioned that Doctor Dubman told mother everything. That wasn't exactly right."

"No?"

"No. When I didn't show up, and he charged her for the hour, he never mentioned that I wasn't there."

"Well, I'd miss you and our conversations if you didn't show up here," I said quickly.

"Thanks," she said, and I was surprised.

I felt that I had survived the test of her fluoroscopic eye and that we were closer.

Later, when I thought about Susan, there was no sense of flight. It was as if the wheels had touched ground.

My next patient that day was a college girl, used to instant service. She kept her finger on the doorbell, as if she knew that I was indulging in inappropriate reveries. "Yes, master" were the words that went through my mind as I walked with deliberate slowness to let her in. My shambling gait was as much in defiance of the passage of time as of her. Though toughness from me was called for if she was ever to build real relationships, maybe she got a little extra toughness that day.

Over the following few months, there was one subject that Lisa steadfastly refused to talk to me about—her cats. I got the sense that she had promised them confidentiality, and that was that. But I also wondered if I had said anything relating to them that she had considered offensive. Apparently not, or at least she didn't tell me. When on occasion I asked her about the condition of Miss Prim, she would always reply, "No change," using those same two words, saying no more and no less. Still I kept asking every so often, since though she was obviously responding in accordance with some policy, arrived at in her private chambers, I felt she expected me to ask. And besides, I was truly concerned. But all that was soon to change.

Because Lisa had never called me before and because her voice was muffled in sobs, I had no idea who was saying, "Hello, is this George?"

"Yes, who is this?"

"Miss Prim's not eating. She's not eating at all. She was starting to eat, and now she won't eat at all. She's just lying there and her tail is thrashing. She's in pain. She's getting ready to die."

"Lisa, we've got to get her to a vet."

"I can't. I don't have any money."

"Lisa, don't worry about money. We have to do our best. Just bring her there. I'll give you the money. Or lend you the money, or whatever you want."

She hesitated.

I had an idea, and told her, "I'm lending it to Miss Prim, all right? Put her in the carrying case with some water and bring her over there."

Still she hesitated.

"Just bring her there. Then you can come here and get the money. Call me as soon as you can."

"Okay."

It was late Monday afternoon, and I prayed they'd be open.

Later she called. "They're keeping Miss Prim. He says he doesn't know what it is. They gave her a shot of fluid. They're giving her fluids overnight. He wants to study the swelling. He's a good man, I think. Doctor Clinger. A very soft man, a caring man."

"That's wonderful."

"But Miss Prim's all alone. Do you think she's scared? She was crying."

"I doubt it, Lisa. She's probably just goofy right now."

The next day Lisa seemed softer. She didn't actually thank me for the money when I handed her the envelope—"a loan to you or a gift to Miss Prim, whatever you want"—but she looked at me admiringly.

Then she said, "I'm afraid to call. I was hoping that . . . maybe . . ."

"That maybe I would call?" I asked.

"Yes, that maybe, I just couldn't—"

"I'll tell you what. You call. We'll turn up the loudspeaker on my phone, and I'll listen. Okay?"

Tremulously, she took the phone. I could help her, but I couldn't live her life.

A secretary told her to wait. "The doctor will be right with you."

We waited together.

Finally, the doctor came to the phone. "I can't tell yet. She's got plenty of fluids. She's moving around a little bit. She's a feisty little character. We gave her an anti-inflammatory. We'll send the blood out tonight, they pick it up at four. There's really not much to say right now about what's wrong with her. Could be any of a number of things. Call back at about six before we close, if you want to see how she's doing." He spoke in a singsong voice, which gave even his most factual assertions the effect of a lullaby.

"Did you say six?"

"Six o'clock. Maybe a little after. We'll be cleaning up then. Okay?"

"Okay," Lisa said, and for the first time I saw her crying.

I felt a great kinship with her, and then I remembered that Lisa had almost fainted over the "death" of her old, torn coat, and I was suddenly reminded of how different we were.

To this day, it has never crossed my mind that my offer of money would have any countertherapeutic element. How despicable are the precisionists in psychology who care more about the operation than the patient! Lisa could only gain by my pitching in. She would know that my heart was in the right place, and when later I took the liberty of admonishing her, she would know that I was not being merely sadistic.

As for Miss Prim, admittedly, I might not have done the same for her under every conceivable condition. But had anyone I knew thrust forth a cat in a near-death state and proved that I was its only hope, I would like to think I would have done the same.

Anyhow, Lisa insisted on paying me back, ten dollars a week, and I was glad.

To our joy and astonishment, Miss P, who had been indeed dying, was quickly recoverable. The vet removed a huge cyst, gave her antibiotics, and sent her home in four days. Seeing that Lisa was one of those who truly care, he charged her a mere two hundred dollars.

After that, everything changed between us. She began confiding in me more and more examples in which she read life into objects like the yellow chair and torn coat. It was as if there were no such thing as an impersonal event. I thought about those primitives who assigned purpose and human frailty to trees and mountains and even the sky above them. The detachment of life from the object to the spirit supposedly residing in it had taken millennia, and the notion of the inanimate had required millennia more. Doubtless, we all indulge in such primitive thought on occasion, but Lisa engaged in such animation as a way of life.

Only slowly did I come to see that in addition to this tendency, she also possessed a keenness of observation, and even of interpretation, that was a whole order of magnitude better than most people's. Lisa had what the Celts used to call "the sight." And because it was coupled with a very flawed sense of what it hurt people to hear, she often got herself into predicaments that were either comical or tragical, depending upon the observer's state of mind at the moment.

For instance, in her job as usherette, a couple in their forties had berated her for not finding them two seats together. For a while, Lisa had said nothing, then when the man persisted, she snapped, "Look, you didn't know each other before tonight. Why don't you sit separately and meet two hours later?"

The two of them were astonished, and the man asked how she could possibly have known.

Lisa had told him, "Well, if she knew you were that short, she wouldn't have worn those high-heeled shoes."

In my office, Lisa didn't laugh but kept looking at me through those same timid brown eyes, as she told me that story and the next, which actually frightened me.

For some time, she'd been lamenting the "decision" by a plant in her building to give up and die, because after a year, a bigger one had been placed in front of it by the window.

She'd left the neighbor a note, but nothing was done. Finally, she had rung his bell and tried to explain, but he threw her out. "Get out of here, you witch!" he'd said.

He was a fat man in a yellowing white shirt and a rumpled brown suit—he looked like a baked potato, she told me.

Shortly after that, the plant had disappeared from the window. In Lisa's words, it had been "driven to suicide."

A month or so later, at about eleven-thirty at night, she'd found herself in the elevator with the "baked potato." He was beside himself because he'd forgotten to press his floor and had to ride up to the twelfth with her. He was peering into the mirror at his collar, distressed and seemingly unaware of Lisa, when she said, "It's all right. She won't know."

He stiffened as if he'd heard a ghastly shriek. "Won't know what?" he asked.

"Your wife won't know you've been with another woman tonight," Lisa said. "I won't tell her."

With that he lost all poise. "Who are you? A detective. Coming to my apartment. I knew there was more to it than you said. Are you a detective? What do you want? No, you can't be. What do you want?"

She just looked at him.

He'd run out of the elevator as if he'd seen a ghost.

I asked Lisa how she knew, and it was simple enough.

"Why would a man look so nervously at his collar, coming home late at night?"

After that, the man tried to avoid her, and when he couldn't, he always tipped his hat and said hello to her politely.

It amused me that if he'd thought she was a witch when she rang his bell, he must be convinced of it now. Then I had the terrible realization that in past times, Lisa was precisely the individual—an unmarried woman who knew too much, a lover of cats, someone who lived an idiosyncratic life without ties— who would have been called a witch. Had she not given the man a near-seizure?

I could see the townsfolk, in a place like Salem, banging on her door, and pulling her from her bed, half-dressed. Some would kill her cats while others tugged her through the streets. The trial would be quick—she laughed inappropriately and had the habit of pointing like a mariner; she might refer to a plant's preference or the inner life of a chair. The "baked potato" would be the chief witness against her and would surely prevail. They would bludgeon her with stones before setting her on fire while the people stood by, fascinated. I pictured her not saying a word. When I wrested myself away from the imagery, I felt closer to her, more protective, and gave thanks that we were here and now, and not there, back then.

A year passed quickly. Lisa was coming regularly, twice a week, and my picture of what had to be done was clarifying. I'd long realized that she'd built much of her personality and value-structure in opposition to Susan. Even before that, there had been the profound injury of her abandonment by her real parents. Her father had turned away in disgust after being denied access to her when he'd been caught in an affair. Her mother, Susan's sister, had bad-mouthed him, and Lisa and her two older brothers had no choice but to stake everything on their mother.

Her two brothers had been escorted across the country to "beautiful California," and Lisa was told she would be collected shortly, that the family would be reunited within the year.

At seven, she had gone to the mailbox daily for good news, picturing the knot of them living in ceaseless harmony, with no one growing up or changing, ever. When no summons came, she could only explain it one way—she was ugly and therefore inappropriate. Susan, her new mother, was beautiful, and by living with Susan, she would make up her deficiency and become beautiful too.

She had loved Susan and always would, but soon had to de-emphasize pulchritude. She was too round, too fat, and the fancier the dress, the worse she looked in it. Especially when at ten she wore braces on her teeth, she crystallized the notion that her benevolent foster-mother was doomed to fail in her effort to redeem and glorify one so hopelessly and irretrievably ugly. From there, a few fiats of the will became the axioms for a new kind of identity, in which beauty, grace, finery, smoothness were anathema. Her comrades were the injured, the by-passed, those not called upon, the voiceless. She had invented for herself Walt Whitman's rule that "Whoever offends another offends me."

She watched Susan date elegant men, successful ones, mostly older, but not the dingy characters in fedora hats that I used to picture pursuing her for sex. One of them gave her a Cadillac "for being beautiful." Their very suavity and politeness to Lisa—some brought her small gifts—made her feel more undeserving; she soon learned to say bumptious things to them: "Are you married?" "Do you love my mother?"

Not surprisingly, Susan slowly elected to keep her out of their company, a decision that seemingly expressed her conclusion that Lisa's path would not follow her own. And, indeed, that was obvious. In trying to be as different from Susan as she could, Lisa had renounced, to a great degree, her concern with anything to do with appearances in the external world.

However, I had come full circle from my original belief that Lisa did not see that world. I gave up my original hackneyed assumption that she had psychically blinded herself to externals, like those ascetics who concentrate utterly on what lies

below. Far from being blind to them, Lisa was a more accurate
perceiver of externals than anyone I had ever known. Possibly
because of her idiosyncratic values, she was able to draw remarkable conclusions from what she saw—about people, and
in the other sense of "remarkable," about animals and even
objects. More accurately, Lisa's outside world, the doings of
others as she perceived them, amounted to a giant and continuous cryptogram. Her accustomed mode of perception was to
decode it, always reasoning from what she saw to its "psychic"
meaning. It was beyond doubt that she possessed a singular
kind of power. She was right stunningly often about people,
and, to my mind, was wrong only when her interpretations
edged too deeply into the realm of the unknowable, especially
the inanimate.

Because adults had so often broken promises and tampered
with her faith, it took a long time for our relationship to solidify. Again and again, she would accuse me, groundlessly I
felt, of secretly wanting her to dress up, to lose weight, to have
sex, to change jobs. And each time she did, I sought to reassure her that, though I wanted her to go on voicing these
charges, I was not guilty.

"If you want any of these things, fine. Maybe I can help.
But you have no grounds for accusing me of trying to trick you
into another life."

I took pains to convey to her that no self-respecting therapist, indeed no one who respects others, should have a single
outcome in mind for another person, whether that other person
is our child, or sibling, or spouse, or friend, or a stranger. We
may decide that for us marriage is ideal or getting wealthy or
keeping up with the neighbors or becoming professionals or
whatever. But to respect someone else requires helping that
person strive to sculpt his own life in accordance with his
deepest wishes.

"Lisa, I'll make a deal with you. If you catch me forcing any
such goal, please tell me. Show me that I'm doing that, and
how, and I'll apologize and be careful not to."

Slowly she became convinced. And because she was so acutely sensitive to even the slightest effort to convert her to conventionality or to any end of one's own, I felt complimented by her acceptance of me.

I liked her enormously. I enjoyed her originality, her burning intensity, though I worried about her welfare, perhaps akin to the way she worried about that of her five cats.

Meanwhile, I kept asking myself, How could I be useful to Lisa beyond the relationship itself? There could be no template for an ideal Lisa. All I could do would be to search for anything that she might secretly want and as yet be unable to attain. To the extent that I could do this, I would be offering more than a mere model of friendship.

However, I felt a curious inability to do this. As I kept asking myself what else I could give her, no answer came.

Slowly I realized that the blanks I drew were themselves meaningful. I had found no answer because Lisa hadn't conveyed any sense that she wanted anything beyond what she already had: her daily routine of caring for the cats, going to the movie house, seeing certain films over and over, and leading people up and down the aisle through the dark with her flashlight. If I were to take this completeness at face value, the most I could do would be to understand her, to bolster her feelings of worth and sufficiency in the life she'd chosen, and to stop there.

This would have to be my plan. It would be presumptuous and unethical to try to sell her on what I considered a better way of life. The therapist's role must never be to undermine life-styles that people choose.

However, one thing troubled me. Suppose that this "failure of personal acquisitiveness" was itself a reaction to Susan's goading, to Susan's own strivings and shallowness. Suppose it was Lisa's way of saying, "I refuse to risk being as disappointed and as unhappy as my mother." If, indeed, she was settling for less but wanted more, then it was my job to uncover that truth, along with others, and to present it to her. Possibly, I could help her pursue that "more," whatever it turned out to be.

I kept this hypothesis in mind, as I continued to study her life, using my own flashlight as I looked into its nooks and crannies.

Apart from Susan, there were few regulars in Lisa's everyday affairs. There was Phil, the waiter at a nearby diner where Lisa would sit, sipping coffee during her breaks. And the others were mostly neighbors who walked their dogs regularly, people with whom Lisa chatted whenever she chanced to meet them.

"Is that the way you want it?" I asked her.

"You mean is it by design or by disease?" she said, and we both laughed.

But she knew what I was driving at. "I think so," she added. "People are so meddlesome. If they don't want sex, they want to criticize you."

"Why? Who does that?"

She had recently been stung by someone's comment that she always wore the same outfit.

"Who said that?"

"Janet. A woman who works in the theater with me."

Lisa's response had been the covert resolution never to talk to Janet again.

"I guess you like the way you dress, and it's nobody's business," I said.

"I don't like it, especially. But what should I do? Get all dolled up, get a permanent, and have people call me a tramp?"

I didn't respond, but of course I thought of her childhood model, Susan. Susan's adorning herself meant prostitution to Lisa, if not of her body then at least of her values. Surely, Lisa was engaging in a heavy projection about what people would think, what they would read into any attempt of hers to beautify herself.

"Sex isn't worth it," she said, apropos of nothing that I could discover.

"That's up to you."

"People would know right away if I put makeup on that I wanted a man. Maybe I do sometimes, but I don't see making an announcement."

It was the first time she'd ever suggested as much.

"What do you mean?"

"They'd see that I was lonely and that things weren't perfect for me, and that's all I'd need. No, thank you. I don't want them to see anything."

I didn't comment, but I was interested in her being so concerned with what people saw, and in her giant overestimation of what they could read about her. She imagined that people could virtually see her motives, infer them from her smallest acts.

That session was a breakthrough. She had trusted me a great deal by divulging to me even a modicum of discontent. She had risked my disdain and my meddling in her private life.

Above all, I wanted her to see that I had no intention of tampering with this treasure, though I would help her if she let me. So as not to appear like someone itching for her to have problems, I didn't refer to anything she'd said that session when I saw her next. Nor did she.

However, a few weeks later, when she again commented that things weren't perfect, I asked her what she meant.

"Nothing." She stopped me cold.

But the following week she told me a sad story. Her one friend Phil wasn't talking to her anymore.

"Why not?"

"He said I insulted him."

"You did? How?"

"He dropped a tray, and I guess I laughed. He always puts too much on one side. It was inevitable."

"And he's not talking to you for that?"

"Nope."

"The first time?"

"No. He says I always make fun of him. But he ought to know I'm not really laughing at him. Phil is a nice guy. But he's very oversensitive, and he's really not a very good waiter."

It occurred to me that if I simply joined her in this indictment of a friend, I might be doing her a serious disservice. She was given to confronting people with their painful inner realities, as if she had no idea she was hurting them. I'd enjoyed it when she'd done this to a few who, in my opinion, had deserved it, but I'd been personally stung by her more than once.

As for Phil, I could appreciate her loss while not siding with her.

"Do you still go there?" I asked her.

"Well, not really."

"But you were friends. You saw him every day. I wonder if anything can be done."

"Do you think it was bad, what I did?"

If there was ever a loaded question, this was it.

I hedged. "I think he was very hurt. I mean, being a waiter is what he does for a living. I guess nobody likes to be laughed at. And he likes you, that makes it worse. But if he never talks to you again, that's really going some."

"Should I go back in there?"

"Do you want to?"

"I guess so. People can dish it out, but they really can't take it."

"I don't know if that was Phil's problem," I said drily.

"What do you mean?"

"I mean he was a waiter, but he couldn't dish it out very well."

She smiled. It was as if she knew I was trying to comfort her by seeing the thing lightly, and she appreciated my impulse, but I couldn't truly solace her.

Still, the door was open enough to admit some light, and I decided to make the most of it.

"Lisa," I said, "I agree with you that a lot of people do get hurt by a lot of things. But it's important to know what's going to hurt people."

"I know," she confessed. "I guess I do hurt people's feelings. I'm aware of that. I say things that hurt them."

"Really? Who?"

She told me that recently several of Susan's women friends had objected to her "mind reading," and would break dates with Susan if she was going to be there. It put Susan on the spot. Usually she favored Lisa, but not always.

And back in college, she had lost her closest woman friend, Ellen, the same way. Apparently, Ellen took Dexedrine and was embarrassed about it. Lisa would know when she'd had some and would comment, "Is it your boyfriend who's so terrific, or is it the Dexedrine?" Or "I see you're on that stuff again, you always make so many telephone calls."

Ellen had demanded that Lisa apologize, but Lisa had refused to, and as a result they never spoke again.

"I can live without people like that," Lisa said.

I thrust the door open a little wider.

"Lisa, I'm sure you can. You are. But you're not the world champion at knowing when you're going to hurt someone by something you're about to say. I mean, if you don't *want* someone in your life, that's one thing. We all drop people, you know what I mean, do housecleaning now and then. But I don't want you to lose a single person you like because you didn't know what you were doing. I mean because you didn't realize that you were hurting someone's feelings."

She didn't say anything, and I couldn't tell how she was reacting.

That weekend I ranged between thinking that my timing had been great and she'd heard me, and worrying that I'd chosen too sensitive a moment to criticize her and that I'd offended her unforgivably.

When ten minutes had gone by and she still hadn't appeared for our next session, I inclined toward the latter view. Or even if I hadn't offended her at the time, it seemed to me, possibly she'd done a slow roast as she thought about what I'd said afterward.

However, she breezed in and told me that she'd apologized to Phil and that they were friends again. She was very happy about it. Apparently, she had weighed my words carefully. She asked me point-blank, "Do I hurt your feelings?"

I wondered how much to say. Then I ventured, "Sometimes, Lisa."

"When? Tell me when?"

"Well, you laugh at me sometimes. Like at my crooked finger. Or the time I dropped my Rolodex when I went to pick up the phone. Or the time I was all dressed up in that dark suit because I was going somewhere formal, and you said I looked uncomfortable."

"Well, you did. You know you did."

"All right, maybe I did look uncomfortable. But, Lisa, you see an awful lot. You have a gift. I want you to tell me everything, that's our deal. I'm just saying that if you tell everybody everything, you're going to hurt a lot of people's feelings."

She didn't reply but looked grim.

Toward the end of the session, she asked me accusingly, "Why did you say all that to me about my hurting people's feelings?" Her lips were pursed and there was a tremor in her voice.

I realized that she was terribly shaken, and I was annoyed with myself for not seeing it coming. But I also felt there could be no turning back. If I deferred to her, she would spot in an instant what I was doing, and would see me as condescending; it would kill her if she thought I was being charitable to her. It was far better to treat her as robust.

So I told her the truth.

"Lisa, I want you to know how you affect people, so you can consider whether to say things or not."

"You weren't trying to hurt me?"

"Not at all, Lisa. Not at all."

That night I kept replaying the hour. The very idea that I would deliberately stoke up anguish in someone so vulnerable caused a terrible sorrow in me. I wondered how she could think so. Had not my loyalty spoken for itself? Apparently not.

I knew she was suffering, thinking about herself and me. I wondered if I'd been too rough. I did my best to console myself with the idea that these things had to be said and that if she thought I had acted sadistically toward her, it was her own import into the relationship; it was, technically speaking, her "transference." But, somehow, even if all that was true, it didn't console me.

I could hardly wait for her to come in, so that I could reassure her.

But if she had been shaken, she'd rallied fast. "You know, I've been thinking over what you said."

"Really?"

"Yeah. Something happened last night that told me you were right."

She'd been sitting near the window of the coffee shop where Phil worked, during her break. Diane, another usherette, was walking by outside with a young man. They had nodded to each other as she went by. Then, after a few more steps, Diane had wheeled around and rushed into the diner.

"Hello. How are you?" she'd said to Lisa warmly. "I was just walking down the street with John. He's my next-door neighbor."

Lisa had said, "So your boyfriend is very jealous, huh?"

Diane had almost keeled over. "How did you know?"

"Well, you never talk to me. You don't even *like* me. You think I'm a nut! So why would you rush in like that? Don't worry, I won't say anything. I didn't even know you had a boyfriend."

"Well, Jim doesn't always understand," Diane had said, before realizing that she owed no explanation. "Okay. Goodbye," she said and ran out.

I was stunned and resisted the words, "Lisa, you're out of this world." Instead, I told her, "Lisa, you've got to recognize that you see a hell of a lot more than other people do. I would never have spotted what you did about—what's her name—Diane. But you scared her half to death."

"I know," she admitted. "But I didn't realize."

I thought I saw a glint of humor light her brown eyes, but she didn't speak.

I went on. "This is a great example of your telling someone a lot more than the person wants to hear."

"I know," she repeated. "But it's all new to me."

For a while, she seemed to be thinking, and I was quiet. Then she said, "Look, I'm going to try. If I say anything that hurts you, please tell me."

I promised her that I would.

Then, as if the idea were hard for her to absorb, she asked, "You really don't see things like that?"

"Lisa, I'm very observant. I see a lot. I'm not stupid. But you're an X-ray machine."

"But you understand things," she said.

I could tell that she wanted me to remain superior to her, to remain her guide. My fall from such a position shook her. If, indeed, there was no one, it would force her to face the terrible truth that excellence must so often confront, the truth of one's aloneness on earth. But despite her gift, I was with her and could still help, and I wanted her to know that.

I assured her, "One thing I can do, Lisa, is to help you see when a comment you might make will hurt somebody."

"Thank you," she said at the end of the hour. I surmised that she was thanking me not for the insight but for my continued allegiance to her. She was more scared than ever, now that she saw herself as someone whose natural style would offend people, maybe even drive them out of her life.

At long last, our therapy had become sharply focused. She was starting to assimilate two truths: that she had a singular and spectacular gift and that it was accompanied by a curious blindness concerning the effect that she herself had on people. I wondered how such sight could accompany such blindness.

And then, as if the data had suddenly assembled themselves, I arrived at a whole new understanding of Lisa.

In marveling at her powers of observation, I had often

thought of Sherlock Holmes's famous line, chiding his friend, "You see, Watson, but you do not observe."

But for some reason, the line suddenly told me something startlingly new, as it sank in. Holmes recognized that Watson, that humankind, saw but did not observe. He was well aware of his own genius. Lisa, on the other hand, had possessed no inkling of hers. She was typically surprised that her comments appeared like miracles to people. Lisa had imagined that others, the majority, everybody, saw as penetratingly as she did. And therein lay her downfall!

I recalled her comment that if anyone saw her putting makeup on, they would know that she had made the great decision to meet men. And her telling me she had worn the same clothing so that others could not infer her moods of the day or her thoughts.

Suddenly it all made sense: those and other comments, why she had chosen to work in the darkness, the only one with the flashlight, who could see but not be seen. In assuming that her own fluoroscopic vision was nothing special, that it was universal, she had taken for granted that other people could read her the way she could read them—in short, she had assumed that she was *transparent*.

Couple this assumption of hers with some degree of self-hatred, easily enough arrived at by any child abandoned by a real mother, and I had a simple formula. Lisa had believed, unconsciously, that for others to look at her was to see what she saw, and to hate her. She had often referred to herself as "ugly."

Ironically, that sense of personal unworthiness was perhaps the strongest element that she shared with Susan, though they had diverged utterly in how they had chosen to deal with it. Susan had adopted the camouflage of style, while Lisa had spent her life trying to avoid the imagined X-ray vision of others. By identifying with others too much, and in that sense attributing to them her own powers, she had constricted her whole life.

It followed that if she could only comprehend, if she could

only grasp the real freedom she had to move among others and
not be pinpointed, not be plumbed to her depths by them, she
might make very different choices—and perhaps much happier ones for her. People were not nearly as formidable as she
imagined them.

Though such a discovery could come only gradually, it
promised to be of profound significance in her life.

My immediate goal, then, was to help her appreciate that
she herself was not transparent, to recognize that, though she
personally could infer deep truths from minutiae, others could
not. Those she encountered in her daily life were, alongside
her, in a trance. She had infinitely more freedom than she
imagined to "reveal" her motives, to commit blunders, to make
friends and lose them, to pursue her goals, without penalty.
She was in a world more merciful, if not in its design, then in
its ignorance, indifference, and even blindness than she'd ever
thought.

As I set myself to helping her appreciate how little most
people saw, she found it hard to believe. But evidence began
to come in. A world in which people saw so much less was an
easier one to inhabit. Lisa began taking more chances with
other people, and one relationship that started about then had
great repercussions in her life.

There was a woman, about thirty, who came to the Beacon
regularly to see old films. Lisa would often take her to her
seat, and had observed in the glare of her flashlight hairs on
the woman's various jackets, some coarse, some fine, and of
gray, white, and black.

One day while seating the woman, she could not help asking, "Your dog gets along with your four cats?"

"Yes," the woman had said. "Perfectly fine. They grew up
together."

She didn't seem surprised that Lisa knew, and Lisa in turn
hadn't expected her to be.

They struck up a conversation when the film was over. After
that, Lisa brought a clothes brush to the theater and would
brush off the woman's coat. She refused a tip, and soon they

were talking regularly. The woman, who gave the name Natalie, told Lisa that she helped out at the ASPCA.

They became friends, and Lisa took her to Phil's diner, where they would sit around, talking mostly about animals. After that, they met about once a week in the theater or for coffee.

The relationship with Natalie became important to Lisa, and I was glad for it. Natalie had said to her, "You're the only person who doesn't ask me a thousand questions about my life." And from that Lisa had concluded, "She's telling me she doesn't want to be asked any questions."

"And thanking you at the same time," I hastened to add. "People really appreciate not being interrogated and not being read."

"I know, I know," Lisa said, as if I had laid on that last piece of advice with the delicacy of an avalanche.

She made several other friends too, still acquaintances from their side but friends from hers. That tendency of hers to penetrate the depths, which at worst expressed itself as startling invasiveness, always left her far more involved with people than they were with her. The disparity was, of course, especially evident in her relationships with inanimate objects, which, to my mind anyhow, gave absolutely nothing back.

Most of her new friends were women who came to see old movies. In general, people were talking to her more often, and I felt sure that this reflected an upturn in her own accessibility.

And there was one man, Tommie, in his early thirties, "frail looking" she said, who was very shy. "I know exactly when Tommie's going to go to the back of the theater to buy candy from the machine. He always goes in *Waterloo Bridge* and in *A Star Is Born* when someone is about to commit suicide. He can't watch. We talk a few minutes. Then he rushes back to his seat."

"You see right through him."

"In a way. I feel sorry for him. He reminds me of Marshall when there's a storm outside. Marshall hides on a top shelf behind some of my books that need the best protection because they're so old. They like their new covers, though. He told me I was lucky to have this job."

"If you tell him that you know exactly when and why he's going to the back of the theater, you'll terrify him worse than the film. He's liable to stop talking to you."

As I said this, the image of the witch being torn to pieces came back to me.

"I know . . . I know. I won't." She put up her hand, like a traffic cop. Then she added, "I started to say, 'You remind me of Marsh—,' but I thought about what you'd been telling me, so I stopped. And when he asked me, 'Who?' I just said, 'A very handsome friend.'"

Over the succeeding months, my task remained to help her appreciate her own impact on people, without ever telling her what to do—to give her civilization without betraying her to civilization.

Hardly a week went by when she didn't astound me with her sight. She was able to read people's past experiences and even their intentions from signs that I would never have observed or properly construed, even if I had. She told me that a neighbor's eleven-year-old daughter was planning to run away from home. The girl did take off two weeks later but was returned by the police. She also mentioned that two men who went to Phil's diner were plotting a crooked business deal, and though I never saw this corroborated, I had reached the point where I did not doubt it.

Sometimes she astonished me by inferences about me, as when she noted that in the past I used to go out with a lot of different women, but could never find happiness. And now—well, now she wasn't sure.

"What makes you think so?"

"Well, you have a little boy's expectations, and you also have a very cynical side."

For an instant, I reverted to being part of that crowd who would have burned her as a witch.

When she asked me, "Am I right?" I was glad for the therapist's asylum of anonymity. I told her for the tenth time that I wouldn't answer questions about myself, and she grudgingly accepted that.

Sometimes I felt that it didn't matter. I was like someone with a submachine gun trying to go through an electric eye. Always I took my own discomfort as a sign that others would be put off by her if she exposed to them her insights about them.

Immediately useful for my work were very dramatic examples of how her powers of perception fed her own feeling of transparency and the terrible dread that accompanied it.

One evening she was talking with Tommie between films and told him about her cats. She mentioned Marshall, his timidity, and added that he needed "special care."

Afterward, she felt sure that Tommie would recall her likening him to Marshall. Hers had been a quick comment made four months previously, and she had not even completed the name "Marshall." Moreover, she had claimed to be thinking about a man friend; the subject had been dropped and never reopened. However, now she felt sure that Tommie would not only recall her comment, but figure out that she had no such friend and had been lying. He would feel mortally insulted and probably would never talk to her again.

I recalled her many references to people as so much trouble, and it was obvious why. If they saw this much and were so ready to recoil in horror, then what prospect had she of keeping any relationship alive?

I asked her how Tommie could possibly be so sure that it was the same Marshall, even if he did recall that comment made a long time ago.

But she was certain.

I had the impulse to say, "Well, you don't have to admit it. Maybe you named your cat after the guy." But her fear went beyond that. To her, it was only a matter of time until he would put the pieces together and disown her.

The best I could do was to get her to articulate that fear, which she did, session after session.

Only slowly did she become convinced that Tommie had seen nothing, or at least that he had made no sense out of her comparison, experienced no slur on his shyness. And once she did absorb this, I made capital of her dire expectation, using it repeatedly in new contexts to help her grasp how radically she overestimated other people's "power of sight."

I told Lisa, "Besides, if they can really see things, they know you have a beautiful soul. They know you're not trying to do them in. They recognize all your acts of caring. No real friend would judge you by a single act, by one moment of your life, and certainly not without talking it out at length."

She listened with a likable and curious openness, and I felt sure I had made an impression.

Feeling ugly and undesirable, Lisa was constantly surprised when Natalie would call and say she was coming to the theater that night. Then one day, Natalie asked her to have lunch. She suggested a sophisticated midtown restaurant, and Lisa went into an immediate panic. Natalie had sensed it. "Don't worry. I'll pay. It will be my pleasure. No problem."

Lisa had consented, but in terror. She felt unworthy of such a friend and such a place, no matter who paid. But she perceived that to turn down the offer point-blank might be interpreted by Natalie as a rejection of her. She told me that she didn't have the clothes or the know-how, and could see the relationship ending with that lunch.

My reassurances fell flat, and Lisa finally decided to talk to Susan, who promised to get her ready that morning. They had their best time together in years, with Susan enjoying the role of expert, and Lisa allowing her to use her savoir faire in a helping way.

Susan had bought her a pair of designer glasses and did her makeup. She sent Lisa off with a list of instructions— "Don't rush your food." "Tell her it's your turn next." "If you get there early, ask the maitre d' if she's arrived. By the way, what's her last name, anyhow?"

Lisa didn't know.

The lunch went fine, and afterward Natalie invited her back home to see her animals. It was a gigantic co-op apartment, where she lived with her cook. Lisa helped prune some of her plants. Probably, it was a pleasant day for Natalie, but Lisa almost collapsed under the strain. Susan had suggested that she call afterward, but she couldn't.

Once again, Lisa was sure she had blown the relationship by some faux pas; she considered Natalie her dearest friend, though the two saw each other only occasionally and briefly.

She was overjoyed when Natalie telephoned her to say she'd be coming in the following Wednesday.

Actually, all of Lisa's relationships were highly romantic and fragile, which made it hard for her to pursue them actively. Yet they were evolving, and it seemed to me that these relationships, collectively, were becoming the true therapeutic force for her now. My own role was becoming secondary. If she could maintain these friendships, I could help her use them to see that people were not nearly so judgmental as she'd thought and that she was in no way transparent.

Then she got a phone call from Natalie, which, though well intended, came like the jagged edge of a hurled knife.

"I'd like to invite you for the July fourth weekend. To my house in Southampton. We're having a small dinner party. I thought you might come for the weekend."

Lisa had said she would let her know.

In my office, she was quivering, and she kept covering her face with her hands. Her words suggested fury at Natalie for not understanding her better. "She knows I can't stand people and fancy dresses and dinner parties." But, obviously, she was terrified.

"If you feel that way, you won't go," I said, as reassuringly as I could.

"I don't even have a bathing suit. But if I refuse, she'll hate me. Why did she *do this to me!*"

I suggested that Natalie meant it as a real option. "Obviously, she likes you, but she can live with your not going, with your seeing her only in the city. Maybe I'm wrong, but I feel strongly that you're underestimating her."

By the time she left my office, she seemed resolved to turn down the offer and take her chances. I knew that the matter of her dealing with invitations was far from closed, that there were some, like this one, that she wanted to accept but was afraid to. Her age-old sense of being awkward and unworthy would sorely crimp her efforts to move toward people until we dealt with it. But committing herself to a weekend with people she considered out of her league sprang up as too high a hurdle; it was not the place to start.

With this in mind, I made a very deliberate decision to let this one pass, not even to use it to investigate her long-standing fear. There would be other challenges, which she could study and deal with, and we would tackle them in the not-too-distant future.

I was satisfied that Lisa's turning down this invitation would do her no real harm. On the good side, she would see, after refusing, that Natalie was still her friend, and this would broaden her sense of the value of friendship. With such an understanding, if later she came up against a truly narrow-minded person who berated her for an innocent act, she could see him for what he was, by comparing him with her real friends. And above all, she would go through life with a sense of what decent people expected of her. We would make the most of her turning down the invitation with thanks.

Then Susan got into the act.

Lisa had been telling her about Natalie on and off since that lunch, and Susan had listened without saying much. But now, all at once, something clicked in Susan's mind: Natalie's living alone with a cook in that huge apartment, her comment that she had grown up going back and forth to Italy, her outspoken love of animals, and finally Lisa's description of her as having auburn hair. She was Natalia K., heiress of a world-renowned wine importer, and fabulously wealthy. Those were real Manets on her wall. "Do you have any idea what that apartment of hers on East Sixty-second Street is worth?"

Lisa didn't.

"Maybe three million dollars, that's all. At least that. And she has homes in Florence and Paris. My friend Margo knows the family. I think it's wonderful that you're her friend."

"I know. She gives a lot of money to animal welfare."

"You really should go for that weekend. I'll buy you some outfits. You really have to go."

Then, after Lisa had insisted that she didn't care, and wouldn't go, Susan trespassed beyond the point of no return: She accused Lisa of settling for a lifetime in her dingy apartment "with all those stray cats of yours."

After that, the breach took only seconds.

"Don't call my cats stray," replied Lisa, sizzling with indignation. "They're not stray anymore. And they're a lot better than your stray men. And don't talk about Natalie either. Just keep your hands off her. I'm sorry I ever mentioned her."

Moments later, she had thrown her keys to Susan's apartment on the kitchen floor, announced that she would never talk to Susan again, and was gone.

She called Natalie and told her politely that she had "too much happening" and couldn't go. "But thank you very much." They arranged to meet in the city the following week.

In my office, Lisa sobbed as she told me that she'd had it with her mother. Indeed, Susan had insulted her far more profoundly than she herself could have fathomed. Susan had conceived of Natalie, Lisa's treasured friend, less as a person than as an acquisition. Unable to comprehend genuine friendship, she had virtually congratulated Lisa for what she saw as connivance in doing so well. And worst of all, she had expressed surprise that Lisa could have endeared herself to someone so select and so lofty.

Lisa had, without putting it in so many words, responded to her mother's tainted view of her and of friendship. It was a view which, I could not help thinking, amounted to the real argument against prostitution in any form—that it reduces other people to the status of objects and relationships to deals. It daubs the universe with gray, muting and destroying the primary colors of whatever it regards.

As Lisa told me about the argument, I got an even better understanding of what she'd been rebelling against over the years.

Even so, as the months came and went, with Susan calling and trying to apologize and Lisa hanging up on her, I felt that the punishment was starting to exceed the crime. Granted, Susan's viewpoint was flawed, but even her misguided efforts to help Lisa over a lifetime had an authenticity and self-sacrifice, and, to my mind, were her purest note. Lisa was the one person to whom Susan gave unstintingly, and with no ulterior purpose. Obviously, this "daughter," disdainful of outward appearances, of social mobility, and of almost everything Susan cherished, had never rewarded her, except by merely being—and by being someone she loved.

In fact, if Susan could have evolved a real understanding of her own, unqualified caring for Lisa, she might have used it as a basis to understand a whole lot else. She could have used this part of herself to grasp Lisa's feeling for Natalie, and for all her friends, including her cats and plants. With such an understanding, she would have gotten on infinitely better with Lisa. And, I could not help thinking, had Susan taken the time to appreciate herself in the one relationship where she was at her best, she might have sung this pure note toward others as well.

Maybe toward me? I really didn't care anymore.

In any event, I felt certain that, despite her tainted view, she loved Lisa and would never stop trying to contact her, and to help her. From what Lisa had told me, Susan had botched many relationships by her shallowness and insincerity. It seemed an irony that here, where she was at her best, she should be suffering the most.

Ideally, Lisa would, with all her power of sight, see Susan's tragedy and avert it herself. But she could avoid Susan's tentacles without murdering her symbolically. Lisa herself would do well by showing mercy in accepting Susan's plea for friendship, even though she did not condone Susan's faults. This would be the final stage of winning her rebellion—her very realizing that it was won.

But she wanted revenge.

About a month later, Lisa announced to me haughtily that she could tell from Susan's slurred hello that her mother was "drinking again," and it was hard for me not to plead Susan's case.

When she said this a second time, I asked her, "Do you think your mother needs A.A. or therapy?"

"She does, but she'd never consider it."

Still, Lisa wanted no part of her.

All the while, Lisa was making better contact with people. Her newly acquired friends now included Natalie and Phil and Tommie—and also Diane, the usherette she had terrified by her mind-reading act. Diane she had won over after a long, emphatic talk about Diane's jealous boyfriend, who finally dumped her because he couldn't tolerate her having men friends. "I remembered your prediction," Diane had said, "and it helped me."

Glad for the contact with this woman, who appreciated her sympathy, Lisa had replied, "I didn't predict anything."

Afterward, in my office, she realized that accurate readings of intentions are often predictions. I told her about the psychoanalyst Carl Jung's prediction that a man would die in a skiing accident, based on Jung's discovery that the man had an obsession to surpass himself and a fanatic desire to ski. Lisa was fascinated.

But even after six months, Lisa's refusal to allow Susan back was as strong as ever. When I asked Lisa if she wanted Susan to stop calling, she was always noncommittal, saying something like, "Well, she can call if she wants to. I don't care. But two minutes is all she gets."

However, I felt sure that if Susan had decided to strike back by not calling, even a month of her silence would have been a sledgehammer blow to Lisa. Both were suffering: Lisa, who was inflicting the punishment, as well as Susan.

She was showing Susan far less mercy than she granted to anyone else, including her cats and even her chairs. She needed Susan. And more than ever, she needed the experience of granting forgiveness, so that she herself would feel the right to it and could move in the world more freely. Besides, granting forgiveness where we can makes us feel like kings and queens.

I resolved, for both their sakes, to keep the subject open, so that Lisa could reconsider it whenever she wanted to.

In surveying her life, I could see that she had cut people off many times in the past, since college days and probably before. As I contrasted Susan's contribution to Lisa with her real mother's indifference, it seemed almost sure that at least some of Lisa's rage was felt toward her actual mother. Because Susan was in her life and her mother was not, Lisa was leveling at Susan the fury she felt toward her mother, and not just the anger she felt toward Susan herself.

Of course, she had the right to banish anyone she wanted, I agreed with her when she made that point.

"So then I have that right, too?" I asked her.

The idea troubled her.

"I won't," I said. "I'm just saying that by your reasoning, it works both ways. I mean that even though I wouldn't do it, I have the right to banish you."

She winced. "Well, if I did something terrible, you could— I don't mean one thing, I mean a hundred," she hastened to add.

"Wait a minute, Lisa. Using your logic, which of course I don't share, one evil could be worse than a hundred and deserve more punishment."

She asked me what I meant, and I reminded her of a number of times when she had dropped people abruptly and never spoken to them again. There was her college friend, Ellen, now married, whom Lisa had "seen through" and then dropped on the spot when Ellen had objected to her remarks. And there were a handful of others.

"Isn't forgiveness a part of loyalty?" I asked. "Lisa, there's nothing you could do that would goad me into never talking to you again."

"So I should call my mother up in California and beg her forgiveness too, huh?" Lisa said sardonically.

"I didn't say that. You don't really have a relationship with her. Not since you were a little child. What she did was unthinkable. But she wasn't Susan. Susan stuck with you and always will, even if she does foul things up sometimes."

"All right, so she's different!"

Though I knew I could go no further at the time, I resolved whenever possible to stress the distinction between her real mother, who had dumped her when Lisa was in her helpless, formative years, and virtually all other people, men and women.

There are psychologists who argue that ultimate evolution always requires coming to peace with one's natural parent. But to my mind, each case is different, and here my selling forgiveness toward Marianne could do Lisa irreparable harm. For Lisa, it was either cling to her sense of outrage or, to the degree that she condoned what her mother had done to her, go on living with the idea that she had deserved that treatment.

By then, I was convinced that her perception of herself as ugly and undesirable had emanated largely out of an attempt to justify the abandonment she had suffered, to make sense out of the chaos. That impulse to see design in our lives, and reason in what is done to us, is for many the worst of our reactions to the mistreatment we suffer as children.

No, I would not defend her real mother—to do so would be lying, anyhow. The plain truth was that Lisa had drawn horribly in the lottery of parenthood. The clearer she could become concerning the whimsical and unusual nature of what her biological mother had done, the freer she would be to trust other people and to forgive them their faults if their intentions were right.

Accordingly, I began to talk to Lisa more often about what Marianne's discarding her had meant to her. Without singling out Susan, or any of those whom Lisa had rebuffed for insufficient reason, I invited her to ask herself, Did she not sometimes treat people as she had been treated? And if so, could not a case be made that she was condoning in her own mind other people's abuses of her, and in particular, the primal villainy of Marianne herself?

I had a sense, as I kept reopening this hard topic with her, touching it gently from as many sides as I could, that progress would have still another benefit for her. Her own refusal to forgive—not just Susan but virtually anyone who crossed her—was restoring Lisa's dread that people would disown her for even an unintentional mistake.

Then the teeming city of New York yielded an experience to Lisa that became pivotal in her life.

A man, perhaps in his late forties, had been coming to the theater regularly, always alone. Lisa could see that he was gentle, and she liked his cultured way of talking; he was one of the few who always thanked her when she brought him to his seat. She approved of the films he came to see, and especially of those he would watch repeatedly.

One evening, during a showing of *Casablanca*, she was astonished to see him heading to the back of the theater, right toward her.

"I'm terribly sorry," he said, "but I can't seem to find my keys. I heard them fall, but I can't seem to locate them. Possibly—"

"I'll look for them," she'd replied.

"Oh, would you? Thank you."

He was delightfully quaint, the way he apologized to those seated near him for disrupting them, as Lisa beamed her light on the keys and he scooped them off the floor.

He thanked her graciously. She said something back, she couldn't remember what. On the way out of the theater, he stopped to chat with her about the film. She thought his observations were brilliant.

The next few times he came in, they exchanged a few lines, those of film characters, as if both of them were too shy to venture forth using their own words. The seedlings of Lisa's infatuation with him were unmistakable.

Then, one especially humid night, the air conditioning was down. Many patrons commented to Lisa about how stuffy it was, as if she were accountable. She would look at them and not respond, even facially.

To her horror, she suddenly realized that this man had just addressed her, and she had been as unresponsive as a stone.

He'd left with the crowd, and Lisa was aghast.

She assured me that he'd never talk to her again. "He probably won't ever come back to the Beacon, ever, even though he wants to see about six films in the festival. He told me which ones they are."

She seemed inconsolable. I knew that I couldn't convince her that she was reading too much into his reaction, though I thought so. No mere assertion by me would help. And besides, suppose I was wrong. Conceivably, he possessed a fragility on a par with hers, and did feel her nonreaction as a hammer blow. But a fatal one? That seemed very doubtful.

In retrospect, I think I was also held back by a lingering fear that Lisa might be right. Not that I thought so: her "sight" was least trustworthy when it came to trust. But it seemed best to let events unfold, and, in any event, the therapist's role is never to make predictions.

The best thing to do, I felt, was to draw her out, to have her spell out in no uncertain terms what she did expect. If she proved right, and he never came back, we would have lost nothing. At best, she would feel less thrown, having anticipated the disappointment. On the other hand, if he did return and spoke to her, I would have provided Lisa with a graphic instance of her pessimism, which we could examine together.

"Do you really think he's that punitive?" I asked her. "That he'd cut you dead for one default, one failure of yours to respond to him, to smile and say something?"

"I do."

"You mean he can't consider that you might have been preoccupied?"

"No. He won't be back and if he does come back, he'll never talk to me again."

We knew that, either way, we wouldn't have to wait long. The first of his film favorites was to be shown the following weekend.

He came in briskly just as it started and afterward went over to Lisa, and they talked. "I'm sorry that I was cranky with you last time," she said.

"Not at all. Not at all. I said something dumb and obvious, and you were busy. You're here all day. It's worse for you than anyone when the air conditioner breaks down."

I was, of course, glad to see her enjoying his return.

Still, I thought, I had to remind her of how sure she'd been that he was never going to come back. This instance of her feeling that a slip would be fatal was indispensible to us. She had spelled out her expectation clearly, only three days previously, and I could still hear her dogmatism. She would have bet a million dollars that she'd destroyed everything, as surely as if she'd dropped a bomb on the city.

Though it might mean interfering with her pleasure just then, I felt I could best use the experience to help her see her tendency to distrust her impact on people, always to think the worst of herself. In the long run, this moment of joy would prove far less valuable to her than to discover this tendency. She could hardly secure relationships in life if she went on expecting the worst from people and punishing them herself when they missed a beat.

I was considering how to break in, when Lisa gave me the perfect opening.

She muttered, "I knew damn well I should have worn that nice, light blue blouse that evening. I was stupid."

"What?"

"Well, I knew that was the showing he was coming to. He always comes for the first showing after dinner."

Could she possibly be that inconsistent?

"Wait a second, Lisa. You swore to me that he'd never talk to you again. You couldn't have been more positive, after what you did to him. There seemed nothing to think about."

"I know."

"You figured, why wear your best when he's not coming anyhow?"

"Okay." She saw the inconsistency too, but I felt it was too pivotal to let pass.

I pushed on. "And you see how wrong you were? You better think that through again. People make mistakes, and they forgive, and very often they don't even notice. You can forgive people's mistakes a little and make a few yourself."

"All right. I understand." I knew she was trying to shut me up, but I wouldn't.

"Lisa," I insisted, "this has got to be a lesson to you. Beware your assumption that people are going to cut you dead. If you don't, you won't give Kenneth a chance. You won't give *anyone* a chance."

Never had she listened so intently, for which I felt thankful to Kenneth. So I went on. "Lisa, you've got to ask, who are the people you care about? Probably they won't write you off for a single mistake, or even two. And you can forgive them too. Otherwise, what have you got? Why don't you give everybody a break!"

I paused, when I realized I had in mind the most poetic last statement on the subject I could find. "You know, Lisa," I told her, "there's something in a poem I love, the *Rubaiyat:* 'Man's forgiveness give—and take.'"

My cheeks seemed suffused with pain, as I remembered reciting that line to Susan, it seemed like yesterday. But of course, Lisa couldn't guess, nor did she say anything at the time.

*   *   *

She began seeing Kenneth regularly, but doubts of her own worth and her self-criticality surfaced—obviously because she cared for him so much. She cursed herself for having few friends whom she could introduce him to, and for her apartment, which suddenly loomed as embarrassingly small and sloppy.

And, probably, long hours of scouring herself for possible deficiencies and worry about them prompted a question she asked me one day, which took me by surprise.

"Do you go for beautiful women?"

"What do you mean, Lisa?"

"I mean, do you judge women by appearances?"

My first thought was that she was accusing me of loving her mother and not her. But then I realized that, of course, she was worrying about her appeal to Kenneth.

I told her the truth. "Just about everyone reacts to appearances, one way or another. You know that, Lisa. But beauty varies, at least somewhat. It doesn't have to be looks exactly. It could be voice, or a certain style, or even intelligence shining through. And people become beautiful to each other, or they start to look ugly. And what's beautiful to one person may not be to another. And, of course . . ."

I could see that she wasn't listening, which seemed fine, because I wasn't really saying anything, just puttering around with words so that she wouldn't feel discouraged.

On occasion, when she got anxious, she blamed Susan. But such blame, it seemed to me, was just a variation on the theme of self-hate, and I combatted it.

For instance, once Lisa said, "She ruined my whole life."

"I don't agree that it's ruined. How could Susan have ruined it? Look what you have in front of you."

The stage had been set for her to reconsider all her relationships.

Then, one night, after an especially pathetic call from Susan, Lisa came in, and, in a quiet mood, asked if I thought she should talk to her again.

I said that it depended on how she felt.

"What if she tells me I'm ugly?"

"That would be awful," I agreed.

"And suppose she attacks Kenneth?" Lisa said.

"Would she do that? She doesn't even know him."

"Yes, she might. She might ask how much money he has or where he lives or how old he is. She doesn't have to know somebody to attack him."

"That sounds terrible. So maybe you're not ready to see her."

"But I think I should. Natalie says that's the way parents are. And I feel sorry for her."

Then it occurred to me that maybe she could renew the relationship on a basis that many of us come to, not just with our parents but with most people in our lives. We have friends of different closeness—tiers of friends, as if they were in a stadium watching our lives from different distances, and we are the ones who determine how close they get.

"Maybe you could see your mother and tell her almost nothing. I mean, don't even mention Kenneth."

The idea had never crossed her mind, it had always been all or nothing with Susan.

"Do you think I could do that?" she asked.

"It's completely your challenge. You'll tell her what you want, and if you tell her too much and she hurts you, then kick yourself."

She seemed doubtful that she could pull it off.

"Well, I don't know for sure," I said. "Maybe I'm wrong. But I think you're both suffering plenty, and I do think Susan loves you, and maybe even you love her."

She wasn't going to admit that, and I didn't need a signed confession. But she decided to have dinner with her mother the next time she called and see if she could stay in control.

She did, and the evening went passably.

When Susan asked her if there was anything new, Lisa told her about places she'd gone to with friends. She and Natalie would go to fondle the dogs and cats, who were waiting execution if they weren't adopted by the end of the week. Even Susan was moved by that.

"Any new friends?" Susan asked.

"No. Nobody. I've been too busy. Absolutely nobody," Lisa had said.

Over the succeeding weeks, I could virtually see her bracing herself against the impulse to brag to Susan about Kenneth. She told me several times in the exact, same words, "The last thing she'll ever get is the chance to mess with him."

Once or twice, I thought, she actually teased Susan by implying that she'd done something interesting, and then when Susan inquired, Lisa stifled her, as she'd often tried to stop me in my tracks, by a wafture of the hand and a blunt assertion, "Let's not talk about that."

Susan obeyed. Before long, it became obvious that she was on her guard not to say anything that Lisa might, in even her wildest imaginings, consider intrusive. She was being so careful that I actually felt sorry for her.

"She got the message," Lisa said with triumphant anger. "She thinks she knows everything but she really doesn't know anything."

Lisa would remain angry with Susan for a long time, and in some respects possibly forever, or until one of them died. True, she had reason. But though Susan's tampering with her over a lifetime was unquestionably a terrible abuse, I felt sure that there were deeper causes too.

It crossed my mind that no one comes tumbling down harder, from greater heights, than the parent who once dazzled us and seemed indispensable. I felt sure that Lisa's fury was in part rage at Susan for failing to live up to the role that Susan herself had pretended to. I realized that I was angry at Susan, too, for that very reason.

Then I wondered, Was Lisa's fury, and was mine, displaced from rage at life itself, which breaks so many promises? What an injustice it would be if, indeed, we all make our parents scapegoats for our disappointment over what life has failed to deliver! If so, was Susan no different from the tens of millions of parents, well meaning and devoted at least some of the time, but also meddlesome, inflicting their foibles and their own, private disappointment on their children?

Lisa and I had certainly thought Susan was different, but we were only two impressionable people when we met her, cutting open an early page of a book with a gorgeous cover and gold lettering. And how many people do live up to our youthful imaginings?

In any event, only by dealing with Susan, by fending her off and telling her what she wanted to, could Lisa evolve the recognition that her life was hers, if she wished it to be.

And so they went on. They fought plenty. More than once, Lisa got up and left the restaurant in fury over something Susan had said, often something she had baited Susan into saying. Susan was the one who called up and apologized.

I worked hard at getting Lisa to see that her perception of herself as an independent adult could proceed only as fast as she stopped badgering Susan. She could tell her nothing about her life if she chose. But with parents, as the Uncle Remus story of Bre'r Rabbit and the Tar Baby tells us, the more you kick the person, the more you stick to him.

She continued to see Kenneth. She told me that he was a researcher, excellent at working with numbers, but too shy for the socializing that would have helped him upgrade his status in the marketing department he worked in. With her at his side, they went to the first office Christmas party he'd ever attended, though he'd been with the firm for eleven years. True, they spoke to only a few people and left fast, but it was an accomplishment for both of them.

Lisa never discussed their sex life with me. She said

she considered what they did in bed too precious to talk about.

Aside from Kenneth, she has many friends now, most of whom have become privy to her incredible gifts of perception and surmise, what I have been calling her "sight." Among them, one woman, an enthusiast of the occult, calls her a "witch" as the highest compliment, and Lisa enjoys it.

It's been six years since I've seen Lisa, though she calls occasionally to say hello and always sends me a birthday card, which Susan signs too. We'd worked together for a little over four years when she decided to stop, with the proviso that she could come back if she needed to.

I thought her stopping was a good idea. Much always remains to be done in a life, and I miss her. But therapy must never define itself as coextensive with the patient's need to solve problems, or with the therapist's loneliness. We were both content that we had accomplished a great deal. She now works for a veterinarian, someone Natalie introduced her to.

By the way, I am sure that she still attributes rich, intense inner life to inanimate objects, though now she gauges people closely before letting them know. Before she stopped with me, we had an exchange concerning that subject, which I'll never forget.

Lisa had been talking about her books being "lonely," now that she was going out more often. In that same session, she commented that her closet "hates to close in the summer" because it's so hot inside. "It likes closing in the winter," she added.

I suggested to her that many people, including those ordinarily thought to be open-minded, might not agree, and would be taken aback by the way she referred to inanimate objects. I'd approached the subject as gingerly as I knew how, saying that I was just telling her how people thought, and that she could do what she wanted with my impression.

The next time I saw her, she came roaring at me, accusing me of laughing at her. "You're not right," she insisted.

When I held my ground, she seemed terribly hurt. "But you'll destroy all kinds of beings, like your plants. You'll go through life a destroyer."

I remembered her dismay over that broken promise to her worn coat.

I tried to clarify to her that I was merely talking about the way other people thought about inanimate objects. I wasn't talking about her. She could think what she wanted, but she should know that her point of view wasn't the prevalent one, that's all.

"Come on," she insisted. "You know everybody thinks that way!" She was shouting and pointing at me. "Come on. I hear them talk. I know what's going on."

And then she half-persuaded me that we, all of us, think the way she did, only she had the purity to stand behind that view, to express it in words, without embarrassment.

"You mean you wouldn't feel bad to see your favorite shirt torn to pieces?"

"I would, but that's different. I mean—"

"What's your favorite shirt?"

I thought for a moment, then told her, "It's a check shirt, red and blue. I wear it in the fall."

"And if I cut it up with a scissors, you wouldn't care?"

"Of course I would, but—"

"I mean, even if I gave you another one, a brand-new one just like it. Come on. Come on. You love it. It's your favorite shirt. It's your friend. You love it, or something is wrong with you, George."

There were tears in her eyes, and she was shouting—even here the voice of the voiceless, the champion of the oppressed.

I knew what she meant, even before she added ironically, "Or your pillow. Or your friendly computer. Come on, George. I'm sick of everybody telling me I'm crazy."

Over those years since I've seen Lisa, I often recall that heated discussion. I *would* miss that shirt, miss it personally, and no replacement would offset the loss. Lisa saw things in

people that I didn't. Maybe she was right here, too, or at least
not as wrong as I'd thought. Maybe we hadn't come as far from
our primitive ancestors, who saw life, human life, in rocks and
stones and trees—in everything.

When I think of Susan, of course it's still of the better version,
though I realize that she is gone. Still, one can't help imagining. As with a sore tooth, one looks for it, hoping it is better
now while knowing that when one finds it, the pain will be
there too.

The best I can do is to regard Susan as two separate people.
The first remains most vivid in a photo that Lisa once brought
in. She was still beautiful in a crisp cotton dress with a plung-
ing neckline, but her eyes, pale and blue as an opal, showed
that all too familiar admixture of resignation about the big
things and impatience about the small. Already she had called
off her journey while imagining that she was enlarging its
scope.

Did Susan really change so much, or had I read into her
nearly all that I saw? Some might say that she was always as
she became, that I was programmed to love, by the forces of
desire—"In the spring . . ."—and so forth.

But my whole professional life, and beyond that, my credo
of existence, is that people do change. They can and do, but
not always for the better.

In this account, I've mentioned only enough of Lisa's spectacular readings of people to convey the depth of her talent.
I've never seen anything like it. At times, in social situations,
when strangers were doing something inexplicable to me, I've
thought about her and wondered what she would make of their
behavior. She remains a quintessential expert in a very special
domain.

One can only guess how many other people there are, gifted
with a clarity and afflicted with the sensibility that attends it,
isolated by their gift. Doubtless, some of these people have

compromised their gift away, in order to belong, to be one of a multitude, rather than remain apart. But others, like Lisa, loyal to their gift or unable to shuck it off, possessed by their special talent, their fate dictated by it, what about them? In this world, it is not enough to know; one must *know* one knows, or the gift can betray its possessor.

KING OF THE BEASTS

Eddie M bore only the slightest resemblance to a lion. For him to see himself as the king of beasts was a feat of imagination, the kind that psychotics can accomplish far more easily than the rest of us. Yet his very presence in the admission ward of a state mental hospital stood as circumstantial evidence that he saw himself this way.

According to the case folder being compiled on Mr. M, he was suffering from psychotic delusions. In the nineteenth century, when things were put more bluntly, they would have called him mad. Or going still further back, the Sunday visitors to the English open-air asylum called St. Mary of Bethlehem (shortened to "Bedlam") would have diagnosed him with a sneer. "Why he's a regular Tom o' Bedlam!"

He had not yet been officially diagnosed at Norwich State Hospital, where I was a psychological intern. My job was to interview and test some of those admitted during the month, and then to contribute my findings to the aggregate of knowledge that would be pooled by the staff, so that an official diagnosis could be made.

I was still a year or so away from my doctorate in clinical
psychology at Columbia, and though technically well educated, I had seen few people with schizophrenia up close. As a
big-city dweller, I'd heard the ranting of diseased minds in the
subways and streets, but to interview a real schizophrenic, to
administer a battery of tests to one and interpret the responses
myself, promised to be the crossing of a threshold to knowledge.

For this reason, I was eager to be the one to interview and
test this new patient. I had read the cursory story of how he'd
been picked up and brought to the hospital, saying he was a
lion. According to the file, he'd growled and actually tried to
bite off the arm of one of the arresting officers. There was little
else in his manila case folder as yet. The social worker's report, the medical report, and the ward attendant's observations
of him were still missing.

The chief psychologist, Dr. Herman Otto Schmidt, seemed
amused at my enthusiasm and assigned me the case.

As soon as he did, I lost no time in assembling my test kit,
which included the Wechsler Adult Intelligence Scale, a test
for visual-motor coordination called the Bender Gestalt, and a
psychoanalytically oriented instrument developed at Harvard
known as the Thematic Apperception Test.

On a whim, I also packed up a memory scale and some
blank paper to administer the Machover Figure Drawing
Test.

Then, after jotting down the name of the building Eddie
was being housed in and the ward he was on, I took off to
see him.

The ward attendant pointed him out to me. He was across
the room, sitting alone, a tall man, dressed in loose corduroy
slacks and a T-shirt. He came over at once, and we introduced
ourselves.

Eddie's acknowledgment of me suggested that the attendant
had told him I was coming to test him. He seemed to realize
that this was the most important testing he would ever un-
dergo. The combined judgment of the staff would decide

whether he was to be kept a prisoner somewhere in that ring of russet buildings or whether he could go home. Never since leaving that hospital world have I felt the same sadness, the same unfair authority vested in me, the same need to make a decision that no living human should have to make about another. The only experience that came close has been that of going to the ASPCA to adopt an animal, when, even as one bestows freedom and the good life on one or two, one knows that those bypassed will soon be injected with a lethal dose of poison.

Eddie followed me quietly to the little cubicle abutting the ward, a room set aside for examinations of all kinds. He was a tall man, gentle, once muscular, with a roundish face and red hair. His eyes were expressionless, as if he felt he had no power over his fate.

While testing him, I was struck most by how evenly he spoke and how sane, how absolutely, even *boringly* sane, he seemed. He spoke flatly and to the point. He took frustrations in stride, as when he ran into trouble on a test item. After he'd flubbed one of the jigsaw puzzle problems, he calmly tried again and got it, just within the required time limit. I wondered, was it composure or resignation?

After the first two tests, we talked. He told me that he lived in New York City and was a bartender at Longchamps. For many years before that he'd run a billiard parlor quite successfully. Having been an avid player in my teens, I engaged him in conversation about the game and its outstanding players, many of whom were employed by the manufacturers of tables to visit and play at the different poolrooms, or "billiard academies" as he called them. He ranked the players as he regarded them, and offered subtle distinctions between their styles and approaches to the game. "There was no one like Greenleaf for bankshots," "Johnnie Irish was the greatest money player that ever lived. . . ."

Then he told me that he had a wife and two daughters, and talked about them for a while.

So reasonable, so down-to-earth, so responsive did he seem

that it actually crossed my mind that a mistake had been made, that the man did not go with the case folder.

I decided not to refer to his lion act or to bring up anything leonine for a while, not even to ask Eddie yet how he thought he had gotten to the state hospital. I was just starting a relationship with him, and any such reference might interfere. Besides, what came from him voluntarily would be more telling than anything I could pry out of him. I could always ask him pointed questions later if necessary.

And it seemed that I'd have to. In the hour we spent together, he brought up nothing about the previous week.

Back in the studio that was my living quarters, I went over his test performances. On the Wechsler Intelligence test he scored 123, which is well above average, especially for someone who never finished high school. However, on the visual-motor test, the Bender Gestalt, he showed a marked tremor and some slight confusion in copying designs. I wondered, could there be something organic, something amiss in his nervous system? And if so, was it real or the temporary effect of too much alcohol?

I resolved to give him the visual motor test again the next day, Wednesday, along with the Rorschach ink-blot test and a few others. I would need my results by Friday when he was scheduled to come to the staff conference and face the fearful judgment of the experts.

By the way, I mentioned that he only vaguely resembled a lion. I smiled as it crossed my mind that in actuality he had very broad shoulders and a huge mane of red hair.

That night, as I strolled across the hospital grounds to my dorm, I again remembered those expressionless eyes and felt badly for Eddie. I pictured him sitting alone on his cot, among about forty other inmates on his ward. I thought of him separated from his loved ones, from his wife and two daughters. It was unlikely that the hospital would allow him to leave after the staff conference met, without some strong argument in Eddie's favor. After all, would anyone in his right mind say he was a lion without thinking that he really was? Yet in my wildest imaginings, I couldn't picture him as dangerous, or even as deluded. Nothing about him seemed forbidding.

But could I trust my judgment? Many psychotics, the textbooks tell us, aren't continuously deluded or dangerous. They move in and out of those states. Would he really have bitten the arresting officer? Maybe, so far as I knew.

Adding to my confusion and uncertainty was something that had occurred in the hospital about a month earlier.

I'd been walking with Ray, a fellow psychological intern, through the passageways that spanned the grounds. A late-afternoon summer storm was in progress, a violent squall with all its pyrotechnics and sound effects. Just outside a window, beyond the shelter of any roof, an elderly woman sat, thinking her own thoughts. She seemed wholly indifferent to, or even ignorant of, the fact that the sky was pouring buckets of water on her.

I'd shouted, "Hey, you're getting soaked. Why don't you go inside!"

She'd responded feebly, but with absolute conviction. "I'm waterproof!"

Doubtless, my rebellious nature delighted in what I took to be a saucy answer from this old woman, almost surely diagnosed in those days as "senile dementia with arteriosclerotic changes." I had relished thinking of her as like Jean-Paul Sartre's prisoner, who, no matter how reduced in circumstances, retains until death the power to say no.

In any event, Ray and I kept on going, our heavy keys jingling at our sides, our minds occupied.

We'd proceeded through a quarter-mile of passageways when I thought about her again.

"Gee, I love seeing someone like that with a sense of humor. That was funny, that comment of hers. 'I'm waterproof.'"

"Funny!" my friend had said. "There wasn't any humor in

that at all. She wasn't kidding. She really *thinks* she's water-proof."

"Come on," I disputed him. "She was putting us on."

He stayed just as insistent.

On a whim, I asked him, "Do you mind if we go back and talk to her again?"

"She'll still be there," he said flatly, as if it proved his point.

With that, we turned around and retraced our steps, opening the same dozen oak doors with our hospital keys, this time from the other side.

I'd thought momentarily that we'd passed the courtyard and that she'd gone inside, but no. She was there, still sitting in the rain, which was just as heavy.

"Say, were you kidding about being waterproof?" I called to her.

"I'm waterproof," she said, as flatly as she had the first time.

"So what does that prove?" I asked Ray.

"It proves she believes it. If she were putting us on, she wouldn't keep sitting there," he said.

I still disagreed, maintaining that we had really collected no new evidence but only more of the same. I sounded persuasive, but even then I began to suspect that I might be wrong.

It had simply been too great a leap of the imagination for me to *believe* that someone was deluded, that anyone could be deluded, could actually believe the unbelievable. The pseudodemocratic conclusion that other people, that *everyone* knew what I knew, had governed me. Or was it fear, outright fear of embracing the fact that a person could be deluded, off course, psychotic? Because that would have meant that I could conceivably be, or even that I was, irrational. If I truly accepted irrationality, what certain psychologists call "frank psychosis," then I would be accepting it as a nearer possibility for myself than I felt comfortable with.

Later, I saw tendencies in many students of psychology

when giving IQ tests to show a similar, motivated incredulity when someone taking an intelligence test couldn't do a simple task. "Repeat after me these three numbers: seven, two, eight." And the patient *can't remember* those three digits in order! The beginner insists that the person wasn't listening. How can anyone who cares fail such an assignment? And yet people do.

It seems that the more we like a person, the harder it may be for us to accept any incapacity in that person. And yet some people do have low IQs and some are psychotic—indeed, a very calculable proportion—whether we want to believe that they are or not.

And so I doubted my doubts about Edward M's insanity, though I'd seen nothing even mildly suggestive of the delusional about him.

My next day was cluttered with paperwork and I didn't get to see Eddie. When I returned to his ward the day after that, I could tell at once that he felt much more defeated. Perhaps he had witnessed bizarre behavior on the ward. Or more likely, he had spoken to someone who had been confined there for many months or even for years. He was starting to feel woeful about his plight.

On the remainder of the test battery, he acquitted himself well enough. Nothing he said suggested psychotic thinking. On the Figure Drawing test, he sketched a rather good likeness of a man holding a wine glass. The woman he drew was well proportioned. Both pictures were even a little artistic. This time, on the visual-motor test, he performed very well, much better than he had two days earlier.

He asked me what that last test was for.

I told him and added that his coordination was excellent.

"Well, it ought to be," he replied. "I've been tending bar for eleven years and I hardly ever break a glass."

For the first time I got the sense that he was selling himself to me. He was scared and he had every reason to be.

I asked him, "What were you doing up in Connecticut last week?"

"Well, I'd saved four vacation days, and I had two days off for the holidays. So I was coming up here to work in the Griswald Inn over the July fourth week."

He told me he missed his wife badly, and the daughter who still lived at home. She would be graduating from high school the next month. "They're probably wondering what happened to me. They don't know I'm here." Gloom came over his face. "They'll find out if I don't get back on time, though. I'll have to tell them."

"I see."

The time had come. Obviously, he wasn't going to mention his being a lion. I would have to ask directly. I picked up the manila envelope and pointed to the page describing his arrest.

I paraphrased. "It says here that when they found you, you were completely naked. You thought you were a lion. You growled and tried to bite the arm of an arresting officer. Were you a lion at the time?"

He weighed the question. "Looking back, I'd have to say no."

Was this dry humor? Who could be sure?

"But you said you were a lion."

He smiled as if he'd suddenly understood something. "And that's why they brought me here?"

"It's part of it. You were totally nude, lying alongside a river." I looked down at the folder. "You were on the bank of the Thames." (Like the locals, I pronounced the "th" and rhymed it with "flames.")

"That I was. I know I was."

"What else about it can you remember?"

"About being a lion? Oh, come on. I was only kidding."

"Eddie, the troopers who picked you up didn't think so. Or they didn't have your sense of humor. Maybe you better go back to the beginning of the day."

"Well, it was Saturday. I kissed the wife and daughter good-bye about eleven o'clock and jumped into the Dodge. By the way, will I get my car back when I leave?"

"Of course."

"So she made a sandwich for me, and I stuck a pint bottle or two behind the backseat. It must have been a hundred degrees already.

"I headed up the West Side Highway and out toward Connecticut. It was a beautiful day last Saturday."

I stopped him. "Was it Friday or Saturday? Sorry, I just want to get it clear."

"Friday. Was it Friday? Sure it was. The traffic, what there was of it, was heading the other way, to the city, and I was almost alone on the parkway. I had this contract with the Griswald in my pocket, and I had to get there to sign in by six in the evening. Friday. Yeah, it was Friday, I was going to start work Friday night. They were expecting a big crowd, a full house for the fourth. Well, I guess you could figure that. So anyhow, it was a gorgeous day—"

"I know that."

"Yeah," he said, and, recognizing my impatience, added, "I know. I'll get to it.

"So when I was well into Connecticut, I took out the bottle and had me some. Not a lot. I pace it when I drive, like when I'm behind the bar. It got very hot and I was tired. So I stopped by the side of the road for a while and had a couple of cigarettes and finished off the bottle. I'm not sure exactly where I was. I guess I had the idea it was Middletown, but I couldn't exactly find it on the map.

"Things were fading out a little, and I'm not the one to kill myself, so I got out of the car. There was a pretty lake. I was thirsty too, you realize. It was goddamned hot. I guess I lay down near that water. At the time it seemed reasonable. And I guess I fell asleep."

"That's where the state troopers found you?"

"Yeah. It seemed like the next minute. My head was killing me. In the front, you know, in the sinuses."

"But you had taken all your clothes off?"

"Yeah. So what! I already told you it was a scorcher, and I was very . . . Maybe I figured I was home in bed. They *surrounded* me. They stood looking at me with disgust, like they'd never seen a naked man before."

"Go ahead."

"One of the troopers, a young guy, said, 'What the hell are you doing here with no clothes on? *What* are you?'—And I thought his use of the word sounded funny. With me naked and with all that red hair on my body, and my big head of hair, and maybe that looked funny to me too, so I said, 'I'm a *lion*.'

"When I said that, they looked startled. So I roared like a lion. That got them really scared. Three grown men with guns in their holsters. And the young one came over to me and handed me my clothes, so I roared as loud as I could and said, 'Don't come any closer or I'll chew your arm off and I'm not kidding.'"

Now Eddie's face was alive, and his eyes twinkled, as if his recall of that day was an alchemy that made him human again.

But just as suddenly, the smile vanished, like the shadow of a bird. "So they helped me put my clothes on, and threw me into the black car and drove me here."

I felt strongly that he was describing events as they had occurred. A drinking problem? Yes. Maybe a severe one. But delusional? A man who genuinely thought that he was the king of the beasts? I was starting to doubt it.

"Do you think they'll let me out soon?"

"I don't know," I told him, as sympathetically as I could.

"Would it be possible for you to call my wife, tell her it's a mistake?"

"That's the social worker's job." I read from the top of the folder. "Ask for Jonathan Scalese. That's what he does. Ask him."

He pleaded. "They told me he's gone until Monday. There's no way you could do it? It wouldn't get you in trouble, would it?"

"Monday? Really? I don't know."

That seemed like a long time for Eddie's family to stay worried about him. And if he got diagnosed as psychotic, he might not get permission to call on his own. The mills of the gods grind slowly, and once you get into a state hospital, if there's no one outside to claim you, the doctors are the gods.

Back in my office, I studied his test performance in depth and went over his case folder, which was fast filling up with input from those who had examined him. His medical report described him as a man of fifty-four in good physical health. There were no abnormal brain-wave patterns, no indications of epilepsy or tumor, though his neurological tests revealed discoordination and the pronounced tremor that I had detected at first. However, his blood was saturated with alcohol, which could explain that tremor, and even the delusions.

If the diagnosis were made solely by the examining physician, without the police report, it would very likely have been "Korsakoff's Syndrome with delirium tremens." Drunks by the dozens came in, got that diagnosis, were dried out, and had sobered up and returned to drink another day. Alcoholics Anonymous meetings on the ward, being compulsory, did much less good than on the outside; very probably, the patient would return, be diagnosed once more as Korsakoff's, and go through the whole cycle again. There were many whose files showed that they'd been through the procedure a dozen times or more over the years, attaining nothing beyond the prolongation of life. For some, there was even the negative effect of their counting on a hospital rescue and using it to permit themselves their indulgences. At rock bottom was the poor drunk who lived so from day-to-day that he had no memory of his previous hospitalizations on the same ward.

Was my lion merely a first-time sufferer from Korsakoff's

Syndrome? I thought so but wondered, because, of course, I so much wanted this to be so.

In favor of this more benign diagnosis was the obvious improvement in his visual-motor skills over the few days he'd been there. The attending physician hadn't the time to examine him twice—there were over eight thousand patients in the hospital and about forty admitted every week. But as an intern, I could check him out daily if I wanted to.

On the other side was the well-known fact that at least some percent of alcoholics and other substance abusers are masking symptoms of far more serious conditions. Some few alcoholics, after they dry out, remain confused, and some become even more delusional; these include people who originally turned to alcohol after the awful discovery that something was grievously wrong with them, that they lacked the common perspective. By drinking, they could hide this awesome reality from themselves, and furnish their own oddness with an ostensible explanation in the eyes of others, who would think they were "on something."

Eddie's case folder, in flux like a ticker tape, took a sudden turn for the worse. In going over it, I saw that the psychiatric resident in charge of the case, who would present his findings on Friday, was young Dr. Carpentier. The urbane Carpentier loved to diagnose people as psychotic. Unlike the more experienced staff, he saw his own attainments as proportional to the severity of what was wrong with his patients. As if his having a case load of dangerous psychotics implied that he could handle the deep stuff, whereas if his case load consisted only of confused or impulsive people, of those simply not up to snuff, he would be just another doctor using a good bedside manner to get his people through hard times.

I'd seen Carpentier contest verdicts in staff conferences before, always maintaining that the patient, even if someone seemed okay, was faking and was desperately dangerous, suicidal or even homicidal. He'd pushed many an official prognosis from "favorable" to "guarded," or from "guarded" to "poor."

My dilemma sharpened. If I were right and Eddie M was nothing more than an occasional drunk who had used humor in the wrong place and with the wrong people, then a nightmare, or rather a "daymare," worthy of Kafka was already in progress.

Dr. Carpentier had taken his early training at the celebrated Salpetrière in Paris. He was slender and darkly handsome, and had just the right soupçon of French accent. If frock coats were still admissible, he would have worn one. Wishing to see himself as a descendent of Jean Charcot and Pierre Janet, the great psychiatrists of the last century, he sought drama wherever he could find it. He would take pride in the case of my lion-man. He would treat the Friday staff conference to a literary diagnosis, concluding that we had here a raving lunatic who must not be set free. And if his eloquence raised serious doubts, the decision would be to play it safe and keep Eddie behind the steel screen.

Against Carpentier's promised deluge of literary language, worthy of the *New York Review of Books* at its most obscure, my only advocate was the examining physician. Dr. Segal was a first-rate practitioner, one who stuck to the facts. And Korsakoff's Syndrome was consistent with the facts. However, Segal, a Hungarian, spoke very little English and was anything but persuasive. Only the previous year, he had been a surgeon back home and had fled his country to escape its despotic Communist rule. With his inability to speak the language and his meager knowledge of psychiatry, Segal would hardly be a match for Dr. Carpentier, who dripped with culture and persuasiveness.

As I went over to talk to Dr. Segal, I thought, "I would rather have them wrestle for the verdict than dispute it with words." Segal was a bullish-looking man, who looked more like a sumo wrestler than a doctor. He took time out from doing his physical examinations to talk to me. When I suggested that Eddie might be best served by being released after the staff conference that Friday, he said ingenuously, "Really? You think so?"

"There's no reason to keep him locked up. He was delusional due to alcohol. Korsakoff's. He has a family, steady work. He could lose his job. We'll destroy him here."

He nodded in agreement.

Far from seeing Eddie as a literary figure who would grace his own reputation by being a dramatic case—a protagonist patient like Freud's Anna O or Shreber—Segal had imprinted in his mind the knowledge of what it was to be a prisoner. I later found out that Dr. Segal's own parents had remained in Hungary, themselves prisoners of their native land.

"So let's work together and get him out of here," I pleaded.

"Okay," he said, and got up. Even before I left the ward, he was involved in shooting a syringe into the arm of a man who'd lost his cool and was being restrained behind a mattress by two attendants.

By Wednesday night, more than my mere contemplation of the facts had convinced me that Eddie had no real lion identity in his mind and that he should go home. My very attempt to rally Segal, the attending physician, had spurred me on. I had long disliked Carpentier (maybe a little extra because when I'd spoken to him in French, he'd always replied in English, as if to say, "You just don't make the grade"). But by then I considered him like a district attorney asking for the imprisonment of an innocent man, one with no previous convictions.

One thing did trouble me, however—Eddie's dry, unusual sense of humor. It made him almost completely indistinguishable from real psychotics, like the lady in the rain. If he said bizarre things without smiling, how was anyone to know the degree of his belief in what he said? Of immediate concern was Dr. Ranger, the hospital's clinical director, who on Friday would preside over the staff conference and make the final decision on all patients brought before him. How could his eminence, Dr. Ranger, despite his considerable experience, possibly know for sure that Eddie was now okay?

I had no doubt that Dr. Ranger was knowledgeable and fair. And he had as a priority not spending the state's resources if a patient could be released. There was nothing grandiose or sadistic about him. He himself was a drinking man, that was in our favor. He didn't seem the "Elmer Gantry" type, who would punish those who reminded him of himself at his worst. But Ranger felt, as most did, that it's better to keep an innocent person in lockup than to release one who, by doing something hugely irresponsible, will degrade the hospital and him. In a borderline case, he could say, almost flippantly, "Let's watch him for ninety days. Contact his family. Schedule him to come up again in October and if he's okay, we'll release him."

I didn't want that to happen.

But that dry sense of humor of Eddie, which by the way I loved, could make it happen. There would be no ambiguity tolerated where delusions were in question. Such humor might go unnoticed, or be entertaining, coming from a bartender serving liquor nightly to drunks, as Eddie presumably did, but not here.

I'd seen evidence of Eddie's "dangerous" sense of humor in many of his test responses. On the Thematic Apperception Test, on which the patient is asked to tell stories about pictures placed in front of him, he had said about a picture of an older woman with a younger one:

"They're in the woods. The daughter looks like she has a *terrible* headache. Her mother has some aspirin and is saying, 'Take these before you go home.'"

I'd asked Eddie, "And what is the daughter saying?"

He'd looked at the picture seriously, as if it contained the answer. Then he told me, "She's saying, 'I don't need to take them now. I'll still have the headache when I get home.'"

Funny? If you look at it that way. I'd thought so at first, but now, in reading the comment again, it scared me. Eddie had headaches, bad ones, and wanted to go home—his identification with the girl, that projection, was clear. But what haunted me now about Eddie's response was the question of whether or not he was really kidding, whether he had any idea that his answer was unusual in any way.

Eddie hovered between comedy and madness. No geographer of the mind had ever precisely located that intersection, though we all assumed its existence. Eddie stood in the forest between the two nations.

The next morning he was glad to see me. I explained that he'd be going up before a staff conference the next day, which would decide his fate. "The hospital doesn't want some nut going out there in the street and doing something weird that could make them look bad," I said.

"I understand. I'll go far away."

Was he kidding again?

"You mean you're going to be weird?"

"No. Not at all. All I want to do is get out of here and go back to New York."

I explained to him that they'd ask him questions, and that he should answer them to the best of his ability. "No humor. Above all, no humor! They won't get it."

"Okay." He seemed confused about the request.

I stamped it in. "I'm putting myself out on a limb. I'm going to say this lion story of yours was a joke, a drunken joke, an alcoholic's idea of a joke."

"No joke?" He looked quizzically at me.

I was upset. I insisted that I wasn't kidding. I was practically shouting, "I don't want to hear another joke from you in my whole life. You get it. Not another joke. You can start right now. Never tell me another joke again. Never say another thing that you even think *might* be funny."

That struck him as funny, and he smiled.

I was furious. "Do you get it? If you say anything you even *think* is funny, you'll be in this place for two hundred years. I'll see to that, goddamn it. Remember. I'll see you at the staff conference tomorrow."

Before I left, he said one word, "Thanks."

*   *   *

That night, I prepared my case like a lawyer, except that I'd had a lot more time than legal-aid counselors, who often don't get to see their client until minutes before the trial. I saw that the social worker's report on Eddie was good. He'd checked Eddie's work record without revealing anything to his employer, and it was excellent. I would make the case for Korsakoff's, and hope that Carpentier didn't go on a tear to prove otherwise.

I had fantasies of Carpentier researching delusions of animal identification and overriding my plea. He always seemed to have an apt quote, or an apt translation of his own—from French or from German. I sometimes wondered whether Charcot or Goethe had actually said half the things Carpentier had attributed to them.

Then a memory flash of something I'd read as a child came to me, and I rushed to the library, sure that this reference, which had so struck me back then, was there and that I would find it. Apt? Carpentier never saw anything as appropriate as this, not in his whole life.

It was there, and I grabbed the book.

The next morning, we gathered in the meeting hall of the Administration Building. The hall was arranged like an old-style amphitheater, where new methods of surgery used to be done before an assemblage. The centerpiece was a sizable mahogany table with scrolled, splayed legs. Around it on generous captain's chairs sat the experts—the modern-day surgeons of the mind. Included were those with firsthand knowledge about one or more of the patients to be discussed and then brought in for a brief interview.

Carpentier and Segal were there, and other attending physicians who had examined patients that week. I and a few other psychologists were there too, and the attendant neurologist.

We few, we happy few, were to be the performers that day. Ranger's chair alone was still vacant.

On about ten rows of flimsy wooden bridge chairs sat the eager onlookers, seated strictly according to rank. The two front rows were occupied by the medical staff, those not involved in the day's activities. Behind them sat the psychologists, even then breathing hard down their neck for a living. Further back sat the social workers and occupational therapists. At the very back of the room, straining to hear, were the nurses and student nurses.

As one went from the front to the rear, the room became increasingly co-ed. In the last rows were those most likely to be young, attractive women. To the doctors, who were preponderantly older men, the presence of pulchritude in the audience was vital, though never mentioned. It was a rare expert who, while discussing a patient, did not strain to project his excellence to the back of the room, and during adversarial moments one felt that the young and innocent were the ones to crown the champion with their verdict.

Unmistakably, Dr. Carpentier was especially concerned with his projection to that last row. He never hesitated to remind the room of his credentials and of his European training, both of which enhanced his charisma. Nor can I say that I was always oblivious of those fleshly, young women in their multi-colored nursing caps, each indicating the school they'd attended. But that day I forgot them as I went over my notes.

Ranger finally arrived. We were ready.

The procedure was for the social worker to start by giving a brief summary of the patient's life and illness-history. The intake doctor would then summarize the findings of his physical exam. Then those who had observed the patient on the ward would speak. Then the director would motion an attendant to have the patient brought into the room.

After hearing about the person first, the collective appetite was usually whetted to see him, especially if he sounded fluky or he had done something violent. The most dramatic entrances were those of people who had to be restrained, and some were actually hurled into the room by a brace of attendants. Needless to say, when this happened it was a serious mark against the person, even before he spoke.

Most usually, however, the patient came in like a job applicant, except that he was applying for his freedom. The clinical director would question him in front of all, and by the person's poise, coherence, and politeness under stress, he would greatly influence the next year of his life—and often even the remainder of his life.

Not until the patient was gone, and the audience had a chance to measure him for themselves, would the psychologist read his report. Those at the centerpiece table would then arrive at a diagnosis and decision about what to do with him. Often this was done fast, but there was sometimes a back-and-forth discussion, in which the psychologist was overruled. That was what I feared would happen with Eddie.

The first inmate presented was a black man, who felt he was hated and discriminated against in Hartford and may have overstated a little. He was diagnosed as paranoid, but released in his father's custody, with a promise that he would come in regularly as an outpatient. The next was an elderly white woman, diagnosed senile dementia, who would probably never go home. Then a very deteriorated schizophrenic man came in, and was unable to understand even straightforward questions. He was put on some medication, with prognosis guarded.

When Eddie's name was mentioned, I began looking at my notes, to be sure I was ready.

A social worker read the story of his arrest. At the mention of Eddie's saying he was a lion, the audience broke into laughter, and I felt bitterly set back. Many in the audience looked forward to those moments of utter madness laid bare. We were in trouble already, but it was inevitable.

Then Dr. Segal spoke in his broken English, and very sympathetically suggested an acute alcoholic reaction, with no organic complications. "You've got to think of Korsakoff's in a case like this," he said. He was one of the few that didn't sound as if he was on television.

While he spoke, I kept an eye on Carpentier, who shifted uneasily in his seat, as if an injustice were being done. He looked especially handsome that day, in his dark suit. He'd had his wavy black hair trimmed for the conference. I thought he was going to speak once or twice, but he didn't. Maybe he wouldn't be a problem, after all.

Finally, Ranger motioned for Eddie to be brought in. He entered well ahead of a single attendant who sat down in the rear while Eddie took his seat at the table.

I thought the audience gasped at the lion-man, but it might have been my imagination.

Dr. Ranger was quite congenial to him during the questioning. But eventually, of course, he had to ask, "You thought you were a lion?"

"Not really. I was drunk and I was kidding."

No humor now, I prayed. Nothing dry. Nothing droll. I wished I could talk for him.

But it wasn't necessary. He was perfect.

When he'd finished, many in the crowd were disappointed. Were they hoping that he'd bite somebody or roar like the MGM lion, that he'd furnish them with a great story to tell their loved ones back home? If he had, they could look romantic, or even bold, for having been in the same room with him, for trying to help such a man, to beard the lion, so to speak.

Anyhow, they seemed disappointed, almost bored, as Ranger's cordial style and leading questions allowed Eddie to talk about his excellent employment record. In response to Ranger's warmth, he boasted about his wife and daughters, one named Kelly and one still at home, Adie. I didn't hear it all, I knew my turn was coming and I went over my notes for the last time.

"Thank you," said Ranger.

The attendant, who'd been half-asleep, stood up and accompanied Eddie out of there.

I felt I was ready, if Carpentier was.

"Who's the psychologist on the case?" Ranger asked.

"I am, sir." I raised my hand.

"Oh, the hospital Ping-Pong champ!"

A few people laughed. At any other time, I would have enjoyed the comment, but at that moment I felt it trivialized me. However, Ranger clearly hadn't meant to disparage me.

"Thanks," I said.

In talking about the case, I made much of Eddie's fine IQ performance, which put him well in the top ten percent of the population. I told them that his ink-blot responses and his Thematic Apperception Test results were those of a very sane person. I explained how his visual-motor scores had gone from poor to good in two days. On the earlier version, the tremor was obvious, but it almost disappeared when I gave him the test a second time, a few days later. "Consistent with his being in a totally drunken state."

Then I discussed his figure drawings and sent them around the mahogany table. "That glass of wine the man is holding tells us a lot. He's a drinker, but not psychotic."

I explained to the assemblage, "His wavy red hair and his being naked were the stimulus for the preposterous but humorous lion association." I underscored what the social worker had already pointed out, and what Eddie himself had told us. "He's a married man who's held jobs, and held them all his life. There's no reason to keep him here, he's never been dangerous. We'd be destroying him."

I was begging, and finally, when Dr. Ranger gestured for me to stop, I started to think it was over and we'd won the day. Maybe I'd overprepared.

But we were far from home. Carpentier was twisting in his chair. He could bear it no longer. With his deep consciousness of himself-in-society, he said, "I disagree."

Ranger looked over at him, and I realized that I had to go to Plan B.

With his half-smile, Carpentier said condescendingly, "I'm sorry, but I've got to say something. I'm afraid you're all being taken in. That lion identity is very serious."

He had a dramatic flair, no doubt about it. I guessed this was to be his showcase for the afternoon. Well, not quite yet.

I launched into my plan. The first stage was to set him up. "Dr. Carpentier, please let me finish. There's something very crucial that I'd like to read. Perhaps you can explain it. It's very short."

That got his attention. What I was about to present was all for him. He was the prodigy. He would have his moment. I was merely introducing him. How could he refuse?

I held up the book I'd taken out of the library. They must have been surprised to see its title—the *Odyssey*.

Even Carpentier was curious.

"If anyone thinks this man's association with a lion is far-fetched," I said to the others, implying that Carpentier knew better, "I want to read a paragraph to you. You all know the *Odyssey*. Perhaps the greatest work of fiction ever written. Its hero, Odysseus, is everyman, the prototype hero."

I felt I had them, and I opened the book to the place I had marked. "Dr. Carpentier, you surely know this passage. Odysseus finds himself alone."

Then I read, straight from the text. "Odysseus entered a thicket, which he found close to the river, with a clear space around it. There he crawled under a couple of low trees, which were growing together, so that the sun would spare him its blazing rays. In this thicket, he fell asleep. He woke up naked and crawled out of the bushes. *Then he strode like a lion of the mountains, proud of his power, who goes on through wind and rain* with eyes blazing as he pounces on cattle and sheep, or chases wild deer."

There was some laughter around the room.

I said, "I'd like to read that last line again."

"Don't bother," said Ranger. "I'm sure we've all read the *Odyssey*."

Then I turned to Dr. Carpentier. Mustering all the pseudo-sincerity I could, I said to him, "What interests me is why this great man thinks of himself as a lion."

Carpentier smiled smugly. "It's an archetype."

"An archetype?" I said.

"An archetype," he repeated. "An image from the collective

unconscious." This time he didn't look at me but at Ranger, as if to imply to the room, "This would-be psychologist is an asshole."

"I hadn't thought of it as an archetype," I muttered, playing the role.

"Well, it is," Carpentier said, and launched into a mighty discussion on the collective unconscious. He was playing directly into my hands. He didn't really have to oppose me, so long as he got attention. I'd given him the chance to use his pedagogical skills, to explain the concept of an archetype. I figured he'd forget about Eddie once he got going. And he really did get going. The more he said, the more he fell in love with himself.

At one point, he mentioned a letter from Karl Jung to his friend Jastrow, who was vacationing at the Zeider Zee. "It's hard to translate from the German, but those messages from the collective unconscious, which Jung made us so aware of, come not only in dreams but in many unguarded moments."

"Fascinating!" I said, like the conductor of his chorus. He could perform all day, for all I cared. After all, he was supporting Eddie's release now. I'd stay in his audience, as long as I could stand it, if only he'd let Eddie out of there.

He was still going. ". . . And Franz Alexander of the Chicago School of Psychoanalysis wrote that 'the superego is soluble in alcohol.'"

A couple of first-year psychiatric residents snickered to show they understood that one. It sounded like a mixed metaphor to me. If poor Eddie had said something like that on a bad day, he would have doomed himself.

"Dr. Carpentier, please explain that," asked someone else.

Now it was Dr. Ranger's turn to twitch. He lit up his third cigarette, as if suicide were preferable to these pedantic diatribes. He'd possibly never heard of Franz Alexander, and considered himself better off for it. But he knew he couldn't stifle striplings like Carpentier, whose flights of fancy made the meetings memorable. Ranger wasn't at all flamboyant, and people like Carpentier drew students and interns to the hospital.

In his sexy style, Carpentier enlarged on his theory that alcoholics are especially open to messages from the collective unconscious, and that this patient was a case in point.

When Ranger could stand no more, he put up his hand. "Thank you, Dr. Carpentier. That was very informative. It was fascinating."

Carpentier subsided in his captain's chair. He had presented himself admirably. Whenever I thought he might be looking at me, I did my best to appear the wide-eyed student learning from incipient greatness.

After a moment, Ranger turned to the social worker, a woman who was standing in for Mr. Scalese. "Is there anyone who will take him out of here, a family member?"

We had truly won now.

The social worker said, "He didn't want to contact his family from here."

Ranger frowned.

I volunteered at once, "I'll bring him back. I'm driving to New York City this afternoon. I'll call his wife and say he's on his way home, if you want me to, to be sure she's there. He can be in my recognizance until then."

Ranger looked at me, surprised. I think he liked my involvement, but he was hard to read.

Carpentier was off whispering to another psychiatrist, presumably adding footnotes to his treatise. Mercifully, he'd already lost interest in Eddie and in what happened to him.

"All right," said Ranger. "If Psychology okays it."

"It's okay," mumbled Dr. Herman Otto Schmidt, the chief psychologist.

Then Ranger said, "Let's move along, can we?"

With my suitcase in hand, I could hardly wait to head toward New York City that weekend. It was four in the afternoon on Friday when I went on Eddie's ward. Most of the inmates were in those gray hospital outfits that epitomized their chances in life, and the ward had its usual fetor—the attempt to suppress the stench of sweat and urine by pungent antiseptics resulted in the new odor of "healthy decay."

At a table sat the perennial card players, some of whom I knew well. There was Peter R, who had once masterminded his own legal case against the state and secured his release but was now back. There was Roger L, who had taken literally the Bible's maxim, "If your arm offends thee, cut it off." Roger still never doubted that he'd done the right thing. There was Chester C, once an outstanding college history professor, who was convinced that the Communists had put him there. He always sat with his back to the wall, in the belief that the Communists wanted to rape him. Actually, the card players were more social than most on that ward.

It was one of the better wards. Many there had a solid chance of release if only a relative or friend would claim them and sign them out. Or even without that, if the person got a promising job offer, he had a chance. Pratt-Whitney aircraft was nearby, and in fulfilling its huge government contracts for aircraft, it offered useful and simple employment. Its agents went over the records of selected inmates and employed some. So did certain of the other conglomerates. Many on the ward dreamed of jobs in those family-organizations, the way millions on the outside imagine winning a lottery and escaping their own private prisons.

Sitting or slumping alone against the walls were the less fortunate. Some of these stragglers in life had never tasted hope and so could not even be said to have forsaken it. A few rose on occasion to walk about, mumbling to themselves, but most stayed patiently in place, holding a single spot of floor-space for their duration here.

Eddie M was wearing his own clothes, a yellow wash-and-wear shirt and light gray slacks, and he looked pretty good. He held some extra belongings in an overnight bag. When he saw me chatting with John, the attendant, he didn't come over but waited courteously until I was ready for him.

My own agenda was to hurry back to the New York City for a big date, the thought of which had lifted me over some dark hours in the last week. I had repeatedly pondered such worldly matters as whether I could get to Zippo cleaners before it closed at seven, because I looked great in the white jacket and charcoal pants that I had left there for cleaning the previous weekend.

"See you Monday," I said to John. Then nodding to Eddie, I went over to him and whispered, "Go out with John, not with me. He'll bring you downstairs. I'll see you there."

Eddie understood at once the value of not being ostentatious in leaving a place where others were confined, some until death.

On the other side of the manicured lawn, I gave his yellow identification card over to the state policeman, and we headed to my car. He would have to return for his the following week.

This man was as sane as they come, and I once again marveled at the terrible injustice that we had so narrowly averted. He got into the front seat with me, and I looked at my watch. Ten to five—we had better start moving.

We chatted about his family, and about billiards. I had questions and he answered them. He had plenty of anecdotes about the masters.

Eddie noticed that I was driving fast, too fast. I had slowed down on the road through Colchester, but now made up for lost time by taking a shortcut behind an old gray church, and I nearly hit it at the speed I was going.

"You must be in a hurry," he observed.

"Yeah, I've got to get to the cleaners before it closes."

"Well, that's important," he said sympathetically. I wondered if he was putting me on.

He pulled out a bottle of something dark, I had no idea where he'd got it, and swigged some down.

It made me nervous. "You'll drink when you get home but I just don't want to see it, after what nearly happened to you."

He put the bottle away.

We flew past Middletown, and onto the Merritt Parkway, the

best road there was in the days before the interstate. The broad road fairly invited me to hurry.

Construction ahead made us slow down. "Damn it!" I said.

While we inched forward, he tried to console me, "Don't worry. You'll get there." . . . "Take it easy." . . . "Ramming the back of that car won't help."

Now Eddie was practically my therapist. His regaling me with stories, and now his role of calming me down, had brought about a real reversal. I was glad for his company, the traffic was getting on my nerves.

From time to time, he sneaked a few more swigs of his rum or whatever it was. As I got more impatient, Eddie became more mellow.

The traffic cleared in front of us. It was close to six, and now I had no time to lose. I must have reached eighty-five, not startling today, but the old vehicles couldn't take it, and our car shook in protest. The parkway had constant reminders that the speed limit was fifty.

Hampden vanished, and then Stratford. After a big curve, when the road straightened out, Eddie observed, "We're gaining altitude."

I could see that he was really hoping I'd make it on time, but he was nervous.

"Aren't the cleaners open tomorrow?" he asked.

"Yeah, but I have a very important date tonight."

The visual illusions on the highway at dusk didn't faze me. I knew which nebulous roads on the horizon were real before we reached them. The parkway was already imprinted in my memory—its every curve, its every narrowing, its every concavity and hill, and we sped over it.

Then far behind us, I saw a speck in the shape of a police vehicle. It closed the gap fast, and soon I saw the black trooper's hat on the driver.

"Oh my God," I said in despair. "He's got me. He's going to give me a ticket."

The loudspeaker voice ordered us to pull over.

Eddie and I waited in the car, both silent as the trooper got out.

Then Eddie undid the top button of his shirt, and I saw that his whole body was tense and compact. I felt horror when he whispered in my ear, "Don't worry. Just open the door when he gets here. I'll bite his head off." He growled.

I looked over at him to see if he was smiling. His mouth was agape, incredibly wide. Then he flexed his jaws, opening and closing his mouth, as if getting ready—

In terror, I warned him. "Eddie, you better not . . . Lions only eat when they're hungry." I didn't even know if *I* was joking.

He closed his mouth just in time, as the trooper arrived.

While the trooper copied down the number of my driver's license and wrote out a ticket, I glanced over at Eddie menacingly, to be sure his mouth stayed shut. It did.

The trooper told me bitterly that I was endangering lives. Of course, he was right, but I was still too worried about Eddie to listen.

"And where the hell were you hurrying to?"

Naturally, I couldn't tell him about the white jacket and charcoal pants. I looked morose and repentant. If the officer had any idea what I was really worried about, he might have locked us both up. Mercifully, Eddie did nothing leonine.

After that, we crept along, even after the state trooper had veered off at the Westport exit.

Had Eddie really believed he was a lion? Obviously, I'd thought so for a moment, when that trooper showed up. I could never again deny that to myself. Could it be that he really saw himself as a lion, who had fooled us in the hospital by playing human—and who was fooling me now?

It pestered me that I would never know for sure.

I glanced over at him as I drove. He seemed deep in thought, and I had nothing more to say. After a while, I consoled myself that, serious or not, he didn't deserve to be kept in the hospital—any more than lions deserve to be contained in tiny rooms, pacing their lives away because they aren't human.

As the headlights came on along the road, I saw it was well past seven. There was no need to hurry anymore. I concentrated on the road and toyed with that impossible question of when is a human being playing and when is he really what he purports to be. I got lost in the abstraction of whether the question itself is meaningful.

Eddie didn't say much more, and I was just as glad. I'd had enough of the imponderable. And I'd certainly had enough of his dry humor, if that's all it had been.

I let him off in front of his home—near Ninth Avenue in the Fifties, my lion-man who would live forever in the forest between pretending and being, between comedy and madness.

WHEN TIME STOOD STILL

Between meetings of the American Psychological Association in Boston, I found myself alone with David Zeaman, the nationally renowned animal psychologist, in the coffee shop of the Copley Plaza. I asked him something I'd always wanted to know. "After the human being, which animal is the most intelligent?"

I'd naturally expected him to say the chimpanzee or the great ape, our immediate ancestor. Or even the dolphin, who was getting plenty of newspaper coverage for its three thousand different vocabulary sounds, its ability to carry out complex tasks, and its friendliness to humans.

Imagine my surprise when he said matter-of-factly, "We don't know. It could be the worm."

"What do you mean, the worm?"

"Well, we have only one way to measure the intelligence of a species. By giving that species precise tasks to do, teaching it by rewards what we want it to do, and then observing what it does."

"So?"

"Well, certain animals, like the chimp, can physically do
a lot more than others. They look smarter. They can show us
what they know. A worm can't. You see, there's only one
kind of intelligence, *functional intelligence*. A chimp can
signal with his hands or feet or tail, can talk in a sense,
go places, fetch things, leave things behind, eat or not eat
something. It can report to us what it hears or smells by any
of these behaviors. The rest is up to us. We find tasks for
it to do, and it does them. Better than a dog or a cat, for
example."

"And the worm?"

"We don't know. Suppose a worm could speak ten lan-
guages, do complex physics problems, could work with
Lagrange multipliers, had the answers to, you name it. How
would we know? We couldn't ask it questions, and it would
have no way of telling us."

It occurred to me that maybe he was kidding me. Though we
were colleagues in a sense, academic researchers have tradi-
tionally had a friendly rivalry with clinical psychologists, one
that sometimes borders on contempt. In those days, they
viewed clinicians as people who couldn't reason as well as
they. Or how else could we buy all that Freudian stuff or work
without the basis of evidence and proof that they insisted
upon?

"So there are worms under the ground, maybe as smart as
Einstein or Pasteur, is that what you're saying?"

"We can't prove or disprove it. We have no way of knowing."

"No way of testing, you mean?"

"Almost correct. They would have no way of communicating
what their true intelligence was."

"But if we study a worm's brain, wouldn't that tell us something?"

"It might *suggest*, but it wouldn't *prove* anything adverse to
the worm. In fact, physiologically a worm is more like a person
than a great many creatures who pass as a lot nearer to us. The
worm has nephron tubes like human kidneys, and even has

concentrations of ganglia like the nerve fibers of human beings."

The conversation ended there. But I kept thinking about the worm, or rather the hypothetical worm, gifted with superior intelligence but with no ability to communicate. For what could a worm do except rise to the surface of the earth or descend, and maybe stretch out or shrink to avoid the incursion of a blade! But this worm knew about birth and death, it had a logical faculty, it apprehended. But cursed with that terrible combination of sensibility and paralysis, it could show us nothing, making no claim for itself.

The professional lecture we attended was boring. On that we all agreed. Maybe our worm could conceive of a better one, though, of course, it couldn't present even the least of its ideas.

Years later when I read William Blake's ironic line, "The worm cleft in twain forgives the plow," I took him literally.

And when I read Heinrich Heine's poetry, written in bed during the terrible paralysis that kept him almost immobile for a decade, I thought of that worm.

> *How slowly Time, the frightful snail*
> *Crawls to the corner that I lie in;*
> *While I, who cannot move at all,*
> *Watch from the place that I must die in.*
> *—from Heine's "Dying Poet,"*
> *translated by Louis Untermeyer*

My reveries about the worm went the way of all metaphors, losing their vividness through prolonged exposure.

Then about ten years ago, when I was well established in private practice, a man scheduled an appointment with me— Mr. Lawrence Fellows we'll call him, a short, fiftyish man with features sharp and pronounced, and wearing a finely tailored dark suit.

"Things are going well, very well," he told me. "I've come a long way. I just don't want to make any mistakes. I guess I ought to tell you a little about myself."

With that he ran over the highlights of his personal history, as some patients find it urgent to do in first sessions.

He'd been poor, married young, started a trucking company that in no time grew to be quite successful. "Then my wife, Ilsa, who was a secretary and had just begun working for us— she was typist, office manager, you name it, she *was* the office—told me that she kept hitting the wrong keys. I mean she couldn't type, she was concerned. So was I. But we didn't dream. She was thirty-two. Anyhow, I urged her to go to our doctor, a very good man, and he sent her to a neurologist, and the neurologist sent her to Presbyterian Hospital for tests and said they'd wait for another doctor to look at the X rays, or whatever they were, of her brain."

His face reddened and he began to cry as if he'd just received the news, and now he was drowning in sobs, and I handed him one tissue and then another, and he tried to continue but couldn't.

"So they sent her for X rays, or whatever."

"An angiogram, maybe?"

"Right, an angiogram, and they operated and said she had six to eighteen months to live. They had told her, too, of course, and we said we'd enjoy them, but meanwhile I still hoped, and of course the business collapsed. Who cared? Well, anyhow, three years after that, I knew I had to do something. I started again. Started all over. So I thought you should know."

"I understand. Is there anything more I should know?"

"Well, yes there is. A lot. I haven't really told you, but I can't right now—" He was quivering, as if it were below zero in the room.

"So anyhow, I have a wonderful business and I'm married again. And that's fine. But I live and die for this business. I do everything myself, except drive the trucks and sometimes I wish I could do that."

His voice trailed off as if his thoughts had turned inward. He seemed drawn into the murky chasm of his past life by a force almost too powerful for him to resist it.

Instinctively, I tried to help him come back to the present. He said his new wife of five years, Mary, didn't work with him but discussed his operation at length with him, and was worried about him.

At the end of the session, when he offered to pay me, I told him my system was to send bills at the end of the month.

"I'm not sure I'm coming back."

"Okay, if you don't want to. Or maybe you want to think about it and call."

Three days later, he called and scheduled another appointment, saying he wanted to see me regularly. "Mary says I'd better. She says I don't trust anybody and I have bad symptoms and I'd better trust you."

But in my office he didn't bring up the symptoms. I had to ask him what they were.

"I sit in a chair motionless, sometimes for twenty minutes, last night for an hour. I seem to lose it, Doctor. The rest of the time I don't trust anyone, I don't trust you. I don't trust my wife. I don't trust myself."

"What do you mean?"

"Maybe I could have kept Ilsa alive. Maybe I'm destroying my business. I need a key person to help me, but there's no one I can really trust. The person wouldn't have to be a genius, just someone I can trust. At this rate, we'll have nothing in a year, but I just can't choose anybody, I can't make decisions when I get like this."

In our next session he told me he'd sat motionless in an armchair at home for three hours, and he was terrified.

"Were you sleeping?"

"No. I know the difference. I couldn't get up. I heard my wife come in. She called to me. She kissed me. She took my hand and sat with me."

"Did she call a physician?"

"No, oh God no!" He looked as terrified as if he'd seen a ghost. "That's why I came to you. You're a psychologist, aren't you? Not a medical doctor. Oh God, no."

Then he stared at me, and, suddenly rising from his chair, said, "Doctor, I'd better pay you now. I may not be back."

"That's okay. I appreciate the offer, but I'll take my chances."

"I mean I may not be *able* to come back." He felt an urge to clarify his last statement.

"No, why not?"

He looked at me skeptically, as if sizing me up.

"Well, for one thing, I'm hearing the chants again, like monks chanting. Music, and not music. I dream about them. I hear them sometimes."

"What are they like, I mean the music?"

He didn't answer.

I repeated the question.

"I'm sorry. There's a lot about the past I just can't tell you."

I deferred, and soon he was talking again about his crisis at work, his desperate need to trust someone before his business went down the drain. "I don't worry about myself so much, it's my wife. I don't want to see her poverty-stricken, and yet I can't make decisions. I can't even get someone to help me out."

After he left, I thought about him a lot. He was decisive about almost nothing—one might say he suffered the curse of limitless options interchanging with those periods of darkness, during which he apparently had no options at all. I wondered, Was he spending his weekend in one of those stupors? And of course, I wondered about his past.

I thought of calling him to see how he was doing. But it seemed wrong to call—he would be more likely to construe my interest as invasive than as an expression of concern.

Then I realized that he'd left me with a sense of inde-cisiveness too. I felt unclear about nearly everything in his life: how he felt about his present wife, whom he mentioned only in passing, how he truly felt about his business, why he couldn't trust anybody.

Even his account of how his first wife had died seemed un-nervingly incomplete. He'd never actually told me about her death, only intimated that it had occurred.

But the more I thought about it, the more it seemed utterly wrong to wait. Though in some cases mere waiting might have therapeutic value, here we had little time. His stupors were lengthening and he was feeling more hopeless.

If I could press him to verbalize as much as possible about these mysteries, perhaps he would uncover more about them for me, furnish a continuity that would make sense out of them for both of us. By keeping me at a distance he would only solidify his distrust of me; unless he trusted me more by action, he would never imbue me with any worth or see me as an ally. A malignant process was already in motion, and a passive approach would play right into it.

I decided to be much more directive and insistent with my questioning.

He said he'd been in four different foster homes after his mother gave him up when he was two. He didn't know who his father was.

"Does that trouble you?"

"I guess I'm used to it. I'd just as soon not know."

One foster home he'd counted on. Apparently, the married couple were very kind to him, and he'd entertained the idea of growing up with them, making a fortune so they could retire. But one day the woman—the only woman he'd ever called mother—had informed him that they were moving to Chicago in a few weeks and couldn't take him with them.

"There isn't space," she had said.

They'd lived near the Cloisters, a replica of a medieval church and monastery, full of artifacts, and he would go there, for hours. "Because it was so sad, I guess. I would sit there on a stone bench sometimes and look at the old coffins, and I used to think how peaceful the dead were. I used to think, 'Maybe if I don't move, nothing will happen, I can stay with the Petrofskys.' But they got rid of me, all right.

"I later found out that they'd kept me only for the money. The state paid them. That's the way it is. Fred—Mr. Petrofsky—he got a job in Chicago paying more, and they didn't need me."

*   *   *

The following Monday he told me he'd heard the chanting again that weekend. His wife had been unable to communicate with him and was terrified. The singing apparently accompanied his interludes of numbness.

That session I must have sounded more like a football coach than a therapist.

"Larry, listen to me. You've got to battle this going into a trance," I told him. "When you see it happening, when you see it even *starting* to happen, when you hear the voices, say something to someone, *anything*. Get up. Move. Do something."

But the harder I exhorted him, the more inanimate he became.

He looked at me with glassy, lifeless eyes and replied merely, "Yes, Doctor." And I knew that others had beseeched him in the past and that I was on the wrong track.

Well, at least I would press him to talk to me.

In response to my many direct questions, he told me he'd been married to Ilsa for ten years. After they married, he'd finished high school at night and got a truck driver's license and drove. "Oh, we had big plans. She'd be a teacher, and I'd have my own business."

Things had gone well for him—he'd bought into the company, and it flourished.

Then, as if he couldn't bear even that much prosperity in his thoughts, he recalled one of the specialists telling him that Ilsa was going downhill fast. By then, the oncologist had guessed she had, "Maybe two months at the upper end."

"I remember that phrase well—'upper end.' She was sleeping peacefully at the time. I begged them not to tell her and they said they wouldn't."

He turned his face away and shut his eyes tight, like an infant in a high chair avoiding a spoon of some unpleasant stuff.

But he went on. "I remember hoping that time would stop so she could stay with me, if only there was a way.

"Then I must have collapsed. I was in an ambulance that was clanging. I couldn't talk. In the hospital, they put me in a room and I sat there, staring out of the window. A woman doctor would come in and examine me. She would shine a flashlight into my eyes as if she was looking for something. Days passed and I didn't move. They fed me, brought me to the bathroom. After a while, nobody talked to me. I didn't talk either. I felt terrible about Ilsa, but maybe I didn't think about Ilsa, I just felt terrible.

"Once in a while, she, the woman doctor, brought in a whole class of students and shined the light and moved my arms, put them in different positions, and left them there. I couldn't move them myself. The students were fascinated. She would ask the class what I was. And usually someone would say 'a catatonic.' She'd say 'right,' and the students were happy.

"Then they transferred me to a big ward and put me in a corner. And I sat there."

"You kept worrying about Ilsa?"

"Not after that. Not once. I had the feeling that things were all right, that I was helping her. That somehow, I guess, somehow my being there was helping her. That it was necessary. Not that I had any choice.

"I used to look out of the window, but I could hear the shouts and the talking, and the doctors would come in, and the attendants. They'd come and go."

"Where was this?"

"At Creedmoor Hospital. I would see a big sign engraved on the building outside. I used to look through that mesh wiring on the windows. Creedmoor Hospital, that was all I knew. A year later no one would talk to me. They would talk about me sometimes. The doctors would bring in students there too, and say 'This is an example of catatonic schizophrenia.'"

"So you were very aware?"

"Aware? I was aware of everything. Every day, of the mornings and nights, the light and the dark, of the snow, of what they said. I used to hear people say, 'Boy, I'd hate to be like that.' I heard a lot. I knew all the patients' names. Their parents and wives would visit them and talk, and they would complain.

"I could see their wives on the steps before they got there, and sometimes I could see a visitor leaving and stop outside the building and throw up a kiss. Oh, I was aware all right. I could even read their lips. And an overweight woman, who always wore red, who visited her son, Mr. Bondy. On the steps leaving, she would always look up at the window at me and cross herself. I could read her lips saying, 'I love you.' Of course, it was Mr. Bondy, her son, she was talking to.

"Then I remember her taking his arm when they left, helping him down the steps to the car."

"You had visitors?"

"At first. A few men from the company. My accountant."

"And Ilsa?"

"No. She never came. I didn't want her to. I had the idea I was helping her. As I say, I could tell even when the doctors would just point to me. With their clipboard, they'd look at me. Dr. Fine and Dr. Clemens and old Dr. Coscarart.

"After a while, they stopped saying hello to me in the mornings. They didn't think I knew anything. They would talk to the others but just point to me. After they stopped giving me medication, they didn't even point, except when the students would come; then the doctor would move my arms around and leave them there. I couldn't put them back at my sides. Even the attendants who fed me didn't talk. That bothered me. Except for one man, Warren White. He would always talk to me."

"He would? What would he say?"

"Well, I don't know how he knew, but he knew I was hearing that music. He would ask, 'How's the music today, Larry?' I wouldn't budge, but he knew."

"Music?"

"Yes. Those monks. They used to sing all the time. I was glad they did. I don't know how he knew. Warren White. He was there six days a week. He told me he worked an extra day because he needed the money. He talked to each patient every day. Especially to me. He would break the rules and smuggle in chocolate for all of us, and every day he'd stuff some in my mouth and it would melt. I loved it, but of course I didn't move my jaws. It had to melt.

"He'd say, 'Larry, I have something for you. Bittersweet.' Now I cry thinking about it. He would shake my hand in the morning and I'd think 'Warren White.' And before he left, after he said 'See you tomorrow' to everyone, he'd come over to me. He'd press his hand on my back. I would always feel his hand. I got to wait for it. Once he forgot when he was leaving. I didn't sleep all night. Warren White, the attendant. Handsome man. Very handsome.

"And the next day he came over to me and he said, 'Larry, please forgive me, I forgot to say good-bye last night before I left. Larry, please forgive me.' He told me he'd had to rush home and he didn't think about me.

"Then something changed. For some reason he would sit, he would pull up a chair and sit across from me and tell me stories."

"What do you mean, stories?"

"About what he saw. About his dog, sometimes. He told me a long story about his mother. She used to cough a lot, he tried to tell her not to smoke, but she'd nag him. One day he told me about his friend Bill, where they went, how they took the dog out to the park. Sometimes he'd laugh in the middle of a story."

"He was important to you."

"Important! I guess I love him. Always will. I didn't show it, but I felt I would die if he didn't say hello. But he always did. He used to say, 'Don't worry, Larry, this too shall pass. You'll get over it. You'll be back some day, this is just a test.'

"I'd been there for two years. Over two years, almost three. They got some new medicine. It made me feel incredibly warm, I didn't like it. But Warren White would sit with me even longer, he would force those pills into me, he would say, 'Sorry, buddy, but this is very important.'

"I started to feel soft again. Not like wood. I was talking! Then I guess it was three months later, and I was really talking. Not great you know, but talking, and the doctors were all coming in to see me and to talk about this medicine. They'd point to me and talk to me and I'd answer.

"And then a doctor said I'd be going home, with Ilsa's mother. I had to take that medicine, and the last day Warren White hugged me and said, 'Larry, I'm so proud of you. I knew you'd make it.' And I cried. What makes someone like him?"

"I don't know. It's a great question. And Ilsa?"

"She was dead. A long time dead. They didn't tell me right away."

"And the voices?"

"They were gone. That's what scares me. Now I'm starting to hear them again."

I had time for one more question. "The music you say you hear these days, it's like that music you heard at the Cloisters, I mean the monks?"

"Yes, it is, come to think of it."

I could hardly concentrate during the first half of my next session. The horror of his story and the threat that it would repeat flooded my thoughts, as a young couple argued over the wife's buying a new living-room sofa without consulting her husband.

That evening, I remembered the image of David Zeaman's worm, his sentient being, aware even of subtleties but unable to let us know. And I thought about Warren White, the exemplar of the goodness on earth that must forever go unacknowledged, because the full recognition that there are such people, that they are not deranged in any way, would inform against us, showing the rest of us, the majority, to be devious, expedient, greedy. And so we deny their existence, or, more diabolically, we deny their goodness, ascribing other, baser motives to them. And psychoanalysis, blinded by their light, charging patients for every hour missed, has led the curse against them, by inventing secret, self-serving motives for them. According to psychoanalysis, they are covering their hidden rage, or seeking power by giving pleasure, or playing God. And then I remembered Baudelaire's line, "To be a saint for oneself, that is the important thing."

Gradually, I pried my thoughts away from these informants, these sublime subversives, resolving that though I was not among their aristocracy, I would at least not deny their existence or damn them by positing less than noble motives for them.

Before the next scheduled hour, Larry's wife called and said he was sitting motionless and couldn't make it. But then she called a few hours later and said he was okay and would see me next time. He didn't want to come to the phone.

The next day, I spoke to the medical specialist, a pharmacological expert, who was trying out different concoctions on Larry. "The Navane isn't doing what it did," he told me. We discussed the possibility that Larry might be getting something out of his torpor.

Two things struck me. One was his not coming to the phone after failing to make his appointment with me. I could view it as his incapacity, or, despite his desperate state, I could view it as an ethical failure. After all, when you stand someone up, for whatever reason, you *owe* it to him to tell him why, not to send a delegate to explain.

When he did return, he seemed strangely untroubled. Instead of showing the terror at his trances, at the voices, that he'd felt in the beginning, he actually told me he liked the voices.

Once more, I lapsed into beseeching him not to give in to them but to no avail. I quit that tactic fast, as it seemed only to prompt an active indifference on his part, as if my espousing the urge to snap out of it freed him to succumb with a full heart, to lose himself in their siren sounds.

*   *   *

The next weekend I scheduled Larry for a Saturday. Not being
Warren White, I resented having to do this, but it seemed
utterly wrong to leave him alone for two days. He seized the
offer, though he probably wasn't aware enough to thank me for
making the time.

I discussed the case with fellow professionals and then studied my own reactions to him as possibly providing a critical
cue. When I asked myself how I truly felt about him, I was
surprised to discover that I actually felt some resentment toward him, along with sorrow for his state. He had a wife devoted to him, a work staff dependent on him, a psychiatrist
studying his medications, and me, seeing him on Saturday.
Yet not only was he making us all feel desolate and like
failures, he never thanked anybody for anything.

As I thought about it, I realized that though his illness cost
him suffering, it was also doing him a thousand services. Indeed, owing to it, or using it, he had arranged not even to be
with Ilsa, his beloved, in her last hours. He had left her actual
death and her funeral to others, arranging—past master that
he was—not even to know when she died.

Was it fair to view him this way? No, if it meant that I
acted toward him resentfully. But yes it was, if such feelings
induced in me gave me real insight, and especially if they
prompted a therapeutic approach that could help him. The
greatest of all sociologists, Emile Durkheim, had dared to
relate suicide to selfishness, and it wasn't hard to view my
patient as selfish, as an immoral worm, quite a different creature from the meritorious worm of Blake. At least, such a
view would give me something to work with, and without it, I
had nothing.

That Saturday, soon after we started, I began, "How come you
didn't call me yourself after you stood me up?"

"I didn't stand you up."

"We had an appointment and I didn't see you. What do you call that?"

"I didn't have a choice."

"Why not? You could have gone to work. You could have called me yesterday. And you certainly could have called to say you were sorry you didn't make it."

I thought I saw his face liven, just a little.

I pushed ahead. "I guess after you got out of your slump, you thanked your wife for sticking with you."

He shook his head negatively.

"You see her crying desperately as if her life is coming to an end because she loves you, don't you?"

"I do."

"So why don't you at least thank her? Why didn't you go to work?"

"You really don't understand," he said to me. "I couldn't."

"Couldn't! You could have. You could have comforted your wife. You could have gone to work. But what did you do? You arranged not to do anything, except jerk off with your music."

He smiled.

Now I was on a roll. "Did you ever hear of Nero? He was an emperor. He played his fiddle while Rome burned. You don't even play the fiddle. You're too fuckin' lazy. All you do is just *listen*."

His answer surprised me. "That's not so. I *try*. I try in ways you don't even understand."

"What ways?"

"I don't know. I can't say, but I try."

"I'll believe it when I see it."

To my astonishment, he thanked me at the end of the hour, and I got the strong impression that he appreciated the tack I had taken with him, that it had some deep, personal validity for him.

Apparently, the tougher I was, the less I believed in his helplessness, his self-enforced passivity, the more understood he felt. Even though this approach was in a sense abusive to him, it was also complimentary. I'd been crediting him with the power of choice, extending that power to him even when he was in his trance. That smile of his was the smile of someone caught out in a secret.

As I thought it over later, there seemed little doubt of it. He'd had a sense that he was, indeed, empowered, more than outsiders dreamed, and he'd *cherished* that sense. To others he might appear like someone who couldn't move, who couldn't talk, who couldn't do anything in his own behalf. But *he* knew better, that was his secret. In some curious way, he'd been attempting a solution all along.

That comment of his, "I try," took on new meaning. But what the hell did it mean? Of course, the mystery remained. I had absolutely no idea what he'd been trying to accomplish by going into his trance, only that it was something.

By the next time I saw him, I had the rationale for my tough approach—an approach that had felt right but that I had hit on almost by accident. Above all, I had to emphasize his sense of freedom and choice.

"Well, did you do anything for anybody since I saw you last?"

"I told Mary that I'd take the medicine Dr. Amols gave me. I'll take it without fail."

I resisted saying anything approving.

I said to him, "Actually, you've got it pretty good. Your own business. You've got a wife who sticks with you even though you give her nothing back, she loves you for some reason. You've got Dr. Amols, he's the best. You've got me working for you, I'm very good myself. You have the money to hire someone to fill in on the job so you could travel, if you wanted to—"

"What's the point?" he broke in. "I can't keep it this way. It'll go down the drain. No one will stick it out."

"What do you mean?"

"Here today, and gone tomorrow, that's me."

"Tomorrow could be even better, asshole."

He smiled but didn't speak, as if he thought of himself as having some profound knowledge about tomorrow, maybe about all tomorrows, that innocent, stupid people like me, weren't privy to.

Now I felt like a fighter who, despite that one left hook of his, had won the last round.

But progress in psychotherapy is typically ratchetlike, improving its grip only to slip back partway and then go forward again. Larry spent the next handful of sessions complaining about his company, about late-paying clients, dishonest ones, and about employees who let him down. His inability to trust anyone and his feeling of powerlessness pervaded whatever he talked about.

I let him go on, content that what he said contained important truths, and also that his telling me anything of importance to him would develop whatever rudimentary faith he had in me and in what I stood for—namely, disbelief in his helplessness and belief in his future.

With a childhood like his, it was understandably hard for him to believe in his own power over his destiny. He elaborated again on how he'd been plucked without warning from one foster home after another. The most seemingly reliable people, the most well-established routines—of when he got up, of when he ate, of when he studied, of when he washed himself—brought him not a hint of the predictability that they afford other children. To be good did not mean to be safe.

Twice he'd been hurried away so fast that he'd left his possessions behind, and when the Petrofskys moved to Chicago, they'd even taken the dog with them, which was more his than theirs. Though he'd sunk into despair, their going had come almost as a relief, so strong had been his anticipation that his best efforts to keep the family together would fail.

I asked him pointedly what those best efforts were, but he didn't answer me.

Like nearly all horrible past experiences that patients report, his sudden abandonment at their hands doubtless sank deep because it was not the first of its kind. The thousandth blow of the ax that fells a tree may not be the sharpest, though it is surely the most memorable.

My factitious anger toward Larry-the-ingrate was hard to maintain as he told me about those early rejections. One family had promised to take him to a ball game for his birthday, but had defaulted at the last moment because it wasn't ladies day as they'd anticipated and they didn't want to spend the full price. He'd wondered where they were that afternoon, and then discovered that they'd gone without him. Soon afterward, that family had dispatched him.

"I guess they figured, why spend the money if they were planning to get rid of me?" He shrugged, as if he understood.

Listening, I was almost seduced into understanding along with him. But I have never found that to understand is necessarily to forgive; on the contrary, often to understand is to despise.

One evening, during the month or so while Larry was going over his past, a woman friend brought me to the home of her brother, an executive at Merrill Lynch, who, with his wife, had given their children all the advantages of money and attention. I was impressed by how little Cynthia, celebrating her eighth birthday, held herself, by how she thanked people for their presents and their compliments, neglecting to do so once or twice and being reminded politely by her mother. "And thank Uncle David for coming. He drove here for three hours from Connecticut."

She seemed to enjoy saying thanks, the way she enjoyed her pink finery that evening, and I could sense the feeling of power it gave her to be appreciative. She was conducting a kind of court and we were in attendance, there for her birthday. Her ready acknowledgment of people, something I did not learn till very much later, stamped in the idea that it *mattered* what she said to people, and that she, at her tender age, could hurt someone or lift someone: her parents, her Uncle David, me. And it was true, there was nothing phoney or constrained about Cynthia, it really did matter to others how she treated them and she knew it.

I thought about several patients of mine whose treatment of others truly hadn't mattered. Why on earth would a ten-year-old Larry say thanks or hello or good-bye? Why should he talk at all, except that by learning amenities and practicing them he could reconvince himself later on, over a lifetime, that what he did mattered. Except, in short, to create his own sense of power, of his importance on earth. But, of course, no one could arrive at such knowledge on his own.

And thus it had never crossed Larry's mind to thank me for the extra time I gave him or to thank his wife for standing by him or even Warren White for being the miracle that he was, for consoling him as he sat motionless in that room.

But not to express such thanks, even now, would be to go on dealing with people as if he were as helpless as he had been with them in childhood. It would be to go on assigning them the role of being utterly indifferent to him. By not acknowledging others, he was still telling himself repeatedly that nothing was for real, that nothing would stay as it was, and that he had no power whatsoever.

That evening, as I took my coat and little Cynthia hugged me and said, "I had a wonderful birthday," I thought of Larry, and knew I would henceforth demand that he do the same thing. What we gave him, even what Warren White gave him, would never fill the void in him. He would have to acknowledge us, give us something back, to create the sense of potency that little Cynthia, thanks to her parents, already claimed almost as a birthright.

So I got tough again. He told me he'd lost a big account and was on the verge of losing another. He needed someone to take charge of things—"an inside man"—so that he could go to the Midwest and close some deals. "He wouldn't have to be a genius. But I can't find anyone, isn't that funny? I just can't find anyone."

"You don't want anyone," I said accusingly. "You'd rather go down the drain with your whole business than have to be disappointed in one more person."

"You're right," he said, and we talked about his childhood when turning to anyone, trusting anyone, seemed always to be the beginning of the end.

"So you'll destroy yourself, just to stay consistent," I said ironically.

Apparently, that touched a cord because he volunteered to start searching for the needed "inside man" or woman before he saw me again.

He was late for the next session and when I asked him why, he said sluggishly, "I don't know."

He talked about the weekend, telling me about his and Mary's visit to friends. But his heart wasn't in what he was saying, and there were long pauses.

After a while, I asked him, "You've done anything about finding the inside man yet?"

He didn't answer.

I knew I was pushing him, but I repeated the question.

During the next excruciating minute, he seemed deep in thought. He looked at me but said nothing.

Finally, I said, "It's really hard to make this kind of decision, isn't it? I mean to find someone you can trust."

"Hard? Everything's hard. Like stone." He stopped abruptly, resting his arms flat on the arms of the chair he sat in, and he didn't move. I would have thought he'd fallen asleep in his chair if he hadn't been staring at me.

Thirty seconds later, I realized to my horror that he wasn't moving a muscle. He was more than asleep. I had never seen anyone so still. He had gone into one of his trances.

In my terror, feeling instantly to blame, I must have asked him a dozen questions at once, praying he would respond.

Still, he just sat there, his eyes wide open, his mouth agape.

I could picture him, motionless in the corner of that ward. Trembling, I asked myself why I had pressured him, what I had done to drive him back into the worst of his psychosis. I compared myself with experts in my field, who would never have done such damage. As he sat there, I felt like begging his forgiveness for having turned him to stone, by asking—no, not by asking, by *insisting* that he commit himself, that he make decisions he could not possibly be ready to make.

Time stopped for me too, as he sat there, unmoving, unforgiving. I waved my hand in front of his eyes, but he did not blink. I recalled stories of how people in such states must have their eyes diverted from the sun or they will go blind, and I switched off the nearby lamp.

Now, blaming myself completely, I saw that my hand was shaking. Should I call for help or wait some more? I decided to wait just a little longer.

But then, mercifully, his eyelids fluttered. A moment later he asked, "How come you turned off the light?"

"I guess I thought it was a glare," I said. "You're okay?"

"I'm trying. I'm trying to help. But it's hard. Everything's hard. Like stone." He smiled faintly, as if sure I understood. He was conscious. He could talk. I felt like celebrating.

"Larry, I know you're trying." I did my best to keep my voice even and conversational.

"The music. The monks." He smiled again. Now he spoke more as if in a hypnagogic interlude, the kind of illusion we have sometimes on the way to sleep or on the way back.

"What about the monks?" I asked. Anything to keep him active, to keep him *producing*.

All he replied was "hard stone," but at least he replied.

He seemed so much safer in the past that I vowed, at that moment, not to mention anything touching his future. I would ask for no commitments. In fact, I observed that the further back in time he went, the more easily he talked.

Maybe he was thinking of those days at the Cloisters when the monks first sang to him. It was worth a try.

"When you used to hear those monks at the Cloisters, sitting on that hard stone. What about them? Tell me anything you can remember. Maybe you can talk about that."

"It was a record they used to play—to help people."

He seemed comfortable once again, even desirous of regressing in memory, as if he needed my companionship over the parts of the journey that he had made so terribly alone, so hopelessly. And his consciousness, his lucidity, his not going into a trance were more than reward enough for me.

"Okay," I said, keeping my tone as nonchalant as I could, "so you were on that stone bench. The Petrofskys had just told you they were leaving. And you went there to sit. Okay, you're on that stone seat, looking at those stained-glass windows you mentioned to me, listening to the record. You remember that."

"It's hard. I was stone too. I wanted to be stone."

"I know you wanted to be stone," I said consolingly. "You still want to be stone sometimes, and you're pretty good at it."

"Goodstone. No. I walked all the way there. It was straight uphill. I used to carry my roller skates there, and I'd roll back down. I could get home without people even seeing me move. I used to pretend someone else was steering me.

"They were gonna get rid of me. They never wanted me, even when I thought they did. Nobody does."

Now he was conversing at normal speed and sounding totally lucid, though I still wasn't sure he knew he was talking to me.

"How awful!" I said.

"I wanted to stay with them, the Petrofskys. To stop all motion. Like just before. So they couldn't sell me. Or trade me. Get rid of me, you know what I mean."

"I sure do."

"I figured if I didn't move—" With that, he stopped all

movement abruptly, as if in illustration. But he'd said enough
to allow me to finish. "If you didn't move, they couldn't take
you."

"That's right. Time would stand still. If nothing happened,
then nothing could happen. Time, everything, would stop.

"I remember I was home when they got there. I was on the
floor, facing the wall. They couldn't pick me up, they couldn't
move me. They thought it was a game, then they saw they
couldn't move me. Mr. Petrofsky, he had a bad back. It was
always hurting, that's why he took the job in Chicago. He
couldn't pick me up, and the neighbors couldn't.

"Some doctor came and he brought his friend. Whatever
they did, I didn't move. By then I *couldn't* move. And mamma,
Mrs. Petrofsky, said it was terrible, and they couldn't go
to Chicago. I was laughing to myself. They kept me a week
extra, I thought it was for good. A lot of people came, and
they shoved food in my mouth, but I didn't shit, I didn't even
piss. They were scared. But finally, they went anyhow." He
paused.

I said, "Larry, it didn't work, just for a while."

"I know, just for a while, but that was good, that was something."

"So you did it again," I said. "You got good at turning yourself into stone so nothing could happen."

"It's pretty crazy, isn't it?"

"Not at all. I think everybody, some time in his life, wants
time to stand still. So why not you? You're just like the rest of
us. But don't do it." I raised my voice. "*Larry, don't do it.* No
time-standing-still, you get it?"

Before he left that day, I put my arm around him, as I
pictured Warren White doing when poor Larry was a lot worse
off. I said, "We understand this thing, and we're going to beat
it. You're going to have a great life. But no making time stand
still, do you hear?"

He snapped his heels together in mock imitation of a Prus-
sian officer before someone higher in command.

We both laughed.

"See you Tuesday," I said. "Don't bother looking for that inside man. Not yet, anyhow. But just don't make time stand still. Call me, if you get the urge. You hear me?"

He smiled, and I felt sure he had heard me. I suspected he had no memory of his trance, and I had no impulse to remind him of it.

I thought about him, reinforcing his tactic over the years, and the phrase came to me *"reinforced concrete."*

Slowly, because he'd forgiven me by recovering, I began to forgive myself for inducing his trance. How I'd done it was easy to see—I'd provoked him by forcing him to commit to the future, to trust. Probably, I would induce that kind of state again if I pressured him similarly. Or more precisely, I would be creating the crisis that he characteristically handled that way.

Some day, if I were to succeed, he would talk about the future, he would commit himself, he would trust. But not yet. Underscoring the resolution I had made, I realized that pressure from me, perhaps even a slip by me, might again set into motion his most primitive device—that of making time stand still.

My next task was to make him so familiar with his tactic that he could never again employ it unconsciously. And to this end, I asked him to remember using it, and to tell me about those periods in as much detail as he could, not once but over and over again.

The more times he recounted the story, the better he could familiarize himself with his tactic and the more conscious it would become. In the future he would become aware of even the slightest stirrings of impulse to use it. I needed him to recognize even his first impulses to freeze, "to make time stand still," to hide from the future by not letting it come.

He seemed to actually enjoy telling me how he did it, as if glad to have someone to confide his device in.

"I would sit there and listen to the music and make sure I didn't move a finger, even when people would look at me. Sometimes people thought I was praying."

I marveled at his expertise.

"So did the monks," he said.

One day I asked him, "And you did the same thing when Ilsa was sick?"

"I think so. I remember I would hold my breath when I walked through her room. She had so much trouble breathing by then. We had oxygen right there."

"You used to wish time would stop."

"Of course."

"So you stopped it?"

"I don't remember, but I used to look at the clock a lot. There were slow days and fast days. I used to hope it would go slow. We had so little time, we had so little . . ."

He didn't finish the sentence, but I could. "And then there were no days at all," I thought.

Strange as it may sound, his method, so logical to him, began to seem plausible to me as he kept telling me about it. Not that I wanted him to employ it, but I could picture someone, with no resources left, despising the future and resorting to such a primitive trick to forestall it, the way a child shuts his eyes to annihilate the sight of something unwanted.

Like Hamlet's curse, "Let no one marry," after his mother's infidelity, like the imprecation of the injured Venus against love itself, "Sorrow on love hereafter shall attend," my patient had set his curse on Time itself. Time, which had brought him so much pain, let it stop! Let no new evils be delivered from its poisonous womb. Of course, Larry was no deity like Venus, who could make good a curse, but only a child still given to infantile fantasies of omnipotence. He could stop time but only by stopping his own process; he could enforce his moratorium, but only so far as he himself was concerned.

Even after he reported not having gone into a trance for six months, I seized every occasion to talk about the tactic—anything to keep him thinking about the device so that he would never again simply resort to it without knowing what he was doing. In fact, I never let a session go by without mentioning his Houdini method of escape, referring to it lightly but often.

Sometimes I would stop him in the midst of an account. "So you turned yourself into stone, eh?" and he would either answer, "That's right, I did," or smile and say, "Oh no. Not that time."

After that, I started creating minicontexts in which he might be prone to invoke it, to congeal himself. I needed to be present at those very moments when he might have used the tactic in the past.

I would ask him small questions about future plans, usually prefacing them by a consciousness-raising statement.

"Hey, Larry, I've got a hard question for you. Do you want to think about it or go into a trance?"

"I'll think about it."

"Are you sure?"

"I'm sure."

"Maybe you want to stiffen up instead."

"No. I don't."

"How do you know? Suppose it's a tough question."

"I *know*. What's the question?"

Only when he was flushed with annoyance would I pose it, being careful to keep it simple and answerable.

"Who are you leaving in the front office when you go to Chicago next Friday?"

At first, when I verged on the matter of trust, he would shut his eyes tight.

"Good-bye, Larry," I said. "See you tomorrow. Maybe next year."

He opened them abruptly. "No, I was just thinking. I'm leaving Louis in charge. Louis."

"You sure he's honest? He won't run away with the books?"

"No. He's too stupid."

Slowly he came back into touch with even his most incipient evasion tactics, emotional fossils of the full-scale trances of his past. And I kept reminding him of them.

"I've got a question for you, Larry. Are you ready to close your eyes?"

Sometimes, when I couldn't think of a way to evoke his impulse, I would simply characterize him, kiddingly.

"Larry, you're a hard man. A *hard* man."

He didn't react for a while, and when he saw the ambiguity, he told me to cut it out. Technically, I was, in my own way, doing what early psychoanalysts called the "working through" of his most primitive defense tactic. That is, getting the patient to experience the tactic over and over, seeing it from every possible angle, so as to develop new feelings about it and mastery over it.

Along the way, he told me that he used the monks' music to encourage him; they had helped him, calmed him as a child. "I know it sounds funny, but I felt I could count on them. They understood me. They'd always be there."

For a whole year, my main focus was on that tactic of absenting himself, and as we kept examining it, he recalled other instances in which he'd used it. Not only did I shy away from the future, I had to resist commenting when he described his business slipping away. Fortunately, a bank loan kept him afloat for a time, but I dared not bring up the matter of personnel; he trusted no one there.

Nor had I any hope that he would trust me as yet. Unlike the overwhelming majority of patients, he couldn't even stand sympathy for the violations he had endured. Apparently, he hated any vestige of impulse it would arouse in him to reach for more sympathy and be disappointed again.

Often when I thought I was at my best, he would snap at

me, "You're just saying that," or "You really don't know what it's like," or "You're off the wall with that, Doctor."

He was so direct, and even brutal at times, that, doubting myself for the moment, I would look back, asking myself how I'd felt when I'd said something to him. Had I been sincere? Had he, indeed, spotted something in me that I disliked thinking was there?

Then I realized that such remarks, though they stung, should be construed as the liberties of someone who utterly disbelieved in the longevity of relationships. Being politic, even courteous, had no utility in the life of someone dumped on one doorstep after another, like a parcel with an address scrawled in an unintelligible hand. Why should someone who so disbelieved in his ability to shape his future, to influence it, bother to acknowledge anyone's best efforts?

He would often anticipate rejection as if he'd known nothing else. After I'd told him I was going to take a two-week vacation the next month, he missed his next appointment and didn't call. Seeing my act as an upcoming abandonment, he was striking first—a tactic not totally new for patients upset by their therapist's taking a break. When I mentioned his standing me up, he snapped, "Why should you care! The insurance company is paying you anyhow."

I consoled myself that at least there were no more trances. Even the most mordant cynicism was preferable to them.

Along the way, his wife called and said that for the first time he was becoming incredibly nasty to her. Though he would apologize afterward, she found it almost unbearable. He had given her permission to call, but still I was afraid that he'd construe any comment I made to her as betrayal. I hurriedly referred her to another therapist, a woman, whom she liked at once and continued to see.

As for Larry, at least now he was announcing his distrust, instead of somaticizing it. He was voicing his thoughts, and not deadening himself to make them go away.

For another year I stuck to my game plan, watching him distrust everyone but at least stay out of his trance states. However, his inability to trust people was threatening havoc on many fronts. Several employees quit because they realized he would never promote them to positions of real responsibility. And because he would not hire replacements and left the business understaffed, it began to go down. A big bank loan went overdue. All this while, Mary was desolate over her inability to get through to him. Unless he looked squarely at his prospects and gambled on at least a few individuals, on *somebody*, collapse on many fronts was imminent.

I knew I had to confront him. There were plenty of openings, but not until I'd actually begun did I know that I'd chosen the time.

He'd just finished saying he didn't trust still another employee.

"Lawrence, I don't think there's anybody in this world you do trust, is there?"

"What do you mean?"

"Well, you didn't believe in your accountant and now he's gone, you don't trust Mary—"

"That's not so, I'm for Mary a hundred percent."

"Come on, Lawrence, you told me you conceal an awful lot from her. 'What she doesn't know won't trouble her.' Isn't that what you said?"

"No, that's not really right."

"Hey, Lawrence, who are you putting one over on! You *know* it's right. You don't trust me. Your master plan is to go through this world alone, and then sulk that everybody let you down. Brilliant!"

"You're wrong."

"It's obvious you don't. Come on. If you trusted Mary, you'd tell her you loved her and appreciated her, the way any human being would. And if you trusted me, you'd express a little appreciation and warmth. And your accountant, Arthur, he'd still be working for you. It wasn't the money. What do you think the guy was half-crying for when he left? He cared about you and you practically called him a thief."

"So what do you want me to do?"

"Nothing right now. Just *realize* that you're playing this

game of life so close to the vest that nobody sees your cards, even you. And who do you cheat? Yourself."

"I see what you're saying."

He might have stopped me at once by closing his eyes and keeping them shut, or by freezing, or even by pressing his arms against the sides of the chair he sat in. But we'd discussed his device of "turning to stone" so often that he didn't allow himself to do this. Even as I assailed him, I was proud of him.

"So what should I do about it?" he asked.

"Lawrence, I don't think you want to do anything about it. Why ask me?"

"Why are you calling me Lawrence, instead of Larry?"

"Oh, I don't know," I said casually. "I figured maybe you didn't want me to get that close to you."

He seemed stricken. "Please call me Larry again," he pleaded.

"Okay, Larry, if it's important."

"So what do you want me to do?"

"Just *think* about it, how you treat Mary and me as if we're your enemies. How you feel sorry for yourself, and how you won't take a chance on anybody."

After he left, I felt I'd gone as far as I could in a single session, or maybe a little further.

That night I resisted an impulse to call, to see if he was okay. Collectively, we'd reached out enough to him; now it was *his* turn to reach out—there could be no real change in him without his expending effort.

Our next session was delayed by one of his business trips, which he talked about much of the session. For half an hour he made no mention of what I'd said earlier, perhaps waiting for me to bring it up. But I didn't. Finally, he asked, "What got into you last time?"

I asked him what he meant.

"Telling me I don't love Mary."

"I didn't say you don't love her. I said you don't let her know. You don't give anybody a sense that they matter to you."

He seemed to be thinking about the proposition, as if he'd never heard it before.

"What do you mean?"

He knew damn well what I meant.

I told him, "Well, I was thinking how different you are from some people. I mean some people really *show* they care, even when they get nothing back."

"I don't understand."

"Well, you take someone like Warren White. I was thinking last night, you're like the *opposite* of him. He stuck with you while you went into your stone routine for almost three years. He never complained. He trusted you, he believed in you. You're the opposite, the *exact opposite*. I guess it takes all kinds. You don't trust anybody. I mean nobody."

"You're wrong," he insisted.

"Oh, am I? He could be dead as far as you're concerned. Even Warren White. I guess it takes all kinds—"

"That's enough." His eyes darted fire at me and I stopped abruptly. I had touched something sacred—not Warren White himself, perhaps, but the memory of Warren White.

I was surprised when he began the next session with an apology. "I shouldn't have yelled at you. You're doing your best."

"Thanks for the kind word. It really means something to me, Larry. I *am* doing my best. But as for your yelling, I wasn't even aware of it. I can take a hundred times as much, as long as we work together, as long as we try."

"You mean as long as I don't go into a trance. My wife says I'm letting my business go into a trance these days."

"Really? That's an interesting interpretation."

"She's a bright woman, Mary."

"She is. And even more important, she's loyal, she's on your team."

"I know," he said.

"I'm glad you do. I'm not always sure."

"I dreamed about Warren White last night."

"No kidding!"

"Yeah. In the dream he said, 'Larry, I'm very disappointed in you,' and I asked him, 'What for?' and he wouldn't talk, he just wouldn't talk."

"Really!"

"And then all the colors ran out of him—they sort of bleached out of him. He was like blank, no color at all, even his clothes. And suddenly the wine glass he was holding up, like he was about to toast somebody, the wine glass just shattered in his hand. It was terrible. I woke up fast."

I could see he was becoming very emotional.

"What do you make of it?" I asked him.

"I don't know."

"Larry, what comes to your mind?"

"I'm afraid he's dead."

"You mean you thought he was dead, in the dream?"

He nodded.

"What killed him?"

Suddenly, Larry's Adam's apple seemed too big for him. He could hardly get his next words out. "I did."

"Really? How? Why?"

"I don't know. But those colors going out of him. I killed him. He used to drink a little at night. He told me it was a problem sometimes. He said he wasn't an alcoholic, but things used to catch up with him sometimes at night."

"He told you that?"

"More than once. He even said I could help him if I pulled out of this, he said that would help him."

"No kidding!"

"Yeah. I want to admit something to you. I've got to admit it to you. He was maybe fifteen years younger than me, a handsome man, black wavy hair. But he was the only father I ever had . . . No, not you . . . you're no father, you're too much like me. You could fall apart just like me. You need too much. But Warren White . . ." He shook his head sadly.

"But he fell apart in the dream."

"I know."

"Even you couldn't help him."

"I didn't try. I just sat there." He seemed deeply sorry, but he didn't close his eyes, and there were no tears. "I just sat there, that's the story of my life."

I kept quiet, while he digested his own invective against himself. Actually, I didn't know whether to underscore it by repeating it, to disagree in order to buoy up his spirits, or to agree and perhaps jog him toward a new mode.

"That's the story of my life," he repeated. "But Warren White must be alive and okay, huh?"

"I guess so, but I don't know the guy."

"I know," he said comfortingly. "How could you know?"

There was another long silence.

"Maybe I'll give him a call," he said. "Just to be sure."

"It's been done before," I said.

I must have been deeply immured in that self-imposed lethargy of his, the one that divorces ideas from acts, which I had assumed as my only mode of helping him—my own defense against urging him to act in any way. When he said a second time, "I think I'll give him a call," I was startled. He *meant* it.

"Interesting idea," I said.

"I know. I just hope I can pull it off."

"Why couldn't you?"

"Maybe he won't remember me. Maybe he won't come to the phone. I just want to thank him, that's all."

"Not a bad idea," I said.

In my enthusiasm, I perhaps sounded a little pompous, but I meant what I said. "You know, in thanking him, you would be saying thanks to a lot of people in a way. It would be great for them, and it would be great for you."

"You think he'll remember me?"

"After three years with you?"

"I know, but he's got a lot on his mind." He hesitated.

"Is that why you don't want to call him, or do you mean you're scared?"

"I'm a little scared about how he'll react."

I didn't say anything.

During the following week, he kept considering whether or not to make the call. I tried to stay neutral when he wavered—the less input from me, the more his contacting Warren White would mean to him.

Finally, he decided he'd make the call, from his favorite office chair. He'd stay on the phone a minute or so, long enough to say he was doing fine, and thanks.

I was confident that Warren White wouldn't let us down.

To my surprise, Larry called me the very next day. "Can I see you, just for a few minutes this afternoon? You tell me when."

He'd never done that before. I had a brief break between patients and fit him in.

Larry was already in my waiting room when the patient before him departed. Even before I'd asked what happened, I knew it wasn't good. His expression was doleful and he didn't speak for a time. In his elegant gray suit, which he wore with a vest, he seemed almost miniature, as if life were finally shrinking him to the nonexistence that he had so often sought.

At length I asked him, "Well, you called him?"

"I did."

"How did it go?"

"He wasn't there. He's not working at Creedmoor anymore. He's not in the hospital system."

"No kidding! That's a shocker—"

He said, "I couldn't believe that he wasn't there. But they said no, he left last year."

I could think of nothing to say but the obvious. "Where is he, I wonder?"

"They wouldn't tell me."

He removed his rimless glasses, took a tissue from the box on my table, and wiped them; then he put them back on, as if some greater clarity might come.

"I just can't believe it," he said. "It doesn't make sense. I just can't believe it."

He was like a man returning to the little town where he'd
grown up, tremulously, expecting to see the same people, the
postmaster, the schoolteacher, looking just as they had, remembering him; he had anticipated the same elms, the same
frogs that he had caught and released in the pond as a child.
He had thought to see all that, but through the eyes of understanding. He had returned full of gratitude, ready to pay the
appreciation he had withheld earlier. But the town was *gone*—
not altered, that he might have accepted—but gone without a
trace, as if it had never existed. It had vanished before he
could beg its forgiveness or reimburse it with his wisdom.

Never had he and I sat so long in silence and been so close
in our perceptions and feelings.

"Well," I said at last, "he's got to be somewhere."

"I guess," he assented.

"He's not dead, I'm sure."

"Why are you so sure?" he asked me. Now his eyes burned
behind his rimless glasses. He looked as neat and precise as a
schoolteacher who had caught me out in something.

But no, I wasn't going to reassure him this time. Suppose I
was wrong.

Instead I waited.

"I sure would like to know," he said.

"So would I."

Then, with sudden resolve, he announced, "I'm going to
find out. I'll track this fucking guy down if he's in fuckin' hell.
I'm going to find him and thank him. You know, we've got
experts for that. A man, some Turkish guy, owed us twelve
thousand dollars for two years. He disappeared. We use a
'skip tracer,' you know what that is?"

"No, what is it?"

"Somebody who tracks people who skip. We don't like people to disappear, we use the best. We got a gay woman, runs
her own agency in New Jersey, Miss Leigh, goes after hus-
bands mostly. She doesn't miss. She got that Turkish guy, I
forget his name. She caught him two years later in L.A. He
was about to sell a house, and boom! 'Twelve thousand dollars
plus, if you please.' He had to pay her fee too. She doesn't

miss. I'll give her ten thousand dollars to start. I'll give her a *hundred thousand* if she wants, so long as she finds him."

I'd never seen him like this. The words seemed to come faster and faster, as if a machine gun spluttered them out. His face moved quickly and nervously.

Even as I listened, he was repeating, "I'll find him. I'll find him. She'll find him." His whole body seemed to glow as if it were radioactive, and the film over his eyes became a trail of tears of rage.

"I'll find him. I'll find him," he repeated. "Thank you, George, you've been very helpful. I don't want to take your time. I'm going to call the office now and get the number. Thank you. I don't want to take any more of your time."

He left hurriedly.

It surprised me as much as him that it turned out to be so easy.

The next time I saw him he exclaimed, "Mary Leigh found him! I've got his phone number."

"No kidding!"

He shook his head disbelievingly. "He was in the Brooklyn phone book."

He'd called her with the information he had, extending his offers of gigantic sums of money, if only she could succeed. Like a real pro, she'd promised to try, at least to ascertain how hard it would be, before asking for any payment. Her staff had checked off everyone with the name within driving radius of the hospital, and they'd found him in an hour. Because Larry's company was a frequent customer, she hadn't charged him at all.

"It's him," he said excitedly. "He worked at Creedmoor. I think they pretended to be from the hospital and needed some information for his pension."

But he was frightened of calling. "I just know something's wrong. I just know it—he never would have quit, he was a young man. Maybe less than fifty. Why is he home?"

I asked him, "How can you possibly guess about a thing like that—"

"Guess, Doctor? I'm not guessing. I *know* he's in trouble. Can I tell you something?"

"Sure!"

To my consternation, he shut his eyes and began to speak with them closed, almost in a whisper. "When I was in Creedmoor—it was Monday—I was at the window. It had stopped snowing but the monks were singing—"

"Open your eyes, Larry, and talk louder while you tell me the rest."

He did. "No, I'm just remembering. It was about five in the afternoon. It was dark out already. The place was grim, forever, the way it is in the winter, especially on Monday. I had the feeling a lot of people were just sitting by themselves. Warren had said good-bye. I could see him talking to some big fat guy who came on duty at four. Warren would talk about us—the medicines, what we were like that day, I mean, if anyone was acting up. I forget the guy's name—a fat guy, he never talked to me, he used to stay in his little room listening to music on his little radio.

"Anyhow, it was dark, I was listening to the monks, I somehow thought it was their kind of weather. And this new guy, he took off those soggy boots, and he threw them halfway across the room against the wall. Shepherd, that's his name! What did I say it was? I remember he used to throw his boots against the wall. And that night, he threw a boot and I heard it thump and it landed near me. I didn't look but I heard, it was right under me, like a fish. And the monks stopped! And I knew it was over. I *knew* she was dead.

"Doctor, I knew. And that week, some time, the accountant, Arthur, we don't talk anymore, he came in, and he looked so sad. He asked me to sign some papers, but I didn't move. I knew she had died, and I had missed it.

"And I know Warren now, Warren White—something is *bad*, man, something is terrible, something is *terrible*."

He rocked back and forth in his chair, and with great spas-

modic motions cried uncontrollably. Larry was a little child
again, an infant in the shape of a middle-aged man, less concerned about what he looked or sounded like than a child
might be.

At length, when he swallowed hard, and I surmised that he
was fighting to recover his composure, I asked him, "Are you
crying for Ilsa or Warren?"

"For both." It seemed the perfect answer.

Then, to my surprise, he looked straight into my eyes hope-
fully and asked, "Can I call him from here?"

At first I didn't answer. His making a call in my presence
would mean that I was participating in his outside life. He was
asking me to commit a major break in therapeutic procedure.

He started to withdraw the request. "I know it's silly. But it
was just an idea. I'm a little scared."

"Sure you can," I said. "Do you have his number?"

He reached inside his jacket and produced a wisp of paper.

His next two words were a crowning achievement for one
who had lived so alone, for so long.

"Help me."

"In what way?" I asked.

"Dial the number, please."

Of course, it wasn't simply that he needed the mechanical
help. He was asking me the way one asks an only friend to go
with him to a doctor's office to hear a biopsy report that might
mean his death. How could I refuse him and ever again tell
him that people were more decent than he thought?

I dialed it and handed him the receiver.

I heard him say, "Hello . . . Mr. White? . . . Oh, is this
Warren White? . . . This is a good friend of yours. We were
together for a few years, at Creedmoor. . . . My name is Lawrence Fellows, I'm not sure you remember me, or maybe you
do, but in a different—You do?"

He was elated.

"'What's happening?' Well, a lot's happened to me. I'm
married, you know, my business is doing well, very well, all
thanks to you, no one else but you. I owe you more gratitude

than everyone in my whole life together, Warren. You gave me
life. You were the greatest single person of all time.

"Just tell me a few words, what's happening to you? . . .
What do you mean 'hanging out.' You're okay?"

Then a cloud came over Larry's face like the shadow of forty
dive bombers. He stood up, holding the phone, and took a
step, as far as the cord would let him.

"Is there anything I can do?" he asked.

"What do you mean, 'Not really'? I've got money. I make a
lot. I'll send ten thousand dollars over there in five minutes,
and you don't have to pay it back, ever.

"Wait a minute, Warren. Wait a minute, Warren, wait a
minute. Give me your address. I've got it anyway. Will you be
there tonight? Give me a chance! Warren, please give *me* a
chance. Talk to me, please. Just *talk* to me. Don't just be
quiet, I can't take . . . Okay. Good-bye. I'll see you at five."

As soon as he'd hung up, he said to me mournfully, "It's not
good." Then, with resolve, "I hope I can fix it. Oh God, I hope
I can fix it."

I just nodded.

He pleaded, "Did I sound sympathetic? I mean, how did I
sound? Did I let him know I want to do what I can, to do
everything in my power? He's all I've got." Then he added
politely, "Him and Mary and you."

After that, he seemed flustered. Often he looked over at the
clock as if hoping the minute hand would advance, so he could
leave.

For decades, at every crucial juncture, time had been his
nemesis. He had done everything he could to halt it. Now he
wanted time to hurry. He was in the kind of state whose only
solace was the passage of time itself. Finally, he was betting
on a winner. Time was a sure thing, though a close second
would be his presence at the door of that apartment in
Brooklyn at five.

He was my last patient of the day. At the end of the hour I
had an impulse to tell him to call me if he wanted to, but I
resisted it.

*   *   *

At ten-thirty or so that evening, my curiosity lured me away from the group of us who went for drinks during intermission at the Schubert Theater. I plunked my quarter in the pay phone and called my answering service. There was a message from Lawrence Fellows, with his number.

"It's not good," he told me. "I saw him. Can I see you tomorrow? We've got to help him."

It was during the week between Christmas and New Year's, a time of elation and suffering, as people counted their blessings or their misfortunes. Larry had come through the early-morning chill in a camel's hair coat with the collar up.

His tone was more purposeful than tragic as he reported, "Someone very close to him died, just like me."

"Oh, I'm sorry to hear that."

"He's in a slump. He just stays in that little apartment of his. It's dark all the time. I know my business is bad, but I have money saved away. I have a pension fund, I have personal credit. And I've got a three-city delivery deal for two years with an option that I think I'm going to close. Mary wants to go to Europe—and, God knows, she deserves it—and Warren White is all alone in that little place. You never saw anything like it. He could use a good lamp or two. He just sits there, in that kitchen with the linoleum half off the floor. He deserves a palace, he deserves to be happy, and look!"

"How long has he been like this?"

"He hardly even goes out, maybe just to buy food. And I don't think anybody goes there. People don't even know he's alive. How long? Ever since his friend died—Robert. Maybe six months. He quit the job when Robert got sick."

There was a pause, and I could see from Larry's pursed lips and sightless eyes that he was back there, contemplating Warren White in that dingy, dark apartment. I waited.

Then Larry said, "You think maybe he's homosexual? I

mean, maybe they were sweethearts. He said Robert was all he had. Is that possibly what he meant?"

"It's very possible."

"It's a tragedy, a horrible tragedy, even for those people. I think they were together a long time."

"It sure is a tragedy," I said.

"I tried to help him. I offered him money. At least to fix up the apartment. He didn't want it. He admitted his money is running out. He has some kind of small pension from the hospital, but not much. Can you imagine? I'm so much better off than he is. I've got to help him."

"He didn't take your money, huh?"

He shook his head decisively, as if to imply that the possibility of getting Warren to take money was too remote to warrant another spoken word.

By evening, after a gray and blusterous day, the wind stopped and the sky was speckled with stars. I was visiting a friend in Nyack and went out walking alone after dinner, aware of a sadness that can seem particularly overwhelming at the end of the year. It was as if I were on one of those stars, seeing this planet through a telescope, bemoaning the obvious fact that virtue is often treated so brutally.

I realized that I wanted Larry to help this man. But I also realized that my concern for Warren White should play no part in my treatment of Larry. One can't employ a patient to do one's bidding, whether it is to settle one's own grievances, mete out justice, or right the world's woes. My job was to study Larry, to understand him, to help him understand himself, to free him to succeed in whatever direction he chose.

Even so, I was proud of Larry. He had already come far. He was utterly involved with his rescue operation, enjoying the tautness that his new mission had given to his life. If he succeeded—indeed, even by trying—he was forging a connection not just to Warren but to all humankind, a bond that the past had utterly denied to him. Such a bond each individual must create for himself. It seemed inconceivable that with Warren in such sore need Larry would allow himself a trance, and that in itself was big progress.

I was pompously congratulating myself for having been the model for this progress of Larry. There had been no parent, no exemplar of the value of effort or loyalty. Then I realized that though I had played a role, I had not been Larry's model at all. The paradoxical thought came to me that Warren White in his prime would have rescued Warren White from the abyss. Warren had been the exemplar, and in this sense the creator of the one person prepared to dive through fire to rescue him. Viewed this way, there was a curious justice. It was as if Warren were saving himself.

Over the following weeks, Larry reported, he went over there regularly in one of his trucks, and visited Warren White while the driver waited downstairs. He would leave food in the refrigerator.

Several times he complained about the ineptitude of his staff. Once in particular, while he was away, his dispatcher had failed to get back to an important account.

He was furious. "I'm gone from the place two hours, and they do something stupid."

I asked him if the mistake had been costly.

"Not this time, but it's coming. You never know. But I can see it coming."

"You just don't have solid, dependable people working for you," I said.

"I can't find them."

"You know there's more to it than that."

We'd gone over his childhood history innumerable times, his fear of trusting anybody, his ingrained expectation that anyone with power over his life, over his emotions, would disappoint him. I had been struggling against his tendency to hide by ascribing the problem to some decline in national or local morality. By highlighting Larry's own, purely personal inability to trust anyone, I had sought for months to start him toward a new view of the world. Though, admittedly, there were plenty of malevolent people, the earth was not uniformly bleak but dappled with kindness. Larry's job was to discern that goodness, to surround himself with the right people, and to learn how to trust them.

That afternoon I was delighted when, after a pause, he said, "I know. The problem at work is a lot me. I can do better."

"You certainly can. There's no reason to live as if you're in quicksand."

"Hey, that's some picture! You're right."

The following week, he reported, "I offered Warren White a job."

"What do you mean?"

"I told him he can come in for six months, as often as he wants. Ride the trucks, learn the business. When he's ready, he's going to be my next dispatcher."

I was taken by surprise. "He agreed?"

"He didn't say anything. But the job's there. And, you know, it's a funny thing. I'm not doing him any favor. I can use him. He could run that place easy. He said I could talk about it some more. Do you realize what a break it would be for me if he came to work with us, if he was there every day?"

He paused to think over his strategy.

"I go there tomorrow night again. Maybe I should bring Morgan, he gets in by eleven. He's paid for the day anyhow. He'll go over there with me and we can talk—"

I told him, "Maybe you're hitting Warren White with too much, too soon."

"I know, but Red is disgusted with both of my checkers right now. He's been telling me to get somebody—"

I put up both hands, like a third base coach signaling a base runner to stop.

"Hey, Larry, I'm trying to say something. I'm not asking you to agree with me, just consider what I'm saying."

"You mean Warren won't like it if we push him?"

"I mean, if you want to help him, you can't just act like one of your trucks. You can't just roll over him."

"I see what you're saying."

"And who was that you mentioned that you were going to bring?"

"Red. Red Morgan, my best driver."

"In addition to everything else, maybe Red Morgan won't be impressed if he sees a man sitting in the corner of a little apartment, in the dark. You know who Warren really is, but he doesn't know."

"Well, fuck Red Morgan then. I know Warren could do it. . . . Anyhow, Red would love him. . . . But I see what you're saying."

"It's a hell of an idea, Larry. It's beautiful. Maybe it would work. I'm not saying it can't. But people don't change that easily."

I could see from his sad expression that this time he heard me. He said wistfully, "You're right. People don't change that easily."

What I next said was not merely to reassure him. I believed it. "Maybe you can do it. Maybe you can lift Warren out of the ditch, but you've got to go slowly."

"I know," he said. "I know you're right."

"How does he feel about your going over there, just yourself?" I asked.

"It's okay. He likes it."

"So maybe, just keep going. You don't have to shove offers at him. Just be with him."

"Okay," he said resolutely. "That's what I'll do."

And for two months that was what Larry did, though he mentioned the job on occasion. "I figured I'd just remind him of it, keep it in front of him, if you know what I mean."

Perhaps on that score he was right, but he was always a step ahead.

One day he reported, "He's watching a little TV. I'm bringing a video recorder over there next time."

And a few weeks later: "He didn't set up the video recorder. It's still in the box. I'm going to set it up tonight. But he's going out for walks. The weather is better, and he's going out for walks. That's good. Very good."

He wasn't a natural therapist, that was for sure. Finally he told me that he'd had an argument with Warren. He'd shouted at him to take the job—"It would be so good for you, you'd be back in the world, you'd make good money. You'd talk to people."

"Why don't you punch him in the mouth?" I asked angrily.

"All he'd have to do at the start is pick up calls and keep track of where the drivers are and where they're going. The guy we got now could write the shipping orders, that's about all he can do. He could learn the equipment. He could learn how to check the highways and read the traffic reports, there's nothing to that. I could teach him. Red could teach him when he's here. We're not asking for miracles."

"I know, but it might sound that way to him."

Then, abashed at my own loss of composure, I told Larry, "Look, you're doing everything you possibly can for him right now. You're saving his life. You have to be patient. You've got to settle for that."

He promised that he would.

For a time after that he seemed more content with just going over to see Warren, once during the week and once on a weekend. He always brought something.

One Saturday Larry had called him before going there and said, "Put your pants on. I'm bringing my wife over. She's desperate to meet you."

He and Mary had brought flowers. But downstairs it had crossed his mind that a bouquet might make Warren think of death, and on the street corner he'd thrown them into a garbage can, to Mary's amazement and chagrin.

Mary had shaken Warren's hand, and told him how much he meant to Larry. "And you mean a lot to me, too. You saved his life. You've saved mine. You're part of our family."

"Warren didn't say anything, but I know it made him feel good. I know it made a difference."

I thought to myself, Larry would know. He was the world's greatest expert at not letting on that he was feeling or experiencing anything. It was an art that he was fast divesting himself of, but he could still perceive it in others.

But Warren's apartment was growing even more sparse, except for the things that Larry brought—a radio, a lamp, some towels. He placed them there unobtrusively, and Warren didn't acknowledge them.

Finally, Larry argued with him again. "Look, if things don't get better, they get worse. You've got to get out of the house. Do something. Come with me. Talk to some people. Start doing some work. It saved me. You won't be sorry."

Larry had even offered to put him on salary at once, he could report when he was ready, but Warren refused. "It just wouldn't do. It just wouldn't do."

"You're right and you're wrong," I told Larry.

"How am I wrong?" he asked ironically.

"You don't persuade people your way," I told him. "Instead of arguing, let *him* tell *you* why he won't start working at your place. Keep questioning him. Let him examine his own reasons, as he gives them to you."

For the first time in our relationship we were on the case together—not as cotherapists, that notion of us would be too small for what Larry was doing.

Under my tutelage, each time he went over there, he would talk generally—about politics, about sports, about the blistering summer heat. "Do you think it's what they say, that it's getting hotter all the time?"

"Maybe."

He offered to have an air conditioner delivered and installed. "My company ships about six hundred of them a week. I get them for next to nothing."

But Warren recoiled as if he'd seen a rattlesnake. "No, I don't want one. Don't do that."

Only at the end of his visit would he mention the job that was waiting, but now, instead of propounding its virtues, he would get Warren to talk about why he didn't want it.

In the beginning, Warren's answers were terse. "I don't know. It isn't for me."

Larry had debated a little. "Well, you tell me what *is* for you then."

But I instructed him to keep questioning, never to rebut what Warren gave him. "Just ask him *why* it isn't for him."

The next time Larry reported, "He says he wouldn't do it, it's too complicated. He's not trained. He never drove a truck. But I didn't tell him that it doesn't matter. I just let him talk, like you said."

"Good work." I told him how to further elicit Warren's unexpressed misgivings. "Hear him out. Don't interrupt, and whatever he says, keep asking him to give you his reasons. Make sure he explains them, over and over."

He did, to the best of his ability.

The next time I saw him I asked him, "Well, what did he say?"

"He said he'd look stupid, he'd waste everybody's time, he'd be stealing money."

That August, I was away and didn't see Larry. But he stayed in New York and didn't miss a visit. He reported that his own business was doing somewhat better, and that he and Mary were making friends, real ones, for the first time.

"There are a lot of real people out there. You're allowing yourself to see a few of them," I said, perhaps a bit pompously.

He didn't respond.

"And Warren?" I asked.

"He's still in that joint, but not quite as down. He did have his brother come over the other day. That's the first person I know of who was there, besides me."

"That's great."

"I know. But he keeps calling himself incompetent every time I bring up the job. Do you know he was in Vietnam, in the army? They give him some money every month too. He's totally against therapy, though."

"Well, he's getting it," I said dryly.

Larry smiled. Without training or a real sense of how our method could work, he had virtually no ability to improvise but was doing well.

His next act was to mention the job lightly, then when Warren refused it and called himself incompetent, to ask, "So what's the worst thing that could happen if you fuck it up?"

"I'm a fraud," was his answer.

Larry had responded, "How could you be! I owe you everything. You can't do me any harm. It's my company. Even if you fuck it up and we have three trucks that get lost for a day, don't you think I'm a lot better off than in the hospital?"

Warren had answered, "Maybe."

"Well, think about it. Just think about it."

"Okay."

In our next session, a half smile broke the usually dour lines of his countenance as he told me, "He said he's thinking about it!"

And in the session after that, he announced. "Warren said he's going to come in. He said, what can he lose. Red Morgan's going to pick him up the first day. Red and I will show him around."

We were inexpressibly happy. We threw our arms around one another, more than proud of the work we had done, proud that life had given us the chance to do it. He had come full circle. This was the completion he had needed, the part of him that no therapist could furnish. He had been the parent he never had.

He stepped back and pointed a finger at me archly.

"Hey, you better look out, Doc. I'm liable to steal all your patients from you."

"That's what I was thinking," I told him. "And I don't like it, Larry. That wasn't the deal."

Of course, there was work to be done, but that was more a benefit than a drawback. Our team would have more opportunity to work together, to express ourselves.

Larry knew without my telling him to give Warren plenty of leeway. Even his offer of a starting salary was limited by the concern not to pressure Warren by expecting too much of him.

The dozen or so inside employees liked the shy, slender, handsome fellow, who knew nothing about the business but never intruded. In spite of Larry's efforts not to favor him conspicuously, the others soon became aware of Larry's eternal patience with him. They saw the softness in Larry's face when Warren came in with a question.

"Let's see that invoice, Warren. You're doing great, but we like the total over here—not at the bottom. Our accountant picks up mistakes better if it's at the top of the page."

They'd never seen their boss ask anyone how the day went, and must have marveled at his "maternal" side. Warren was always there early, as he always had been at the hospital. Without being told to, the others answered the phone, even when he was nearer to it, as if sensing his fearful reluctance to go public. For months he ate lunch alone and remained an isolate, asking questions only when necessary.

Then, possibly because Red Morgan always asked to speak to him at the ends of his phone calls from cities across the country, some employees imagined that he was a family member of Red. One man, a clerk, cutthroat by nature, insensitive and too ambitious, had planted the idea. Unable to conceive of human ties other than mercenary ones, he had concluded that no one could be supportive without a profit motive unless it was to a relative. However, no one dared ask Larry about his relationship to this fledgling stranger, and whatever comments there were stayed in the realm of the covert.

Gradually, Larry began talking less about Warren. Though Warren kept working there, it became obvious to Larry that he couldn't force a more personal relationship, after several invitations from him and Mary were turned down. His seeing Warren five days a week would have to suffice.

The whole adventure brought Larry and me closer than we had been. I often thought of St.-Exupéry's definition of love as "Not two people looking into each other's eyes, but two people looking ahead in the same direction."

Then, on a day reminiscent of that gray, snowy afternoon when the monks had stopped singing abruptly, the day Ilsa had died, Larry came bursting in, elated.

"Warren's really getting it. He got on the phone today and saved an account. Could you believe a driver went into a ditch right outside Fort Worth and didn't call for six hours? We had an empty vehicle in Dallas that could have gotten there, and he waited till they all went home. They didn't want the order. Warren got on the phone with the customer. I don't know what the hell he said, but he saved it. This is the guy I need. Do you realize that this is the guy I need?"

"No. It never crossed my mind."

A year later, Warren White became Larry's dispatcher and still is at the time of this writing. He and Larry are still not major social friends, but they did break the final barrier: Larry yells at him, "You fucking moron, how could you let two trucks do the work of one?"

And when he feels badly afterward and apologizes, Warren is quick to forgive him.

Larry still comes in to see me once a month. He still sometimes goes off the deep end with anger. And he still has considerable learning to do about stepping back and letting things run without him. But that problem is only the vestige of a mistrust that, we both know, nearly buried him alive.

I sometimes muse that if Warren White had been gifted with the creativity of a great artist—the kindness, the love, the prescience—he could hardly have created a better finale. And then I correct myself and realize that he was, indeed, a "mute, inglorious Milton" who possessed all those gifts and put them to their ultimate use.

THE TABOO SCARF

Owing to an egg's shape, a beast banging on it from the outside will have great trouble breaking it open. But the slightest tap from inside the shell can shatter it; when the chick is ready it can pop out and get started. Nature in its selective wisdom thus favors the new generation—for instance, the unborn ostrich over a pride of lions, who can slam an egg halfway across the Serengeti without being able to open it. Nearly all the leverage is from within.

By the same token, a patient, *any* patient, tapping even lightly, can accomplish more personality change than even the best therapist working alone from the outside.

The appreciation of this is ushering in the next century of psychotherapy. The therapist is no mere surgeon, providing relief or cure to the patient lying on the couch. That picture has already given way to a new one of the patient as blocked but striving, as potentially able to identify his own feelings and to act in new ways, and ultimately as the one who must crack the shell of his own problem.

Beyond our offering warmth and insights, we must find

places where each patient can tap, even gently, against the
surface of his container. We encourage effort. But only by the
patient's own exertions of will, by his or her acts, can real
change be produced.

I saw an unforgettable example of this some years ago. Had
the patient not tried something whose importance we both un-
derestimated, she might never have made the discovery that
changed her life. Beyond that, Maggie's case illustrates that as
we go forward, we also go back. To hide from the future is to
hide from the past—to venture ahead is to delve into both. In
this sense, we either live many periods of our lives simultaneously, or we don't live any at all.

Maggie was twenty-seven, tall, attractive in an angular way,
with dark, intelligent eyes. She was a graduate student in
paleontology, and she loved her subject so much that I think
she would have talked about it the whole hour unless I'd broken in.

She had already gone looking for fossils in the United States
and was eager to travel to Africa, where, she told me, all human life began. "Though right now what I'm doing is mostly
cataloging." She smiled engagingly.

Her problem was unusual.

"Doctor, I've been going with a boy for three years. I love
him, but I'm terrified of marrying him. I just can't." She
paused, as if gathering the courage to continue. "And something else. I know how silly this sounds. But I'm afraid to kiss
him on the lips."

She looked into my eyes for anything possibly condemning but found nothing, and went on. "Some people can't
have orgasms. I do, most of the time. I enjoy sexual inter-
course with David—at least, I would a lot more if it wasn't
for this."

She reiterated that she loved David. "But this is just impossible!"

She was becoming agitated. "He wants to marry me, but I

don't see how I can. The way things are, I don't see how I can."

"He's upset too?" I asked.

"Of course he is. He was married once—for two years. He loves me. He wants to marry me, or at least he did. But I keep putting it off. I mean I said, 'Wait until September,' and that was last year. Then July. Now it's October. I'm just very afraid that if I marry him—" She stopped.

"Afraid of what?"

"I don't know. We had a terrific fight last summer. He left me in the car and took the train home alone, from Massachusetts. I really thought it was over. We didn't talk for a long time, two weeks. Then I broke down and called him. He was glad. I love David, that's what's so crazy about this, so wrong!"

"When you picture yourself married to him, what comes to mind?"

"I don't know. I've done that. I don't know. Death, maybe. I can understand why he's so upset. He's thirty-seven. He really wants to have a family, and he's a wonderful person."

She sighed deeply.

"You've had this problem before?" I asked her.

"From the time we started. He tried to kiss me goodnight, the first night. I couldn't. And even after that, I just couldn't."

"I mean with other men."

"Well, I've always had the problem—I guess you'd call it a phobia. But I never realized how severe it was."

In the past she'd imagined that she just wasn't fond enough of the man. "But I love David."

Near the end of the session, she asked me, "What do you think my chances are?"

"I don't know for sure," I told her. "Probably good. But we're going to have to dig."

Only after she was gone did I realize that I'd drawn that metaphor from her own calling, though in sessions to come I sometimes did this deliberately, to summon her exuberance.

But digging wouldn't be so easy, as I learned the next time. There was something else unusual here. Maggie could remember virtually nothing about her life before she was ten.

When, at a recent birthday party for her mother, an aunt showed her photos of the frame house the family had lived in, it was barely familiar. She had only an indistinct memory of trees peering into her bedroom window and of her father being downstairs. She was told that she would run over to him when he got home at night, that she would take his jacket and bring him a shot of bourbon, and that he loved her. But even this was hearsay.

In his photos he was handsome. She knew that he was a powerful union leader, and that he had provided well for the family. They'd lived in Weston, Connecticut, quiet, friendly, more rural than neighboring Westport. According to her mother, they would all go to Westport for Sunday brunch—she and her parents, and her mother's parents, who lived in Fairfield, a half hour away.

It had been a paradise, but then her father left, suddenly and forever.

Maggie and her mother had quickly relocated to a dingy downtown sector of Fairfield, not far from her grandparents, and they strove hard. She recalled her mother sitting her down in the new, smaller kitchen. Her mother had said, "It's up to us now. We have each other and that's more than enough. We'll do fine."

And in a sense they did. Her mother took a job as a saleswoman, and from then on it was urban life. Maggie saw more of her grandparents than of her mother, who was off working much of the time and came home exhausted. But she knew that her mother was toiling for her welfare, and she felt taken care of.

Remarkably, her amnesia covered the first period of her

life, in Weston, and seemed nonexistent after that. That it conformed so precisely with that phase, touching nothing else, argued strongly that it was psychogenic. It could hardly be that all her powers of observation and retention had suddenly developed on the day they moved to Fairfield, and yet her memory of the new apartment, of the friends she made, of begging permission to stay overnight with one, of the local school was excellent—she was, if anything, more detailed and precise in her retention of these experiences than most adults are.

She could vividly recall her grandfather's taking her to New York City on a few occasions. Once they went to a ball game that he wanted to see, and she fell asleep. But another time he took her to the Museum of Natural History, and the sight of the dinosaurs on the first floor was something she never forgot. "He saw how fascinated I was and bought me a big, colored picture book on the subject."

Especially graphic to Maggie was a cartoon in *The New Yorker* that appeared when she was eleven. Two scientists had pieced together the foot, up to the knee, of some gigantic prehistoric creature. One of them, looking at the random array of bones remaining on the floor, was saying to the other, "Well, I'm willing to say the hell with it if you are."

Maggie told me that she'd found this cartoon a riot and had kept the page. She smiled when telling me the caption, and I could not help wondering if it expressed a part of her own thinking, an impulse not to reconstruct, that might dovetail with her not remembering.

Later, when I mentioned to a colleague that Maggie's amnesia "fit her first decade like a glove," my mind free-associated to so-called "glove anesthesia," in which the person experiences numbness and sometimes total paralysis of the hand up to the wrist with no other symptom. True neurological damage would never impair only the hand and nothing else; it would follow certain pathways called "dermatones," and thus involve not only the hand but the arm. For this reason, we can always diagnose glove anesthesia as psychosomatic. Numbness of the whole hand—and only the hand—attests to the use of will.

Similarly, the fact that one period of Maggie's life was utterly blanketed by "forgetfulness," while the rest was wholly available to her, was altogether too neat to allow any explanation other than a psychogenic one. The evidence seemed strong that Maggie could not remember because she unconsciously chose not to.

Because her amnesia "gloved" the era of her father's presence in her life, I especially wondered about him. Any information about how Maggie had perceived him or felt about him when he was around promised to be valuable. Indeed, even random facts about him were welcome at this stage—whatever we learned might be suggestive since up to now we'd had virtually nothing to go on.

My best information, it seemed, would have to come from another source. I would have to study how Maggie behaved with me. Though she could remember nothing about her father, she had spent hundreds of formative hours with him. She had developed through him some sense-of-herself-in-his-presence, that is, a sense-of-herself-in-a-man's-presence, and that had led her to some theory about what men are like and about how she should behave around them.

Almost surely, she would reveal those early-formed beliefs in her dealings with me. There would be some commonality between her reaction to that primary man in her life and her reaction to me. Perhaps I could uncover at least something of her picture of her father from the way she perceived me—and acted with me.

Studying the so-called transference to learn about a patient's father or mother is a common technique relying on this transfer of reaction. If we are distrusted, we may suspect that the patient distrusted a parent. The patient who constantly repeats himself to us possibly had a parent who didn't listen. The patient who always anticipates harsh judgments from us may have gotten them from one or both parents. Reasoning backward, we can often infer what a patient thought of a parent from how the patient perceives us and treats us.

Usually, of course, the therapist has the patient's memories to compare with his own experience of the patient. In this case, however, having only Maggie's treatment of me to start with, I would have to reason entirely backward, trying to ascertain from it how she might have perceived her father. I would have no corroboration for this backward inference— at least not for a while. So far, the transference was all I had.

At first I imagined that I was seeing nothing in the way she dealt with me. Maggie's mode of treating me could be best described as polite and factual. She always arrived on the dot and was never curt with me. She never joked. She asked me for nothing, except at times for my opinion as to whether she could be cured. She simply came, and talked, and left. Only slowly did I realize that what I had initially taken as non-response toward me on Maggie's part was a very real response—namely one of extreme caution.

It might follow that she had treated her father with the same deference and conformity, that she had kept him at the same respectful distance, that she had admired him but never kidded with him or taken any kind of liberty. If so, and if this early acquired formality of hers had been adopted as a defense against closeness, why had she adopted it? What had she been afraid of? Was she guarding against a love for her father that felt illicit, or against encouraging his love? I wondered if anything had taken place between them that had motivated this guardedness.

Any such inferences of mine, had, of course, to remain only a hypothesis. Her diplomacy with me might have a simpler, more recent explanation. I had seen many graduate students like Maggie become overly deferential in dealing with their professors, who make the ultimate decision about whether they get their degree. Perhaps Maggie's diplomacy with me was merely an extension of a daily style that she'd adopted at Columbia's department of paleontology.

I decided that, though she didn't remember her early life, I would at least get her to tell me everything she'd been told

about it by other family members. Over the next few weeks I
asked her a great number of questions.

Maggie told me that she had no idea why her father left.
Only one thing was certain—that he hadn't wanted to go and
that it had been completely her mother's choice. After leaving,
he'd tried desperately to come back, but her mother had remained adamant.

Maggie told me, "My grandfather said that in the beginning, my father used to call every day and beg her to let him
return. Sometimes twice a day. But she wouldn't even talk to
him."

"Really!"

"Yes. Even after he left Connecticut to live in Chicago, he
used to tell my grandfather he'd come back in a minute to see
me if she would let him. Even if my mother wouldn't talk to
him, he'd come back to see me."

"I wonder why she was so strong on the subject."

"She even gave up his financial support, because then he
would have had the legal right to see me."

"Why did she throw him out?"

"I don't know."

"You must have thought about it. What speculations did you
make? What crossed your mind?"

"My mother's sometimes very strange. All at once she just
couldn't stand him. That's what my grandfather said. She just
wanted no part of him, and he left. He left like a man."

She said this glibly, almost proudly, as if she'd been over it
often, as if she were reciting a foregone conclusion. But I
could tell that a lot of emotion was still bound up in her simple
narrative, that perhaps Maggie suspected more than she
wished to disclose. Maybe he'd been caught with another
woman, but I had no evidence, and I surely didn't want to
venture such a guess.

During the next few weeks, she went on to portray her
mother as close-lipped, honest, and given to a life of stoic
resignation. If the woman, now in her sixties, enjoyed anything, she certainly didn't let Maggie know. She had only a few

friends—women—including a cousin whom she went on vacations with. Maggie felt sure that there had never been another man in her mother's life; she hadn't even dated anyone.

As a girl, Maggie would sometimes ask her mother if she was ever going to remarry. Her mother would snap, "I don't have time to waste on another man. And besides, I've never met a man good enough for my daughter."

"I used to be glad," Maggie told me. "Now I worry about her being alone in old age. But she's not an easy woman."

That seemed like an understatement.

"And even if she had wanted to marry again," Maggie explained, "because she's a devout Catholic, I don't think she could have without a lot of hullabaloo."

"And you never heard from your father again," I said, partly by way of summary.

"Never. My mother wouldn't let him contact me."

She said this so emotionally that I brought the subject up again the next week, in case there was more to it.

"He tried to come back?"

This time she didn't respond, which I took to mean that the answer was, decisively, no.

The next two months yielded little. Her early life seemed like a lost city that, if we could even glimpse it, could tell us an enormous amount about her contemporary life—in particular, about her symptoms.

I decided to change my approach. Instead of continuing to inquire about her past, I began looking into her *attitude* toward the "forgetfulness" itself.

"Does it trouble you that you can't remember those early days in Weston?"

"I guess it does."

Her words said yes, but she sounded almost blithe about having lost touch with those first ten years. Such indifference, if I read Maggie correctly, provided virtually clinching evidence that she really didn't want to remember that early period—that she was forgetting it by a strong act of will.

The more I discussed it with her, the surer I became that I

was seeing what the nineteenth-century psychiatrist, Pierre Janet, termed *"la belle indifference."* Janet was the first to identify such indifference as a telltale sign that the person is producing his seeming incapacity by an act of will. The sufferer is getting something he secretly wants out of the disability, be it paralysis or numbness, for instance—or here, in Maggie's case, memory failure.

I had worked with Maggie for three months and now was certain that, in her "loss" of the past, she was unconsciously achieving a desired effect. And by that time I also felt almost certain that her amnesia had to be related to the inhibitions— against kissing and marriage—that had driven her to seek my help. Maggie's was one of those rare and classic cases in which "lifting the veil of amnesia" would, indeed, prove crucial and perhaps tantamount to her resolving her symptoms.

Even after those three months, I had no idea what she thought of me personally or how she felt about me—whether she considered me warm or cold, competent or a disappointment; she showed no curiosity about me. Indeed, there seemed nothing particular about her response to me. I got the feeling that if I told her that she would be seeing a replacement henceforth, someone with my credentials whom I had completely briefed, she would not have batted an eyelash. She treated me with the impersonality of a doorman or clerk, except that my status was professional, which she constantly reminded me of by calling me "Doctor" without using my name.

Beyond my frustration about not knowing her past, I could sense myself becoming demoralized at being so completely discounted as a person. Here, too, it was as if her unconscious knew all the lines of communication with the past, and she had severed this one systematically. Had she permitted me a relationship with the usual understandings, annoyances, and fondness if not love, such exchanges might have taught me about her and evoked memories of other involvements, including her earliest one with her father. But so far, that too was missing. I decided to ask her outright how she felt about me.

"I think you're very good. You're experienced. Very professional."

She couldn't have given less if she'd refused to answer the question.

"No, I mean what feelings have you had about me? I mean, are there times when you get angry with me? When you're sorry you're here, or when you're glad?"

"No. I don't think about that part."

It was almost as if she didn't know what I was saying, though, of course, she did.

However, she had strong reactions to her professors. One woman, a geologist who had recommended her for the dig she went on in Arizona, she described as a wonderful, warm person. And she said about the man who sponsored her thesis, which she was just starting, that "he has a great sense of humor and is a lot of fun."

She liked David's parents, but not his brother Robert, who, she said, "thinks he's great and he isn't. He just isn't. I can't stand to be around him."

"What is there about him?"

"He just got married. His wife Sonya follows him around like a trained dog. That's what he wants, apparently. She was pregnant. He had to marry her. Their little girl is about a year. I pity her."

"How does Robert treat you?"

"He's always trying to kiss me goodnight. I think that's half the reason Robert and Sonya call us, so we'll go over there, and he'll come over and he can trap me at the door and kiss me. It's a battle at this point. I keep away. Who wants him slobbering all over me!"

"David knows how you feel?"

"Yes. I tell David everything. He protects me. He'd better. Last Saturday night Robert said I looked sexy. He said, 'I love all those low-cut tops you wear. It's great that you wear those prim, little white blouses and then keep half the buttons open.' What's great about it?"

"Do you have an impulse to button a few extra buttons?"

"No. Never! I wouldn't give him the satisfaction. I have an impulse never to see him again, that's all."

When she was gone, I tried to reconcile her utter non-response to me with her detailed and often volatile reactions to just about everyone else in her life. I could hardly believe that she really had no feelings about me. On the other hand, if, as seemed likely, she had rich and complex reactions to me and what I said, why would she hide them from me, even when I asked her outright how she felt about me?

The most likely answer was that she saw me as a sleuth, and though she had sought my help, now she wanted to withhold anything from me that might "aid my investigations." I began to think of her, more than ever, as a person divided, like the patient who goes to a physician because of a tumor, but then, afraid that it is cancerous, conceals it from him and hopes he won't find it.

In a curious sense, I was as dangerous as Robert—he because he would molest her sexually, I because I would uproot truths that she strongly wanted to keep concealed. Were they sexual truths, so that in a sense Robert and I were counterparts, intruding in different ways? That seemed distinctly possible.

I had the impulse to say, "Hey, Maggie, there's a lot you're not telling me. For instance, you're not telling me your reactions to me, and you're not really trying to jog your own memory. Maggie, you're keeping us in the dark."

But it wasn't the way. Maybe Maggie truly didn't know, consciously, what she was doing. She might have looked at me blankly, as if I were crazy—and then retreated further.

Besides, it sounded accusatory. She was under terrible strain as it was, hating herself for an incapacity that seemed utterly out of her control. Rather than blame her as a way of relieving my own frustration, my next step would have to be to reveal to her that, in spite of how it seemed, she was working against discovery.

*   *   *

Things were going downhill with David. He and Maggie had
some terrible fights.

"He got me a pearl choker. I found a jeweler who turned it
into a two-strand bracelet. I had to lengthen it a little. I paid
for that. We were going out to dinner with his parents, they
were in town, and he asked me to wear the necklace so they
could see it. His mother loves jewelry. She thinks she knows
everything about it. When I showed David the bracelet, he was
furious. He asked me why I didn't tell him.

"But I had told him. He knows I don't like necklaces. I
should have said something when he gave it to me last fall, but
I figured I'd be nice. I'd take it and surprise him. So that's
what I did.

"It went okay with his parents. I knew I shouldn't have gone
back to his apartment that night, I just knew it. But he
pleaded with me. Oh no, I forgot. His mother said, 'I guess
you two have your reasons why you're not getting married, it's
none of my business'—something like that anyhow. I didn't
say anything. That came up too, in the fight."

The fight had started over the necklace, he'd been terribly
hurt that she'd altered it.

"Then he lost it," she said.

"What do you mean, 'lost it'?" I asked.

"He started screaming and making fists at me. How everyone expected us to get married, and how humiliated he felt
that I wouldn't kiss him. That sometimes he felt like killing
himself. I told him I loved him. I think he was a little drunk.
He said he didn't want to sleep with me anymore until I did
something—"

Up until that point, Maggie had been curiously reportorial,
like someone watching a city burn down from afar. But I could
see that the next thing he'd said really hurt, even before she
told me. "He said I made him feel ugly. He said he wanted to
date other women. He said, 'Maybe I'll find someone who
doesn't think of me as so ugly.'

"I started shouting at him, accusing him of telling his parents that I had this problem. I guess that comment his mother made really got to me, I didn't realize it at the time. I called her a bitch, and he got very hurt. He just lay on the bed and he cried. He just cried and cried. I told him I thought he was beautiful, and he tried to kiss me, but I just couldn't. He knows I'm going to you and that you'll help me. Do you think you can, or am I just wasting your time?"

I got the sense that she was seething.

I asked her, "How do you feel about me right now, I mean, when you just said, 'Do you think you can?'"

"No feeling. I just wonder."

"You're not angry with me at all? You're not disappointed with me?"

"No. I'm disappointed with myself."

"You're never disappointed with our work here, or with me?"

"No. We're doing what we can."

I had no choice but to let it go.

Then, pleadingly, she asked, "Doctor, do you think I'm crazy? I mean, about this fear of kissing."

"No. Of course not."

"I know David is right. He really loves me. He even apologized the next day and said he would always love me. He said that was why he got so upset. It would be worse with anyone else. I'll do anything. I really will."

At that moment, I thought of her as a wounded deer, who had run from hunters magnificently and now felt utterly at their mercy.

But though I had no desire to rush in for the kill, I knew I had to go forward.

Trying not to sound cruel, I said, "You say that you'll do anything. But I get the feeling sometimes, Maggie, that there are things you know, or maybe that you suspect—or let's say this, things that you *think* that you really don't want to talk about. We need all the information we can get. Nothing's irrelevant, you know what I mean. It's like on a dig. I don't know much about your field, but I know that you people find things that don't even make sense for a long time, I mean not for a while, and then they do."

When she was gone, it crossed my mind that there was a way she could prod her memory—perhaps she could go back to that home in Weston, if it was still there. I knew from my own experience of returning to my street in Washington Heights how evocative such a trip could be. I hadn't remembered merely people and places; ascending the hill toward my house restored a kinesthetic sense of myself as small, and recalled a time when that hill was painfully hard to climb. From the neighboring courtyard and the sight of nearby buildings, some new but others starkly familiar to me, I got a sense of my own childhood that transcended words. I could approximate it as marked by poverty, enthusiasm, an impression of adults as giants, and of my own helplessness. The memories themselves clamored for attention.

During the next session, Maggie talked about tactics in dealing with her Ph.D. committee. The faculty liked her, she worked hard and had a good mind. It was a matter of getting them to agree about an assumption she was planning to make; she had to persuade two professors, competitive with each other, to consent to be on her committee so that she could proceed. It would have been obtrusive to bring up Weston.

But soon after that more trouble with David created an opening. In despair, Maggie actually suggested, "Maybe I should just give it up."

"What do you mean?"

"I mean leave him. It just isn't worth it."

"Maggie, you yourself told me that things wouldn't be better with anyone else. Do you still love David?"

"I do."

"Well, we're not going to quit, just because there's more we need to know. I've been thinking about you, and about all this—a lot."

"Really."

"I have an idea."

"What's that?"

"Maybe you could take a one-hour ride back to that house in Weston. I mean, take a look at it from the outside. Even knock on the door. I bet you'd remember an awful lot."

Her face flushed, and she blinked hard.

"Would you go back there?"

"Is that really psychotherapy?" she asked. Her question was dipped in irony.

"Whatever it is," I said, "it's a sound psychological principle that might very well start your memory going. You might remember at least some things about your life back then."

She restored tranquillity to her face, but, I felt, only by a great effort of will. "Well, I'm mounting samples right now. For microscopic analysis. These are the fossils I was telling you about from the Arizona sample. Two people are waiting for them for a monograph."

"Well, maybe some time later on," I said casually.

"Of course."

I let her divert me easily. But it was as if I'd asked her to cut out her left lung and hand it over, and she replied with a smile, "Not now. Another time for sure."

The next time she came in she was more distraught, presumably expecting me to pounce on her. Now I was really running the risk of being another Robert, of trying to kiss her at the door.

I didn't mention Weston again, and she softened. She went on to talk about David and her.

When, a few weeks later, I again brought up the subject of Weston, she told me smoothly, "I don't have a car. It's hard to get there."

"Would David drive you?"

She winced, and I knew I was being obnoxious again.

"Of course. But I don't like to ask him. He's got a lot on his mind with his CPA exams."

"Maybe an hour on Sunday?"

"Do you really think that's going to help?"

"Maggie, I don't know. It might. Are you opposed to going there?"

"Well, not exactly opposed. But it seems pointless."

The following week she announced that she thought therapy was making her worse, not better. "A lot of phobias I thought I cured years ago are coming back."

She told me that when she first came to New York City, she was afraid to walk alone in the streets at night. She'd gotten over it, but now she was frightened again. She'd had to call David several times to pick her up at the library. "Also, I'm afraid to drive his car without him. I'm getting upset in restaurants. And I'm starting to have terrible nightmares."

She'd had several dreams that she was helpless, shouting for David, but he was gone, gone forever. In one of them, a man had said, "You know you made it impossible for him, just the way your mother did for your father."

The man was obviously me.

I felt certain that even the *thought* of going back to Weston was activating these fears, and I despaired of asking her to do it.

However, there was one thing that we had accomplished and that I would not let go of. A truly compliant Maggie, the good little girl she'd pretended to be, would have driven to Weston the instant I'd made the suggestion. Finally, we had an overt act, a refusal on her part, that we could point to.

We could forgo her return to Weston. It was a great gain that we had uncovered both her fear and her active efforts to keep something buried, whatever it was. We had exposed the Maggie who was simply refusing to delve into her life.

I did my best to show her that I understood her fear and did not condemn her for it.

"Maggie," I said, "I'm not asking you to go back to Weston.

I mean, if you wanted to, that would be great. But I see how horrible it is for you even to think about it."

She nodded.

I went on. "I mean it would be easier to go on a dig in the African jungle than to go back there. And that means something."

"What does it mean?" She sounded flustered and angry.

"Well, if there's anyplace else, anything you can tell me that you remember or *can* remember, please tell me."

She seemed to be thinking very seriously. Then she said, "Doctor, I want to tell you something."

"Yes?"

I felt instantly excited, sure that something new and valuable was forthcoming.

But I was wrong.

She said, "You know that if you dig brutally, you destroy the data. A tremendous amount of data, artifacts, bones, records, God knows what, have been destroyed by brutal digging. . . ."

Was she really embarking on this moral lecture? It seemed so, and I would have to listen as she went on.

"Heinrich Schliemann probably destroyed ten times more material than he unearthed. . . . He went in with a bulldozer to excavate the site of ancient Troy. People thought he was wrong. . . ."

She was talking to me as if I were a student in an elementary class and I behaved like one, blacking out for much of the lecture.

I felt like saying, "All this about incompetent methods of digging is your way of burying and reburying, Maggie." But I didn't and let her go on.

When she'd finished, I said, "Maggie, I get the impression that you're pretty angry with me."

"Well, you've been pushing pretty hard."

"I have. But Maggie, I'm really on your side, though maybe it doesn't look that way. I'm not really a bulldozer."

"I know," she said, and I could tell I'd been forgiven.

Then she said, surprisingly, "That was a lot of bullshit about archeology, wasn't it?"

We both laughed.

When she was gone, I realized that my reaction to her had changed considerably. Almost since I'd known her, I'd had strong, mixed feelings about her. There was a detached, cut-off side to her. She had been injuring David by much more than her refusal to kiss him on the lips or to marry him.

I too had felt her pushing me away from the beginning. And yet, all along, I'd pictured her as the kind of person whom I could like, if only she would change that trait. Now that we'd surfaced that repressive part of her, and I was sure that she saw it, I suddenly felt different. I both liked her and felt sorry for her.

I realized that feeling as frightened and defensive as she did, it must have been incredibly painful to her to come to me at all. And yet she had come, session after session.

Most important, something in her attitude told me, even before she came back the next time, that we had finally raised our anchors and were on our way.

She began the session by talking about her grandfather. "I guess my relationship with grandpa was the best one I ever had with a man. He always lit up when he saw me, and we trusted each other completely. I think we both felt misunderstood. I even loved his polished bald head. I used to rub it with a cloth and we'd both laugh."

She went on to say that "when grandma Dorothy died it was sad, but I could live with it, she did a lot of nagging. But when Julian passed away, I lost something tremendous."

I wondered why she'd decided to talk about her grandparents so much that day, but it seemed best not to ask. I had a strong sense that she was headed somewhere and, very possibly, she herself didn't know where.

She said, "Grandpa was never himself when he was with her. She was very scowling and critical."

"Critical of what?"

"Of where he took me. Like to a football game when it was cold, or to his office. Or when he talked about wines to me. She was really tough. She scowled all the time and broke in on him if he was telling a story."

"What do you mean?"

"I mean we were having a big Thanksgiving dinner. A lot of people were over there, I think I know who they were, I'm not sure. And he was starting to tell a story, like, 'So I was driving up the West Side Highway at about forty-five—' and she'd break in, real tough, nasty. 'You were not, Julian. You were going sixty!' It might not even have been relevant to his story. And he'd look so sad, and he'd stop and he'd never finish the story. He'd just quit and then wipe his face with a napkin and excuse himself from the table."

"What did you do?"

"Maybe sit there if my mother wouldn't let me get up. Or maybe, I think that day, I followed him into the study. He'd show me the wine labels that he was importing, red and gold with pictures, like big stamps. They were pretty. And he'd say, 'Maggie, this one's really good.' We were outcasts, now that I think of it."

"So, in a way, he was really like a father to you, wasn't he?"

"Yes. Maybe because his marriage was so bad. But he really loved me. I was everything to him, everything to Julian. He used to brag about me to the people he worked with, to the truckers and stuff. I didn't appreciate him at the time."

In other words, I thought, the first two marriages she'd witnessed, the only ones for a long time, had both been variations of hell. I recalled her response a while ago, when I'd asked her what being married had made her think of—she'd replied, "death." Her father might as well have been dead.

I think she saw the beneficent look in my eyes as she talked about her grandfather.

But then she suddenly corrected me. "No. You said he was like a father. But he wasn't. He was never like my father. I always thought about my real father, out there, somewhere, thinking about me."

This was new, and I was pleased to receive it.

"You thought about him a lot, Maggie?" I asked her.

"All the time. When I got a top spelling grade. When I put on a fancy polka-dot dress, I remember, to go to my friend Paula's party. Other times. A lot of times. I guess I wanted him to know what I was doing, how well I did, all the time."

"Too bad he didn't," I chimed in.

"But he did!"

Could I have heard her correctly? No, that was impossible.

"Say that again," I asked her.

She moved quickly and nervously, and color came to her cheeks. Half-choking, she repeated, "But he did."

I would have thought it was her imagination, but her eyes were moist with tears, and she seemed unable to talk.

I handed her the box of tissues, and she wiped her face with them but did a lousy job. I waited for her to compose herself.

"This was the big secret between my grandfather and me. I promised him all my life I wouldn't tell. All his life. That he wouldn't tell, and that I wouldn't tell. I mean that we wouldn't tell my mother or Dorothy."

She looked at me plaintively, her eyes glistening with tears.

I got the unspoken message and assured her. "Maggie, I promise you I'll never talk about this. Not to your mother or to anyone. You know that. But I promise you again."

She nodded.

"Anyhow, grandpa kept in touch with daddy. Daddy insisted. No matter what my mother said, he had to know what was happening with me. He used to call my grandfather at the office. He couldn't call me. He was afraid I'd say something, I was so young. He said we'd be together, he'd meet me when I grew up."

"He was living in Chicago?"

"Yes, I didn't know his address. But he had a big union job there. Grandpa knew it, but he told me he gave daddy his word not to give it to me. So mother wouldn't get it. If mother knew, we would be ruined. Grandpa used to tell me that all the time. He'd call me aside and remind me. He used to whisper, 'Don't forget our secret.' Sometimes when we were alone, especially if I looked sad, he'd say, 'Hey, Maggie, how's our secret?' and I guess I'd cheer up and I'd smile. Or maybe he'd just put his finger to his lips, that was the signal, I'd do the same thing. We even did it in front of Dorothy and my mother at the table, and we'd know."

"Did you ask if you could talk to your father?"

"No. He told me I couldn't. But daddy would always send me a birthday card, care of my grandfather. I could see the address. He couldn't mail them directly, naturally."

"How come you didn't tell me all this before?" I asked Maggie.

"I guess I didn't trust you. But now I do. I guess I felt funny about it. Oh yeah, he used to send me Christmas cards too."

"What would they say?"

"They were very beautiful. But very simple. Like, 'I love you, Maggie.' Or 'I'm always thinking about you, Maggie.' Once he sent me a note, 'Congratulations on getting three A's and a B in school, and have a great summer. You worked hard. You deserve it.'"

"That must have meant a lot."

"A lot? It was everything. My mother didn't know a damn thing about school, or my homework, except that I had to go there and do it. Oh yeah, I used to ask my grandfather, 'How come daddy knows so much about me?' and he'd wink. He was a wonderful man, Julian. Once he went to Chicago on business and talked to my father."

She stopped abruptly, her face crimsoned and she almost lost her balance. She was sobbing profusely.

It crossed my mind that all that emotion missing during our first four months and then some was here, coursing through her all at once, as she remembered.

She told me, "When Julian went to Chicago . . . he had dinner with daddy. . . . And daddy said he wanted to see me. . . . I was fourteen. He hadn't seen me in years. . . . But grandpa said, 'You can't. That's the deal. You promised my daughter—that's my mother—if you come to New York to see Maggie, and mess up her life, I'll shoot you.'"

"My God."

"I was so upset. I didn't talk to grandpa for a month, maybe a whole month. No, maybe it wasn't that long. He was so sad. But finally we became friends. He said he had to do it for me. If there was trouble, he'd lose touch with my father altogether."

"You were kind to forgive him."

A half smile broke through. "Yes, well, grandpa bought me a dress and said daddy had sent him the money for it. But I don't believe it. I think grandpa just bought it. But I guess I'll never know."

"And after your grandfather died, how old were you when he died?"

"Seventeen. After that my father couldn't contact me, not directly. I guess that was the deal. So I lost two people at once, two men, two real people. . . ."

She was all tears now, her body had gone limp. And I knew that she would say no more. Our time was up, and I suggested that she come in the next day, instead of waiting.

Heroically, she stood up and said, "Thanks, I don't have to, though. I'm glad I told you."

When I saw her again, she seemed softer, and her attitude suggested that she was readier than ever to talk about anything I asked her about. I felt relieved. Still, I was careful not to assail her with questions about what she'd told me last time, so that she could see that disclosing deeply personal truths was not like giving a pack of dogs the scent of the quarry.

She didn't mention her father at all. Nor did I bring him up, though, naturally, I had a bevy of unanswered questions, most of which had risen out of what she'd told me the last time.

David had just taken his CPA exams and felt sure he'd passed. In any event, his study ordeal was over, and Maggie was making plans with his parents to give him a surprise party at their home. She was busy with the menu and with buying presents for him.

For a week or so the two of them had been getting along well. But she was becoming very anxious, and it wasn't hard to find out why. While David had been so engrossed with preparing for the exam, as Maggie put it, "He didn't worry about what was wrong with us, I mean with me. Now he'll start thinking again. And if he passes and opens his private office, which he's planning, I think the pressure will be on like mad."

"You mean for you to marry him?"

"And that kissing on the lips. Why is it so important to him? You know, a lot of societies, like the Eskimos, they don't even do that."

Some look of mine, maybe an involuntary frown, must have stopped her.

"I know that's bullshit," she said.

I certainly hadn't meant to stifle her by a facial expression. Anything a therapist wants to say, he should say, not insinuate it so that a patient obeys without knowing what's going on. I didn't like myself.

"No. Go ahead!" I said to her.

"No. But it *is* bullshit," she insisted.

"Why?" I asked her.

"Well, David put it right, when I said that to him. He said it wasn't just the kissing itself. It was that kissing me on the lips mattered so much to him, and I wouldn't. If anything mattered to me, if it mattered even a little bit, he would do it for me. It just hurt him that I wouldn't, that I didn't want to. But I can't. I think I'd pass out if I did."

I told her that I understood.

"Then, of course, everyone will expect us to talk about our plans. 'What about your plans, your *future plans*?'" She said this in a piping, mocking voice. "'When are you two *getting married*?' I've got to deal with that. Robert, I can handle. Last time I kept calling him a 'great man,' over and over, and I think he's afraid of me. David said I was terrific, and he didn't mind at all."

"Well, the party isn't really the question, maybe. It's how you feel. It's what you want," I told her.

"I know."

For two weeks, there wasn't a word about her past or her father. Then she told me, "I'm going up to see my mother in Fairfield this weekend."

I had the urge to ask her to ply her mother with questions. I could easily have given her a list.

But I limited myself to saying, when she had only about a minute left, "Maggie, have a good time up there with your mother and with your friends. And if there's anything you can find out, that would be great."

"David's going with me," she volunteered.

"Oh, that'll be fun," I said.

"For protection," she said.

I was preoccupied that weekend and didn't think about Maggie until shortly before she buzzed in.

"I can see why my father left," she said, as soon as she'd sat down in her favorite chair.

"What do you mean?"

"Well, as David said, my mother doesn't have a good word for anybody, and she doesn't enjoy anything. David said it's amazing that I came out as well as I did."

"What did you talk about?"

"Mainly Fairfield. Her church. The shopping center. The fact that prices are going up. Brilliant stuff like that."

"What do you mean, not a good word for anybody?"

"She kept saying that I looked thin, not once but fifty times. And when I asked her about grandpa, she said he always spoiled me and that he was a 'hail-fellow-well-met,' or something like that. I asked her what she meant, and she told me that her mother, Dorothy, was always the brains behind his making a living."

"Do you think that's true?"

"I don't know. I doubt it. But why *say* it? I reminded her that grandpa always had so much good cheer, and she was always so depressed. She said, 'That's true, but it wasn't always like that.'

"I could see where she was going. I told her, 'You better not say one word about my father. You've done enough. Do you hear me? Not one word. You drove him out, and you messed me up, that's enough.' Doctor, if David hadn't been there—"

"What would have happened?"

"I don't know, but I'm not going back next week. That's for sure."

"You were invited?"

"No." Maggie smiled. "Christmas, maybe. She really has obnoxious habits, even when she's not putting me down."

"What do you mean?"

"She talks to me as if I'm incredibly stupid. She knows I'm going for my doctorate. I can't be a total idiot."

"I don't follow you. What did she do, for example?"

"Well, for instance, our doctor has a daughter, Lydia. I've known her all my life. We were, well, maybe not good friends, but we knew each other for ten years, pretty well. My mother said to me, 'I don't know if you remember Lydia Gibbons. Doctor Gibbons's daughter. She's getting married. Do you remember her, darling?'

"I said, 'Mother, how the hell can you ask me that! You know I knew Lydia for ten years. Lydia Gibbons is tall, not too bright. She wanted to be a doctor. You remember we met her on the street and we discussed her being a dietary technician. Mother, we must have talked about it at least five times.'

"My mother does that kind of thing to me over and over again. In different ways. This one's father died, and that one's wife is sick. Things we already talked about. She's weird. She talks as if I never heard of the people. I think she's getting senile."

I didn't reply, but it crossed my mind that possibly her mother had become repetitious because she'd seen Maggie forget things so often. Conceivably, Maggie's remarkable forgetting of Weston and everything that took place there was only one example of a phenomenon that her mother had witnessed time and again. If so, that must have been terribly upsetting to her mother. I could picture even a sensible mother being utterly confused over what Maggie remembered, and what she didn't.

Then I realized that I hadn't noticed Maggie's forgetting anything that took place in my office. It seemed strange.

Maggie said, "I've been thinking about my father a lot."

"In what way?"

"Well, it's a funny thing to have a father, and not to have one. I don't know if he's alive or dead. Maybe I should find out."

"You mean look him up in Chicago?"

"I don't know what I mean."

She wasn't up to that. But even so, I realized what a long way she'd come if such a thought had dared suggest itself to her.

Maggie said, "When I was in Fairfield, I remembered looking up at the sky when I was little. We must have just moved. I saw those elms on Sunday. David and I took a walk. It's funny. I remember looking up through those elms and thinking, 'It's so far from Weston and so far from Chicago, but daddy must be looking at the same sky and thinking of me.'

"He thought about me a lot. In school, sometimes when I used to start a test and do real great, I pictured him looking at me—proudly, I guess. Or even when I was just sharpening a pencil. That sounds stupid, doesn't it?"

"Not at all."

"When I used to walk in Fairfield Park, I thought of him. I'd pretend he was talking to me. Once a couple of boys, we must have been all about twelve, were giving me a hard time. I thought, 'I'll really call my father and he'll come back and crush them.' But that was fantasy. I knew I couldn't call him. I once had a fight with grandpa. He wouldn't tell daddy something about me that he said would upset him. Later I was glad he didn't."

"You still picture him looking at you?"

"Sometimes. But I turn it off. He doesn't know anything about my life anymore."

"Do you think he'd like David?"

"I *know* he would. They're so different. Daddy's not educated. But he was smart. David was what he wanted for me, I know that. Did I say 'wanted'? I mean what he wants for me."

"He'd like you to be married to David?"

"He would. And to kiss him, too. I know what you're thinking." She smiled. "You know he wasn't educated but grandpa used to point to his picture and he said, 'You know, your dad likes two things.' And I asked him what. And he said, 'Cigars and big words.'

"Grandpa said that once when he and daddy and some people were waterskiing, someone had the rope around him real loose and the boat was going, and daddy cut the rope fast, while the boat was going, and whoever it was fell in. And they said, 'Harry, why did you do that?' And my father said, 'Are you kidding, if that rope gets loose, it could go around your head, and you could get'—he wanted to say decapitated—but he ended up saying 'decapitulated,' and grandpa corrected him, and he said, 'Well, decapitulated is a bigger word, and it's even worse.'"

"Is this the first time you thought about that story in a long time? You never mentioned it before," I asked her.

"I think it is." She reflected. "But now I realize I used to think about it often."

"You mean the big word or his sense of humor?"

"No, I used to have dreams about it. Bad ones. About somebody having his head cut off by accident. My mother used to come in and calm me down. Isn't that amazing!"

"What?"

"That I forgot so completely that I used to have these nightmares. The same one, over and over. I guess I was little. It wasn't long after we moved."

"Your mother was really comforting then, huh?"

"Yes. She was. Yes, she really was. She was always there. I think she felt terrible about kicking daddy out and being so crazy."

When the time was up, Maggie seemed astonished. "Gee, I feel I've been here only a minute. It's really over already?"

On the way out she looked radiant. I realized that the early impression she gave of angularity was not merely geometric or aesthetic. It had been in her gestures, in her whole style, which seemed marked by sudden impulses and reverses of direction.

Now she was open, eager. Her inhibitions remained, but now they seemed like isolated incapacities. She was freshly accessible, and on my side—on *our* side. It was as if we had stopped a poison from spreading, by confining it to a few places, by localizing it. But how would we get to the source? That was still unclear.

I often wondered about her father, not as he had been in Weston but afterward. With all that power of his, and that curiosity about her, why hadn't he insisted on seeing her? When I touched upon the subject with Maggie, she reminded me of her grandfather and his gun.

"He would have used it, he was kind of a nut, I'm sure he would have used it. And my mother, when she was angry, she didn't need a gun. I'd like you to meet her some time," Maggie said caustically.

But after Maggie made these discoveries, her symptoms got worse, not better.

"Doctor, I can't believe it. I'm so damn phobic. I had to call David twice after class to pick me up, and last Saturday I got so upset in a restaurant that we had to leave. Then I had another nightmare and I woke him up. It's worse."

"What was the nightmare?"

"I don't remember, but I was screaming for David. He said he felt good that at least I wanted him when I was desperate. I guess that's something. I can't believe it. Why do you think I get so afraid of things, like when I was thirteen?"

"Maybe we're removing layers. I mean, we're heading back that way."

"Through time?"

"Possibly. The truth has a way of squirming sometimes, as if it's trying to make a getaway when we close in on it."

"What do you mean?"

"I mean not really the truth, but the part of you that doesn't want to find out."

She looked upset. "So, what do I do?"

"Maggie, you're doing great. Just like your doctorate. Stay tough. I mean, stay dedicated. We'll get a break."

"You mean like after a rainfall when a fossil pops up?"

"Oh, I didn't realize that. Is that the way it happens a lot of the time? After a heavy rain?"

"Every rain changes everything. It gives you a whole new chance."

"Well, in a way, then . . ."

She saw my hesitancy. "I don't mean it's just luck. You have to go over every square yard of ground. I mean a team does, for miles, after the rain. I mean, I know what you're saying, George. You have to work."

"Well, we're working, Maggie. Keep it up. You're doing great."

Perhaps because David could see how much Maggie was suffering and how hard she was trying, he softened a great deal. For the time being, at least, he dropped his deadlines with Maggie. That helped considerably. David's becoming so patient with her made Maggie herself more impatient than ever for cure.

It wasn't simply that she'd been opposing him in the past. She wasn't negative, in that sense. But while he'd been hammering at her to change, she'd conceived of her task as having to change for *him*. Now she was assuming the burden much more as her own.

I could see that in her present state of mind, she would leave few stones unturned. But I also knew that this feeling of urgency on her part was temporary. One bad evening and David might lose his control, and Maggie her hopefulness. I was eager to find something she could do—almost anything, soon—that might teach us more before that inevitable setback.

In retrospect, I think that a sense of this being an optimum time for me to exhort her, and for her to delve into herself, accounted for the single session in which we finally broke through the shell.

It was unusually cold for early November. Flakes of snow eddied under the gray sky and were starting to cover the heavily trafficked streets. Several of my out-of-town patients had canceled late-afternoon sessions that day, being snowed in, and there was a general feeling in the city of people wanting to go home early and stay there.

Unlike my other patients, who layered themselves with sweaters under heavy coats, Maggie seemed to enjoy defying the elements. She had on a well-tailored beige coat that was belted at the middle; it had a huge fur collar that left her neck very exposed. As she hung up the coat on the rack in my hallway, it crossed my mind that she must be cold but I didn't say anything.

The session was full of subject matter, mostly her studies.

When it was over and we walked to the door, we noticed a sumptuous red-and-gold scarf lying on the couch in my waiting room.

I commented that it was a shame that my previous patient had left it, she must be cold, and then mentioned how pretty it was.

Maggie didn't say anything, she just scrunched up her face.

"Maggie," I asked, "you don't like the colors?"

I had a sense of her pulling back as if they were the colors of a poisonous reptile.

"I hate scarves. I never wear them."

"Really?"

She'd spoken with such finality that I was taken aback. Trying to soften her attitude, she added, "I just don't like wearing anything around my neck."

I remembered her battle with David over the necklace that she had turned into a bracelet, and I had the natural impulse

to let the whole thing go. I felt like closing the office and going
home. Besides, I had a personal rule that once a patient left
my office, even if I did choose to follow that person to my
waiting room, the session was over. I was no longer the person's therapist out there.

But I suddenly had a fierce impulse to push further. In
retrospect, I think I sensed that Maggie's quiet negation of
scarves had a megaton of force behind it, and that made me
curious.

"Maggie, why don't you try it on? The woman who comes
here ahead of you couldn't care less. I'm sure of that."

Maggie knew her by sight. More than once they'd exchanged
pleasantries in my waiting room.

"I know, but I hate them."

"Maggie, then don't," I said. "But I almost get the sense
you're afraid of that scarf. Anything you're afraid of is probably
worth doing, just so we don't widen the circle of those fears
that you hate yourself for—"

She headed toward the scarf, picked it up, and then draped
it around her neck, so that the ends fell loosely on her shoulders. "This is the first time in I don't know when . . ." she
said blithely. And then she collapsed onto my couch, the scarf
still draped over her shoulders.

For an instant, by the glaze of her eyes I thought she'd had
an epileptic seizure, or passed out entirely. "I'm sick. Very
sick," she said. And then she repeated flatly, "Doctor, help
me. I'm sick. Very sick."

I removed the scarf at once, but it made no difference. She
seemed dazed. "Oh, dear God, help me!" she said. She was
addressing no one in particular, at least no one present.

I sat down in a chair across from her.

"I'm sick. I'm very sick," she repeated. "I remembered
something, I don't know if it really happened. No, it couldn't
have. Oh my God, dear God, please help me."

I just waited. As a child, she'd told me, she was religious.
However, I'd never heard her say the word "God" before.

She went on. "A fat guy, Blecker, stopped him. Oh, thank
God for Blecker."

I looked at her but didn't want to disturb her memories, even by asking who Blecker was.

Her return look was acknowledging. "Blecker was daddy's bodyguard. A giant. He used to go to work with daddy. He used to sit outside the house. Oh, thank God he was there. Oh, thank God he was there! I remember the screaming and screaming." She stopped.

"Who was screaming?" I asked.

"Me. I was screaming and screaming. He was choking her. With a scarf, like that one. Not red. She was wearing it. We burned it. Grandpa and me. We burned it when he was gone. Could I have some water?"

"Of course!"

As I rushed out to get some, I was struck by how incredibly dry she seemed. She hadn't shed a tear. She was in shock. No, she was more like someone being choked.

She gulped the water down. "My daddy was, he was *choking* her with the scarf. She couldn't scream. She couldn't say anything. Screaming and screaming, I was screaming and screaming, and Blecker came running in. He thought something had happened to daddy, and he saw and he shouted, 'Stop, Harry. Stop.' I thought daddy was going to kiss her. I think he was. He put his hands on her cheeks, the way he used to, he was so tender. The way he used to kiss me when I went to sleep. But he was strangling her and she fell down. He was strangling her with the *scarf*! He didn't know what he was doing."

She looked up at me as if to ask, Could I take it? Was it acceptable that she was saying all this? Were things safe now?

At least that was what I must have thought because I said, "It's all right, Maggie. It's all right now. Tell me whatever you want."

"And Blecker picked up the big glass table, the whole gigantic glass table, and he smashed it on my daddy, on his back, and daddy let go." She breathed, reliving the relief, the recognition that it was over.

"My daddy was sitting in a chair. He was dazed, that was the last time I saw him. And I started to run to my mother, she was lying on the floor, and Blecker picked me up and he threw me in the bedroom, on the bed. And he must have locked the door, I don't know. And then mommy came in and said, 'Maggie, I'm all right. You're all right. Don't worry.'

"And the next day they told me daddy and Blecker were gone. My mother was gone too. She went to the hospital, but grandpa said she'd be fine, it was just a checkup. I asked him, 'Is daddy coming back?' and he said, 'I don't think so.'

"I remember grandpa and I went into the living room. It was a cold winter day, like now, and we lit a fire, and the glass table was cracked down the middle, and I saw the scarf on it, and I cried, and grandpa picked me up and said, 'No more scarf. No more scarf.' And I was crying. And he put it in the fire and we watched it burn. We watched it burn up. And daddy was gone."

"That was the last you ever saw of him? I mean actually saw him?"

She nodded yes.

She felt sheepish. I thought it was because she thought she'd presumed upon me with all that emotion. And I said, not knowing what else to say, "It's all right, Maggie."

But she clarified. "I've been so unfair to mommy."

"I'll be home tonight," I told her. "If you want to call, you can."

This time she took my number, just in case.

When I next saw her, she said to me, "Sometimes I pretend to myself that it never happened. Or it sort of fades from my mind. I'm not sure."

"It was a long time ago," I said.

"I know. But how could I have forgotten?"

"It's not the most pleasant memory."

"I know. I was telling David that now every time I think about it, I feel more sure that it really did happen. You know what I did?"

She told me that she'd put on a friend's necklace "just to prove I could do it."

"And how did it feel?"

"Scary. But I kept it on a half hour."

"You had thoughts of being choked again?"

"I don't know. I don't really know. But I'll tell you something amazing. When I had that necklace on, even though I was scared, I knew, more than I ever knew, that I'm going to marry David. And stay married."

I shared her excitement.

"Exactly why should that be?" she asked me, as if psychology were the kind of exact science that could yield a single, precise explanation, which, of course, it can't.

The best I could do was to guess. "Maybe, Maggie, maybe in a way all men were your father. I mean, deep in your heart, in your spirit, you expected them to choke you."

"David won't. That's pretty obvious," she said.

I thought, I've never seen her so much on his side.

She said, mostly to herself, "How could he put up with all this garbage? My mother too. I've got to talk to her. I've just got to. I've been very unfair to her. I mean, she can be pretty impossible. But I can't believe what she went through . . . and she never mentioned it."

I told her that I could really understand why nobody wanted to talk about it.

"I know," she agreed. "My grandfather took a chance on me. He used to say six times a day, 'Don't tell your mother about that birthday card. She'll go crazy. Do you want me to hold it for you?' More came back to me. We had a broken piece of wood on the floor of that porch. We used to lift it up and keep the notes there. That was like part of our secret. Isn't it funny how that porch came back to me the other night, when I was with David? I think that's why my father kept so much in touch with me."

"What do you mean?"

"He must have felt terrible about losing me. I guess it all makes sense. Why he asked about me so much. Why he always sent me a card. Grandpa said he used to go crazy for details. He used to say 'more and more details.' He used to say

'Give me the facts. Don't just tell me she got a B on a history test. What kind of history? What did she get right? What did she get wrong?'"

I asked her, "How would you say you feel about your father now?"

She said, "I know it sounds funny. But I love him. Mixed, I guess. I know what he did. But at least he kept trying to get in touch."

I knew exactly what she meant.

A few weeks later, she reported that David had kissed her on the lips.

"How did it feel?" I asked her.

"Funny. I can't say I enjoyed it, but maybe I will."

I thought of Jean-Paul Sartre's concept of "a world in which all is permitted." Maggie hadn't yet ascended to that world, but she was climbing toward it fast.

I suggested that whenever possible, she should do things—anything—that might be hard to do because of the past.

"You mean like kissing David?"

"Or wearing that necklace, the way you did. Or even a scarf, if you can. If you can't, you can't. But if you can, then do it."

She looked puzzled.

I tried to explain. "I mean, all those avoidances, those fears, were ways of burying the past. But you're not back there now, Maggie. You're not back there anymore. We can put the past to rest, and you can have a fantastic life."

But she wasn't buying it. I was surprised to hear her say, "You know, I miss my grandfather."

And I realized that my little speech about the past was too simple. It actually upset her. For if she was truly here, here for good, and the past was gone forever—even if the past was soon to go, then her grandfather was going too. Her beloved grandfather was going away forever—at least that was how it seemed. He was more than just a link to her father, she needed his love for the big adventures ahead.

I did my best to assure her, "He was a great person and always will be."

"He will," she said forcibly.

Of course, I hadn't meant her to forget him or lose his voice within her.

We were almost there. She had the upper hand. In the months to come, it would be up to her to slash at the remnants of her fears, wherever they manifested themselves.

It was a Friday in the middle of December. She and David had scheduled a Caribbean trip for Christmas week. In lieu of spending the holidays with her mother, they were going to Fairfield this weekend, right after her session with me.

We both knew that the chemistry between Maggie and her mother had to be different. Maggie felt very much warmer toward her. She felt touched, even chastened by the fact that her mother had never defended herself when Maggie would attack her bitterly for driving her father away. Maggie's own maternal feelings were surfacing, and she had them toward her mother.

And Maggie also had questions to ask—not all at once, she had vowed, but she would ask them. How much would her mother be willing to tell her?—that was unsure. However, toward the end of the hour, with David waiting outside in the car, she told me firmly, "I'm ready for whatever she tells me."

I felt proud of her, my dauntless paleontologist of her own life.

But the road to discovery had still another turn to take, and Maggie and I were scarcely prepared for it.

On Monday Maggie prefaced her recounting of her conversation with her mother: "You won't believe it."

"I won't? Why not?"

"Because I didn't. But, of course, I do."

"Friday night," she began, "we just talked about a lot of nothing. She was being very nice. Maybe because of David, she looks up to him. We went to some antique stores on Satur-

day, and she and I went back to cook dinner. David went to
see some friends of his, Roger and Phyllis, two people I can't
stand. My mother and I were getting along pretty well, and I
poured her a drink—she can drink sometimes but she doesn't
like to admit it. Well, it's her only pleasure, really, that and
going to church, and we sat down in the living room. It's hard
to get her to stop doing things and sit down. And I *told* her, I
didn't ask, about my father trying to strangle her and her kicking him out. I said, 'It really happened, Mother, didn't it? And
she admitted that it had.

"And I told my mother, 'I could see why you kicked him
out, and why you never mentioned him and his very name
upset you. I could see that.' And my mother said, she said,
'No, darling, I didn't kick him out, he told me he was going. I
begged him not to go.'

"So I asked her, 'Why did he pull the scarf around your
throat?' 'Your father was crazy,' she said. 'Anything could set
him off. It was when I begged him to stay, for you if not for
me. But he didn't give a damn about you. There was another
woman. I don't know, dear, if we should discuss this.' 'Mother,
we *have* to,' I told her."

As Maggie reported this dialogue between her and her
mother, she seemed to have an effortless recall. It was almost
as if her memory of recent events made up for all that her
memory of remote events lacked. I reflected on how with the
elderly, their memory for long-ago events, the details of their
childhood, sometimes seems miraculously astute, as if com-
pensating for their inability to remember what just happened,
such as why they went into a room or where they mislaid their
watch. Maggie's compensation was just the opposite.

"So my mother said, 'If we have to, we have to,' and she
gulped down a shot of scotch straight. I was surprised. And,
oh yes, that's how we got into it. She said, 'Your father didn't
give a damn about you, that's what killed me. He was sleeping
around with those women in Hartford where he used to go.
Okay, maybe he got tired of me, I was never much of a pros-
titute.' I'd never heard her talk like that. 'But you! How could

he leave you? How could a man leave his child? And you so fearful all the time, so sensitive, as grandpa would say. That's when I told him what I thought. I said, "Harry, as God is in heaven, you're a rotten bastard if you run off now and leave us with nothing." And that's when he came over to me—'"

"I thought he was going to kiss you," Maggie had said.

"'He did kiss me. Yes, he kissed me to shut me up. But I wouldn't shut up, and then, dear God! I thought he was going to strangle me, but Blecker—I don't know if you remember him, that big Jewish bodyguard of his. Blecker came in just as everything was going black, and that was it. Your father packed his bags, and we've never seen him or heard hide or hair of him since. We did just fine without him. We did just fine without him!' She'd finished her second shot of scotch and was getting loose."

Then Maggie had said, "Mother, I have a confession to make."

"What's that?" her mother asked, looking at her blankly.

"My father kept in touch with me all those years. I just never told you."

"Kept in touch! That's nonsense!" her mother said. "He didn't give a damn about you."

Maggie had told her, "Mother, he did. He really did. Grandpa would talk to him. He'd call grandpa on the phone, but grandpa never told you. He knew how hurt you were."

"That was your grandfather's *dream,* may he rest in peace. He was a good man. A kind man. A lazy man. But he loved me, and he loved you, Maggie. But that was just his dream. He was a dreamer."

"Mother, you're wrong!" Maggie insisted. "He talked to my father all the time."

"Nonsense!" her mother repeated.

"Mother, will you please stop saying 'nonsense'! Mother, he even threatened him in Chicago."

"Who?"

"My grandfather. My father wanted to come back and see me. He wanted to see me. He would always ask about me."

"Chicago!" her mother had said, in astonishment. "Your grandfather once went to look for him in Chicago. We needed money when you were sick, you don't remember. Your father was a union organizer there. Kind of a union judge or something.

"Your father wouldn't even talk to him. He wouldn't even see grandpa. Grandpa was a dreamer. Your father had another family by then. He wanted no part of us. He didn't want the likes of us."

"But Mother, I hate to tell you," Maggie had insisted. "I used to get Christmas cards and birthday cards from my father. I mean, he never forgot. And he used to mention my life. I mean, he knew all about it. How can you deny that?"

"Child, your grandfather made them up. He used to sign your father's name. We thought he was crazy, my mother and I. We asked him why he did it, and he said you needed a father. He said a child needs a father and you shouldn't be deprived of one. So you had one. We let it go. It couldn't do any harm. He used to say so long as he was alive, you'd have a father. So you had one, God knows it wasn't much."

At that moment, she'd caught sight of the time. "Good God, we have to do the carrots, it's getting late. What will David think if he gets home?"

"One more question, Mother. Please, one more question," Maggie had begged. "How come you never talked about Weston or any of this?"

"Talked about it? We didn't see any reason to. It was bad enough, and you were happy. You know, after you moved, you were a happy child. We worried about you at the time, but you seemed to forget everything. I mean when we moved. We overheard you telling your friend, Paula—do you remember her from across the road?—that your father went away to work and that the whole family was moving to Fairfield because you wanted to go to a big school. So we went along with it. Why not? You were happy. It never came up again. We never brought it up."

"Do you think my father is still alive?"

"No. He died before your grandfather did. Maybe a few years before. An auto accident, your grandfather said. Someone called him from Chicago. It was in the papers there. He was drunk at the wheel.

"Maggie, you and David, be careful when you drive. Who does the driving?" Maggie had replied, "He does, mostly." "That's good. He doesn't drink much, does he?" Her mother had repeated, "Come on, we're not going to get the vegetables done sitting here. David'll think you're a real do-nothing."

Maggie had defended herself, "Mother, he knows I'm not." But she noticed that her mother's carping no longer bothered her in the slightest, the way it used to.

I expected Maggie to be jarred at hearing her mother's account of what actually happened the day her father left. And I imagined that she'd be in shock at learning that he'd never written those cards or asked about her—that he didn't care about her at all. I guess I imagined that she'd be as stricken as someone else whose parent had suddenly died. But Maggie had none of these reactions. It was as if her will had been strengthened by the work she'd put in over the previous months and now she could face the truth without wilting.

Her grandfather's love was still there to offset the loss, at least somewhat. Even allowing for his deception of her, she could still see him as loving, as steady, and, if anything, as more imaginative than she'd pictured him. In every sense, except that of having actually sired her, her grandfather was her father, for better and for worse.

Her discovery freed her to experience the rage and disappointment in her real father, which most children face immediately when a parent leaves without contacting them. The self-hate, the curiosity, the fury of the child abandoned—these are almost as inevitable as breathing. Rarely does a child suppress the truth as well as Maggie did, which means that few have to wait as long for the facts to emerge. First ruefully, then stoically, and finally with the optimism of re-

birth, most children make peace with the past and move into
the future. And that was what Maggie did, belatedly.

What made Maggie one of those rare children who at the time
utterly refuse to face what has happened to them? Her father's
attempted strangulation of her mother just before he left, the
horror of it to Maggie, was probably a factor.

And those around Maggie took special pains to reinforce her
forgetfulness. Neither her mother nor her grandmother had any
impulse to remind her of life in Weston, her life before her
father left. Untutored in psychology and deniers of reality
themselves, they never considered that such pervasive denial
as hers could have harmful effects. They treated her as if what
is forgotten is gone.

As for her grandfather, Maggie's mother was certainly apt in
describing him as a dreamer. Although well-intended, he was
the architect of a ruse that reached the proportions of a life-lie.
Over the years, Maggie had lived with the falsehood he had
contrived and had attempted in every way she could have to
sustain it.

Together, Maggie and I studied her methods of supporting
the lie her grandfather had bequeathed her. Not only was this
the best means of weakening it, but as patients become conscious of their methods of bolstering falsehoods, they delude
themselves less. Denials thrive in darkness, and we wanted all
the light we could get.

While growing up, Maggie had come upon many evidences
of the truth, which she had found ways of discounting. Her
family's very relocation to Fairfield was a reminder that they
had much less money than they used to, and that her father
wasn't contributing. Her telling friends that they'd relocated
for her to go to a better school substituted for that reminder.
Her father, she would often explain, was on extended business
in Chicago, where he was a very important man. This presentation also reinforced her own fantasy that her family would do
anything for her and that they were close-knit, even though her

father was away. It helped her forget that her father was never coming back.

As with most untruths, and especially a life-lie, the need for constant surveillance to stamp out reminders of the reality is the chief cost. For Maggie, these reminders were everywhere. No wonder she thought of death when she thought about marriage.

Because marriage meant strangulation, she would tell her girlfriends that she was never getting married. "I'm going to be a career woman, instead," she would say in high school.

Years later, she remembered, she felt great disappointment when a close woman friend of hers announced her engagement. Maggie had rationalized this as dismay over discovering that her friend wasn't as serious about her career as Maggie had hoped.

Kissing was a desperate reminder of what had happened, one that she'd worked hard to banish from her life. Even more than marriage, "a kiss on the lips" meant to her "the kiss of death." The loss of voice, the loss of freedom, the loss of life, were, not surprisingly, all bound up in the kiss. She did her best to be sure that no one kissed her on the lips.

She remembered having been very distraught the year after her father left when her girlfriends would talk about kissing. They would ask her tauntingly if she'd ever kissed a boy and once when she'd told them no, a friend had said, "I'll show you how to do it." Maggie had fled in horror. For many years, she'd refused to date, and when she did go places with boys, she was careful to choose the shyest, the least aggressive, and if possible even a boy who was physically weaker than she.

And that waterskiing story her grandfather used to tell, in which Maggie's father couldn't find the word "decapitated," was far more loaded than either Maggie or her grandfather imagined. She would beg her grandfather to tell the story, which she described as so funny that it made her sick. I could see why it did. Though she loved hearing anything about her father, the story itself was a stern reminder of the last day she ever saw him, in that it linked her father with strangling.

I got her to tell me that little anecdote many, many times, which she did quiveringly, until finally she could relate it to me without a trace of discomfort.

That winter our sessions evoked many memories of her childhood in Weston before her father left. He used to go away for a few days at a time, and she would miss him. But on his return, when she would hear the sound of his car on the pebbled road, she had mixed feelings. She would run out to him and he was always delighted to see her. But then her mother would scold him for being away, and trouble would start.

"What kind of trouble?" I asked.

"Big trouble. I used to beg her not to yell at him. I used to say, 'Mom, maybe he won't come back at all if you keep yelling at him.'"

"What would he do?"

Then she remembered his habit of going over to her mother angrily and kissing her so hard that she had trouble breathing. It was his way of shutting her up and of seeming to say, "I'm still attracted to you. I love you."

I wasn't surprised that he'd done this many times. His performance with that scarf could hardly have been an isolated act. Maggie had witnessed not one kiss that verged on strangulation but many. Traumas are less often isolated events than heightened instances of a repeated activity. The single dramatic, loaded incident stands for many incidents, some perhaps lesser in degree but all of the same kind.

Maggie's relationship with David kept improving. She enjoyed kissing him, and her misgivings about marrying him lessened until they were no greater than those of any sensible person contemplating marriage. They married eight months later. Getting her doctorate would still take at least a few years, but

Maggie enjoyed the work immensely and there seemed to be no great hurry.

I can still remember a card she sent me from London where she'd gone to take some courses the following summer. She'd had a dream that she was digging in her backyard in Weston, looking for fossils and studying the dirt around them. She was wearing a Sherlock Holmes hat. She'd found something, it was unclear what. There I was, complimenting her, and she'd said to me, "Sedimentary, my dear Watson."

We ended our work the following year, though Maggie and I still talk on occasion. She and David have two children.

In evaluating the great lie that Maggie's grandfather told her, I think that people would always differ. Some will argue that his performance was inexcusable, that the ends never justify the means, and that even the best-intended hoax is immoral. It cheats the listener out of the chance to deal with the reality. Certainly, the costs of dishonesty are like ever-widening circles, and no one can ever know for sure what they will disturb.

Maggie's grandfather had no way of reckoning the impact on Maggie of what he was doing. Nor were his motives totally altruistic. He himself profited a great deal from his lie—his status with his granddaughter was something he enjoyed nowhere else. She became utterly dependent upon him as the only conduit to her father, as the coholder of their secret. As with any lie, it is hard to know to what degree the teller was motivated by derivative benefits.

On the other side, that of "pious fraud," there is the likelihood that in at least some ways his lie improved her life radically. Having a father out there may well have done much to give Maggie a feeling of worth and helped her define herself. Conceivably, she would not have persevered in school without a sense that someone was following her progress and cared. She would not have accomplished so much. The sorry thing is that this "someone" could not have been her grandfather himself.

One thing does seem indisputable. Her grandfather's invention of a father, the figure he concocted, was a masterpiece. It must surely have been the creative act of his life, his detailed rendering of this unwavering, sensitive, caring man.

I sometimes think of that imaginary father, shouting at Maggie's real grandfather: "Don't just tell me she got a good grade in history. What kind of history? What did she get right? What did she get wrong?" It seems a shame that so much of the credit for caring about Maggie went to that figment rather than to her grandfather himself.

Naturally, I never mentioned to the woman who'd preceded Maggie in my office that her scarf had been, figuratively, an instrument of cure. But I had that thought when I handed it to her the next time, and mentioned how pretty it was. Three months before Maggie would not have dared to touch that scarf, much less wear it. Though she didn't know it, in picking up the scarf and trying it on, she was going back to Weston and reliving some of her early ordeal.

As her therapy made evident, Maggie had, all along, been expressing her "memories" of childhood in many of her likes and dislikes, which passed as mere matters of taste. Her favoring V-necked coats and open-necked blouses seemed nothing for anyone to question. Nor did her dislike of necklaces and scarves. The adage is that one never disputes matters of taste. Only when Maggie was challenged to reconsider these preferences, could she see how strongly she held them, and how terrifying it was even to think about giving them up.

Of course, Maggie's childhood was more traumatic than most people's. However, even the best-adjusted of us are repressing fears behind habits that pass as mere expressions of our likes and dislikes. Ordinarily, we go a lifetime without having our daily preferences subjected to scrutiny. It is only when they are challenged that their dire importance to the person starts to surface. They are not the quiet habits they seemed to be, but devices to tamp down painful memories of the past. Like Maggie, though less dramatically, we are all repressing the past and fleeing toward the future, by unconsidered habits that pose as mere preferences.

This means that only by daring can we invent the future and discover the past. No one can do this for us.

THE KINDLY PROFESSOR

Professor Edgars was a tall man, with an arrogant look. He had a thin, carefully trimmed mustache, impeccably styled white hair, and a Vandyke beard. His two shining eyes held a certain dominance over his face.

"I need your help," he told me, as if I had little choice.

"With what?" I asked.

"I want you to tell my young wife that she has multiple sclerosis. I should not be the one to tell her."

Had I heard him correctly? I wondered at once how he knew, and she didn't, and of course, why he couldn't tell her himself.

"There's a lot I don't understand," I said.

"If you'll only be patient, you will." He smiled condescendingly. "If you will only listen, young man, you will understand. It would be best, therefore, if you can help it, not to break in."

I took a deep breath. I always felt short of breath with "don't-interrupt-me" people, and he was a major offender. I subsided into my chair.

"Meeting her was the pivotal event of my life, you might say."

"How long ago was that?"

"Six years. I was forty-four, she was twenty-two, exactly half my age. I was with Professor Lefert. He's in my department, and we'd left a noisy restaurant for some place quiet to talk. We'd often go somewhere after dinner. It seems like yesterday."

He blinked and rolled his eyes, and then recomposed his face, all so quickly that I wasn't sure of what I had seen. Then he went on.

"We tried a new place, but it was anything but quiet. It was dark with neon lights, crowded as could be, cheerful enough but with plenty of hubbub, voices, and rock music in the background. Henry's a stodgy type. He wanted to leave at once, and I was ready to.

"It was there that I saw Donna. I still remember her, tall, with dark hair. Her long hair bounced as she twisted and turned on the dance floor. She smiled continually and seemed lost in the music. I guess I was hoping she wasn't too attached to the boy she was dancing with, and I hoped she was older. I'm forty-four, you know. I mean I was forty-four when I met her, she was only twenty-two. I was hoping she was older so it wouldn't be so preposterous."

"Preposterous?" I echoed.

"Will you let me go on!" He became agitated at my breaking in. His reminiscing was apparently like having sex, and I had opened the door and interrupted him.

"Doctor, I knew that she would free me from my creative lethargy. Does that sound insane? That I could create with her in my life. No. Really. Does it sound insane?"

Again that blink. I was sure it was a facial tic.

"Not really, Professor. Go on," I said.

He did. "In that crowded, buzzing, neon hive of a place where you could see and not see in rapid alternation, despite the noise level, where everyone seemed so young except Lefert and me, after a single glance, I couldn't take my eyes off her. She was a wonderful dancer. I never thought I'd say that. I know so little about it. You know, I'll never forget that yellow dress. Does it sound insane now?"

It was a trap, and I wouldn't fall into it. "Go on," was all I said. I hoped that I wouldn't get into trouble with that.

"No," he went on. "You can't judge it adversely. The French call it *coup de foudre*—a powder burst. Goethe called it 'elective affinities.' I knew that I had to meet her, to speak to her—Lefert wanted to go. He had papers to mark. And ordinarily, I would have, too. But her smile, her *abandon*. I knew, even as she twisted and turned on that dance floor, surrendering to the music as she seemed to create it, I knew that she could be my whole life. I might as well tell you. My *whole life*."

While he was masturbating in memory, I realized that I seriously disliked this man, who had negative charisma. I began wondering whether I should work with him. Should a therapist try to treat someone who elicits so much discomfort in him, so much dislike?

"Well," he said, "Lefert was shoving his way to the door. I was behind him. He expected me to follow him through the crowd. But I waited. The music stopped, and she had to come right past me. All I could think to say was, 'You're a wonderful dancer.'"

"She answered you?"

"Just 'thanks.' That was all she said. I pressed. 'Where did you learn?' I think I asked. Or something like that. 'How did you get so good?' Something awkward. The collective babbling of the student body in that place was enough to mask almost any sound. She said she was a professional dancer, with the New York City Ballet. 'Oh, that explains it,' I said. 'No,' she laughed. 'Very few ballet dancers do this kind of dancing,' she said. I felt stupid. And ancient. Yes *ancient*, in my sleeveless sweater under a Burberry jacket.

"But I stayed long enough for her to tell me that she danced in Balanchine's company. I knew nothing about Balanchine, except the name. Out in the street, I remember, I told Henry Lefert, 'I met a young woman. I'm going to be her lover. I'll marry her. My *life* depends on it.'"

I started to say something, but his eyes hardened, and he raised his voice and went on, faster, as if in sexual excitement.

"It was dark, the middle of winter. I wanted to say, 'Henry, please have coffee with me somewhere else. Please stay with me awhile. I've got to talk.' But he said to me in surprise, 'Edgar, you're married as it is. Don't you think this is a little sudden?'"

I asked, "What did you want to say to him that you didn't?"

"I don't know. I wish you wouldn't interrupt me. I am known as a very fine teacher. I won't leave anything out if it's at all relevant. Don't worry." He smiled, and paused to collect his thoughts.

In that instant, I could trace my dislike of him, my feeling of suffocation in his presence. He was trying to control me and the hour—and everything that was said in it. In short, he was a controlling bastard. My feeling short of breath, my disliking him, didn't come from any special bias of mine. Nearly any therapist who worked with him would have felt that way. If I wanted to continue, I was as qualified as anyone.

After that, I made sure to let him talk. Because of his insistence on running things his own way in sessions, and oddly because of his Vandyke beard, I found it impossible to think of him as anything other than "the Professor."

"Here's the interesting thing," he continued. "I had been writing almost nothing, contributing nothing by way of scholarship, for some years before that. But I knew that if I could go out with her, I knew that very night that, if we became lovers, I would become as prolific—I almost said as prolific as Samuel Johnson himself. He is the person I specialize in."

"Samuel Johnson?" I asked feebly.

"Yes, do you know who he is?"

"I've heard of him."

"Well, I should think so. I specialize in the Johnson circle. Don't confuse him with Ben Jonson," he warned me.

"I'll try not to."

"Sometimes I feel I'm Johnson's embodiment, his descendant here, in this age. Anyhow, I knew that I would become creative, prolific. Fulfilled in love, I would convert my immense studies, my extensive reading and analysis into great works illuminating Johnson's period and his life.

"So I attacked the problem of meeting her, of winning her, as if it were any other challenge, in academic or real life, but it was different."

"How did you do that?"

"I began studying ballet, I mean writings on the subject. I contacted my brother Ollie, a dance teacher, whom I had not seen in years, an admitted homosexual, but nonetheless knowledgeable. I learned all I could as fast as I could. I bought tickets regularly. I sent her flowers. Finally I went out with her. We had coffee, then dinner. We talked.

"To my astonishment, she did not hold my age against me."

"For a time, I did not tell her I was married. I couldn't afford to. She was too important to risk losing. I read poetry to her. We talked about ballet. I met her friends. They were all from the company. She knew few men apart from her ballet friends. I talked to her about history, about the ancient Romans, and about Napoleon, about a world beyond anything she had dreamed of.

"We would meet late at night, after the ballet, and spend a few hours together. I would tell Emily I was going for a walk, to think. More and more I explained to Donna the world beyond ballet, and she was enthralled.

"Then, one night we made love, and I knew I would be leaving Emily. Naturally, I had to tell Donna I was married. When I did, she was startled."

At his saying that, the facial twitch returned in much greater force, this time dominating his face. It was a horrible sight. It began with a blink, after which he rolled his eyes and grimaced. His face froze and then returned to normal. Seconds later, it was as if he had willed himself to consign that moment of disfigurement to oblivion, and, as he went on, he expected me to do the same.

"I swore to her I would get a divorce. And the next night, I told Emily it was over. She was brokenhearted, but she was less surprised than I thought she would be.

"It was a whirlwind courtship. I thought about nothing else, nothing but Donna and my writing. We were soon living together. That year I wrote scholarly papers on Johnson, on

Boswell, on Oliver Goldsmith, and completed another. It was the dream that I had not dared to cherish.

"Of course, many of my fellow faculty members and friends were jealous. Donna was so beautiful—and so young. But it made no difference. She was grace itself, with sea-green eyes, a dancer's figure and walk, a delicate flower on a long stem. Our making love was wonderful, but our just being together— we needed nothing else. I would meet her backstage. Life had begun again for me, in every way."

Somehow, he broke into his own story and talked about his childhood, his growing up, along with Ollie, in a very poor family in The Bronx. Their mother had died painfully from cancer when Ollie was eleven and the Professor was twelve. With the father away working all the time, Ollie had spent a year and a half at her bedside, hardly going to school.

"I think his closeness to her is why he became a homosexual," the Professor conjectured. Then he smiled wryly, "Well, you would know more about that." In any event, he and Ollie had pursued vastly different lives and had seldom talked in recent years. Apparently, the Professor had resumed their relationship to learn what he could about dance, for the sake of his courtship.

The session was nearing its end. I told him there were only a few minutes left, and asked him if he had anything special he wanted to say before leaving. He questioned me about my credentials. Where had I gotten my degree? With whom had I studied? Was I licensed? What had I written, if anything?

I felt it my obligation to answer those questions bearing on my professional status. However, I was suspicious of the questions he asked about my personal life, deciding that his aim was to learn about me in order to control me, or at least to have an excuse to discount what I might say, if he didn't like it.

I told him it would be best if I didn't talk about myself. He seemed annoyed but made no comment.

When the doorbell rang, and it was clear someone else was coming, he said to me bitterly, "I guess you have to stick to your schedule." We hadn't yet gotten to his "young wife's" multiple sclerosis, or his assignment for me to tell her.

We scheduled another hour. "I think that will be enough," he said.

Afterward, the irony of it all occurred to me. With all his success at finding the woman who could inspire him, at engineering his marriage to her, at structuring his world, there was one thing he could not control, which nearly everyone else could—namely *his own face*.

Suddenly I saw that tic, that horrible grimace and loss of mastery over his eyes and lips, as mocking him. It was as if another creature inside of him were making faces at him, saying "This is all a fraud."

Although I didn't like him, I was fascinated by him. Perhaps if he weren't coming to me for help, paying me for my time, I would have found him utterly intolerable. But in reality, he was soliciting my help. Perhaps the same goblin within him that twitted him about his insufficiency was pleading with me to feel some sympathy for him. With that in mind, I actually did.

He began the next session by handing me two monographs he had written on Samuel Johnson, as if he wanted extra credit. I thanked him, and promised to read them.

"What is there about Johnson that appeals to you so much?" I asked him.

"That's a good question," he replied. "Donna didn't appreciate him at first, now she loves him. He overcame odds, much as I did. He spanned the ages with his knowledge, wrote poetry and literary criticism, and has never been properly appreciated."

"You said you identified with him last time," I reminded him.

"Well, I did." He smiled faintly. "But I guess now I am appreciated, by Donna and increasingly by scholars in my field. I'm luckier than old Samuel."

"What do you mean?"

"With Donna. There was no healthy love in his life. He was separated from Tetty, but he found no one." He returned to his narrative. "I should say that when Donna and I first made public our relationship, many people scoffed at it."

"What do you mean?"

"Once we began living together. There were professors and their wives, people who'd known Emily and me for many years, who refused to invite me anywhere with Donna. Some, like Lefert, were curt with me, though at a few college functions when I brought Donna, those same men, in their late forties and older, looked at her enviously, even lasciviously.

"By then, our friends were mostly ballet people. I met dozens of dancers, young boys and girls. They were polite, but the age difference and our difference in interests made things difficult. They became little more than nodding acquaintances, but Donna preferred to leave them and come home—to be with me. I was very protective of her."

"What do you mean?"

"Well, she would become distraught, and at times even devastated. After Mr. Balanchine—the kids, you know, called him 'Mr. B'—would criticize her. For some reason, he was a god to them. I would console her, and tell her he might not be right. Dance wasn't everything. The music and the glittering multicolored stage was exciting, but not equivalent to life."

The tic came and went. I set myself to try to identify his particular comments or thoughts or attitudes that might trigger it. Though I would have to mention it some day, this did not seem to be the time.

He told me, "I came to see that with her delicate beauty went almost complete inexperience of the world."

"What do you mean?" I asked him.

"Well, for instance, once we were driving somewhere in Connecticut—I was driving, she didn't drive—and we saw a dead animal on the road. It was in her mind for hours. She kept asking me, 'Do you think it died instantly?' I told her it surely had.

"I protected her in many places. That became my role. From the sight of a dead squirrel when we went for a walk. If I saw someone on crutches or in a wheelchair, I would suggest another direction, or block her from the sight. The world has enough tragedy. She represented beauty, and I would protect her where I could. I constantly recited poetry to her. I have a superb memory, as Johnson did, and I had many apt quotes, to make the world as beautiful as I could."

"I see," I said, but in a sense I didn't.

"I was only giving back to her what she gave to me," he explained. "She gave me beauty and new life, and I . . . I became her nervous system. She relied on me. She *listened* to me."

He paused to remove a fleck of lint from his wool pants, and deposited it in my wastepaper basket.

I could see that in removing this symbol of imperfection, he was grappling with strong feelings concerning what he was about to say. His face became anatomized by the effort he was obviously making to keep it under control.

"Then she fell onstage. She *fell*. Her left leg buckled under her. It meant nothing to either of us at the time. The ballet mistress consoled her and rubbed some liniment on it. Mr. B wasn't there at the time, but he replaced her for a while.

"A few days later, we'd been married about six months, she woke up one morning and told me that she saw spots in front of her eyes. I sent her to my physician. He examined her. I called him, with her at my side. But all he could say was that he'd made an appointment with a neurologist for her, Dr. Tomasso, that Friday.

"Donna was upset. She'd planned on getting back to dance. Her friends were all rehearsing. I stayed with her, and canceled my classes to go to Tomasso with her, to keep up her spirits.

"He scheduled her for tests at Columbia Presbyterian. He said it could be a lot of things. 'We just don't know.' They had to get an angiogram and some other tests.

"Now she was really upset, and so was I. But I didn't let on. This may sound funny, but I felt I was failing her."

Of course, I knew what was coming, even as I asked the Professor, "So what happened then?"

He stopped, and I waited for the tic. But it wasn't there. His face became rigid, but when he spoke, it was soft and his eyes were reassuring.

"She was sleeping after the last test when I met the doctor in charge. I followed him into his office and he told me what it was. MS. 'That means she'll never dance again?' I asked. I couldn't believe it. There seemed like an infinitude of time between my question and his answer. Some time in there I had the thought, What crime had I committed to bring this about? Finally, the doctor answered, 'I'm afraid it does.'

"I didn't accept it. Who would? 'But you're not positive?' I demanded to know. 'Well, positive is a funny word,' he said. He hedged. 'We think so. We don't know what else it could be.' He was so pitilessly calm. I blew up and demanded the records. Of course, he agreed to give them to me at once. 'Does this mean she'll be paralyzed?' I asked him. 'I mean, in a wheelchair. Or worse?'

"'No. Not at all,' he said. 'It might be. Each person is different. MS, if it is MS, is progressive,' he said. He explained what it was, lesions in the nervous system that just appear, appear inexplicably. 'She may never get worse. Each person is different,' he said. But by that time, I couldn't hear him.

"Of course, I felt the terrible injustice. Why her? I begged him not to tell her. When he said he had to, I told him that we were going elsewhere with the records. I pleaded with him, and told him that the next physician would tell her, if indeed it proved as he had said. But not yet. It was as if it had happened to both of us.

"Of course, the second doctor told me the same thing. I haven't told anyone. I haven't wanted to know," he said, looking at me beseechingly. "Why destroy what we have, what I've *given* her? But now I must tell her. I can't bear it alone."

I wondered exactly what he had given her, this man who was

"her nervous system," this man who had veered her away from all human frailty, who had played God but in the end hadn't even come close. And now he wanted to pass the role to me, the way Atlas had tricked Hercules into carrying the sky when he had felt it was insupportable.

I asked him, "Why do you want her to know now? I mean, why now as opposed to any time in the past?"

His answer surprised me. "Because she's out long hours in the evenings, taxing her health. I'd persuaded her to return to college. She did for two years. She limps slightly now. Learning would be so good for her, but I think she's demoralized. She did badly on a few exams. But we all have. That's no reason to stop.

"She's out more than she's home. She doesn't respond to me the way she did. I think she's depressed, very depressed, over the limp. She hardly answers me. She doesn't want me to read to her anymore. I know she's depressed."

"It's been a terrible burden for you, hasn't it?" I said.

"Yes, it has."

"May I call you Donald?" I asked him, though I didn't know why I thought of it then.

"Yes. Certainly. Please do."

"Donald, why won't you tell her yourself?" I asked him.

"Because I've protected her for so long. I cannot betray her this way. I feel so foolish about everything now."

"What do you mean?" I asked him.

"The contact lenses I bought. The plastic surgery I had around my eyes, so I could look younger. The exercise program. The losing weight. We don't even have sex anymore."

"No?" I was surprised.

"She doesn't want to."

I started to ask him, "Do you think your wanting her to know about the MS is a kind of"—the terrible word "revenge" came to my mind, "revenge for her rejecting you." But I paused and didn't say it. I backtracked, and asked simply, "Well, I agree she should know, but why now?"

He stopped in thought. "Because I'm afraid she'll hurt herself. She's too much on her own. She needs me. She needs different values, a different emphasis. She's still a child. More of a child than ever. Will you tell her?"

I pressed. "Donald, is that the only reason?"

His eyes were hooded in pain. "Well . . . I really can't . . . I can't bear it alone. It's too much for me. I need her to bear it with me now."

"I know," I said, as consolingly as I could. I thought, "Now you're seeing the downside of running the universe." But for the first time I felt terribly sorry for this man who would be God, but lacked the equipment.

I told him, "Maybe I can help, but not that way. At least I can't promise that. There's a lot I need to know to help you."

He asked, "Well, at least, will you see her?"

To my surprise I said, "Yes, if she wants to see me, and you really want her to come in."

The tempo of those last five minutes between us had slowed down to a fifth of what it had been. Our third-person relationship had given way to a real one. We were, for the first time, two human beings.

An hour after he left my office, Donna called and made an appointment, saying it was at her husband's request. She was pretty, with the leggy look, the slender neck and high cheek-boned face that Balanchine so preferred in dancers. But not beautiful. Her eyes seemed gray, which was curious, because I'd remembered her husband saying they were green.

After glancing around my office and saying that she liked it, she remarked, "I'm sure Donald's been telling you how much he worries about me. But before you give me a lecture, Doctor, there's something I want to tell you."

"Of course," I said.

"I've been thinking, since I called you. And I might as well tell you the truth. I should be as honest as I can, shouldn't I? There's no sense in my coming here and playing games."

"I agree with you," I said.

"All right. Before we go any further, Doctor, there's somebody else. My marriage to Donald has been a mistake. I've been the last to know it. But I know it now. Are you stunned?"

"Not really," I said. "I really don't know enough about you to be stunned."

"That's good. That's good. I guess he told you I'm a dancer. It's my whole life. I mean, I was a dancer when he met me. With the New York City Ballet Company. And I still am, even though I don't dance because of the MS. I'll always be a dancer. I guess I should get that straight."

So she knew. I made no mention of the MS so as to see how she fitted this fact of her existence into her outlook.

I told her, "Yes, your husband did say that you were a dancer. And I do understand what you're saying. There's no contradiction."

"Good, because that's important. I was twenty-two when I met him. He came on very strong. Very strong. Not that I blame him, but he came on very strong. I shouldn't have gotten involved with him. He gave me everything he could. He would pick me up after performances. He would talk to me about anything that mattered to me. But my friends were right. It was ridiculous. I just didn't know it."

"Why ridiculous?" I asked, I thought innocently.

"You don't believe me." She seemed alive with fire and passion.

"Donna, I didn't say that at all. I'm just trying to follow you. I'm not doubting anything you say."

She folded her arms in front of her. "Can I tell you a story?"

"Sure."

"One day, I'd known him about three months, there was a ballet I love called *Medea,* by a Danish choreographer. The company had done it years ago. Melissa Hayden was brilliant in the role. Jacques D'Amboise and Violette Verdy. Since those three, we hadn't done it. Mr. B's mind was on other things.

"Anyhow, I had the musical score, and the ballet mistress remembered most of it, and we, three of us, rehearsed it and did it for a bunch of the kids. They liked it, it was fun, but there were suggestions, naturally.

"Then Donald came in and stopped everything and gave one of those English lectures on the myth of Medea and what people said about it. Everyone had to stop and listen. And he said, he said that unless we really researched the story and the interpretations, we shouldn't be doing it. *We* shouldn't do it. I was so embarrassed, in front of everyone. I was mortified. They thought he was crazy.

"I know what you mean."

"He was *always* embarrassing me—embarrassing me where it counted most."

"It's interesting that you married him," I commented. "Do you think you were in love with him for a while?"

"That's a good question. I'm not sure. I thought I should be. At first I thought he was quaint. I wasn't sure. He knew so much. I never went to college, you know. I thought I should be. He knew a lot, but he hated anything physical. Sexually, well, it didn't work too well, but I thought it was me. I think he brainwashed me."

"That's a strong statement," I said.

"Maybe it is. But he had strong opinions. The kids would walk home. He didn't want me going with them. He said it was a dangerous neighborhood. Oh, I don't know. He's always comparing one dancer to another, or one ballet to another, this one is better than that. Are you following me at all?"

"I am. I really am."

Her face suddenly clouded in sadness. "Oh, I don't know. It was my own fault. But I never should have moved away from my friends, even if I couldn't dance anymore, because of the MS."

"I gather that you and he never discuss the MS," I said. It seemed a violation for me to tell her outright that he'd thought she didn't know about it.

"No. We never do. I think it's very painful for him. He hates the idea of being weak or old or crippled or sick—or dying."

So it was *him*. I could believe that. That story he'd told of leaving his mother's death to his brother. His very hatred of himself for getting older, which made him such a travesty to his friends, that had led him to her in the first place.

"Yes, he would never mention it. Maybe he thinks I don't know. I don't know what he thinks. But Bruce doesn't care, and we talk about it. We talk about everything."

"Bruce?"

"Yes. I told you there was somebody else. I've been seeing Bruce for six months. He's shy. He's not so sure of himself. He's thirty-two, but he's not so sure of himself. Maybe that's why I love him.'

"He's a dancer?" I asked.

"No. He works on sets. At first I felt guilty seeing Bruce. I drive to his house, in his car, an old beat-up Ford." She smiled. "My husband doesn't know I park it right in the neighborhood. He doesn't even want me to drive."

"You don't have sex with your husband anymore?" I asked.

"I can't have sex with him. No. Even though he's my husband, I would feel unfaithful at this point. I never enjoyed sex until Bruce. I'm very inexperienced, actually. Do you think I'm a terrible person?"

"That didn't cross my mind."

"I guess I'll have to tell him it's over," she said.

I told her, "If it is, if it really is, you will when you want to."

There was a long silence, which I broke by saying, "It's one of those things, like tying your shoelace. After a certain age, no one can do it for you."

She laughed. The darkness left her face as she said, "I was afraid you'd be like Donald. But you're not. Not at all. Do you like ballet?"

"I do. But I really don't go very often."

She smiled. "I don't either. Not enough. But I'm going to."

She told me a little about her childhood. She'd always been close to her father. He'd accepted the marriage, but "he was

never fond of Donald." Then she said, "Well, I guess I've got
to untie my shoelace."

I must have looked at her in befuddlement, because she
hastened to add, "You're the one who said that. I mean, I
guess I have to tell my husband it's over. Maybe we could
come here together, and I could tell him then."

I thought about that one. "No," I told her after a while.
"This isn't really a place to make big moves in your life. That's
something *you* really have to do. Just you and him, together."

She squinted, as if in disappointment. "But suppose, I
mean, maybe . . . I mean maybe afterward, if I have to, can I
see you?"

It didn't seem that I could promise that, at least not on the
spot. It would be wrong to see both of them if they were sepa-
rating—he'd be coming half to find out about her, and my
work with her would be contaminated by my seeing him regularly. After all, he had prior claim, if he wanted to stake it. It
was bad enough that he was losing her. I didn't feel I had the
right to drop out of his life, inexorably, at the same time. But
maybe if they were still together, no matter what loomed in
their future, I could see them together . . . I didn't have time
to think it through, but gave her my best answer.

"Well, maybe before you break up, if you really are going
to, and if you both want to, I could see you both, if it would
help."

She told me, "I think it really might. Would it be okay?"

I assured her it would. But when she left my office, I still
wouldn't have bet with certainty that she'd be leaving. Such is
the strength of unseen ties, and unseen fears, that one can
never be sure.

I got a message from him that night. "Call me back, no matter
how late, under any condition, please." His voice sounded
feeble and slow, as if he'd been stabbed.

When I reached him, he said, "Doctor, I don't know what
you said to her. But she told me she doesn't love me anymore.
She wants to leave."

All I could say was, "Really!"

"What did you tell her about me? Did you tell her to walk out?"

"Absolutely not," I assured him.

"I'm calling you because she promised to see you with me. Can we possibly make it right away? It's very important."

"Is she there now? We can figure out a time," I said.

"No, she isn't. We had a terrible argument, one of our worst. She's out tonight. She's sleeping at a friend's. But she promised that if I could reach you and set up a time, she'd be there. She'll be calling me in the morning."

Instinctively, I scheduled them to come in after my last patient the following day. It wasn't shaping up like the kind of session where one could stop abruptly. After I hung up, I realized what an eternity it would be for him until he saw her again. I wondered if he had any idea that she was with another man, which she almost surely was. She had all the leverage now.

They came in less than a minute apart, and sat on opposite sides of my couch. She wore a frilly green dress, had a lot of makeup on, and was in high-heeled shoes. She looked much prettier than she had, and by contrast, he looked much older and without resources. He seemed rumpled. He had drawn his youth from her breath, and it was there no longer.

He glanced over at her, almost as if he wasn't sure he knew her. He began with a curious formality. "It's not important what you said last night. What is important is that you're very unhappy, and you want me to change."

Again he looked toward her, but she kept gazing straight ahead. He went on, as if she were there with him, completely. "And there are many ways in which I *should* change," he announced.

"I don't want you to change," she said sharply. "Stay exactly the way you are."

"Yes, you do, darling," he reminded her. "You said there was a lot wrong with me. And you're right. May I explain—"

"Your explanations make me sick," she said flatly, still not looking at him.

Then, very softly to me, she said, "Doctor, I tried to tell him last night that it just wasn't working. I said, 'Donald, I've been very unhappy. It just isn't working for me.'

"But every time I tried to talk, he said, 'Darling, you're very troubled.' He wouldn't hear me. Oh God, he wouldn't hear me! It's impossible to feel sorry for him."

She covered her face with her hands. A moment later she removed them, and asked me for a glass of water.

I left the room and came back with one. She took it and drank while he waited patiently. His vacant, dismal look somehow made me think of a home, once boisterous but now gloomy because the children have come of age and moved out.

A long silence followed.

He broke it, "I know I'm not the easiest person—"

"Hah!" she said. "That's a laugh."

"I was starting to say something, darling."

"Say whatever you want."

"Darling, please let me finish," he pleaded.

"I'm sick of your finishing. I'm sick of your explaining. Your explanations make me sick."

He spoke with a modulation, strange for one who felt that his whole life was at stake. "But I *am* worried about you, and I want to change." He leaned toward her and extended his hand, as if to rub her back. She retreated stiffly out of his reach.

However, he pretended not to notice and went on. "Darling, you've changed since we met. *You* have changed considerably. You've mellowed and learned and evolved. You've mastered so much. Yes, darling, you have. Don't you think that I . . . that I . . . deserve the same chance? . . . Don't I?" His eyes were clouded with tears.

She softened for an instant. But she held fast. She said sharply, "Don't worry. I'm not angry with you. I'm just sick of being your dream, of getting marks from you. I'm sick of your twitch, of your not mentioning it. Did Samuel Johnson mention his terrible twitch? It was so ugly that parents wouldn't even let their kids go to his classes. You're not so perfect!"

"Darling," he sought to appease her, "I realize that. I realize it. I realize it more than ever."

I was still stunned at the revelation that Johnson, his hero, had a terrible twitch, and I had to wrest myself away from that, to listen, as she went on.

"Now I know what you meant, that the past is so great. You're from the past. *You are.* Back in the eighteenth century, or whenever it was, when men would compliment their wives, and protect them. Big shots, cheating them out of the big things. Everybody was like you back then. But not anymore. You don't love me. Come off it."

Suddenly he was crying like a baby. "Darling," I think he was saying, "doubt my strength. I doubt it, too. But don't doubt my love. Please, don't doubt my love."

I looked over at her, and she was crying too. But she pulled out a handkerchief and recomposed herself. Even before she stood up, I realized that her agenda was to end it, here and now. This whole session was a formality, an official ending, as if written in the fancy calligraphy of the eighteenth century, his favorite: "With deepest regards. Always. Your affectionate servant. Good-bye."

"Thank you, Doctor," she said to me. "I'm leaving. I've had enough."

And to him. "I won't be home. I'm not coming home anymore. I'll send some people for my things." Her pocketbook had spilled some of its contents onto the couch, and as he started to help her collect the assemblage of lipstick, compact, keys, and change, she said icily, "Thank you. Don't bother."

I followed her to the door, and for the first time saw the slight limp. Perhaps the tension had brought it out.

He was sitting there inertly when I got back. "Doctor, I have the terrible feeling that this is the beginning of the end for me," he said. "Maybe I should see you for a while, if it would be all right."

"Of course," I said. "I expect you to. But let's think of it as just the beginning."

It wasn't easy bracing him. For months, he kept hoping Donna would come back. He had several dreams in which she whispered to him that she loved him, and told him that she'd only been trying to scare him. Why hadn't she sent her friends over to pick up her belongings? he asked me. I refused to speculate.

Then, finally he did get such a call, and they came over. Generously, he added some items that were truly his but that she'd always loved. Or was it generous? Perhaps he was still hoping she'd see the light. Even after that, he would rush to the phone when it rang, expecting to hear her voice.

He often rationalized, saying not that he wanted her back, but that he was worried about her health. Not that she couldn't take care of herself. But it tortured him that he didn't have her phone number and address so that he could call her just to make sure she was okay. "No matter what she does with her life, I have to know that. Suppose some day she gets into real trouble, how will I know?"

Apparently, she'd mentioned the MS during their final argument—the very first doctor had told her. When she'd told him, Donald had been taken aback, even felt betrayed by that doctor. But now he was glad she knew. "And suppose the MS gets worse?" But, obviously, she knew how to reach him and simply didn't want to.

Then the divorce papers came. He signed without delay, being resolved not to deter her. Within days, he started writing again, though he saw no connection between this release from her and his having his own life back again.

In his better moments, he regaled me with literary stories and references, but he was the Professor through and through, complimenting me for knowing things, "That's good, that's good," or asking with surprise where I had acquired some fact.

With a twinkle, he would ask me what a word meant, or recommend some book or method of self-improvement. He would sometimes use an obscure word, and then define it, or worse yet, ask me if I knew what it meant.

I played into his system, and he liked me. When he lectured me, though, I felt a tinge of repugnance. I also felt that I should listen, and for a time be his junior, since he had so little left. As we got to know each other better, I studied him. Soon I would need a therapeutic strategy, but at this stage, keeping him afloat was more than enough purpose for me.

Here was an incredibly lonely man, whose professorial style could at best attain admiration from others—never love or genuine sympathy. He was a man alone in the pitchy night, spouting aphorisms, while others, despairing of perfection and of eternity, embraced and comforted each other. What he needed was love, or better yet, simple understanding and acceptance. But early in his life, having decided that he was unworthy of it, he had settled for admiration, for fame—the pursuit of which had separated him more and more from ordinary people, who were far ahead of him.

His mother, it turned out, was a cruel woman, who never touched him physically and spoke admiringly only about highly accomplished people. At a very early age, he had dreamed of writing a masterpiece and winning her that way, his only way.

I set myself to revealing to him, as quickly as I could, how he kept people at bay, crushing them by his erudition. He could never become God, but he could take possession of his weaknesses, allow them to be seen, and prove to himself, once and for all, that they were not disqualifying. An important step was his facing his friends, including some he had renounced, and telling them that his marriage was over. Rather than make up an excuse, it would be better to say simply, "It didn't work."

He was stunned that this proved good enough. Henry Lefert, whom he had known since college days, had a few laughs at his expense. But that was all part of living. Meanwhile, each time he did something condescending—acting surprised that I knew something, or defining a word for me unasked, or speechifying—I pointed it out. By that time, I truly no longer felt put down, but observed to him that other people, who knew him less well, would.

For some reason that I never understood, the facial tic disappeared. I had postponed mentioning it, because he seemed

too vulnerable, but I'd planned to have a neurologist examine
him eventually. When I finally asked him about it, and observed that I hadn't seen it lately, he told me that it had begun
when he was in his twenties and working on his Ph.D. thesis.
A few of his friends had noticed it. It had disappeared, then
returned toward the end of his second marriage.

"Actually," he explained, "this twitching or jerking of my
facial muscles became most pronounced when things started
going sour with Donna."

If it did return, he could use it as an indication that he was
under excessive pressure, I observed.

Later we discovered a curious correlation. The more completely he sought to control a situation, or another person, as
in graduate school or when he'd felt Donna slipping away, the
more blatant his facial tic became. His relinquishing sovereign
control over outcomes guaranteed that the tic would disappear.

Why a facial tic and not some other symptom? That we will
never know. Freud often commented that one of the impon-
derables in many cases is what he called the patient's "choice
of symptoms." But remembering Donna's comment that Samuel
Johnson suffered from a facial tic, I bought a recent biography
of Johnson, and read it avidly. After all, Donald's tic had first
become manifest during his studies of Johnson, and it is well
documented that many tics are learned by imitation.

What is technically called "echokinesis" refers to stereo-
typed imitation of another person's movements, and thus many
tics run in families. If this was, indeed, a case of echokinesis,
it had the miraculous extra feature that the copying was done
not from someone the person saw, but from someone the person had read about—a case of echokinesis that had taken
place over a span of two centuries.

It took several years for Donald to soften his approach, to
allow people to know him, to touch him. It seemed an irony
that Donald, awkward, elderly in style, a perfectionist, sought
the exact opposite of all these traits in the woman he had
loved. He had sought consummate inspiration in the grace of
the dancer, the optimism, the humor, the innocence that he
would never accept in himself.

But many of us seek in lovers traits that we ourselves do not embody. We import what we do not produce. What made Donald so interesting to me, in the end, was not his irrationality or his striving, but his belief that he could control all the elements. Only as he gave up this belief, and allowed himself the innocence and optimism he had always denied himself, could he give a woman a real place in his life. The youthful gazing into the future—innocently and optimistically—would have to be his own.

I became relentless at showing him how he sought control over people. A man who can't be interrupted is a man that nobody likes. Though I often sounded harsh to him, I was begging him to come back to us mortals. Slowly I began to feel more relaxed with him, less confined and better able to breathe. He was giving me space. Some of his old friends returned, and he made a few new ones. He went on with his scholarly writing.

He saw Donna again, only by accident—in the street, on a few occasions, and once when he went to the ballet with a woman friend. They were cordial, though his heart beat fast. He came to remember her, not as the greatest failure of his life, but as his first childhood sweetheart, which in a sense she was.

UNFINISHED SYMPHONY

Donald T was too intense for the world. Or more precisely, the world, since cooling down, had lost the fervor that Donald required of it. An oversized, black-haired man in his sixties, he kept his beard too precisely cut, and he wore dark, very well-tailored suits.

He recounted with childlike animation the great and terrible things that had happened during his life. He had been a Marine and loved it, especially Iwo Jima; he still went to the yearly reunions of his division, meeting with men who would accept no less than victory. The death that dwindled the ranks of those who appeared each year was the same enemy, the same death, that had killed so many of his buddies in the South Pacific. He goddamn well wouldn't yield to fear of it. Let it come when it would come.

As he went on, you could see that he was a man of vast culture. He knew history and law, especially that of years gone by. And he knew music and loved it. Loved it? That was an understatement. His love of music was one reason he had come to see me. It had confronted him with an enemy bigger than the "Hibernian bear," the animal, he informed me, most feared by Roman soldiers, the centurions who extended Julius Caesar's realm.

This enemy was so great because, like death, you couldn't fight it. The enemy was noise. Not just any noise, but the infuriating, interruptive, sound of a page rustling four feet in front of him. These pages were being turned by a little, white-haired, elderly lady on alternate Saturday evenings, but just at those zeniths that Donald had waited for, while the great orchestras of the world were playing the music that matched his intensity, that understood him, that even anticipated him, that gave him life.

The *Tannhäuser* Overture interrupted! Haydn's *Clock* Symphony marred by extra sounds, unwanted sounds, *loathsome* sounds—irritating turnings of pages of something (was it a program or an actual score?) that not only did their mischief like stab wounds, but sent my new patient into a series of fantasies of revenge against someone so brutal, so uncaring, as to destroy what he had waited longingly for over the two-week period since the last concert.

For Donald, the interval was not that refractory period between Handel and Bach, when he and his wife would chat with other couples while the orchestra rested. (Six of them, good friends for many years, had season tickets and all were great music lovers.) For Donald the real interval was that two-week span between concerts when he would anticipate the coming to New York City of Von Karajan or Colin Davis or some other great conductor who would cast his brief spell over the hushed assemblage and who would transport my patient into the place of beauty and truth and harmony where all was right and ideal, and which, especially when the Chicago Symphony Orchestra played Wagner, would send him home drenched in tears.

But now, instead of Mozart's Clarinet Concerto running through his head, every note of it, Donald was haunted by the apprehension of the white-haired lady turning pages. He was tough enough on the big things. He had braved infantile paralysis with his young son, spending every day with him keeping up his son's good cheer. He had influenced his local PTA and had made runways for wheelchairs a requirement in the state, though his son didn't need one. Eventually, thanks to Donald's dauntless optimism, his son had become a confident professional man who had just married. My patient had braved bad times too, in his hardware store, reading the classics and listening to music when no customers were there. Now he was successful. He loved Nancy, the woman he'd married three years after his first wife had died of breast cancer, though music especially summoned up his deceased wife's memory, renewing his desire for her to be with him and to hear it.

The big question in his life now was whether he should sell the hardware store and retire. There were the usual problems with employees, but business remained good and he loved the dealings. He told me one of his chief reasons for coming to therapy was for help in making that decision. His wife thought he was overreacting to problems that arose in the store, but he wondered if he wouldn't be better off without the strain.

Of course, in the store and elsewhere, the problem was his uncontrollable anger and need for perfection, a sense of himself as cheated, which lay too near the surface, a readiness for rage that had precipitated him into several fistfights with customers who he thought were rude. Ultimately, I would have to understand the rage, the disillusionment that had doubtless given rise to it, the sense of something undone, something discordant within him that gave even small frustrations their incendiary power.

But, as Donald kept reminding me, there was an immediate problem, one that he had to solve or somehow dispose of, one that demanded attention. Apparently, the woman in front of him, like my patient himself, owned an expensive yearly subscription and would renew it perennially. She would sit directly in front of him until one of them died. When he called me, he had been beset by thoughts of strangling that diminutive lady with the white hair, whose rustling of pages was doing far more mischief to his brain that she could ever dream.

Of course, he wouldn't actually murder her. His obsessive

visions of her during the start of that last interval had, from the moment he called me, given way to the more benign imaginings that she would just die on her own. There would be absolute silence while the sad and stately Clarinet Concerto, K. 622, held the room in its sway. He would wait for the page to rustle, but nothing. He would wait and wonder. Still nothing. At last he would enter the serenity of the music (a piece that, he informed me, was Mozart's real requiem for himself, as opposed to the one known officially as the *Requiem*.)

When the lights went on the people would rise, but that white-haired head would remain resting on the back of the chair in front of him. Someone would peer over at her. "Are you all right, dear?"

"Lady, you okay?"

"She's dead," someone else would say flatly, as my patient headed for the aisle smirking. Donald had done it. And if God loved music, He would not blame him. And so her unfortunate death, besides being timely, would be a reaffirmation of God, of justice, and of music. Not incidentally, it would also cleanse his tickets to the rest of the concerts that season, and those he would get when renewing his subscription over the years to come.

"I told my wife this fantasy. She says something must be wrong with me, and I know there is," he admitted.

In the next session he went into more detail about what his hardware store meant to him. He had built it from scratch. While he had worked tirelessly, the Connecticut town he had toiled in had grown up around him. His very property had multiplied fivefold in value. Now his business was flourishing, thanks to his expertise and the growth of the town. He could unload his store at a huge profit. The question was, should he?

He told me about the irksome aspects of his work, the unwarranted complaints about his prices, which were more than fair. He trembled when he started talking about one very wealthy customer, with a fine colonial house on a nearby estate, who would string him along on a bill for some small amount not worth a lawyer. Recently, my patient had fantasies of storming the man's home with a marshal and snatching an oil painting or two done by a grand master while the stingy millionaire looked on aghast. "I'll hold this until you send me my seventy-five dollars plus interest. And until you apologize," Donald would tell him.

But the law was worse than slow, it was costly, and "those millionaire skinflints probably have batteries of high-powered advocates there to help them steal."

"Aside from those occasional injustices, do you like running the store?" I asked.

His answer was strange. "My wife says I do, and I guess I do. Of course." Then he seemed to build up steam as he described what he did. "There are widows, people whose families I've known for forty years. I've got a couple of good college kids working for me. It's family. The people in the town need me, they *really* need me."

Then suddenly he drew his lips back and bared his teeth like a trapped animal. "But those bastards. It only takes a few bastards. Sometimes one. They should be taken out and shot. Court-martialed and shot."

He seemed incapable of expressing opposition, or even conceiving of it, unless it was violent. And because he would not permit himself to indulge in such force and had no alternative, he was peculiarly helpless, bully-able, and at everyone's mercy.

He commented, "I'd shoot them myself if I could."

"Would you?"

"Yes, if they were court-martialed and it was my job. With pleasure. When I see those people in the street who owe me money—" he broke off the thought. "They destroy the town, they destroy everything."

A little later I asked him, "How does Nancy feel about your retiring?"

"She says I'd be lost without the store. She says I love it, even the arguments. She thinks that I love the involvement, but she's wrong. Not that kind of involvement. She doesn't realize . . . So what do I do about the white-haired lady? I guess I can't smash her with a tire iron, can I?"

He looked into my eyes as if hoping I'd say something like, "Go to it. You're in the right. I'll declare you legally insane, and you'll beat the rap."

As he anxiously rubbed his beard with his hand, I could feel his anguish over having an option that was so alive in his mind that he needed energy to defeat it, not just once but over and over again. It was as if that little lady of seventy or so was a messenger to his brain, a marathon runner who'd come streaking down a long, winding road to declare to the teeming city of his mind, "The world is imperfect, full of blotches and blemishes. See! Here is one. And worse than merely in the world, this blemish is in your *ideal world*. There are blotches in the world of Wagner, in that of Mozart, in Haydn's *Clock* Symphony, there are irregularities in time itself, do you hear, in time itself, which supposedly heals all wounds."

I wondered why this man, so intense, so romantic, lived so much in the ideal world or rather in so fragile an ideal world, one in which any hint of static was louder than perfect musical forms. How much he must have suffered in the past to have required such a flight into the ideal, and how his torment must have followed him, like the cruel hounds of hell chasing him right through the unstable paradise he had sought to erect on earth. Why was his outer layer so permeable?

I would have to learn this, to learn how to help him keep his heaven but develop membranes to protect it.

Shortly before the session ended, on a whim I asked him, "So what did the white-haired lady say when you told her not to turn the pages?"

"Well, I didn't really ask her, I just gave her a look."

"You never asked her?" Now I was the one aghast. "Do you think you should?"

He shrugged his shoulders. "She knows. She's got to know. There's no point to it. She just doesn't give a damn."

Hard as it was for me to absorb it, I realized that he was afraid to ask, afraid perhaps because then the humiliation would be complete. This man, with all his power of mind, of imagination, and of body had no idea how to use modicums of force, scintillas of energy, to adjust the real world. He was in danger of throwing everything away, rather than seek to adjust things rationally.

The next week Donald told me that he'd been very agitated, and a friend had recommended a psychiatrist who might give him something to calm him. I was alarmed. I knew there were certain physicians who would solve his problem much the way ordinary drug pushers do in schoolyards. "Things are tough, huh," the streetwise pushers say understandingly. "You'll like this. Straight from Colombia. No markup. You'll be in *heaven*." The physicians in question put it differently, but their gist is the same. "You're suffering from an impulse disorder. Anxiety reaction. Very acute. DSM. Three hundred-oh-two psychologically. I've seen a number of these cases. Try this. It's called Xanax. I'm sure it will help you." That last "I'm sure . . ." is part of the treatment, a placebo sentence, to make doubly sure that the Xanax, or whatever the drug-of-the-day happens to be, gets its full chance to set up an extra barrier between life, and pain.

Sure enough, when Donald told me the psychiatrist's name it was familiar. I'd know the man somewhat, a primping character, given to making arrogant assertions. I could still see him, holding forth in hospital conferences, talking about the psychodynamics of a patient he'd never actually seen, full of jargon. I remembered him sneaking out a chapstick, guiltily, and rubbing his lips with it when he thought no one was looking. He was afraid to do it openly, as if it were connected with his preparing to kiss someone on a big date. Dr.——was a trivial character if there ever was one, a minor player, especially alongside my patient, whose intensity was a challenge, not merely an obstacle.

Although so-called antidepressants are often useful, I was against them here. Under their effect, my patient might no

longer be bothered by the turning of a page. He could take
solace in that, but neither would he weep at the music or be
transported by it. Along with the rustling of the page, the music itself would be gone. And how could he possibly determine
the value of keeping his hardware store, answer the big question that had brought him into treatment, if he didn't have
access to his feelings?

I offered him the name of a different physician, a more con-
servative one. But then I told him that I saw tranquilizers as
only a last resort, and, I hoped, an unnecessary one.

"That's how I feel, Doctor," he replied at once. I could see
that he felt relieved. I did too.

Actually, he enjoyed the complexity of running his store, his
dealings with merchandisers, the constant influx of new kinds
of tools and gadgets, his giving quick explanations to customers on how to use them, his encyclopedic knowledge of where
everything was. He could in a wink answer his employees'
questions about which jack or Phillips-head or bulb or screw
was right for some function, and about where to find it.

He writhed only at the thought of those occasional customers—not the openly disgruntled ones, he could handle them,
but the opulent, disdainful people who took for granted his
store and his services. They would thanklessly march over him
as if he were the earth itself, misusing him as if he were there
only for them. He assured me that he had money. He wanted
to travel. Why should he go on submitting to them?

His wife had once again cautioned against his giving it all
up on the spot. "Donald, what will you do? You love it, Donald. You'd be lost if you were home all day."

Slowly I saw that his helplessness in the store was akin to
that at Lincoln Center. He seemed without recourse when a
customer who owed him money came into his store for some
item and didn't offer to pay the amount still owed.

"Do you bring it up?" I asked him.

"No. Oh no, I never do that," Donald said.

"Not even with those customers about whom you have fantasies of going to their home to seize their goods?"

"No, never. I wouldn't give them the satisfaction. I'd rather blow up their car."

"Why's that?"

"I'd look poor and needy to them. That's just what they want. Do you think I should sell the store, Doctor?"

"You'll know what you really want to do when you understand yourself better." I wasn't being evasive, it was the truth, though it perhaps seemed as if I were ducking the question.

I commented, "It sounds as if those customers are just like the lady who turns the pages. Your nemesis. You never really told her to stop."

"I gave her some dirty looks at intermission."

"That's it? She might not know what they were for."

"Come on," he responded. "She knows she's disturbing us. No one else does that."

"And suppose she doesn't know *how*."

"She knows."

Poor, decent, violent-minded Donald could express aggression but not in small doses. Like a single nerve fiber, he was all or nothing—in his case, murder or silence. He was a giant so afraid of his own aggression, of crashing into those who blocked his path, that he routinely submitted as if he were a helpless dwarf. And because his very outrage was itself grotesque, he could do nothing with it except be consumed by it. But he could learn . . .

He seemed deep in thought, and I was mulling over how to surface the problem when I sprang back in alarm. He was bellowing, "That goddamned fucking woman, whoever she is . . . I *know* what I've got to do."

"What's that?" I asked.

"Return the tickets. Get my money back for the rest of the subscription."

I said something, but he didn't hear me. He was doing calculations in his head.

Then, mostly to himself, he muttered, "That's four hundred and twenty-two dollars they owe Nancy and me. I'll get it. That's all. I'll get it."

He nodded silently, firming up his resolution, and then looked straight at me. "I'll get it. That's all. But suppose they don't give it to me?"

"What do you mean?" I asked him.

"I mean, suppose I go and complain and say how *impossible* it is and how much this means to me, and they still won't give me the money."

"Who?"

"Whoever's at Lincoln Center. Some official. Some petty bureaucrat, I don't know who. You know, some clerk, probably a woman, most of them are. She'll see that I'm in a spot, I mean I'm *compromised*, and just because I'm in a spot, I mean *stuck* with the tickets, she'll say no. Maybe she's instructed to say no. I mean, why would they be kind enough to give us back our money? This is New York City, you know. Nobody gives anything away here. I mean, I can imagine her saying, some woman of fifty in a blue suit with a hat, behind some desk, I can just hear her saying, "Too bad, boy! You bought the tickets, you live with them." Why should she do *me* a favor? Did life do *her* any favors? Apparently not, or she wouldn't be behind some desk carrying out orders, you know what I mean?"

Now he was trembling, his face red, his Adam's apple bulging, but his fists were not clenched. There was no sign that he would convert his frenzy into any form of violent action. Instead, he seemed almost on the brink of getting a heart attack, so divided was he by his own fury clashing with his anticipation of injury and his feeling of futility. I had the visual image of him splitting in half.

"Come on, Donald. How do you know they'll refuse?"

"Goddamn it, they will. They never make things that easy. As soon as I explain the problem to that executive, man or woman, I know what the person will say. He'll say, or she'll say, 'Well, you bought the tickets. The season's almost half over. What do you want us to do? It's *your* problem after all. We don't want to lose the money on a real purchase. It's too late in the season to find anyone else for those tickets.' Well, the hell with them!"

I nodded and started to say something.

But my patient was already on his feet. "Look, it's six blocks from here. The box office is open. I'm going over there right now. I'm going to talk to them, I've *got* to."

"But—" I tried again. "Donald, we ought to *talk* about this."

"No. Thank you," he said. "You've been very helpful. I'm clear about what I *have* to do next."

And with that, he stormed out as if he were staking his claim for the good guys on Iwo Jima.

The next session, even before he sat down, I knew that something major had happened. He took pains to fold his trousers under him, preserving the crease, a thing he had never done before. Instead of asking solicitously how my week was, a habit of his, he shook his head sadly. He seemed absorbed in a contemplative calm, as if he had found some answer.

"I'm not giving up the store," he informed me quietly. "I'll find a way to live with it. I get too much out of it."

I nodded, to show I understood. "What led you to that conclusion?" I asked.

"Oh, nothing special. Just thinking about it."

But there was more. I had no idea what, but clearly some notch in the tumbler had been turned and the safe had opened, revealing at least some of its contents.

"Uh-huh," I said, assimilating his mood and waiting for him to go on.

There was a pensive silence, as if he was considering changing the subject.

"By the way, what about these tickets?" I asked.

To my astonishment, I thought I saw a veil of moisture cover his eyes.

"Oh, them," he responded matter-of-factly. "They took them back. That's all."

"How did it go?"

Apparently he had rushed to the box office and stood on

line, waiting almost apoplectically for his turn. The ticket
agent was a brown-haired college girl, presumably a student, a
few years younger than his own daughter. She was quiet, effi-
cient, and very busy with customers.

While waiting on line, Donald's mind churned with expectation. He did everything but grab the cage like Gargantua while
preparing his plea for reimbursement. His rehearsed diatribe
included such statements as "This lady who sits in front me is
a *maniac*." "We've *got* to get our money back." "It's
unbearable." "Please, have mercy!" "Who do I talk to if not to
you?"

But Donald never got that far. When he finally reached the
booth, he had begun, "I have this subscription for two, and
there are five more Saturday nights on it, and it just isn't possible—"

The college girl had interrupted. "You'd like to return
them?" she asked politely.

"Well, yes. I would."

"Oh, that will be fine. Leave us your name and address. We
have a thousand people waiting for those tickets. You'll have
the money by Friday. Would you step over there, please, and
fill out this form, and we'll give you a receipt."

He'd stepped away from the long line, and she'd immediately begun talking to the next customer.

"And how did you *feel* at that moment?" I asked him.

"Relief? I felt tremendous relief."

But I could surmise even then that there had been something unusual. Even before he'd returned the form, he'd had a
foretaste of sorrow. The giant, the Wagnerian adversary that
he'd rehearsed for, turned out to be merely a bright, honest,
capable schoolgirl, not at all interested in his nightmares or in
his pulsating sense of injury. She had given him exactly what
he had wanted. Or had she?

On his way through the lobby, it crossed Donald's mind for
the first time that he was not going to hear the Chicago Symphony Orchestra at all that season. Would they return next
year? Probably. He hoped they would. And Isaac Stern? Gone

too. Rampal? Maybe there were still tickets for him. Individual ones if not two together. He'd rushed back and waited on line once more, though he'd burned with embarrassment. He would salvage something. But no: "Sorry sir. Those performances are all sold out."

"Sold out!" The words resounded through his mind as he drove back to Connecticut. "Over. Sold out. Dead. Used to be. Not to be."

He'd turned the radio on and recognized Rossini at once. Too bright for the moment. He switched it off. When later it occurred to him that the white-haired lady would be there with the masters every other Saturday, he was surprised to discover that his anger toward her was gone. "It wasn't her, it was *me*," he'd thought. "Good luck to her. May she live forever!"

At least one thing was clear. He would keep his store, he would delight in his storehouse of items, in his ability to understand new gadgets, in his memory, and above all, in the daily exchanges that made his life full. No handful of annoying individuals would cheat him of that. He had too much to live for.

Next year Donald would send in his subscription request early. There would be other concerts, many of them. He would learn to push his way forward softly, but only by staying in the real world long enough to make that discovery.

The Mathematician

Peter K was the first person on earth ever to invert a skew symmetric matrix by pressing a button—that is, he was the first to develop a program for computers to do so. Now Peter stood trembling in front of a dozen select leaders at the brokerage firm that employed him and demonstrated his accomplishment.

His witnesses were nearly all men, vice-presidents or better in the multibillion-dollar firm, in custom-made gray chalk-stripe suits and ninety-five-dollar silk ties and wing-tip shoes. They sat in stuffed, upholstered chairs, in a thickly carpeted, wood-paneled room, trying to pay attention but understanding nothing, as Peter, a twenty-eight-thousand-dollar-a-year man, gave them a presentation fit only for university professors, and even then, only for specialists in the then newly invented field of computer science.

Peter, a squat, thirty-eight-year-old man with unruly hair, was in the vanguard of applied mathematics. Still, he sweated profusely in his beige sleeveless sweater over his white shirt and brown tie, and he stammered and repeated himself. He might as well have let all his verbalizations stand, right or wrong, instead

of repeating axioms, propositions, theorems. To those movers of
modern society, Peter was perfect—a mathematical genius
whom they could boast about to clients at lunch or over the
phone. Or on the company plane, they could casually pass the
four-page glossy on Peter's work, put out at great cost by
the company, to some representative of a client company.

No one understood a word or a term or a symbol, but the
inversion of matrices by machine was at the cutting edge of
stock-market science. This they had been told. Now the
moguls puffed on their cigars and listened courteously as Peter
reviewed what he had done and why, and when it was clear he
had finished, they applauded politely.

At the end of his presentation, Peter almost fell down. He
had misused the word "cofactor" twice—that is, he had used
the word as Niels Abel and Leopold Kronecker might have in
the last century, and he had failed to state that his system held
for negative skew symmetric matrices as well as merely for
positive ones. The journal *Psychometrika* would insist that he
clarify that. Suppose the boss, the soft-spoken, mustached,
former army general, constantly in the news, had realized his
mistake. But no, mercifully, General——came over after the
twelve-minute presentation and shook his hand. "And no one
ever did that before?" the general asked.

"No sir. It's not in the literature. I developed a certain
transformation using Jacobeans to allow for—"

"I understand. Congratulations," exclaimed the general.
"Do you drink?"

An assistant who had overheard all this took the question as
a command and hurried toward the refrigerator in the corner of
the room, a glorious, old-fashioned enclave with egg-and-dart
moldings and a chandelier, and club chairs around a solid oak
coffee table—all indicating how long the company had been
there and would be there.

"No, I don't drink, sir," said Peter. "I have very high blood
pressure. Was it all right?"

"All right! It was excellent! Our downstairs staff says you're
the best thing that ever happened to us." The general turned to

one of his top executives, a million-a-year man. "Don't let Pru
Bache steal this fellow, whatever you do."

"No sir," said the tall, redheaded Irishman. Peter was the
only Jew in the room, and was dimly conscious of it. But they
treated him well, and he was not the sort to compare himself
with anyone else, or his salary with another person's.

Lunch, in the executive dining room, with all those waiters
hovering behind him, observing his table manners, was a
nightmare for Peter. Recalling his wife Emily's advice, he
tried to finish slower than usual, but could do so only at the
cost of downing a few bites of roll between mouthfuls scooped
from his plate of sole almondine with a meager portion of string
beans. He calculated that two bites of roll for every three from
his plate would clear his plate right on time with the crowd.
He had always been good at related-rates problems. Even so,
it didn't compare with the comfort of eating in the cafeteria.

That evening on the A-train home he did some jottings. Anyone who wished to peer over at them would have seen Fortran
language, Greek symbols, vectors and matrices, written with
love on a yellow pad. But Peter was sweating. The previous
day he had promised a computer solution to a problem in from
the Chicago branch. A vice-president had come by after leaving it with him for no more than a half hour.

"How long will it take?"

Peter had responded nervously, "Three weeks."

Later, in my office, he assured me that no one in the country
could do it faster, even working overtime on his own and grappling with it on Saturdays.

But the vice-president had looked crestfallen. Not understanding one syllable of the problem except the plus sign, he
had shaken his head sadly. "Three weeks. That's a long time."

"What about the project that I'm on?" Peter had asked tremulously.

"Ginder's project? Forget that," the VP said consolingly.

Peter had peered at him through his thick, rectangular

glasses with the silver rims and, as if someone had spoken for him, had volunteered, "All right, I'll see if I can do it in two, but I'm not sure."

"That's better," the VP had assured him. "I'll tell everyone two weeks. I knew we could count on you." Then, heartily: "Kalinkowitz, you're a good man. A very good man."

I said "maybe," I didn't say "definitely," Peter had thought to himself the instant the VP was gone. But even the sound of his unspoken voice to himself as it sped through his brain was a whimper. Moments later he'd stood up reflexively and felt dizzy. That terrible high blood pressure. He'd sat down carefully and downed two more green pills with the cup of water he always kept on his desk.

On the train, recalling this, Peter reflected that he had just been robbed of the next two weeks of his life. He had promised Emily, "No more Saturdays or Sundays. Evenings with you and the kids."

"Good," she'd replied. "They miss you. You've got to be a father. *I* love you."

Now he wondered to himself, "What did I do to deserve such a loving wife? And look what I promised. I don't even know if I can get it done working day and night. Today was lost with that presentation and being sure I wouldn't stutter. And that lunch over the fancy tablecloth, and last night getting it ready. I might as well be dead— No, don't think like that."

The sooty train squeaked to a stop between stations, and Peter redoubled his efforts with his style pen on his yellow pad. The lights went out as if in protest. But Peter's mind kept producing the first of the needed axiomatic equations and when the lights came on again, he wrote down his findings.

Coming up the stairs among the people at the Hundred and Sixty-eighth Street station, he realized that he would never be allowed to finish the other project he had started. He had undertaken that one in panic, also with insufficient time allotted, his own stupid promise then too. It had been chaos at first. His

blood pressure had skyrocketed to one-fifty over ninety-one.
He had staggered home, eaten, and gone off to sleep, and then
sprung up with a set of insights at three in the morning. As if
the muse of mathematics had shown him the solution in his
sleep, he could suddenly imagine getting the job done in time.
Panic had been given way to optimism, to the mathematician's
elation, and he had become eager to work, to see the fruits of
his invention.

But now he never would. That problem was gone. They'd
called it unimportant. "Forget that one," the VP had said, and
Peter had not thought to protest, "No, *I* need that one. I solved
it. I want to see my solution—to materialize it."

He felt painfully deprived. The realization that his brain-
child had been stolen from him now boomed in his head. His
unfinished labor had been replaced by an impossible task.

The booming grew louder as he turned toward Haven Avenue near the Hudson—those were the mental images that accompanied the blood rushing through his temples as his
pressure rose to a perilous one-sixty over ninety-five.

Alarmed by his dizziness, Emily had called the family physician, who went over at once. After a brief examination, the
doctor had told him, "This is more than a physical problem.
You need psychotherapy."

Peter had at first objected to such self-indulgence. But Emily and the doctor were insistent.

As a result, Peter was in my office the next week, recounting a
life of incredible challenges that he'd consented to, virtually
volunteered for. "Even Hercules had only twelve tasks," I
thought. "This poor guy has a limitless number ahead of him,
because he keeps assigning them to himself."

He told me that his parents had come here from Poland and
had toiled for years, saving money so that he could go to college. They were proud of him. Emily and the children were
proud of him too, but he always seemed worried. He would
typically rush home from the zoo or any Sunday outing that

they'd looked forward to, and coop himself up doing problems that the Great Stock Brokerage Firm paid for.

"Suppose you simply told them at work, 'I can't do it in two weeks. I really need four,'" I inquired. "What would happen?"

"I couldn't do that." He shook his head.

"Why not?" I asked as casually as I could.

He paused in thought, squinting at me curiously. "That's interesting. I don't know."

On the good side, he was a logician to the end and would never avoid a question. But he could tell me only that the thought of saying no to them felt tantamount to jeopardizing his whole career—worse, casting it into the flames.

Meanwhile, he worked around the clock to finish his assignment on time.

"And suppose you brought it in late, what would they do?" I asked.

"I don't know."

"Would they fire you?"

"Maybe. No . . . I don't think so. No, but I couldn't."

After that first interview I got a phone call from his physician, a friend of mine since early childhood, who had given Peter my name. The gist of it was simple enough. Peter's blood pressure was reaching life-threatening numbers, despite his medication. Only his wife had been informed of how close to the edge he was: there seemed no sense in scaring him.

The doctor told me, "His father died of a stroke related to high blood pressure, you know. If he doesn't slow down, he's on the way out. He's quite brilliant, I understand."

"I got that impression," I said.

That call left me very despondent. Here I was, anchor man for this very good, devoted—all understatements—bizarrely dedicated drone of a genius, and his family. His kids and his wife relied on him and now he relied on me. The burden seemed more than I could lift.

I asked myself why I felt that my arms and legs were so heavy. For a time I failed to recognize that this malaise was something that Peter had induced in me—or more precisely, a state that I had assumed in overidentifying with him.

However, slowly it came to me—once again my profession had played its favorite prank, almost as if it had a mind of its own. I had put myself too much in Peter's place, and looking at the world through his eyes, I had lost my own perspective. Like him, I was feeling that I had undertaken an impossible task, with a time limit.

Then I realized that just the way Peter took on too much of the burden at work, I'd been construing the problem of his recovery too much as my burden alone. The problems put on his desk belonged to his company, and not to him only. Nor was I alone in having to cure Peter. I had him. The better he got at refusing excessive burdens, the lighter my load would become.

I felt easier at the very idea of holding him responsible for at least part of his cure. After all, he was superbright, with a love of logic, and he was willing to work.

I would devote myself at once to discovering and revealing to Peter his own hand in his fate. We couldn't afford to sit back and study his past in a leisurely way. Though people misperceived him and put pressure on him, he was doing the real harm to himself, signing those impossible contracts, one after the other. My immediate aim was to have him see this.

Though Peter readily answered any questions I asked, he never mentioned a feeling. Even when using the words "I" and "me," he retained the emotional detachment from himself of someone hired to write a brief biographical sketch of a long-deceased figure for an encyclopedia. When I asked him how he'd felt at some moment, he could respond with only a flat statement of what he'd thought. Apparently, he blotted feelings out of his mind and retained only his thoughts.

"How did you feel when you realized you'd agreed to do the job in two weeks?"

"I thought about how many hours I'd need, and I started to calculate where they'd come from."

And later. "When your wife cried because you canceled Saturday night movies with her, how did you feel?"

"She was right."

"I mean, when you saw her actually crying, how did you feel?"

He squinted and ran a hand through his hair. "I had to do the job assignment."

I thought I saw a wistful look in his eyes, and I pressed. "You have a wonderful wife, children who love you, and you're not with them. You're constantly disappointing them, cheating them and giving yourself high blood pressure, scaring them to death. We've got to find out why."

"Why what?"

"Why you put the job, the VIPs, and everyone there ahead of your wife and your kids and yourself. Why you'd rather spend Saturday night making the corporation happy than give warmth and love to the people who love you."

"That's not the way it is."

"Come on, Peter. Those VIPs are with *their* loved ones, making love or telling stories to their kids, or on outings, or in the car together visiting friends. They probably don't even talk about work."

Again he looked wistful.

I went on. "They have *you*. Why should they worry? You're conscientious, they know that."

At the end of the hour I said, "We're just defining the problem. You've been making a lot of choices here. It's important that we identify what they are."

"I understand," he'd said dutifully, as if it were Advanced Math 202: Differential Equations for Engineers.

Naturally, I wondered, what in his past had led him to obliterate his feelings the instant a moment had passed? That mechanism made it impossible for him to take care of himself.

He pictured all his family members—the way an army ant might if it could talk—not as loving or as cruel, or as feeling anything, only as doing their job. It was a colony of four. His father was a waiter in a local diner who did what he was told, which often meant working long overtime hours. His mother took good care of them, but Peter couldn't recall her ever getting emotional. Her attitude was perpetual concern that the kids behave well and not get in their father's way when he came home exhausted, which was every night.

Peter spent his childhood watchfully. His brother Ralph, two years older, was the athlete, the outgoing one. Neither of them talked to their father much, or to each other—Ralph was usually off playing basketball in the schoolyard and Peter would stay in his room reading. I had the impression that Peter had assumed from his parents some of the humility that they felt befit their status as immigrants. Ralph overcame that image by assimilating through athletics, but Peter, a lonely child, did not.

Peter was ten when his father died, and he had felt awful grief. "But what could I do?" He shrugged. Growing up, he seldom dated. Emily was the only woman he'd ever slept with; "It was wonderful and still is."

From what I could gather, Emily was a gracious woman, dedicated to him and the kids. She had come to New York City from New England to study music. She'd been married before, for three years to a lawyer who'd had a lot of affairs. With Peter, she had accounted for both sides of the courtship; she still played both sides of the court in arranging all their dealings with friends.

Interestingly, Peter's kids, both boys, were rambunctious and happy, and Peter loved seeing them frolic around the apartment as he himself never had. "Isn't it wonderful to have an emotion?" I had said, when he told me that. I remarked that only when talking about his wife and children did he show genuine pleasure.

"It's what I wanted most and I have it," he agreed.

I wondered, how many years of yearning for some redress of his own impoverished childhood had gone into that want?

It was February and the flu season, and many on Peter's floor were out sick. Included were Mark and Joan, low-echelon em-

ployees and the worst offenders at breaking in on him with
questions. Apparently, they'd found Peter the only person who
was accessible and could answer their questions. Their ab-
sence enabled him to finish his assignment on time. He'd also
had the benefit of two national holidays.

I could see that he was somewhat less tense even before he
told me, "My wife says that therapy is making me a little better
already."

"Maybe," I offered, "but I'm afraid of coincidence."

"What do you mean?" I could always count on his curiosity—on his underlying belief that "All facts are friendly."
He was a scientist, down to his very DNAs.

"I mean you got lucky," I told him.

"Lucky?"

"Right. Mark and Joan were sick. They left you alone. No
credit to you. If they were there, you would have let them
crash in and you'd still be hysterical. And the extra days to
work. They were also a gift."

He nodded, and I could see him processing the implications.

We went back to his childhood, and again I wondered why
he'd felt so constrained to obey every order, to comply with
every suggestion. Neither parent ever hit him or used scare
tactics. His brother Ralph was amiable and in no way a bully.

Even so, we were now sure, Peter's fear of offending people
had already become acute by a very early age. An incident
showed that vividly.

Once when he was nine, after he'd taken his brother's
mashed potatoes, mistakenly thinking that Ralph had already
finished his dinner and gone out to play basketball, Peter felt
paroxysms of regret and doom. He'd been eating alone and had
shoveled them onto his plate and devoured them, when Ralph,
three inches taller, freckled, and handsome, came in cheer-
fully, sat down, and yelled into the kitchen, "Mom, more potatoes."

There weren't any more.

Another kid might have felt sorry momentarily, but the incident stabbed Peter with remorse. Afterward, he could hear Ralph's trusting voice over and over again, and his mother's reply, "Sorry, there are none left." Peter's mind replayed the sight of the empty bowl, and Ralph's moment of disappointment. Again and again, Peter felt horror over what he had done to his innocent brother. The incident so obviously bore the stamp of his morbid fear of doing harm that I wondered about it.

Evidently, early in life, along with the adage, "All facts are friendly," perhaps even higher on the list went the axiom, "Never infringe on another person." No one else had even remarked about what Peter had done—Ralph had run off to play basketball and forgot the whole thing. Yet Peter kept remembering it all through his childhood. The question was, how had that household instilled such fear in him?

Two events in the office that month both had real impact on Peter. First, Mark resigned. An immature young man, Mark had never really caught on or seriously tried to. Finally, he had simply told a supervisor, "This kind of work isn't for me," and had quit with no notice.

Because of Mark's intrusions at least twice a day Peter had broken off his own work, and upon returning to his desk had lost his own way and had to recover it. Sometimes he'd been on the verge of solving an important problem, but still when the knock came, he'd dropped everything. He had treated Mark's interruptions as commands, though Mark had never been appreciative.

I tried to make capital of Mark's quitting, asking Peter how he felt about it.

"Nothing much," he replied.

"Well, it's the first thing you told me, coming in."

"I know."

"You gave him a ton of time, how do you feel about that?"

"I guess I feel bad. What bothered me is that he didn't even come in to say good-bye."

"I guess the problem is that you give an awful lot without thinking about it. We both know you're going to have to ration that generosity of yours."

"I know I am, but it will be hard."

It seemed like progress, not major, but the kind of ground-work therapists must always do in advance of revolutionary changes.

The second event that same month was nothing short of miraculous.

Word came that the general himself, one of the three chief officers of the whole huge brokerage firm, wanted to see Peter. The floor buzzed with talk about his arrival. It would have to be today, the general's assistant had said, he was in New York City only until five o'clock.

At three sharp, there he was, emerging from the elevator, looking much as he had in those March of Time films during the war years. A tall, silver-haired man in his late sixties, still trim, with blue eyes, a reassuring voice, and inspirational poise, he stopped only long enough to ask someone where Peter's office was. The two people who shared the computer room with Peter left but not before stealing a glimpse of him coming down the hall.

Peter hurriedly typed instructions to the big printers to stop spewing out papers and let him in. They must have been quite a sight together—the general with his classic features, worldly, stately, privileged, the quintessence of style in his blue suit, and Peter, intense, overfocused, superbly accomplished but awkward, the product of New York City's bustling, free school system.

The general pulled up a chair. It was perhaps the first time in decades that no one had actually invited him to sit down. "I'm curious about what you do," he said, and Peter explained.

The general drew a cigarette from a silver box and lit it as he listened. Peter, characteristically assuming that everyone knew as much as he did, or would ask to clarify anything they didn't follow, used a variety of terms that the general never questioned.

After a while the general asked him, "Is there a form of, uh . . . how would you put it, uh . . . mathematics, or statistical work, uh . . . in which you don't look at the whole history of a stock or company, but only at its recent performance . . . in which you choose your parameters, as you people call them, events in the last few weeks only?"

Peter felt his pulse quicken. He had no idea what the general was talking about, and had the fantasy of losing his job on the spot. It was a desperate moment.

But as always with Peter, truth won out. He told the general he didn't understand.

"That's all right, young man. I'm not a hundred percent clear myself," the general said reassuringly. "For instance, on the Murmansk run, we had a master plan. We were sending seven kinds of supplies to the Russians in a limited time frame. There were tanks, trucks, ammunition, fuel . . ."

Now Peter felt petrified that he might forget one of the seven— It was hard to know which one was crucial, maybe all of them.

On rambled the general, saying something about the North Sea and how long a man shot down could last in ten-degree weather, and giving numbers and details about the Wolf Packs, which, he explained, were German submarines.

"Is it all right if I get a pad and write some of this down?" asked Peter.

"Of course," said the general. "But it's not really critical. I'm just trying to give you the feel of the thing."

Anyhow, the Murmansk run was a slaughter, and the general contended it was because of too much reliance on original expectations and not enough flexibility to base judgments on new information. He reached his question, "And what branch of mathematics or computer science bases judgments on the latest results, one that might have saved us at Murmansk?"

After asking, the general smiled brightly.

Peter was silent. He felt completely muddled.

It seemed an eternity while he thought, but he was so speeded up, it was probably seconds. Then, falteringly, he suggested, "Well, sir, there is a branch of mathematics, it's a kind of probability theory, sir. It's called Markov Processes."

"Excellent!" the general said, as if his whole world had been put in order. "Say that again."

"Markov Processes," Peter repeated, a little louder. "You make predictions based not on initial expectations but on recent developments."

"Excellent!" the general repeated. "Just what we want. Mr. Kalinsky, you're a very bright young man."

Kalinkowitz, not Kalinsky—but it was hardly his place to correct the general. Peter was stunned, hearing the general repeat, "Very bright. They're right about you."

With that the general rose to his feet and extended a hand.

Not knowing what to do, Peter seized it and shook it. He followed the general to the door, where the general turned, and looking through bright blue eyes at the former City College student, said warmly, "You've been very helpful. Markov Process, have I got the words right?"

Peter told him he had.

He left hastily, and anyone who saw him leave saw a warm smile.

That afternoon the usual interlopers on the floor gave Peter a wide berth, and he was able to resume his computations in peace.

Peter was perplexed by the visit, but it was not without effect.

When Peter's next assignment was given to him, Nick, his supervisor, must have been surprised to hear Peter say, "I don't know how long it will take. I have to do some computations. I'll get back to you."

"When?" Nick asked him.

Peter hadn't expected the question. "I'll let you know in an hour."

"Okay," Nick said grudgingly and left.

Alone in his room, Peter estimated that four weeks would be reasonable. But as he sat there, amid the huge steel cabinets with spring reels of tape drives, it got harder to say so. His

actually saying the word "four" seemed dishonest—even brutal. Later, he told me that he'd pictured Nick's shoulders dropping, as they often did. It would be like delivering a terrible
blow to the solar plexus to ask for that much time.

Thirty-five minutes later, while Peter was still wrestling with
himself, there was a rap on the glazed door. It was Nick again.
"Well?"

Peter looked into Nick's lined face and saw—pain. Disappointment and pain, even before Peter had told him anything.

"I can do it in three weeks," Peter said and was surprised to
hear the words come out.

The instant he'd spoken, Nick said mournfully, "You're sure
it will take that long? They're waiting for it, Peter."

Peter's cutting a hand off had availed him nothing with
Nick. But he was becoming enlightened. He had despised
himself on the spot.

We were making progress. Though he was still doing the
same things, he was no longer doing them blindly. He no
longer saw himself as merely a victim. At last he was beginning to feel, in his very nerve fibers and proprioceptors, that
he was doing all this to himself. The general's visit had left
him with a glimmer of a sense of entitlement. Somebody up
there loved him. As Peter sat in my office, he writhed with
self-reproach over his sacrifice.

I pressed him to tell me why he'd given in, and what he'd
felt.

For a moment he had no idea. Then, to my astonishment, he
volunteered that he'd felt *sorry* for Nick.

"Sorry for what?" I asked.

"Well, for one thing," Peter said, "he's got a drinking problem. You know, he was in AA, almost lost his job. And he's
back drinking again."

"Any other reason?" I asked.

Then, little by little, Peter presented an impression of his
supervisor that I never would have imagined. The gist of it was
that this poor, sandy-haired man in his fifties, in the pale,
pinstriped suit, really knew next to nothing—Nick's dread se-

cret was that he was an impostor. Only Peter knew it. Here he
was, thought Peter, making a hundred and sixty thousand a
year and in a terrible position, being utterly reliant on me.
"On *me*!" Peter thought. Seized by a sense of Nick's fragility,
and embarrassed by the power he himself had over his boss,
Peter had bent himself to doing the job as fast as he could, to
make Nick look good—to prop him up.

"You're a good guy, Peter. You feel sorry for people," I told
him. "Even those who kick your brains in."

He smiled feebly. "I know what you mean," he said.

The sessions that followed left no doubt of it: Peter's constant
self-destructive acts were driven by the delusion that people
were fragile and would collapse, and that only he could save
them. For example, he would volunteer to drive people home,
all over town from family gatherings, when he was exhausted
and they could easily take a cab. He acquired financial information for friends and for distant relatives, set up their hi-fi
equipment; he built a fireplace for an aunt who, besides being
thankless, had always been curt with Emily.

All these things he offered on impulse. The minute someone
expressed a need, and often before, there he was—rushing in
to fill the void. And, nearly always, just before he'd gone
ahead, he had felt sorry for the person. He would see the
person as frail and unable to cope—such was his visualiza-
tion, even of those quite capable of doing things themselves.
Peter imagined himself in a world on the brink of crumbling, it
was as if no one could cope with anything without him.

I sought to steep him in awareness of this rampant pity of
his, bringing instances of it to his attention. He was stunned to
appreciate how often he was behaving with that motive.

When it came up, I would simply label it, "You sure feel
sorry for people."

Or merely observe, "You sure are propping people up all
over the place."

"I know," he said.

Sometimes I would actually start a session, "Well, tell me how you played God this week."

He usually could.

Soon afterward, Peter came to see that no performance of his could satisfy Nick, that being disappointed was Nick's stock-in-trade, it was his way of getting more out of people. But even knowing this, when Peter did displease Nick he felt like an ax-murderer.

One weekend Peter had the recurrent daydream that he'd driven Nick back to the bottle for good.

"In other words, you're the only thing that stands between him and total destruction," I said, and he smiled.

We were discovering a secret grandiosity in Peter. It had been easy to miss because he'd felt so defeated and looked so glum. But it was there, the sense that he had the power to make or break other people.

I still had no idea where this inappropriate pity came from. Why did he see people as so fragile? On this, we were as much in the dark as when we'd started.

The next month Peter noticed that several executives in the company were especially friendly to him. They would greet him cordially in the hall, and one dropped by with coffee just to chat. "Sorry, I can't drink coffee, I have high blood pressure," Peter had told him.

We couldn't figure it out until word came that the general had mentioned him to several VIPs in Washington. He'd done so more than once and especially at a breakfast meeting at the Hay-Adams. The general, while extolling the firm in his usual intimate, nonchalant way, had talked about the need for "instantaneous prediction," and had repeated the words "Markov Process" amid his lengthy, airy comparisons between the stock market and war, which, after all, was his first love. Several times the general had confided to his listeners, "We've got the leader at this kind of abstruse mathematical work." And with a sly but friendly wink, he had added, "I won't tell you his name. It's top secret right now."

Those in attendance hadn't understood a word of the general's ramblings about war or finance. Nor had his partners. But the general had style, and they knew he'd meant Peter. The entire firm imagined that the general's famous visit to the little computer genius must have been the first of many.

I was thrilled. Peter went into a state of shock at not knowing enough. His wife kept complimenting him and told their kids and all their relatives about it. She insisted that being so prominent, he go in at once for a huge, well-deserved raise.

He asked me what I thought of the idea.

"What's the downside, as you people say in the market? Can you use the money?"

"She says I should ask for forty-five. I'm making twenty-eight now."

I didn't comment.

The person he'd have to ask wasn't Nick but a man named Don Beagan, a former All-American linebacker. Peter had seen him in the elevator, a hulking, freckle-faced, redheaded man. When he resolved to do it, there was a lightness of spirit about Peter and I felt we were really on our way.

That week, while documenting his accomplishments to support his case for a raise, he had a series of lurid and horrible dreams. In several there was moaning over someone who had died. The worst was a screaming nightmare of a penis growing and swelling, and turning red, and finally exploding, with blood gushing out of it everywhere. Shadowy adults wouldn't tell him who died, but he knew it was a man with whom he had a secret pact and who trusted him without reservation. Worst of all, he realized that he himself had somehow killed the man. No one else had figured it out, but he himself was certain of it. He knew that he was a murderer.

Almost surely, his new approach toward people was activating these thoughts. I wondered if the moaning was sexual—and what relation he imagined there was between death and sex.

I warned him, "You may have these dreams whenever you start asking for what you deserve. It can feel as if you're committing murder, but that's just your fear coming to the surface. You're going against a deeply ingrained pattern."

He asked me what I meant.

I explained, "A deep fear of yours is crying out against your doing these things for yourself. But that doesn't mean you should turn back. You won't always feel this way. You'll kill these fears if you push ahead. It's only that what you're doing now is new."

It was meager consolation. But what real comfort can one give to a person bravely opposing a lifetime pattern? At such a time, there is no escape from the terrible sense of loss, except that afforded by returning to the repetitive but confining life that one is trying to renounce.

Mr. Beagan's secretary took Peter's call and set up the appointment. "Do you think he knows why I want to see him?" Peter asked me.

Only half in jest, I asked Peter, "Do you think it'll kill him when he finds out what you want?"

He replied immediately, "I thought of that."

Then, because critical moments in a life often recall past ones, I asked him, "When you used to go to your father, I mean, to ask him for something, how did he react?"

"You mean money?"

"Oh, money, or permission to do something, or you wanted him to play with you, or to watch you do something—to pay attention to you."

"Oh," Peter said, "he was always very good. He loved me. I don't remember doing that much, but I guess I must have."

"Did you see his penis, do you remember?"

"I don't remember . . . No, I think my parents always kept their clothes on. Even Richard, and me too. My wife and I are different that way. No, we were never naked around each other."

So much for that hunch of mine.

*   *   *

Peter was due in my office at seven on the evening of his big meeting with Beagan, the linebacker. At a few minutes to seven, I made a phone call, prepared to hang up the instant he got there. But he didn't. At a quarter after seven, I realized that I'd been prolonging that conversation because I was worried. He'd never been late. I hung up and shuffled some papers.

The phone rang. It was his wife. He had collapsed and had been rushed to St Luke's. She'd been kept in a waiting room for hours, while the doctors did tests.

I was almost as frightened as she was.

With no one else due, I told her I'd be right there. When the elevator reached his floor, she was inside his room and they were talking.

"The pressure is bad, but they didn't find any damage," he told me, obeying his first instinct, even flat on his back, which was to take care of the other person.

His wife said, "You've got to stay overnight, anyhow, darling." She took his hand.

I stayed only briefly, being obviously in the way.

In the hall I saw my old friend Richard, his physician. We walked down the corridor, out of earshot. Richard whispered, "We've checked him for hemorrhage and for P-wave abnormalities. Fortunately, we haven't found anything. There are no vascular changes in the heart or kidneys. They're okay, we think—"

"That's good."

"Not so good," Richard said. Richard was middle-sized, slender, a handsome man with black wavy hair, a meticulous dresser, married to a fashion model, and very conscious of the impression he cut, even as he said, "The pressure is just as high. He's going to have left ventricle failure soon if this goes on."

I felt awful.

"Can't you keep him calm?" Richard asked me critically.

We were heading back toward Peter's room and stopped talking until we passed it.

I said, "We're going to make headway soon. But the thing is that to reduce his pressure, he's got to do some things that might make it temporarily bad. He's been putting himself under—"

"Operation successful, patient dead," Richard said. I realized that I liked Richard a lot less than when he was a kid and we'd gone to see a magician together and practiced doing some of his tricks afterward.

"Let's hope not." That was all I felt like saying to this man, who had long ago disowned me for making less money and aging worse, as if both were symptoms of my lesser rank.

"You know," Richard said, "his father died of high blood pressure when Peter was ten."

"Yes, I know that. It must have been terrible," I said. "He really doesn't like to talk about it, though he's just starting to."

"A hereditary vascular problem. The sons have it too. But it doesn't have to be fatal. I was a resident when they brought the father in. No chance. It was as if his head exploded. Mike Garlock, the chief, used to call it 'vascular blowout.' Like the old flat tires. We want to do an EEG in the morning. George, maybe he's not a case for you."

"I guess we're both feeling bad. Your medications don't seem to be doing much good either," I said, holding my ground.

St. Luke's released him the next day, with all tests negative. After staying home only one additional day, he went back to work.

I asked him to recall for me what happened the morning of his collapse, in as much detail as he could. In terror, he'd gone upstairs to see Mr. Beagan, a brute of a man physically and reputed by some to be brutal toward employees.

Beagan had greeted him at the door. "I hear wonderful

things about you, Mr. Kalinsky. We're proud to have you aboard."

Somehow, they'd gotten onto the topic of Peter's wife and kids, whom Peter praised to the utmost. "Steven's already taking piano lessons, but I think he'd rather play the drums. They're louder."

Mr. Beagan found that hilarious.

When Peter told him he needed more money, Beagan replied, "Well, I've been looking at your record, and there's a note here from one of the senior partners. You certainly deserve more. Why didn't you come here sooner?"

Peter had been astounded. He told me that he'd suddenly felt like a little child. "You should have seen the size of Mr. Beagan's arms and hands. They must be four standard deviations above the mean."

When Mr. Beagan asked him how much he wanted, Peter had glanced down at a note he'd brought with him, to be sure that he stuck to his mission. He read from it, "Forty-five thousand a year and a third week of vacation."

"Hmmm," said Beagan . . . "Fine. As of June first. Is that okay?"

It was the middle of May.

"Of course," Peter said. "Thank you very much, sir."

That was all there was to it.

He'd called his wife with the good news. Then excitement rang in his ears and racked his body, as if he were being shaken in a lion's mouth. He'd tried to resume his work, but the numbers and notations seemed to throb on the page and he couldn't. Lunchtime had come. It was a gorgeous day, with hardly a cloud in the sky, and he'd decided to go out for a walk. He strolled half a mile through the ubiquitous grid of streets and into a little, neon-lit diner, where he chomped down a submarine sandwich, hoping that the food would calm him.

But coming out, he still felt funny, a stooping, insignificant figure wending his way back through the garrulous crowds. The

idea came to him that it had all been too easy. "I felt like . . .
I felt that . . . I got the idea that Mr. Beagan was *afraid* of
me."

"What do you mean?" I asked him.

"Well, Roy and a couple of other people said he was mean,
that he was tough. But with me . . ."

He paused, and I waited a moment. Then I asked, "What
are you thinking?"

"I don't know. I had some thought I wanted to tell you, but I
lost it. Anyhow, I started to shake, the way I did on one of
those blood-pressure medicines, one that they told me to stop
immediately."

"What then?"

"Oh, I did what I always do when I'm anxious. Mental calculations. They calm me down if they're hard enough."

"What were you computing, if you can remember?"

"Well, I like to look at buildings and estimate their dimen-
sions—their surface area and volume. I calculated the volume
of all the buildings on one street and added them up."

"Did that calm you down?"

"Not really. The buildings were too easy. They were too
easily reducible to contiguous parallelopipeds, mostly just a
bunch of cubes set on top of each other. After that it was just
compound addition. Maybe I felt a little more relaxed, but I
knew I was very nervous.

"Then I got to a good one, the New York Stock Exchange,
do you know it?"

"Not really."

"It's a beautiful marble building. It's an interesting calcula-
tion. It has six columns in front, three stories each. Right
circular cylinders, volume 'pi r square h.' I remember adding
in that triangular pediment on the top. I added that in.

"Then I stepped back to estimate the roof, which had one of
those balconies, and I pictured him, Beagan. It sounds stupid.
He was trying to hold on but he was falling off the roof, and I
looked over the street and there were people who wouldn't be
able to get out of the way. I think I must have moved my head

too fast, looking up and then down. I got dizzy all of a sudden. I must have sat down on the sidewalk, so I wouldn't hurt him, I know it sounds crazy. And I passed out.

"I remember they brought me inside, through the columns. Someone said it was a heart attack. And someone said, 'Here comes the ambulance,' and they brought me to St. Luke's. That's where Dr. Murdock is connected. The whole thing was ridiculous. It could have been a good day, but I ruined it. I ruined it."

"Why do you think he fell off the roof?"

"I don't know. It was just a thought."

"Well, Peter, you've been having dreams of people dying, and this is, let's call it a daydream. But it's not that different."

"That's right. It's not."

He ran a hand through his hair nervously, and I took this as a signal to stop. Almost instinctively, I switched the topic, asking him about his older son, who had taken a Cub Scout test the previous week. I could feel Peter inhale with relief. Moments later, while talking about Steven tying knots, he seemed animated and was as close as he ever got to being joyous. Soon the time was up.

That evening I made the quiet resolution to myself not to push him too hard—either by asking about those murderous daydreams of his or by asking questions that might impel him to pursue more in his life, and possibly collapse or even die in the effort.

By then it seemed certain that his acts of asserting himself, even in small ways, were evoking his fantasies of murder. Like anyone who steps forward into a personal abyss, waking the dogs of antiquity, Peter had stirred memories that would never have risen had he merely sat still and tried to recall his early life. But pushing ahead to learn still more would be small consolation if he died in the search.

Even more than before, I felt defeated. Suppose Peter *did* actually die? In my own daydreams I heard Richard Murdock saying, "Operation successful, patient dead." Had we reached an impasse, now that in fear of killing my own patient I'd become afraid to invite him forward, and even afraid to inquire too much about his past? If so, what remained? For me to become merely his companion, his well-behaved interrogator about trivia?

There I was, holding my breath, utterly controlled by a patient—not by a tyrant, but by a totally open person, an "all-facts-are-friendly" fellow, a *scientist* to the core. Still, he might as well have been a tyrant.

Only then did I realize that Peter, as a small child, must have felt much the way I was feeling toward him. His father had been afflicted by life-threatening high blood pressure until he died. Especially just before the end, Peter's mother, devoted and terrified both, had done everything she could to avoid turbulence. Peter could hardly have failed to connect expression in the home with supreme selfishness—or even murder.

Through my own present fear of doing harm, I could imagine the strictures on Peter while growing up. It dawned on me at last, the nature of the tyranny. "To do no harm," that first principle of the doctor's Hippocratic Oath, was surely a primary force shaping his earliest days. "Careful. Your father has high blood pressure." How could he have escaped such continual warnings or the example of caution that his mother set? And what repercussions that message must have had! And *still* have. And now, to Peter every authority was still a father whose very life depended upon giving him the most meticulous and respectful treatment.

I could imagine how his brother, Ralph, might have averted Peter's fate. Ralph had been older when their father's blood pressure problem became acute; moreover, Ralph was by nature outgoing, and he lived for sports outside the home. Peter was introverted, and his very poor eyesight perhaps contributed to his hesitancy. In any event, Ralph had seemingly escaped, but Peter had not. Paradoxically, Peter's *father's* blood pressure problem was killing him, every bit as much as his own was.

I could also imagine why Peter so enjoyed his own kids

raising a hullabaloo. Their storming through the apartment sig-
nified a new era, and may even have implied to him unconsciously that his own condition was not so serious.

For the first time I linked that dream of a penis expanding,
turning red and exploding, with Richard's comment that the
father's burst blood vessel in the head was a "blowout." Peter
had been away at camp when his father actually died, but at
many other times he must have seen his father's face redden,
as he must have seen his own penis swell and turn red—and
explode. Had he seen his father's penis, in actuality? How
could one know? But he had pictured it, surely.

It didn't seem warranted to speculate that Peter had truly
felt wrongful, or in any way accountable, for his father's death,
the classical combination of desire and guilt that Freud attributed to all sons as part of the Oedipal experience. The fact
is that few sons come out being so fearful of any form of assertion. Few develop so strong an unconscious association between asking for what they want and murder. So the damage
was done to Peter during the years just before his father died.

So murderous were Peter's wishes that they could extinguish
lives the way one blows out candles—witness mighty Beagan,
clutching the balustrade but still tumbling to the pavement
below. No, not his father's death or any single event could
stamp in such an association. But *years* of being careful, of
solicitude in boyhood, of watching his father redden and collapse on his bed, could instill the connection—and did.

I'd become sure that the pieces fit even before I saw Peter
next. I thought of T. S. Eliot's line "Do I dare/Disturb the
universe?" Well, Peter would dare, I resolved, and maybe this
new discovery would help him dare, would help him dissolve
that incredibly inhibiting association between asking for what
he wanted and murder.

I had an urge to tell him, "Fellow scientist, look what I
found!" But, of course, I would have to move ahead cautiously,
to corroborate my discovery, and above all, if it were accurate,
to help him grasp it at his own rate. I would have to return
mentally to where we had been together. I wanted him to consider this insight and not go plowing forward until he did.

*   *   *

In my office the next time he looked different physically. The muscles in his cheeks were like cords, which suggested the strain of his recent life. His body seemed rounder; his arms, more in motion as he spoke than I'd remembered them, led me to imagine more arms, many—I pictured him as a spider, weaving an invisible web in the air in front of him. His indifference to creating an impression, so detrimental to him in the world of tricksters and illusions, seemed admirable.

He told me about his last few days at work and at home. He'd taken some time for himself and gone to a Little League game that his older son had played in. "He struck out twice, but he came a lot closer to the ball than I ever did. He'll get it."

I was still at a loss concerning how much to tell him, still mentally retracing the steps that had brought me to my insight, which had put me far ahead. I knew I was back with him when I said, "Peter, you're a problem-solver. Let me tell you my problem here. I'd like to know what you think."

"What's that?" He smiled at the reversal and waited.

"Well, you've been pushing ahead, asking people to give you more. Asking for more things you wanted. That's been good. You have more time too—and you're getting more respect maybe than you ever had. Most important, you're giving yourself a better sense of . . . uh . . . self-esteem."

I stopped abruptly. I knew I was rambling. How does one say what came next? I wondered. Only by saying it. "But Peter, I'm worried that these efforts of yours, I mean asking for more, like the raise—"

He broke in to help me. "You mean, you're upset about all those nightmares, those terrible fantasies of mine?"

"Yes. Well, no, Peter. Not just that. You can live with those. They pass. I'm worried. I'm worried that in doing what you have to do, you're going to mess up your blood pressure. I mean, do more harm than good."

"You mean that I'll collapse. I'm going to die."

Of course he was right, but I held off. "Well, Peter, I didn't say that, but we don't want to create such a jolt on the way to cure. And we don't want you to keep suffering either where you are. You see, it's—"

"Don't worry about that," he snapped back. "Don't worry about my pressure."

"Well, you did collapse."

"I know, but my pressure at its height even then wasn't as high as it got many times before."

"Peter, how can you be sure?"

"I'm sure. My wife takes my pressure regularly. I have a nurse take it at work too, twice a week. I'm keeping a record. You're doing great, George."

"What do you mean?"

"Well, you see I've been drawing a continuous curve of the systolic and diastolic, just to see how I was doing. Not just recording periods and maximum points. I've been doing something that has never been done before—at least so far as I know."

"What's that?"

He smiled. "I've done a Fourier analysis of the function."

"Peter, I don't know what that is."

"I'm sorry. It uses complex variables. You see, Fourier reduced all periodic results like this to sinusoidal functions, and that reduction gives us a lot of information on the spot—"

"Peter, I'm lost. What are you saying?"

"That since I started coming here, I've been doing steadily *better*. Not just the mean amplitude and the maxima, but the periods . . . I'm sorry." He smiled again. "My blood pressure is very much better, so have no fear."

"That's fantastic. Really?"

"Really. So let's keep going."

On the way out I thought, he was no spider. That reassurance of his that we were making progress made a huge difference. That evening I floated a foot above the ground myself.

Obviously, to take care of me wasn't his function, but rather his disease. But, this time, it hadn't been his intention either. He was taking care of himself.

*   *   *

I could hardly wait to peer at his early life through my new lens. But even so, I wouldn't hurry him. Surely, there would be openings if I looked for them. "If it's important, it will come up," the psychoanalyst, Leopold Bellak, used to tell our class in his Viennese accent.

During the next session Peter spent a lot of time talking about his kids. The younger was to have a birthday party, and Peter's mother was coming in from Philadelphia to stay over for a few days. My inquiry would have to wait.

Meanwhile, I listened for any hint that he might be restraining his own sons by inducing in them concern for his health. If I could find even one instance of that, I might use it to help him remember how he felt growing up, and he could use it to better understand his present fear.

But he simply wasn't doing that, in any way. The kids acted silly and shouted themselves hoarse, even during evenings while their father lay on his bed inside, throbbing and unable to sleep. He and Emily had decided not to burden them with their father's condition—they wouldn't understand and it seemed pointless to worry them. The day Peter had collapsed, they'd stayed with Emily's sister and were told only that his parents had to go somewhere.

I asked him how his mother got along with the kids. He replied that they loved her, but that she often annoyed Emily by telling her to control them more.

"How?" I asked.

"By insisting that they do their homework early. By making them put things away. I was always very neat growing up."

"And quiet compared with them?" I asked.

"Right. Very. My mother says they make too much noise."

"You knew about your father's high blood pressure, didn't you?"

"Sure."

The hour was drawing to a close, and this was hardly a topic to pursue with three minutes left. I suggested, "Peter, there's some information we need. If you get a chance, when you're alone with your mother, ask her about your dad's high blood pressure, I mean how much you knew about it, and what it was like to be with him."

He said he would.

There was some comic relief. The very afternoon that Peter's mother was due, the general had dropped by again, just to chat. He'd asked about Markov Processes. "Was Markov a Russian?"

Peter didn't know.

"No matter," the general had said. He rambled on about battles, somehow managing to relate Peter's work to the invasion of Tarawa, to Rommel, to Darius, and to Caesar. Once again the general thanked him prodigiously. "We're proud to have you aboard."

On the way out he'd asked Peter not to discuss what they'd talked about, which was easy, because Peter had no idea.

It struck me that the general's mind might be dimming, but his reputation certainly was not. Word had it that the general's wisdom was worth tens of millions to the company, and, I surmised, conferences with his little genius in the computer room had become part of his myth.

I was surprised to hear Peter say, "He makes me feel good."

"How?"

"Well, for instance, I was going to switch off the machines. They whir a lot, I don't hear it. And they have a lot of blinking lights. Nobody can stand it. But he said, 'Keep them on. They're important. We've got to stay in the trenches.' It was funny."

More than funny. The general's sturdiness, which had inspired millions, was especially important to Peter. Here was one man he had no fear of crushing. Dimming or not, the general was still a general, and even his use of Peter was starting to make sense.

*   *   *

Peter's mother corroborated that his boyhood home was filled
with concern over his father's health, to the point that all expression seemed constricted by worry over upsetting the delicate, high-strung man. After talking with her, Peter could
recall his early dread of committing an atrocious blunder; it
was a fear made ominous by the sense that since he didn't
know what he was afraid of doing, he would have to guard
against—everything.

Then came particulars. Milk poured into a glass with an
unsteady hand, spilling across the dinner table; a voice too
loud; a book left in the bathroom; homework still undone—
these felt not like mere lapses of performance but like near-
misses, like planes passing too close together over the Atlantic
at night, acts dangerously close to destroying life as Peter
knew it. Exactly why they did wasn't clear, which made the
threat more ominous by its being curiously ineffable and irre-
futable. Of course, it was that any of these things could wreak
havoc on his father.

In my office he recalled rushing home to get there ahead of
his father. He'd once left a museum ahead of his school class
to be there in time. It wasn't so much that his father wanted to
play with him, or missed him, than that things had to be in
place, including him. "Everything had to be orderly." As he
spoke, I commented, "Just as in mathematics."

Later he remembered that not having kids over to play was
in response to an unspoken family rule. That included Milton,
another budding scientist. Peter had been hard put to explain
to Milton why he was unwelcome. He felt terrible about it, but
he wasn't sure himself, and so he made up a skein of different
excuses when Milton seemed on the verge of inviting himself.

Peter's mother had merely to look glum or put a finger to her
lips indicating that daddy was inside lying down, and Peter felt
instantly overwhelmed by the need for silence, for submission
in whatever form was expected of him.

While he told me about his mother, I came increasingly to

suspect that, though the poor woman obviously suffered, she
had also made unfair capital of her husband's illness, and ultimately used the illness to enhance her own control. Her real
motives back then would remain to some extent a mystery.
But, certainly during this stay with Peter and Emily, she was
quite a different woman from the one he had portrayed. She
was thankless and found petty flaws in Emily as a mother and
as a host. After the main course on Saturday night, she told
Emily, "It was good chicken, dear, but you spent much too
much for it." Then, as soon as the kids had left the table, she
whispered that high blood pressure runs in the family, and that
they would get it too some day.

Peter suddenly saw how oppressive his mother was. He wondered how he could have failed to notice it before. He felt
sorry for her, but he understood why Emily would always count
the hours until she went home. So it wasn't merely the fact of
his father's precarious state, but her uses of it, that had made
him so afraid of doing harm.

Peter and his mother had chatted for hours one evening during that weekend visit, while Emily and the kids were inside.
She had lowered her voice and confided in him, "I sometimes
think that Ralphie killed him. Not you, but Ralphie. Your
brother was so badly behaved." She apparently still used her
older son like a kidney to collect the poisons of her own self-
doubt and whatever guilt feelings she had.

We could see why Peter had always been afraid to ask his
father for anything. As a boy, he'd had no idea why, but finally
we knew. He'd had no fear of being turned down—his father
always sought to give him what he needed and never got angry.
It was rather Peter's confused apprehension of danger, dinned
into his head by his mother's constant warnings that the frail
man should not be disturbed at any cost. It was mainly those
warnings that had imbued Peter with an eerie sense of his
father teetering on some edge and subject to disaster if
pushed.

Fear of a despot is a weak inhibitor by comparison. One can
kill a tyrant, one's day will come: myths tell of heroes becom-

ing kings. And even if one does nothing but merely wait and grow strong, succeeding some day far from the home, the grip is broken, the era is over. But there can be no ritual killing of someone next to death, no later success, no independence or self-affirmation or even self-approval; the mere impulse for these proves one's unworthiness, one's ingratitude to the sorrowful tyrant for his gift of life and protection.

Peter was astonished when I interpreted for him that he was displacing his early fears of toppling his father onto people in authority over him now. For someone so timid around superiors, his courage to have long talks with the general as equals had seemed a miracle to his fellow workers, but, of course, it wasn't. Had Peter simply feared being crushed by those with power, he might have cringed at the prospect of talking with this world-famous leader. But his real fear was of frailty in men, not potency, and so the general's status posed no threat to him at all. Quite the contrary, it was reassuring.

So long as Peter catered unthinkingly, propping these "fathers" up, he could avoid his mental imagery of their collapse. But the instant he crossed one even in his mind, the imagery was there. Finally, he could see all this.

But such knowledge was still theoretical. He would have to break the grip of the past by becoming what he feared most, not once but many times. Ahead still lay the need for Peter to assert himself repeatedly with those in authority, and to experience that terrible childhood imagery. Beyond a doubt, those murderous fantasies would come, but without their mystery. He would recognize them as the past staking its claim. And as he plunged ahead in spite of them, they would disappear as surely as they would appear for a while.

I could, of course, not tell him directly what to say or do. Were I to give him assignments, I would become simply another authority whom he feared displeasing and injuring, no matter how useful my advice proved to be. He might earn more respect from people, and even improve his income, but if his motive were to sustain me by being a good son, nothing basic in him would change. Unless he acted out of self-interest, evoking his own demons and slaying them, he would remain the same inside, fearful of causing death by displeasing— except that this time it would be fear of displeasing me.

Armed with his new understanding, he resolved that hence-forth in the office when he was doing calculations, he would send intruders away. Even this took stamina and rehearsal at first. Minutes after saying, "I'll talk to you later," as he sat at his desk, he felt a strong urge to hurry, to break off his work and rush to see what the person wanted. He could actually identify his idea that he was doing irreparable damage to the poor fellow outside.

It took effort for Peter not to apologize when he finally was ready for the person who'd knocked on his door. But he would have to cease doing even that—there was no need to comfort people, especially intruders. I told him that he would feel bet-ter about himself much quicker if he made the demands that he had to without apologizing.

I did my best to keep reminding him of what he might be afraid of in those exchanges, on the grounds that he could best appreciate the irrational nature of his fear if it was a very conscious fear. I was counting on what the psychoanalyst Karl Jung called, "the antiseptic power of consciousness."

I knew that what struck me as my own overstatement would not strike him that way, because I was describing his inner experience. Once, when he was debating with himself whether to ask Nick for an extra assistant to get a job done fast, I observed, "Even if you need him, isn't it dangerous?"

"What do you mean?"

"Well, you don't want to give Nick a stroke, do you?"

And very often I would ask, "Did you kill any fathers this week?"

He would usually say he had, and recount some incident in which he'd asked for something, or turned down a request from a higher-up. We would talk about his fantasy afterward.

As I'd hoped, after a while my lighthearted anticipations of danger came to his mind, almost whenever he wanted something and felt afraid.

After three months he was actually starting to enjoy an aspect of his exchanges on the job, watching himself and waiting to see what he would feel when he held his ground.

In six months it had gotten much easier. He was doing some things automatically that had been excruciating for him to do in the beginning. The fantasies did come sometimes, but weakly; they were mocking reminders of his childhood now, a childhood he was leaving forever. He no longer felt the terrible trepidation that accompanied them.

Once again the general dropped by, his bronzed skin, his physical fitness, his plentiful gray hair belying his age. This time he had given no warning, and when Peter started getting up from his chair, the general said with his usual charm, "No. Keep working, please. Finish what you are doing."

Peter had no idea what was expected of him, but not wanting to disobey orders, told the general he needed four more minutes.

"That's perfectly fine," the general said and stood silently behind Peter as he clicked away at the keyboard. When Peter said, "That's it," the general pointed to a V-shaped array of symbols on the screen and commented, "That looks very much like Alexander's phalanx, with the crossed swords. Is it related?"

Peter was unable to make the adjustment.

"Alexander the Great," the general said. "We have Peter the Great."

Before Peter could even respond with befuddlement, the general told him, "I need you to join me at a lunch with some very old friends. They happen to be important clients. They've chosen us to handle their national pension fund. They know we're in the vanguard. Explain to them what a Markov Process is. Just define it for them. Let them know you're aware of it, so to speak. Don't say too much. They're not mathematicians at all, but very decent people. Very decent. It's this Friday."

Peter felt some of his old panic. He had the fantasy of calling a former professor, now at Princeton, for a quick reading list, and of studying around the clock. But Emily reassured him, "You heard what he said. Just define it. Not too much."

That night he had a dream of the general masturbating in a movie theater. The general's penis swelled, grew red, and he could hear the general say, "Ahh," in pleasure. He woke up frightened, and then laughed. We had discussed the imagery of redness and explosion, and the death of disappointed fathers so often that his fear itself exploded and was gone.

"But what was so funny?" I asked Peter.

"Well, when I woke up, it crossed my mind that the general is just jerking off with all those wars and with the Markov Process."

Peter found the lunch tense but bearable. One of the heads of the client company was a former governor in the South and another had served under the general. Actually, the general cut short Peter's memorized definition by asking for the menus.

Afterward, the general thanked Peter for his help. It crossed my mind, as Peter described the meeting to me, that though Peter himself probably added nothing important, the general's use of Peter almost surely bolstered his own image and that of the firm.

Months later, after Peter had become thoroughly capable of recognizing the dejected look, the helpless gesture, the shrug of the shoulders that had so long controlled him, he made a discovery. People showed hardship much more to him than they did to others. For instance, Nick would lose his temper with others and threaten them, but with Peter he always came across as hanging on for dear life.

Even beyond his misperception of people, Peter had unknowingly trained people to play pathetic with him. Whether consciously or not, they found that the technique worked, and so, ironically, Peter had created a world of infirm people around him and confronted daily the very kind of "father" he dreaded most. People unconsciously select tactics that work and drop those that don't.

When I explained this to Peter, and he saw that even friends and relatives did this to him, he was furious—first at them and then at himself. He doubled his resolve not to submit. During the year that followed, he came to see that people were indeed much more robust when they had to be.

I stopped seeing Peter after about two years. His blood pressure had gone down from its dangerous level, though he still took medication sometimes. He was not a sentimental person, but shook my hand as if we were colleagues who had solved an equation together and now had to move on. In a curious way, I felt that the adventure of our working together was more a high romance for me than for him. He was not one to romanticize experience, though he was very capable of love.

Some years later I saw his name in the catalog of a prominent university as a full professor. Almost surely, he was doing research as part of his employment; in any event, I pictured him surrounded by inspiring experts and traveling to present papers to people who really understood them, and I felt that he at last had an audience worthy of him. I've had an urge to call him, but in this profession one does not do those things. The needs of the therapist for personal closure and for friendship must be satisfied elsewhere, and in that sense I guess we are like mathematicians.

KILLER

By April those inside the sprawling state mental hospital could hear the sparrows twittering and the bluejays beeping in the brightness of very early morning. Summer is toughest for the patients to take—the days are longest and sexual stirrings make each russet brick building a prison more confining than in the winter.

They would huddle on the porches behind the meshwork, watching the cars arrive with attendants and nurses and doctors who had enjoyed their freedom the night before and soon would again. For most patients, the only hope was gradual promotion leading to discharge. Each improvement to a better diagnosis meant transfer to a "better-behaved" building with a few more freedoms—more outings, more privacy, a more trusting staff; then the chance for still another promotion as the reward for good and lucid behavior, until finally the day of discharge. That discharge depended partly on who was waiting outside and willing to take responsibility for the person—a family member, a loyal friend, or a benign employer who would dare hire a former mental patient.

I'd driven to the hospital as a consultant and was chatting with a half-dozen attendants in their white overalls, in a sparsely furnished room, with thick glass windows looking out on the grounds.

"Doc," one of the attendants, named Andy, said. "We got to talk about Slav. I know he's a schizophrenic, but he's a mean motherfucker. We don't know what to do."

Another guy I hadn't met before, who introduced himself as "Armand the Barber," showed me a missing tooth. "See that. Slav! And he knows what he's doing. Believe me, he knows what he's doing."

"Look, lemme me finish," said Andy. "Slav was a prisoner of war. The Russians had him. He's a big bastard. Strong as an ox. He'll punch an attendant, and if you hit him back, he says he'll sue. He'll cost you your goddamn job. Meanwhile, he takes shots at everybody."

"And when the doctors question him, he talks only Polish, like he can't understand anything," said someone else.

"If it wasn't for everyone else on the ward stopping him, I would have been a goner," said the first guy, Andy, himself about six-two, wiry and seemingly very strong.

"We moved him to about three different buildings. He pops people, other patients, attendants, and then he pulls that legal shit. He's problem number one. He's got to be," Andy said.

"Get me all the records on him you can," I said, and they called downstairs.

We went on to talk about a few other patients, a kid of fifteen who cried nearly all the time, and then someone else. After a while Andy reached into his shirt pocket and then fumbled in his denim pockets for a cigarette. Not finding any, he went to the window and shouted through the bars down to the lawn. "Hey, Killer! Come up here."

Moments later a black man of forty or so, with a perfect build, in a white T-shirt that showed enormous muscles and stovepipe pants with a waist no bigger than a size thirty-two, came in so lightly that he hardly touched the oak floor. He must have sprinted across the lawn and practically hurdled the few flights of stairs as if they were half a step.

"Hey, Killer!" Andy shouted and suddenly went into a boxer's stance, weaving and bobbing his head. "Would you run to the store and get me two packs of Camels? Be back as soon as you can."

Killer smiled beautifully, showing some gold teeth, took the bill Andy handed him, and was gone.

"He's a patient," someone explained. "But not really. He works on the grounds. He has total freedom."

"He doesn't *want* to leave," said someone else.

"It's about a half mile each way, and he has to check past the first guard. He'll be back up the stairs with the cigarettes in about six," Andy said. He looked at his watch.

I was impressed.

"I'm afraid Slav is gonna kill somebody," Armand the Barber said. Armand's face was lined, and once I got past his beautiful head of wavy black hair, combed and oiled in the fifties manner, I could see that he was a lot older than the rest, maybe fifty-five. He had a slight French accent, Canuck to be precise.

"I feel so goddamned frustrated," someone else said. "We could put him in the hold, but he'd be worse."

A messenger brought up Slav's folder. The papers gave the diagnosis: "Paranoid schizophrenic: traumatic psychosis due to the war." The Slav—I truly don't remember his name—had reportedly been in the German army and was captured by the Russians, one of the ten percent who survived Stalingrad. After the war he had somehow found his way to the United States, the land of plenty, and had kicked the shit out of people for no good current reason.

The folder had nothing to offer by way of insight or clue. But I perused it as if it did because I saw that the attendants were watching me and were scared. I recalled a woman physician telling me that when she went to accident scenes in an ambulance, even if what she saw were inert bodies sprawling in blood on the sidewalk, her first rule was to look confident to disperse the crowd. She could be puking inside, but she had to appear in command.

And these attendants, utterly devoted men, were frightened

onlookers too. They could have buried poor Slav forever in one of those hospital buildings never visited by the press or by administrators and seldom by doctors, sent him to a ward where people live and die, babbling, eating their own excrement, unable to keep their clothes on, where the attendants themselves are pretty far gone, and have to be, or they'd prefer a job in the Gulag somewhere to the stench and the decay. Every state mental hospital still has such wards—receptacles for little children as well as pallid, senile adults unable even to count the days.

No, it was to the credit of those attendants that, despite their fury at this man who pounded on them and claimed insanity, they were still not reconciled to his removal to one of those places. They knew that patients had often sued individual employees as well as hospitals. And though most attendants subtly arrange for protection from clusters of inmates in case of assault, there have still been plenty of bones broken and hospital employees have been stabbed and murdered.

Killer returned with the cigarettes. Andy unwrapped a package and handed him one. Then, pretending to look displeased, Andy said, "It took almost six minutes. That's some mile, Killer."

The black man beamed. He knew a compliment when he heard one.

Andy told me that Killer had been a top middleweight contender. "Number-two and fought for the title, in fact. In the Garden. Right, Killer?"

Killer nodded. He looked like a figure in *Sports Illustrated*. He was no longer a middleweight, he must have been a hundred and ninety. But he was still perfectly proportioned.

"He had him, but he lost in the eleventh," Andy explained. "Killer went for a knockout, and he wasn't supposed to. He didn't have to."

I caught on finally. Killer was punch-drunk, and no one wanted him. So this was his home.

Then Andy got up, looking real serious. "Come on, let's box, Killer."

The black man smiled, and when Andy stepped toward him and shot out a left hand, Killer pulled his head back just enough for it to miss. The others started shouting, "Get him, Killer," as Andy went after him with left jabs and a few wicked rights. "Get him," they yelled, as Andy kept missing.

Killer's hands stayed low, and he went on bobbing his head and ducking. But he didn't throw a punch, and as the others kept shouting, "Get him, Killer," I knew this was a familiar scenario.

Killer kept shuffling and evaded everything Andy threw at him, but once Killer blocked a right jab with his forearm and Andy shouted "Owww!" in real pain. Andy, with a gangling style but some technique, was soon breathing hard.

Then Killer faked a left to the midsection, which Andy went for, dropping his guard. In that instant, Killer touched Andy's left temple ever so gently with the knuckles of his right hand, and we all knew that if Killer had wanted to put something into it, Andy might be sleeping for a long time, if not forever.

"You win, Killer," Andy said, very winded. "I'll get you next time." And then to me, "What do you think? Do you want to try him?"

"Thanks, no," I said. And Killer went out and down the stairs and back across the grounds to resume his work watering the trees and the lawn.

The next week the Slav tried to put a fork through an employee in the dining room for refusing to give him a second helping of mashed potatoes until everyone was served. The medics shot him full of barbiturates and put him to sleep for a day or two. What next?

The attendants were perhaps hoping that my advanced studies would suggest something of value, but I was sure that the answer was not to be found in books. I had given them some good insights, I thought, about the other patients the guys mentioned. But if I were an attendant on a ward, facing the

Slav for eight hours a day, or worse, *turning my back to him*, what would I do?

"Hire a hit man." A terrible thought! One obviously prompted by fear, but it was the only answer that came to me each time I thought about those guys going off to work in the morning, kissing their wife and kids good-bye.

I wondered if Andy had told his wife the problem, and I wondered how frightened he really was. They never showed fear. Hire a hit man. Of course I wouldn't do it, but thoughts are free. Anyhow, that was my reaction.

Then, all of a sudden, a possible solution came to me—a *real* solution. I resisted it at first—it had to be only a frightened schoolboy's wish fulfillment, a fantasy. No, I couldn't recommend it. It seemed better and better as I went over it, but I'd be ruined if they put the idea into practice and it got connected with me.

I was back at the hospital early for my next bimonthly visit, in that same big room with its sparse aluminum chairs that were more interested in being stacked than being sat in, around an oak table a century old.

"The guy's a problem, all right!" Andy said and told me once again in detail what the Slav had done.

A couple of them were ready to see the clinical director.

"This guy has got to go to a back ward," one man said.

"I don't ever want to see his ass again," said Armand. "Nobody sues from back there."

I remembered going into a wrong building out of a blinding snowstorm at another state hospital, and entering one of those wards. The chaos, agony, and the stench of bodies drove me out fast—a perpetual train wreck of humans and animals.

They were talking about making a formal request of the clinical director.

"We're not up to that yet," I heard myself say, with more authority than I felt. "I've got an idea."

I knew that I didn't want to make it explicit. It could spell major trouble for me and my license if it were perceived as my idea. Yet it felt right.

"Let me tell you a story," I began. "I used to teach fourth grade. I had a kid, Stuart, a big kid. Smart. Careful. He was scared, but he was also mean, and he was on a bad track. I don't care how scared he was, he acted superior to the other kids. He'd criticize their shoes or a spot on their shirt. They hated him and he felt terrible. He didn't know what he was doing. He would tattle. He once told another kid out loud that he could get me to lose my job. Can you imagine that? A lot of kids his age don't even know that a teacher is someone with a job. They just think he's a teacher, like a cop is a cop, your mother is your mother. Like you're born that way.

"If I left the room and two kids talked, Stuart would make an announcement first thing when I got back. 'Robert and Mary were out of their seats.' 'Timmy cheated on the test.' He used to turn kids in like an SS guard. He knew all the rules but he had no friends. He was eight and he always talked about his rights."

"A prick with ears," somebody said.

"Right. So I solved it," I told them. "There was another kid—Robert. Not nearly as smart as Stuart but bigger. He was basically a good kid but a terrible behavior problem. In fact, I got him because some of the women teachers didn't want him. Both of Robert's parents were in TB sanitariums. He was staying at his grandmother's house.

"The only time I could get Robert to study was during a test, when it was quiet, like a spelling test. Robert would put the spelling book on the floor and turn the pages with his feet and look up the words. It was cheating, but at least he was studying.

"One day Stuart announced that Robert was cheating. I tore up Robert's paper in front of the class. 'You got a *zero*. Stuart says you cheated. Zero.'

"At the end of the day I dismissed the class, one by one. I used to do that so they'd be quiet. I'd pick the quietest kids, one after the other. They'd strain to sit frozen quiet, then they'd go down the stairs without a word or I'd call them back. That's a big way they judge a teacher—by how quietly his class goes down the stairs.

"I was getting down to a few kids left, including Robert and Stuart. I could see Robert ready to lunge at Stuart, praying they'd be left alone together, he could hardly stay in his seat. I let the others go, and then switched off the lights and left, as if I'd forgotten the two of them. I had a glimpse of Robert flying over an empty row of desks.

"Stuart's mother was the only parent downstairs who insisted on waiting inside the school building for her little darling, the future president of the United States.

"'Where is my son?' she asked when she saw me. I always left last, like the captain of a sinking ship.

"'I don't know,' I told her innocently. 'I thought he was gone already.'

"By the time she got up the stairs, Robert was on top of Stuart on the floor, punching the shit out of him. Who was Stuart gonna sue? You get it. Robert was eight years old. Boys will be boys. The principal got them in his office, and Stuart didn't say a fucking word. After that they became friends. I had Stuart go over Robert's spelling with him in the back of the class."

They enjoyed the story.

"So who?" asked Andy. My parable came out more nakedly than I'd wanted it to.

"Who?" someone else asked.

"What's Killer up to these days?" I asked.

"He don't hit anybody," Andy commented.

"Maybe if he took a real shot in the head, he might," someone else said.

"So we'll move Killer to my ward for a while," Andy said. "If you recommend it, I think they would."

"That's an interesting idea of yours, Andy," I said, thoughtfully. "Maybe it's worth a try."

"It really is," someone else said.

"All right," I said, as if I were giving in. "If you want me to fill out the transfer for Killer, I will. He won't mind?"

"Not at all. Killer doesn't mind anything," Andy said. "He's outside in the summer anyhow. Everybody knows him. He's outside from six to six."

"Any chance I can see this guy Slav, just for a minute, next time I'm here?" I asked them.

"We'll bring him up right now. You got another few minutes?" They were in an obvious hurry to get the ball rolling, especially Andy, who was living with this thing.

Of course I could see him for a few.

"We'll bring him right up," one of the attendants said.

"I got to take off," said Armand the Barber apologetically.

Andy went to the phone and called in. "The psychologist here wants to see . . . We're in 3B . . . The Ad Building . . ." Then to me, "He's coming right over."

Two burly attendants brought in a robust man, about forty, with a stubby blond mustache, blond hair, his chin lifted a little too high. He had the kind of face you see on a ship's deck through a periscope in war films.

They had led him through the underground route, from which there was no escape. It meant opening and closing heavy oak doors every seventy yards or so. They stood right next to him.

I introduced myself. He didn't acknowledge even understanding me.

"You can sit down if you want," I said.

He didn't budge.

An attendant shouted right in his ear for him to "Sit down," and he did.

"I hear you do a thousand push-ups a day," I began.

No response.

"He hears you," one of the attendants said. "He thinks this is the war."

"He don't think shit! He just hates everybody," the other attendant said.

"He was captured by the Russians," said the first guy. "He has a number on his arm. They must have tortured—"

"A number on his arm. Let me see that—" I broke in.

An attendant rolled up the Slav's left sleeve, revealing a

multidigit number. The Slav held impressively still, he might as well have been a statue.

"Wait a minute. The Russians didn't put numbers on people. Only the Germans did," I said. "I don't get that story."

They shrugged and looked at me as if to say, "What are you making a puzzle out of it for? Who cares, Germans, Russians, Martians. He's a bad head. What kind of history do you need?"

"But a lot of people pretend they aren't German. If he was in a German camp . . . What the hell is he talking about?"

They looked at me as if I were crazy, even for being curious. Slav wouldn't talk, and that was that.

On his way out, I got a sense of how big he really was.

"Well, that was useful," I commented, mostly to myself.

"All right. We'll tell Carboni"—he was the clinical director who had authorized my visits. "He may want to call you to verify," Andy said.

I agreed.

It didn't take long. On my next visit about four of them broke in and tried to tell me the story together.

It had happened on a Sunday, which is always the hardest day in institutions. Sundays, some people get visitors and others don't. Andy and another attendant had put the lights out at the usual time—nine o'clock—and the fifty or so inmates on the ward were stretched out on their metal cots with mattresses. The dormitory room was a testimony to the modern idiom—form follows function; the mattresses came off easily enough for use in restraining a violent person. But that evening there had been no trouble. Things had gone smoothly.

The two attendants had gone into their little office room abutting the ward and were filling out papers and talking. They had a few hours to go before midnight.

There had been only one noise from the ward, the intermittent moaning of a boy about twenty. He'd kept saying the same thing, "Two hundred million years on the rock. Two hundred million years on the rock. Two hundred million years on the rock. Oh God, two hundred million years on the rock."

Andy and his cohort had gone over to the boy's cot several times. They'd talked to him and had run their fingers through his hair to calm him down, and then come back in the darkness through the forest of beds to their little office. They knew what his outcries meant. It was obvious. The boy's parents, who used to come regularly every Sunday to see him, had started to miss a Sunday or two, then more of them. He would pray for them to come, falling to his knees next to his bed, clasping his hands in prayer until they turned white. He would stay up all Saturday night. But the visits had dwindled, diminished, and now it looked as if they were never coming.

"Two hundred million years on the rock"—that was the biggest expression he had, the statement that did most justice to his plight.

Ten minutes of silence. Then from their little cubicle, they could hear his keening again. What the hell could they do? Andy went out and talked to him as warmly as he could. "But Billy, I know. Billy, I know. But you're keeping everyone awake."

Already the chorus had started of "Shut up," "Keep quiet," and an occasional "Quiet or I'll kill you."

The Slav was evidently sleeping after his workout. He was staying fit for the revolution. Killer, as always, had gone right off to sleep too. But now each new rupture of the silence by poor Billy lamenting his eternity was being accompanied by a wider range of voices telling him to "Shut the fuck up."

Then at eleven o'clock, just when they'd felt sure he was asleep, Billy began again. Andy and his buddy heard a thud, an unidentifiable sound, and then the single most horrible word imaginable—"Fire!"

Accelerating like running backs, they were out of their office and onto the ward, but they saw no fire, only a scuffle going on in the corner. Everyone was awake, and two men were fighting furiously—two white men and neither one was the Slav.

"Where's the fire?" asked Andy. The other attendant was already back inside phoning for help.

"Fight," said the Chinese inmate, and it sounded so much like "fire" that Andy realized at once why he and everyone else on that ward had sprung awake so fast. It was as if the big, wooden gymnasiumlike room had tilted to one side, its inhabitants edging as far away as they could from the Chinese guy, who alone had seen the fire. By the time more recruits came, Andy was calming them down and also yelling at the Chinese man, "Don't you know how to talk?"

He gave the ward ten minutes extra with the lights on. The fight had begun by someone hurling a shoe in the direction of the kid to shut him up. The shoe had hit someone else who was half asleep. He had lunged in the direction from which the shoe came, and that was it. No one was hurt. It wasn't worth anyone's time to go over the incident.

The recruits left soon afterward—a pleasant job, troubleshooting in a mental hospital—and Andy and his cohort returned to calming down the combatants and the rest, under the bright bulbs that quashed their vestigial nightmares. Killer was strolling around the place talking to no one, with the physique and ease of New York Giants linebacker Lawrence Taylor between plays. As far as he was concerned, nothing much had happened. Most of the others were back in bed. Andy invited a few very troubled stragglers into his office and was doling out cigarettes, which, technically, was against the rules after nine.

Billy had come in, and he and Andy were chatting together and smoking when the Slav blocked the door of the cubicle. "You're not supposed to smoke. Give me a cigarette," he ordered Andy.

Following the first rule of safety on the ward, which is never to be blocked from a phone, Andy himself stayed in the little office with Billy. He called across the ward to his buddy to come over at once.

"I want my cigarettes," the Slav demanded and looked at the packs of different brands on the shelf in the office, which belonged to various inmates. None of them were his. He never bought any. He wasn't actually a smoker. This was straight trouble.

Andy stood up, looked him in the eye, and said, "Slav, you don't have any cigarettes here."

"He's smoking. That guy's smoking too. And he's smoking," said Slav, pointing to different inmates on the ward and lastly to Billy inside the office.

"Hey, Killer!" Andy called. "Come over here. You got this guy's cigarettes. Why did you tell me he shouldn't have any?"

Slav eyed the black man as he approached.

"Killer, he wants to box you," Andy said. Then to the Slav, "He said you were a motherfucker, that you're a Jew or a Gypsy or something and you were never even in Russia."

Slav glowered at Killer, and Killer looked back at him curiously and smiled.

All at once Slav threw a murderous right hook to Killer's midsection. It landed solidly, but Killer backpedaled away and avoided a wicked shot to the head. Now Slav went after him in earnest and it was surely one of the strangest fights in history, the white man grunting, throwing hooks and jabs, frustrated and furious, while Killer, not knowing Slav was any different than an attendant, bobbed and wove and slipped punches, and finally touched Slav on the nose with a right so gently that Slav hardly felt it. The ward was on its feet again, hating Slav and most of the inmates not even recognizing Killer, who'd been there only a day or two.

It was good stuff according to the attendants, Slav landing an occasional punch but doing no damage and getting more crazed each time his opponent danced away from him and touched him on the cheek or the side of the head or the stomach. He took Killer's mock style of fighting him as the profoundest insult of his life, as almost unendurable. And now he went after the black former contender, snarling and with a hatred on his face that made the attendants worry for their champion.

Once again Killer slipped a punch and touched Slav's forehead, and this time held the pose, but instead of stopping as the attendants did, Slav countered with a shot that landed ferociously somewhere, the attendants couldn't remember where. But they knew it had registered. Killer backed away and a broad grin came over his face. This was for real. Like the old days. In the Garden. *You're a champion again*. Killer's was a smile of recognition, of revelation.

In he came and slipped another punch, and Slav was down. The attendants thought it was a short left jab to the head. It must have had terrible leverage. Slav didn't move.

"Lie down champ. Just go to bed," Andy whispered to Killer, who stood over the prone man. Finally, he shoved Killer back to his cot. Andy had the impression that moments later Killer forgot the fight. It was possible. With frontal-lobe damage, remote memory stays—Killer would never forget his forty-six professional knockouts—but this was too recent, another event in the penumbra of forgetfulness. By the time the medics came, Killer was asleep, though Andy swore he had a smile on his face.

The Slav went to the infirmary, where they cleaned him up and reset his nose. Apparently, he'd taken at least another blow that nobody saw, which had broken two ribs. When he returned a few days later, Killer was back on his own ward, doing his gardening, shadowboxing, and roadwork by day, and sleeping like the peaceful child that he'd become at night.

Slav had no one to sue and was no trouble after that, at least so far as I heard. He could hardly imagine the life on a back ward that he'd been saved from by that short left jab, or whatever it was that Killer had delivered so mercifully.

Later they established that Slav had actually been a prisoner of the Germans in Koblenz and had been released, half-starved, after the war. The numbers and letters on his arm told more of his story than he did. What had led him to pretend, to *believe* that he was a German soldier? Possibly, a mechanism exposed and given to us by Anna Freud, daughter of Sigmund and also a psychoanalyst, provides our explanation: *identification with the aggressor*.

Anna Freud observed that little children when subjected to brutality by adults sometimes resort to this identification. The little boy beaten by a boarding-school master adopts his facial tic, as if to say, "I am an extension of you. You may beat the others, but spare me. I am like you." After that it's a short step from "I am like you" to "I *am* you."

The child's adoption of this defense mechanism must surely help explain why so many battered children and victims of parental incest go on to treat their own children the exact same way. Here was the victim of prolonged brutality, surely a proud man before it all began, surviving psychologically by pretending that he was the aggressor and not the victim. Clinging to this pretense, he came increasingly to believe it.

For a while the attendants were afraid to challenge Killer again, fearing that having drawn blood, he might forget they were playing. But Andy, sensing that those sparring matches were main events in Killer's emotional life—his way of giving and receiving affection—took the chance. Killer instantly resumed his comic-strip style, and the other attendants soon began sparring with him too.

There were no further incidents, but now when he throws his punches, it isn't mere speculation about how good he really was. The attendants still tell the story of his real fight, and at least some tell it with more than admiration. They tell it with gratitude.

THE TRIUMPH OF FRAILTY

I recognized Ken's voice at once, and he seemed glad. It was a cheerful voice, of good timbre, though a bit overexplicit in its confidence and articulation, like a radio announcer's. Some years ago, Ken had constructed his personality and approach to the world very deliberately. I had watched this construction and played a part in it.

I was both pleased and sorry when he said, "I've got to come in and see you." I always liked talking to Ken, but this sounded a little too urgent.

His next sentence told me I was right. "I finally went for the AIDS antibody test. They were supposed to call Monday but they didn't. When it's positive, I've heard they don't call right back. I have the feeling it's bad."

I did my best over the phone. "Ken, this isn't like you. You're jumping the gun. There's a lot of red tape in these places. I don't see it."

"I know, but it's Thursday. I'm sorry to bother you, but I'd like to come in."

It was going to be one of those painful sessions, with my not knowing what to say. So many of my gay men patients from out of the past were calling, just to talk—some were nearly broken by recent bedside vigils with friends; others would come in mourning loved ones; one or two were themselves near death and had trouble getting around. But the hardest sessions were those with people who had just gotten bad news about themselves and still had it before them, unshunnably, to assimilate.

These were tidings of nightmare proportions, but the kind that didn't go away when you woke up.

Eight o'clock the next morning was the only time I had, and Ken was glad to come that early.

I had breakfast alone at a local diner on Broadway and tried to read the paper, but it was hard not to think about Ken, not to worry about him. It was a September day, sunny but already cool. The leisurely sense of summer was gone. On the streets the people bustled toward their destinations as if all life depended on their promptness. I realized that in the colleges—Ken was a teacher of English literature and drama— September was an optimistic month, a time for new learning, a fresh chance for good grades and to find new comrades. Ken must be seeing youthful discovery all around him.

I wallowed in the thought that the death of someone who has learned to struggle and care and appreciate life is every bit as tragic as that of any novice. No. I stopped myself. I was already prey to Ken's way of looking at things; it was as contagious as the plague itself. We had no evidence. The verdict wasn't in, and even if the worst diagnosis came to pass, the last thing Ken would need from me was morbidity.

He was at my office door when I got there, and we were happy to see each other. I deliberately didn't scrutinize him but got the impression that he had aged considerably. He was about five-ten, with black curly hair and delicate features. His slender physique argued his youth, but there were semicircles of fatigue under his eyes.

I decided that irrelevant chatting would only add to the tension, and went to our subject at once.

"Why do you think you're AIDS positive, Ken?"

"I've had a bad throat all summer. And I've suddenly been getting a lot of cold sores. It seems like I haven't been able to fight off simple colds. I *never* used to get colds. I always used to make jokes about how healthy I was, that I never got a chance to use my sick days. George, there's a lot I don't know, but I do know myself."

"You've been having sex with a lot of people?"

"You know I don't do that. Last night I was figuring. Over the last six years, it was five people."

"That doesn't have to be so dangerous."

"It only takes one."

"I know, but probabilities change."

I was doing what I'd resolved not to—looking for favorable signs. It wasn't my role and it wasn't helping. We'd find out soon enough.

I asked him, "When are you going to call them back?"

"I decided I'd wait until Monday. I got the bill from my doctor yesterday. They were fast enough with that."

"Are you involved with anyone these days?"

"No. Not for two years. I was living with someone, but it wasn't right. He thought I was boring, and I started to think *he* was boring."

I asked him, "How long has it been since I saw you? Ten years?"

"Yes, can you believe it? Eliot's been dead close to ten years now."

I could hardly imagine it had been so long.

Ken said, "I'm sure if Eliot had been going to you, it never would have happened." He stood up and took off his jacket and laid it carefully on the couch.

I commented that it was a pretty fancy blue blazer.

"You know us gays. We dress well and we're house-proud. We're cultured. And, unfortunately, we're public-enemy-number-one."

"You mean you make the wanted lists?" I asked him.

"Only the AIDS list. God's vengeance, you know. He's trying to upgrade the community."

"You're getting a little morbid, aren't you?"

"Well, what are we supposed to do? I mean, what am *I* supposed to do, while I wait for Monday to come around? Go out dancing?"

"Why not? Why do you make 'go out dancing' sound so ridiculous? I'm worried about you. You're turning into one of those notorious, prissy, college professors. I guess every school needs one. 'Hates himself for being homosexual. Therefore teaches the young as a way of atoning. Very precise. Waiting to die.' That's not the Ken I knew. You need about six sessions a week. You better sign up."

Even before he responded, I knew that my getting tough with him was the best thing to do.

He said, "You're right. I guess I've stopped living these days."

"That's your old problem, Ken—"

"But George, this is real. It isn't like just finding out you're homosexual and that everyone's going to hate you, your friends, your parents, the community."

"Why? They hate you at the college?"

"No," he admitted. "Not really."

"They know you're gay?"

"They expect the college English and drama teacher to be gay. It goes with sensitivity, doesn't it? Sensitivity and early death."

"Ken, in your case it goes with self-pity."

I could understand his falling into that mode, but I wanted no part of it. My clobbering him for his attitude seemed like the best way out for both of us. I continued, ironically, "Poor Ken. He died early. When were you born?"

"Nineteen forty-eight."

I said, solemnly, as if reading an obit, "'Ken Cameron. Nineteen forty-eight to nineteen eighty-eight. Self-pitying homosexual. May he rest in peace.' How's that?"

"I guess you're really enjoying yourself," he said sarcastically.

"No, you are. You don't even have any evidence about yourself yet. I can understand why you're so afraid. I can really understand it. But meanwhile, nothing has happened to you. So far as we know, you're not even a carrier of anything—except self-pity. I mean, I never thought you'd come back, wallowing in self-pity when nothing has actually happened to you."

"What do you mean?"

"I mean suppose there's nothing wrong with you, Ken? Look what you're doing to yourself."

He said, "But suppose there is. This reminds me of old times."

"Me too. We went through a lot didn't we?" I said, closing the gap.

"We did," he agreed. He fell silent, and I surmised from his constantly changing facial muscles that he was back there, remembering something. After a while I asked him what he was thinking about.

"Oh, getting beaten up in the street. Right on Madison Avenue. And saying to you that maybe I should try to convert. Become heterosexual."

I told him that I remembered his black eye, but that I couldn't recall much about how that session went.

"I'll never forget it. It was the turning point of my life. When I talked about becoming a heterosexual, and you said you couldn't help me. And I asked who could you recommend. And you said you never saw a gay person, man or woman, become really heterosexual as a result of therapy, so you couldn't recommend anyone. You said I'd have to find the person myself.

"I carried on that if I could only find Miss Right and settle down, it would work, and you said, 'Poor Miss Right.' Of course, you knew what you were talking about. I would have only messed up some woman's life if I made her part of an experiment. It's a lot easier to be yourself and be disliked by a lot of people than to be nobody. I guess Eliot found that out."

"I don't know what he found out."

I didn't like to think about Eliot, but he intruded. Over the years, a decade if Ken was accurate, he'd hovered in the background, like the Grim Reaper himself, whenever I worked with a gay patient, though only a few like Ken actually knew Eliot and knew his story.

Then Ken said, "I wish I was stronger."

"Ken, you *are* very strong," I said. "I've always thought of you as a tower of strength. Just because you don't go through the streets with a leather jacket and brass knuckles. I mean, you don't have to be a weight lifter to be strong."

"I know. But you're right. I haven't even got bad news yet and I feel like I'm going under."

"I think anyone in your position—I think every gay man in America and a lot of other people—are nervous about this. How can you possibly run yourself down for being scared? Especially if you have anything that even looks like a symptom."

"That's true. You'd be nervous if you were me?"

I felt a little cornered by the question. He was asking me for an exact probability statement about his chances, which, of course, I couldn't give him.

I told him what I could. "Even if I had one chance in a hundred of having AIDS, I'd probably be nervous. I don't know your odds. I don't think anybody does, Ken. That's the lousy part. Of course I'd feel shaky, and if anyone told me I shouldn't, I'd tell him to go fuck himself."

"I understand. So what would you do?"

"That's easy." I said. "I'd call someone who's a tower of strength. Maybe someone like you—and talk. But that's not saying you have AIDS. I wouldn't want to go up in a twin-engine plane in a storm, but that's not the same as a crash."

"Right." He looked straight into my eyes, and though he had a baritone voice, there was a hint of the suppliant about him as he said, "I feel a little better." Then his eyes twinkled, and he added, "I was about to say, 'I appreciate the transfusion,' but these days every transfusion is dangerous, and it wouldn't be fair."

"That's not funny," I said.

We talked a little about his parents, on in years but both in good health. "I speak to my mother maybe every two weeks, and my father gets on at the end to say 'hello' and ask me in a low voice if I need any money. He always says the same thing, 'I know a teacher's salary isn't much.' That's about it. He never really could appreciate my being homosexual."

"What's to appreciate?" I asked him. "You are what you are."

"You know what I mean. He could never accept it, he'd still rather not know. He and my sisters are in constant touch. Oh, I forgot to tell you. They're both married. Helen has two kids, boys, and Margie has one on the way. A girl."

"How modern, to know in advance!" I said.

"I know. Her husband is a stockbroker. Maybe he deals in futures." Ken smiled for the first time.

"So do we," I told him. "We've got great futures."

"You haven't changed much, George, have you?" he said.

Before leaving, he surprised me by asking, "Have you got any words of wisdom?"

It was the kind of question I get asked often and never answer. As a therapist, there to elicit as much of the whole truth as I could, to understand it, to clarify it, to hold up the mirror, it wasn't my province to give guidelines for daily life. Ken knew that as well as I did. I had an impulse to remind him. But it would have sounded like my saying, "Best of luck. Now fuck off. I'm within the rules." Obviously, he hadn't come to me for that.

He'd told me he was going to be alone in his apartment over the weekend, mostly listening to his opera records and preparing his lectures. How easy it is when you're alone for possibilities to feel like realities, for thoughts to assume the status of accomplished facts. The whisperings of ideas echo loudly when there is no other voice in the room. And in a case like this, waiting without knowing is in some ways worse than knowing the worst. I felt I had to say something, if only so he would have another voice in the room with him.

I told him, duplicating the tone of someone who just made

an arrest and is reading the suspect his rights, "You have the
right to be terrified. But you have no right to conclude that you
have AIDS. You *don't know*. Get a calendar for nineteen
eighty-eight. Write down the number of minutes you spend
each day in self-pity. You'll get better control of it if you do."

He commented, "Okay. I'll do it. That self-pity sounds
pretty disgusting, doesn't it?"

I stayed official-sounding. "Let's not condemn it. Just look
out for it."

At the door he suggested scheduling a session for Monday,
after he was to find out, and we set one up. The time, three in
the afternoon, became more indelible in my mind than it was
in my date book, where I wrote it with a black flare-pen.

I'd gone over the question "Do you call or don't you? Do you
bring up the topic or don't you?" so often with patients in
trouble that I didn't need a special inquiry to decide against
calling Ken that weekend to say "cheer up" in any variation.
He had friends for that. Suppose I caught him in a moment of
good cheer, of laughter, of forgetting. I'd be doing the exact
opposite of what I'd intended. In that case, my very voice
would be a reminder of AIDS, its existence, its prevalence.
Besides, I had nothing special to say.

My own weekend became a whirligig of thoughts, of memories, of Ken, and of Eliot, the friend who had long ago become
disaffected with him and me, and finally with life itself. We're
all distorted by this thing, I thought—not just those who have
already been sentenced or love somebody who has, but anyone
who cares about the millions under siege. And yet, in spite of
the press and video coverage and the talk, it was as if few
people knew—knew emotionally—outside of those directly
touched.

It wasn't just a matter of caring because you could be next.
It was caring because you ought to care because you're human,
and because caring can still become the human's signature,
the way placid strength is the elephant's or reaching high al-
titudes is that of the tern.

*   *   *

I wanted not to think about Ken or Eliot that weekend. Though nearly every therapist does productive work in off-hours, my thinking about them didn't promise to help anyone.

But I didn't have any choice. Once again, I saw how ideas that we want to suppress and people we'd like to forget can, with what seems like a will of their own, make appearances in our lives in other forms—almost as if they chose candidates close to us to lobby for them.

Saturday afternoon I played tennis with a guy named Burton. He'd been a fair player, but his tennis lessons were destroying him: He was concentrating on so many things—bending his knees, getting his racket back in time and such—that he couldn't hit the ball. As a result of his lessons, I beat him easily, using whatever strokes I could muster.

Burton seemed to have no fun playing the game and probably never did, though he nurtured the illusion that some day when he did everything right, he'd be wowing them somewhere. He lived every day as if only tomorrow mattered. In the locker room, he discussed his new strokes in detail. He extolled his coach and handed me the man's card, which I took politely.

On the way home, I kept hearing Burton's ravings about the fundamentals of the game, and then realized that I was thinking about Eliot. Though Burton was less dramatic, less tragic, and far less attractive and talented, he and Eliot were both advocates of what I deemed "the school of postponement and perfection." As nonmembers, Ken and I were left down here, embracing our own condition, our imperfections.

Lolling in the back of the cab, I took one of the tennis balls I'd won from Burton out of the can, and in some kind of primordial, superstitious way, I squeezed it and I thought of Ken, as if we shared a triumph. It was the Ken of more than fourteen years ago, at least by his count.

AIDS was unheard of back then, in 1974. What is today known widely as the "gay movement" had just started to attract atten-

tion in the United States and elsewhere. Thirty states were
empowered to seize anyone for even a consensual homosexual
act with another adult, and to put the person in prison for five
years or more. And these were no idle threats. I'd met gays
who'd spent a lot more time in jail than many murderers do.

What stays with me most of my first impression of Ken was his
lack of outrage over what had been done to him. Here he was,
his face blue from a dislocated nose and his arm in a sling
from a blow he'd received when he'd tried to block a punch.
Four or five hoodlums had pulled their car to a screeching
halt, poured out, and amid shrieks of "faggot" and "pansy,"
had punched him and kicked him and then driven off.

In my office he didn't curse them or seem to suffer from that
terrible sense of impotent rage that is usually a delayed conse-
quence of having been manhandled.

I asked him, "Did you go to the police?"

He said that he hadn't, there was no point to it. Nor had he
thought to try to remember the license plate of his attackers'
car. He didn't think that way, this boy of twenty-six, who had
been in the big city working as a waiter and trying to get acting
jobs for two years. He'd come here from Iowa where, he said,
"Everything was football, and it wasn't for me."

He'd struck me as handsome, despite the discoloration of
his face. And he was almost too pleasant for someone beaten
up so badly less than a week before that. He wasn't especially
effeminate, but one could guess that he might be homosexual
by his attention to detail, his fastidiousness, and by what
seemed like a lack of personal force, which typified some gay
men—in particular, those whose homosexuality troubled them
and drove them toward an overcompensating conventionality.

Ken, like many, suffered from the fear that to show emo-
tionality, or even intensity, might cause him to appear much
more evidently homosexual than he would if he remained mod-
ulated, even under stress.

He must have repeated five times the phrase "right on

Madison Avenue," as if the truly astonishing thing were that this avenue of fashion and of consummate luxury had failed to awe the thugs or deter them.

When I asked him how he felt about his assailants, he hesitated. "How do I feel about them? They're stupid. They're wrong. What do you want me to say?"

His tone was almost nonchalant. It was arch at most, not angry.

It wasn't hard to conceive of a possible explanation for his lack of real outrage. Ken himself harbored some of the hatred toward homosexuals that his assailants had given vent to with their brutality. He was a young man divided, being homosexual and hating himself for it. The two hemispheres of his psyche were at war.

I saw further evidence of this conflict as we went on. In an apparent attempt to distance himself from his own homosexuality, Ken would make derisive comments about others who were gay. He sneered at a fellow waiter who was gay and rather obvious about it. "All he needs is a dress," Ken said.

And when some friends of his had complained about a bank's refusal to hire a woman who couldn't get bonded because she was a lesbian, Ken didn't stop to consider if there was an injustice and where it lay. Not wanting to take sides, he simply let the air out of the issue by saying, "I guess they have their reasons."

His was an unconscious program to make his own homosexuality go away by pretending it wasn't there. He imagined he would some day fall in love with a woman, marry her, have children, and settle down—and never have to endure another moment of attraction toward a man. Not that he wanted to do any of this, but his present state seemed intolerable.

He had close women friends, and one night the previous year, had found himself in bed with one, who seemed bent on converting him and saving him from hell. However, he couldn't get an erection, even when he'd tried to imagine that he was with a man. Though he liked her personally, the very thought of having

sex with a woman was as upsetting to him as performing homosexual sex acts would be to most heterosexuals.

Ken's dreams, his fantasies, his ambitions were all linked
with romantic feelings about men. He would write a great play,
inspired by a male lover, who would be in the first row on
opening night. Nothing seemed to matter if he had to give up
homosexuality. He'd had his first romantic-sexual fantasies
about males when he was nine or ten, and they'd been recur-
ring ever since.

But his feeling of urgency about banishing these feelings
was also very strong. A civil war was raging within him, and
Ken wanted it to be the war to end all wars—if only I would
help him to stamp out the opposition, the upsurgents.

In about our third month he said to me, "I want you to help
me battle this thing!"

"What do you mean 'this thing'?" I asked him, though I felt
sure I knew what he had in mind.

"My homosexual side. I want to get rid of it, once and for all."

"In other words, you want me to save you from yourself?" I
paraphrased.

With seemingly no compunction or feeling of strangeness,
he answered, "That's right. I do."

I told him that I couldn't do that. I could very probably help
him overcome his fear of living, his lack of belief in himself. I
could help him understand who he was and what he wanted. I
could help him enjoy life more and work more effectively—at
best. But he would have to choose his own goals.

He seemed dissatisfied.

That was when he started talking about Eliot, a new acquain-
tance of his. They'd met through a friend of Ken who had been
in love with Eliot but got rejected. Ken said he could see why
his friend was in such pain. Eliot was good-looking, sure of
himself, with a beautiful smile. He was an athlete, he would
run great distances in Central Park, and afterward, at eight in
the morning, would drop into the restaurant, where Ken would
serve him orange juice and corn flakes.

Eliot was a last-year medical student and was to begin his psychiatric residency soon. His plan, he told Ken, was to go into analysis during that final period of training, using it to eradicate all traces of his own homosexuality in order to become a first-class psychiatrist.

Ken himself was close to being in love with Eliot, and had no doubt whatsoever that Eliot was going to succeed. "Of course, you can do it if your analyst is good," Eliot had promised him.

"Well, I think my doctor is very good," Ken had replied.

"Has he got good credentials?" Eliot had asked.

"I think so," Ken had said.

Eliot had explained, "Homosexuality is a stage. It's what we call a 'passing-through stage' on the way to healthy maturity. It's a matter of going back to your childhood to understand where you got blocked." Eliot spoke in a way that admitted no contradiction, and anyhow, Ken was not one to contradict.

Within recent weeks Eliot had become Ken's second authority, he had almost the same status that I did. He was more dogmatic, he sounded surer.

Ken was surprised and delighted when, one morning, Eliot asked him, "So who is this doctor of yours? What's his name? I'd like to see him."

He had told Eliot proudly, but when he'd mentioned that I was a clinical psychologist and not a medical doctor, Eliot had winced.

Even so, Eliot was going to call me, Ken said. As if fearful that I wouldn't work with Eliot, he praised him and assured me that he would have absolutely no misgivings if I tried to help Eliot as well as him.

A few days after calling me, Eliot breezed in, everything about him suggesting fitness and comfort. He told me that his father was a big surgeon in Boston, and therefore he himself wanted to try another branch of medicine. They were Jewish, but the family had changed their name. He told me that "In many professions, it's not that good to be thought of as a Jew."

I asked him the standard questions, what did he want out of therapy?

His answer was cagey. "To know myself better. Yes, that's it. To know myself better."

I got more specific. "What would you like to change about yourself?"

He became facetious. "Well, I'm growing a beard, as you see. I'd like to change the way I look."

I let him divert me. "Is this the first time you've had one?" I asked him.

"No. I've grown one and cut it off a number of times. I like changing my appearance."

I just waited.

"Oh, another thing," he said. "I've had some . . . some homosexual experiences. I'd like to stop those."

"I see. Why don't you?"

"Well, it hasn't really been that important to me, but now it is."

Eliot spoke as if everything were under his absolute control, and to doubt him would itself be derelict.

"I grew up with three sisters, and a very strong mother. But I've slept with women too, of course. Women are very attracted to me."

"You enjoyed it?"

"Not really. I never have, but I can satisfy them. I can always get an erection, I mean, unless the woman just lies there."

"You've enjoyed sex with men?"

"It's a sickness. How can you enjoy it? I've done it a lot, I guess, but mainly when I've been under a lot of tension. It's a kind of release. I want to stop doing it."

"How old were you when you started those experiences with men?"

"When I was a child. I guess I've always had them." He smiled, and I got the impression that he was studying my face, perhaps even hoping that I would find myself attracted to him.

At length he asked, "Well, Doctor, what do you think?"

I told him much that I had told Ken, describing his erotic reactions to men as his particular sense of romantic beauty. But he insisted that he had to change.

"That's not something I can promise."

He got impatient. "People come in here in agony over their problems, and you say there's nothing wrong with them. That's because you're not as well trained as psychiatrists. You can't go as deep." He went on to say that psychologists are shallow alongside medical specialists. "I guess you just don't go deep enough."

I said, "Obviously, Eliot, not everyone agrees. But I've never seen therapy change someone's erotic preference. If a man is attracted to fat women instead of thin, or old ones and not young ones, that's a very special form of erotic-romantic arousal. Therapy can't change it. And if a person is homosexual, that's not something we can just shift. Therapists are divided on this, you know, Eliot. I have my view and I can't promise—"

"If you knew enough, you could."

"I can't debate that, but from what you say, your attraction to men goes back so far, I'm not sure you would really even want to change, except that—"

"I absolutely do. I'm not a hopeless case."

"I didn't say you were. I was going to say, except that society is so tough. I mean, if you were convinced you would find love and happiness, be effective in your profession, have friends, have your parents' acceptance, whatever—if this didn't depend at all on your changing, would you even *want* to change?"

"But you're talking nonsense. That's not the way it is. You're really a very limited man. Has anyone ever told you that?"

"Yes, Eliot, they have."

He followed up strong. "And you're also a very hostile man."

Taken by surprise, I kept quiet, since my only mistake could be to counterpunch. But he was so apparently out of control that it was easy for me to guard my composure.

A moment later he softened his tone. "May I ask you a question?"

"Of course," I said. "I'm not sure I'll answer it, but sure."

"Are you a faggot?"

"Do you mean am I homosexual?"

"Yes."

My first thought was that what I am is nobody's business, but I decided to be truthful, for his sake.

"No, I'm not. Actually, I've never had a homosexual experience. My head doesn't go that way. But it doesn't make me any better than someone who is."

"You mean me?"

"Eliot, we don't have to battle. Obviously, you think I'm pretty deranged because I don't consider your homosexual desires to be sick. You'll do what you want."

I stood up.

"Yes, I will. I'll find someone with a lot more knowledge and better training than you obviously have. You don't have to walk me to the door."

He was the proverbial youth who had never tasted defeat. He would find some professional easily, a man or woman with the right credentials, who shared his view that he was diseased and should make an all-out effort to change. There were plenty of experts who thought he could—and should. Only in recent years has psychiatry reversed its official stand on homosexuality as an illness and have those who attempt conversion become a minority.

When Eliot was gone, I could feel his contempt even more keenly than when he'd been sitting in front of me. I experienced his distrustful eyes, his swagger, and his sneering pretense of certainty. I felt as glad that he was out of my life as he must have felt to have me out of his.

But as I was to learn, Eliot was far from out of mine. Ken was to keep me apprised of Eliot's doings and of his opinions—on occasion at first but increasingly over the few years that followed.

I'd half-expected Eliot to run me down to Ken at their next meeting. Possibly he had started to, but Ken was an advocate of mine, and there was no such report.

My therapeutic strategy with Ken in that early phase included bringing to his attention any comment he made condemning himself—or condemning other people for being
homosexual. He was astonished to see how often he did this.
He took quickly to the formulation that he was in conflict, that
his yearnings were for love and affection from men but that he
felt queasy and unspeakably wrong for this.

Living alone and not yet a success at his chosen work also
played into his self-hate. I saw him as courageous for having
come to the "big city," and for his willingness to fight the
odds, but he didn't see himself this way. He saw himself as an
abject failure. Not simply because he was homosexual, but
because his acting career was yielding little beyond some audi-
tions, a showcase performance that led nowhere, and a non-
paying role in a play done in an uptown church.

He had plenty of time to contemplate, not being by nature a
goer to bars or parties. Alone in his room at night, he would
experience that terrible sense of isolation that is incident to the
human condition. He would hear the night marching outside
and would picture a mass of people at a party that he wasn't
going to be invited to. And he would attribute this sense of
isolation, which all of us know, to the fact of his being homosexual.

I tried to help him appreciate how much of that ache is
universal, how, doubtless, we all have a sense of some promise
broken—the promise of a closeness that must remain imaginary. Call it existential disappointment, if you will. It tran-
scends the details of any individual life, being the essence of
life itself.

He felt heartened by my helping him stop attributing that
universal feeling to his being homosexual. That kings and
princes, and all of us, feel this way meant a great deal to him.
It took time for him to absorb the idea that even his family
members must feel similarly, and that unbroken certainty of
one's way is swagger—not real strength.

He'd had urges to tell his mother that he was homosexual.
In fact, just before he came to me, he'd considered revealing it
to her in the context of announcing that he was going to a

therapist for cure. As he saw it, that would take the curse off it. However, since I had proved so uncooperative on the subject of "cure," now he couldn't say this in good faith.

"I don't want to lie to her," he said. Ken didn't like lying to anyone.

His younger sister, Margie, had no idea. She'd always admired Ken, who had been like a father to her, and he writhed at the thought of her ever finding out. But Helen, his older sister, could take it. In fact, some comments she'd made suggested that she might already have guessed but was waiting for him to inform her officially. Ken's realization that he was isolating Helen, as well as himself, by his secrecy, edged him toward taking the chance.

Telling almost anyone would help. Ken had lived as if virtually everyone he knew would consider him a leper, except for certain gay men, who, being accomplices in degeneracy, could ill afford to pass judgment on him.

"So the honest part of your life will be spent entirely with gay men," I observed.

"It sounds terrible, doesn't it?" he said.

It was a curious paradox. Hating himself as he did, he felt uncomfortable in the company of nonhomosexuals, and because he saw his own reflection in homosexual men, he felt uneasy with them too. Women seemed the most forgiving—or, as he thought of them, the least unforgiving. And so Ken spent a lot of time with women, the waitresses in his restaurant and with fledgling actresses who took classes with him.

In about our sixth month, I pressed him on the subject of whom he could tell and whom he couldn't. I had little sense of how close he was to divulging the truth, but his answers would help us gauge exactly how accepted he felt by different people.

"Ken, suppose you had to tell one person in the world that you think you're gay, I don't mean a stranger, I mean someone you care about, who would it be?"

As I'd expected, he said Helen.

"And who in your family would you *least* want to tell?"

Again, I wasn't surprised. "My father."

"How do you think he'd react?"

"It's very simple. He'd go crazy. He's gotten much more surly than he used to be. I mean he loves me, he'd give me nearly anything. But, George, if I told him I was gay, he'd break my nose."

"Really!"

It hadn't been very long since that gang of toughs had smashed him in the nose. It crossed my mind that to Ken they were—in a perverse way, of course—a gang of fathers.

We were making progress. He was differentiating people in his own mind on the criterion of how accepting they were.

A few months later Ken flew home to Iowa for a visit. He went for a drive with Helen and told her. She was sympathetic and thanked him for trusting her, and said nothing about having thought so. Perhaps she had known but had the diplomacy not to alarm Ken with the idea that anyone could tell.

She said that she had no idea how their mother would react if Ken told her. If anything, she felt even more strongly than Ken did that their father would go berserk if confronted with the fact. "I've been watching him," she told Ken. "He was always bad, but he's getting worse with his arthritis. The other day mother made a suggestion about how he should plaster the wall, and he wouldn't talk to her for two days, until I begged him to."

Recalling our sessions, for the first time Ken considered his father's irascibility as a sign of weakness, not strength.

He returned from Iowa triumphant. It wasn't just that he'd reclaimed a loved one. If Helen could accept him, so could others. He had struck a blow against his unconscious premise that decent folk would never welcome him if they found out he was gay.

I kept him talking about this conviction of his. Sure enough, he saw men, women, children, adults, people of all races and creeds, as a homogeneous mass, cohesive and agreeing on the loathsomeness of people like him. To recognize that he felt this way further freed him to reconsider the idea and what he did.

He took another chance, divulging that he was homosexual to a fellow waiter who had just gotten married. The youth seemed unperturbed, and they remained friends.

Ken's confidence was growing. He talked somewhat less urgently about "curing himself" of his homosexuality. His priority shifted toward accepting himself, and pursuing his career. If some of the people who were going to find out would hate him, that was their problem. At least that was how Ken felt on his good days.

However, he continued to have bad days, too, days when his doubts surfaced and he hated himself. And his friend Eliot knew precisely how to stir up those doubts.

For a while Eliot didn't drop by. Then he started coming in again, not in jogging clothes but in very fancy three-piece suits. He didn't come in alone but with other young people, whom Ken took to be fellow students of his. They would talk politely and in hushed tones.

"There's something different about him," Ken said. He couldn't pin it down, but Eliot was much less communicative. Eliot spoke to him only to say hello and to order his meal. He never acknowledged Ken on the way out.

Then, according to Ken, one day Eliot dropped in alone, and another waiter served him. As he sat over coffee, he summoned Ken over to his table. Thinking at first that he wanted service, Ken whispered to the youth whose table it was, but Eliot beckoned him again and Ken saw that he wanted to talk.

Eliot started out by asking him how his acting efforts were going, and when Ken implied not so well, Eliot suggested it was no surprise.

With great assuredness, Eliot commented, "It's stopping you. You have to get past it, or I don't see how you can succeed." He stirred his cereal as if unaware that he'd dropped a bomb on Ken's life.

Not unexpectedly, Ken pursued him. "Do you really think so?"

"Of course. It's rather obvious, but I assume you're making progress."

"You mean at not being homosexual anymore?"

Eliot didn't answer. He knew that his implication was clear, and let Ken do the work.

"Why . . . do . . . you say that?" Ken stammered. "You're overcoming it?"

"Of course. May I have another napkin please."

Ken scurried to get one.

Eliot said, "Actually, I never really was homosexual. I've been in very intensive psychoanalysis with one of the top people in the field, and he doesn't think so. He's very expensive. Four times a week. He wants me there five. I've learned a lot about my childhood. I haven't had a homosexual contact of any kind for ninety-five days."

"Really!" Ken was confused, but delighted that Eliot was taking this much interest in him.

"No. I've been dating several women. It's really very much better."

Ken was drawn away by requests from patrons at other tables. When he finished, he expected Eliot to be gone but he was still sitting there, reading his newspaper and dawdling over his coffee.

Ken returned, as if magnetized by both beauty and truth.

"You're still seeing that same doctor?" Eliot asked.

When Ken told him that he was, Eliot commented flatly, "It's a mistake."

"What do you mean?"

"I had a weak father. I chose an analyst who is quite strong and very different. The choice of doctor is crucial in these cases."

"'Choice of doctor'!" It was all Ken could do to echo the phrase.

"Well, if you really want to know—"

"I do," Ken had insisted.

"No one who doesn't want to be homosexual has to be,"
Eliot said smugly. "You're going to the wrong man."

"I am?"

"Obviously, he's not fully analyzed or properly trained.
Maybe you ought to consider changing."

With that Eliot looked at his watch and rose from the table.

Ken got busy and didn't see him leave. Afterward he felt
desperate to ask him some more questions.

Ken didn't report that conversation to me for weeks, but it
threw him into a quandary. He went home and swigged down a
few beers and felt sorry for himself. His life was a mockery.
Eliot had told him only what he already knew—he could travel
the world but his flaw would always be there, until somehow he
burned it out of his soul.

Eliot was the figure he wanted to be—young, handsome,
rich, rising, educated, and correct in his assertion that homosexuality hobbles even those with talent and desire. Eliot was
making the sacrifice for his career as a psychiatrist; others had
made it. "It's stopping you. You have to get past it"—the
words drove Ken to another beer and still another. The phrase
seemed both to epitomize his life of suffering and to explain it.

Finally, Ken seized his jacket and went down the two flights
of stairs and into the street. It was eleven o'clock at night,
and, in his muzzy, half-anesthetized condition, Ken imagined
that everything he saw confirmed his status as an outcast.

On Broadway he saw young couples, dressed casually, going
home, arm in arm, and he pictured them with children in bed
already asleep, their lives arranged and full. He saw elderly
couples, presumably together for years and who would remain
so as long as they lived—heterosexuals, normals, *real* people.
There were also occasional men, walking alone, some of whom
he took to be homosexual, and when one or two looked hun-
grily into his eyes, he turned away.

At Fifty-ninth Street he headed eastward, across Central
Park South, pausing to look up at the broad curtained windows

of the Plaza, where the privileged were spending the night. He imagined that no first-rate hotel would permit two men in one of their suites, and he felt they were justified.

Past the Third Avenue singles bars he went next, envying the lines of young healthy boys and girls, whose very animation and youth made him feel as if he were long dead and coming back to look at the world. He had once dreamed of redeeming himself with a great acting career, but now even that seemed impossible.

On First Avenue, the furthest one east, he veered downtown and ambled past the hospitals with their huge iron gates. With only an occasional person on the streets, he felt more able to experience the sad truth of his isolation. It was as if he had never been in my office.

He was vaguely aware of a gang of toughs, in jeans and sneakers, standing in a dilapidated park, and he strode past them. The next thing he knew they were surrounding him.

"Faggot, you want to suck me off?" one of them said. He was a chubby fellow with a crew cut.

Ken tried to pretend that he wasn't there.

Another blocked his path.

There were about six of them, blacks, whites, Hispanic— later when I asked Ken to free-associate about them, the first phrase that came to his mind was "United Nations."

The chubby fellow grinned and pulled loose his belt and brandished it. Ken thought another one of them was holding a switchblade. He sobered up at once and pictured his death right there.

"Look, leave me alone. I'm not bothering you"—that was all Ken could think of to say.

"You *are* bothering me!" said one of them. "Take your jacket off. I want it."

"It is off," said the chubby fellow. "He doesn't ever put his arms in it."

"Maybe he has no arms," said someone else. He slapped Ken on the face, and somehow they got hold of the jacket.

They began closing the circle.

Just then a police car came into sight, its red lights flashing, and the thugs backed off, trying to look inconspicuous. The police must have recognized what to them was surely a common tableau. An officer sprang out of the patrol car and raced over.

"What's going on here?" he asked.

"Nothin's happening, man," said the chubby fellow.

Ken spoke up. "Can I have my jacket back, please," he demanded of one of them, who handed it to him. Then Ken said to the officer, "I'd very much like to get out of here."

Several of the thugs grinned, and the policeman said something nasty to them. Only then did Ken notice that all the while the officer had kept his hand on his holstered gun. He was alarmed that the officer really thought he might need that gun.

The officer told them to break it up, and they made a show of scattering. He escorted Ken to the patrol car and sat with him in the backseat.

"You homosexuals ought to have more sense," said the other policeman, who was at the wheel. "You make it hard for yourself, and you make it hard for the law."

"Well, in any case I'm certainly glad you came along," Ken said. It crossed Ken's mind that nearly any young man who sounded at all cultured and strolled in that neighborhood could be taken as gay.

Then a radio call came in. A woman had just witnessed a robbery uptown. Ken had the thought that someone standing at a window, probably in the high rise across the street from the park, might have been looking down and made just such a telephone call, alerting the police and perhaps saving his life.

After that he avoided me the whole next week, calling in and saying he had the flu. When he did come in, he was subdued and reluctant to talk. I pressed him to tell me what was on his mind, but he said only that he felt hopeless.

It took two sessions for me to drag out of him what had

happened. When he told me about his close call, I had him reconstruct everything that had led up to his going out that night, starting with the moment he woke up in the morning.

He hesitated before telling me what Eliot had said, but there too I insisted on as many details as he could possibly remember. Even his serving Eliot and rushing for the napkin meant something—it underscored his role as a second and Eliot's as the one calling the shots. Eliot could beckon him over or dismiss him, could compliment him or tear him down. And with Eliot's various gifts and accomplishments, and especially his sovereign certainty of himself, it was easy to see why an uncertain Ken would be so swayed.

As Ken came to see that Eliot had driven him to his six-pack of beers, and utter disapproval of himself, I once again took stock of a sorrowful truth. The harsh words of authorities who demean us have a curious impact on our psyches that is often greater than the encouragement of friends who believe in us. Ken was still reeling from Eliot's comments, as well as from that evening.

But I knew, too, that though this had been a brutal setback and our work together seemed lost, it had not truly been lost but only eclipsed for a time.

The following week we came to the matter of why he'd made his way into that murderous vortex, so far from civilization that even his shouts would be lost in the night. Granted, Eliot's comments had a terrible effect on him. But why had he gone there?

When he told me he had no idea, I asked him to free-associate, to tell me whatever came to his mind.

"I don't think I started out to go there, but then I felt I should. I just felt like going over that way."

"Why there?"

"I know this sounds ridiculous, but the United Nations is over there. Wow! I must have been a lot more drunk than I realized."

"What is there about the UN?"

He hesitated. "I guess I was pretty drunk. Well, they have a lot of power, and they bring peace."

"The UN does," I agreed.

I was in a territory that made no sense to me, but since Ken was the one who had brought me there, I counted on his unconscious having a map.

"What kind of peace?" I inquired, partly to break the silence.

"I don't know . . . Then I saw those hoodlums, of all those nationalities. I just couldn't stand the pain . . . Maybe they'd bring peace."

It was frightening, but I had to put the worst possibility into words. "You mean by killing you?"

He thought awhile, seemingly not sharing any of my alarm. "I know it sounds funny, but . . . Maybe not kill me, but punish me."

"You mean beat your homosexuality out of you."

"Maybe. I can't believe it. But now that you say it, it seems right. I think that's why I wore my jacket European-style—you know, over my shoulders, not putting my arms in the sleeves. So I'd look homosexual. God, I don't know what got into me."

I was stunned that he didn't seem especially shaken, even now, by the realization of what he had done.

"What scares me, Ken," I told him, "is that you could do it again. And you could get killed next time."

"I know what you mean."

But his words still sounded flat.

With our session coming to an end, I had an impulse to clang an alarm in his head, though I wasn't sure how.

I repeated, beseechingly this time, "Ken, you will if you want to. People who hate themselves drive cars into trees, or die of some accidental overdose. Every day people find ways because they hate themselves. I hope you know that, Ken."

"I've got to deal with this, don't I?" he said.

I had barely time to say, "You really do." We were already into someone else's hour.

*   *   *

When he was gone, I realized that I'd been concentrating on too narrow a problem, in studying what his homosexuality meant to him. He had come to hate himself so thoroughly that he hated all his feelings—he hated everything about himself.

But to my delight, Ken had apparently absorbed much more than I'd thought, because he came in next time very angry with himself. "I must be weak. Very weak. I never should have let Eliot do that to me."

This time I was ready. I had thought about Ken a lot since seeing him, and the answer was on the tip of my tongue.

"He didn't do it to you, Ken," I said. "*You* did it to yourself."

"How can you say that? He broke me. Even if it is a sickness, how could I react like that, get so crushed?"

"Ken, did you *feel* crushed? I was afraid you didn't," I said, and he was stunned.

"What do you mean?" he asked.

"I mean, while Eliot was talking to you. While he was there. I was afraid that you didn't feel anything. What did you feel at the time? You tell me."

"Well, I don't know. I guess I was interested. I was curious."

"That's the problem," I explained. "It takes courage to feel crushed, humiliated—right on the spot. To say 'I feel like garbage.' You didn't say that to yourself. You didn't register what you were feeling."

"What do you mean?"

"You did it to yourself. You pretended you weren't feeling anything. And then when you went home and started to feel, you tried to drown your feelings in alcohol. And you did a pretty good job."

"Well, who wants to feel horrible about himself?" He still didn't get it.

"No one. But Ken, if you feel like shit, any time, anywhere, I want you to have the courage to know that you do, to say to

yourself, 'I feel like shit.' Knowing is going to be your trump
card. If you have the courage to feel bad, if you knew this guy
made you feel like garbage . . . If you knew it *on the spot*, you
wouldn't have tried to punish yourself or distract yourself when
you got home.

"That night your feelings told you what to do because you
didn't know what they were. They controlled you from behind
the curtain."

He said a number of things indicating that he understood me
and agreed, and I was astonished at how quickly he seemed to
assimilate the concept until he explained why.

"You sound like Vladimir, my acting coach. Vladimir's always saying to feel it before you do anything. 'Feel the part,
know it. Know what you feel. Then decide how you want to
show it. That's the fundamental of method acting.'"

"Well, I'm saying the same thing, Ken. I'm talking about
'method living,' if you want to call it that. If you knew that you
were feeling like garbage, you could ask why. Who was making you feel that way? *Why* were you feeling that way?"

"Do you feel that way, sometimes?"

"What a question! Of course." I was delighted that he'd
asked; it gave me a chance to repeat that if you know you're
feeling low, at least you can make rational choices and maybe
discover why you are.

That quiet session proved pivotal for everything that followed,
and I could sense it when Ken was gone. I had discovered
perhaps the single, most critical fault in his whole approach to
life—his fear not just of homosexuality but of all his feelings,
and especially of any indication that he was weak. His equat-
ing intense feelings with weakness was prompting him to deny
any such feeling much too often.

I had no doubt that Ken got the message. Now if only he
could take his bearings properly, his emotional bearings, we
would really be on our way.

Our project was no longer the local one, of how he felt about being homosexual. He was burying his feelings a mile a minute, and that would have to stop.

I underscored this whenever I could.

Once he said, "Maybe I shouldn't talk to Eliot anymore."

"That's up to you. But just be able to register if you're hurt or angry, so you can deal with the person or the issue and not bury yourself alive."

I noticed that Ken never acted annoyed or displeased with me. One day I started a session very late, and he said it was okay. When I pressed him, he admitted he was slightly piqued, but even his letting on that much upset him. He recalled his father's refusing to talk to him once when, after getting hit by a baseball, ten-year-old Ken had cried. Both of his parents had sometimes scolded him for boasting. "Pride goeth before a fall," they were fond of saying.

Later he recalled great embarrassment when he'd been asked by his sixth-grade teacher to go to the blackboard but couldn't because he had a hard-on. He'd grown up so under wraps that showing almost any feeling seemed as dangerous as letting anyone see that erection. Doubtless, Ken would have emerged from this straitjacket, as most children do who start out that way, but at twelve he made the discovery that demanded that he redouble his efforts at secrecy; after that, he never let up.

This was the discovery that he was different, that his interests were at variance from those of most boys, and that he was emotionally and sexually attracted to other boys and not girls. Suddenly, it was as if this dread reality explained the inadmissibility of his inner life. Now it seemed that his showing any emotion was a potential giveaway of his dark secret.

Ken feared that people would see his anger as unmasculine, his excitement as effeminate, his interests as strange, his fear as childish, his indifference to dating girls as freakish—and, of course, his loving feelings toward men, he thought, were the most bizarre part of him.

And so he'd begun keeping his emotional life a secret—even from himself. Having severed his relationship with his

own inner life, he became everybody's potential victim. He
would move toward people who disdained him and stay with
them; he would fail to appreciate real acceptance and love; he
would hardly know what he wanted to do—these were prices
he paid for self-alienation.

As we kept discussing his reactions, he began to spot them
more readily, at first not the instant he had them but somewhat
later. Little by little, he shortened the time needed to identify
them. By the end of a year-and-a-half's therapy, he could recognize his reactions of injury and humiliation within seconds.
Being able to do this greatly improved his flexibility of choice
in dealing with people, and his confidence.

A by-product was that his acting improved considerably,
enough for him to get a part in a low-paying off-Broadway production of William Inge's *Bus Stop*. However, to his surprise,
when acting became an everyday affair, he didn't enjoy it
nearly as much as he'd hoped to. He preferred the company of
writers and critics and scholars to that of actors. He began to
suspect that he'd used acting as a pretext to come to New York
City, where he'd always wanted to live. And that he'd also
used it as a vehicle for expressing emotion when he'd had no
other way.

While in the play, Ken hatched the idea of finishing college
and preparing himself to teach literature and drama. A new
friend, a former director who had gone back to school, was
influential in Ken's choice to get his transcript and return for
courses.

Over this period Eliot would pop into the restaurant at un-
predictable times, with men friends and with women too. Then
one day Eliot came in alone, and whispered to Ken that he was
engaged to a woman named Phyllis, "a therapist and the
daughter of a very prestigious family from Newark."

Eliot announced, "I've never been happier."

Ken felt the blood pulsing through his cheeks, but recognized the sensation at once as either great pain or fury or both.
Though he was far from prepared for all variations of onslaught, this one came from a charted direction: We'd been
over that last terrible exchange with Eliot innumerable times.

Ken had scrutinized Eliot and himself, while Eliot was describing the expensive wedding to be given by his bride's family in the very near future. "We're having three hundred people," Eliot said.

Ken's heart sank at the thought that he wasn't even considered worthy of an invitation. But he watched it sink, as one might see a ship foundering in the waves. He knew at once that Eliot had induced this feeling, and that Eliot was using his urbane presentation to convey, "I am going forward, and you are not. I belong to the acceptables and you do not."

With an impishness that I had never known Ken to express, he said to Eliot, "So I take it that you're not homosexual anymore?"

Eliot threw back his head charmingly. "No, Ken." Then he drew closer and whispered, "She's pregnant."

"Well, I really wish you the best," Ken had said to him.

In retrospect, we felt that Ken's one mistake was letting Eliot be the one to end the conversation, which he did conspicuously by picking up a newspaper while Ken was still standing there. Ken would have done better to busy himself elsewhere once he caught on to what Eliot was doing.

Probably as a result of that ending, the conversation stung Ken more than it needed to. Even so, he felt buoyed by the recognition that he had spoken up. He could find absolutely no self-destructive urge after that conversation.

To Ken's astonishment, Eliot came in again the very next day. Ken could not remember his ever appearing two days in a row before, and as soon as Ken saw him, he felt triumphant.

Within minutes Eliot signaled to him. Then for no apparent reason, Eliot said, "I'm not homosexual anymore. I would say 'gay,' but those people aren't gay."

Ken answered at once, what he knew to be true. "Well, I'm a real homosexual."

His saying that sent a message to his own mind, not of homosexuality—that was a simple fact—but of self-possession, which became an invaluable precedent for his future outlook.

After that, when Eliot came in for lunch, they didn't talk, doubtless because each wanted to protect himself from the other's opinion. Someone told Ken that Eliot's wedding had been spectacular, and soon after that, Ken heard that Eliot's wife had given birth to a daughter.

Meanwhile Ken stayed on the only path that seemed viable for him, acceptance of himself as homosexual. It dawned on him that he'd known this about himself since he was twelve. He'd come to New York City because he'd yearned for the tolerance that he thought a big, diverse city could offer him. In any event, Ken saw that for him to pretend that he was anything but homosexual would be like walking on his hands.

Being homosexual seemed far less unpleasant when he realized that the drawbacks were not inherent in *who* he was, but owed almost exclusively to the status of homosexuals in the world. It was relieving for him to assimilate the truth of his own nature. He kept on telling selected people that he was gay, and made new friends as well as some enemies. But a few friends, whom one sees regularly, are stronger than a multitude of ill-wishers in the penumbra of our lives, and Ken was happier than he ever had been. He was achieving his goal of creating an extended family, one that knew him and welcomed him.

For a long time there were no lovers. Ken's homosexuality remained a vision of life rather than a mode of living. He had always associated sex with love and was very wary of casual, unemotional contacts. Then he had an affair with a man in his fifties, a professor at NYU, where Ken was getting his bachelor's degree. The relationship didn't last, but during it Ken affirmed his desire to study drama, to teach, and some day to try his hand at writing plays.

For a time Eliot disappeared. He came back friendlier, but still bombastic. He used the trick of making a pseudo-complaint to contrast his rich, forward-going life with Ken's dereliction. He told Ken that "Having this psychiatric residency, studying for the boards, and not being able to sleep because of a little child is very difficult." He didn't ask Ken a single question about his life.

On the bus home Ken felt dismal, and came up with the

explanation that he loved children and was hard put to accept that he would never have any of his own. Back then the laws against a single man's adopting a child were iron-clad, and even gay people who had formerly been married were losing custody of their own children in the courts. It was a real penalty in Ken's case.

I was seeing Ken once every two weeks at the time, while he went for his master's degree. Money was tight, and he clearly didn't need me the way he had. He would rush from his waiter's job to his classes, and he had a cadre of friends for support. He was planning to go out of town, if possible on a teaching fellowship, while he studied for a doctorate. Though, of course, much remained to be done, he characterized his life as going very well.

Then one day he came bursting in with news about Eliot. "Remember Roger, the guy who works in the fur district, who was having an affair with Eliot?"

I vaguely recalled the name.

"I just wanted to tell you. You won't believe this. He and Eliot are lovers again."

"Really!"

"I'm not kidding. Roger says that Eliot visits him there about twice a week. It's like a big thing. Not for Roger anymore. Roger says he can't take it. Eliot goes running over there, and then gets disgusted and says the whole thing is sick."

Seeing my expression, he said, "You're as surprised as I am."

I resumed my therapeutic attitude and asked him, "How do you feel about it, Ken?"

"I think it's funny. With all those lectures."

I observed, "Well, now we know why he had to keep giving them. They must have been aimed at protecting him against his own impulses. I guess they were as much for him as for you."

"More," Ken corrected me.

I asked Ken for any other reactions.

"I think I'm annoyed at him. My friends think the whole thing is ridiculous. They think it's funny. But I guess I'm annoyed at him. He's an imposter. Yes, annoyed. Very annoyed."

The topic gave way to Ken's wanting to rehearse a big moment coming up soon. He was finally going to tell his mother that he was gay. He thought she suspected and in any event, he wanted her to know. He couldn't stand her asking him, over the phone and when he was there, about girl friends and if he ever planned to get married. "She seems to think that she hasn't done the job unless I do," he said to me.

When he went back to Iowa and told her, she was silent. She didn't say anything the next day either, and it was almost as if she hadn't heard him. But then, while he was packing up to return to New York, she came in and begged him not to tell his father. He'd agreed at once, but then felt sorry he had.

In my office he arrived at the decision not to tell his father for a while. But he also realized that the choice of whom to confide such a thing in can never belong to anyone but the person himself. There would be major implications, whether he told his father or not, and it was not his mother's domain to make the decision. He was sorry he'd agreed, because perpetual secrecy would isolate him forever.

I asked him, "Suppose your father were to die and never know. Would you be sorry?"

He answered instantly that he would. "We're so far apart. I've got to give him a chance. For his sake and mine. I'm not a child molester, after all." He smiled at the allusion to his former lover, who was so much older than he. But he also decided that this was not the time to tell his father. It was enough that he'd told one parent. He would live with the problem a little longer.

Meanwhile, I had the sense that he wanted me in his life, if only for an occasional session, as the "good father," and to be in his corner if his actual father went off the deep end when Ken told him.

Word came that he got his assistantship at an upstate university and would be going there the following year to study
and teach. His departure would provide a natural end to therapy with me. I'd been working with him, on and off, for about
four years.

Then it happened. Ken came into my office in tears. He reported that Eliot was dead. "Everybody's talking about it. It
happened in Chicago."

"How?" I needed time to assimilate it.

"We don't know. We're trying to find out. Last weekend
some time. We think he was murdered, maybe. He was only a
few months from taking his psychiatric boards, from becoming
a full-fledged psychiatrist. I just don't know. We just don't
know. We're trying to find out."

Three or four people that Ken knew had heard about Eliot's
death, but were all in the dark as to the details. His parents
were not reachable, and anyhow, no one saw fit to ask them
about it.

Then they found out it was suicide.

Eliot's sister, who had always been very close to him, got
the facts. Apparently, Eliot's psychiatrist, who was both treating him and supervising his work, was one of those utterly
convinced that homosexuality is a desperate illness, which any
aspiring psychiatrist would have to overcome before going into
full-fledged practice. Their master plan had been for Eliot to
achieve his total conversion in time for his psychiatric boards.

As the day drew closer, one can assume, Eliot got increasingly depressed over his failure to comply. Much will forever remain a mystery, but we do know how he spent his last
day. Late on a Friday afternoon he went over to two uniformed
policemen in the Loop in Chicago, and made a sexual proposition to one of them. He touched the policeman's shoulder, and
as he must surely have expected would happen, the officer
arrested him on the spot. In court, when it came out that he
was a medical doctor and had no previous criminal record, he
was released without bail in his own custody.

No one could have found a more brutal custodian. Eliot called his wife and told her he was stuck at the hospital and would not return until much later. Then he took a room in a motel and downed a lethal dose of sleeping pills, ending forever the question of whether he was homosexual or not.

One can only imagine the agony that Eliot must have suffered. His going to medical school, his becoming a psychiatrist, his marrying and having a child, his very living must have come to seem to him an imposture and a travesty. The boy who had everything was nothing.

When word came of his death, Eliot's sister put through a dozen phone calls to the psychiatrist who had been treating him. He was either busy or had other things on his mind because he answered none of them. Finally, he came to the phone but was curt. "Homosexuality sometimes runs this course," he said.

More properly, self-hate sometimes runs such a course, and had he conceptualized the problem that way, I think, Eliot might well still be alive.

Ken was still in shock when he thought about the whole thing a month later. The case had become somewhat of a *cause célèbre* among psychiatrists. Together with a few others it got discussed behind closed doors a great deal, especially during the months just before psychiatry changed its official stand toward homosexual patients. And today there is a division of psychiatrists, many of them professedly homosexual, who patrol the profession so that such tragedies will not recur.

I will always remember Eliot's cold, expressionless eyes— what I took to be his hatred of me when he was in my office. But, of course, it was really hatred of himself.

The real question, as originally posed by Kinsey, is why some people in a loathed minority hold their heads high and live, while others adopt the encircling view and condemn themselves. No one—not even the gang of toughs who surrounded Ken that night in the lonely park, not a whole society—can be as brutal or belligerent an enemy as the internal voice in some people that says, "You are hateful. You do not deserve to live."

Instead of trying to make everyone look the same, and act the same, competent therapists always study that internalized voice, and when it is full of hatred, they seek to soften it, so that the patient can live in peace.

A few months after Eliot's death, Ken said to me, "It's funny. I always thought that Eliot was strong and I was weak."

I reminded him for the last time, "It takes far more strength to disappoint society, if life calls for that course of action, than to please it and sacrifice oneself needlessly."

Soon afterward, Ken told his father that he was gay. The man reacted in a way that neither of us predicted or could have envisioned. He told Ken simply, "No, you're not." Ken never mentioned it to him again, concluding that his father had heard him and would do what he wanted with the truth.

Off he went to the university and got his doctorate in education, majoring in the teaching of theater arts. He specialized in Restoration Comedy.

For a while Ken kept in regular touch with me. Then, as with perhaps the majority of patients, the tugs and tides of life drew him away, although we retained each other warmly in a kind of preconscious sensibility that remained timeless. Perhaps that was why I recognized his voice so quickly when he called.

It was Sunday night, and Ken was to get his medical report the next morning. He must have felt like a convict on Death Row, waiting to see if the governor would grant a reprieve. What would he have offered to convert that unknown probability fraction into certainty that he was not a carrier! Not that being one is equivalent to dying. Far from it, but for those awaiting sentence, or those who already have gotten bad news, it can sometimes feel that way.

Once again I wondered, should I call him? How could he be

thinking about anything else, even for a minute? No. He might be. I decided that my impulse was selfish. I wanted reassurance from him that he was in good spirits and still robust. I've spent more than my share of time with the dying, and I know that trick of rushing into a room, the kindly visitor, whose real motive is hope that the patient has magically lost his malady and is sitting, propped up, waiting for the signal to leave and return to everyday life.

I didn't call and woke up a few times, knowing what Ken must be feeling.

The next morning my first two patients thoroughly engrossed my attention. At ten-thirty, the red light was blinking on my answering machine, and I went to get the message.

"No sign of AIDS. Good news! I'll see you at one." It was Ken, though this time, for an instant, I hadn't recognized his voice.

Then it sank in, and the world seemed young again. He had won in the lottery.

Later I thought about the inadvertent mischief of modern science, in enabling us to see death or paralysis or blindness years away, like an invading horde on the horizon. At this stage, we can do much, though not all we would like; however, that time may not be far away.

Ken brought me a lavish bottle of champagne as a present. When he left he said earnestly, "Let's stay in touch."

We knew we always would, one way or another.